'Set during the war, but it's not about that. It's not military fiction. It's a story about people. It's about coming of age, love, memory, guilt, fear, and suppression: the human condition with all our vulnerabilities. Powerfully emotive nary, Sunderland

'Unputdownable.' Helen, Exeter

'Great story loved it he instinct for survival and the ha ere. A touching and affecting story.' David, Folkestone

'A page turner, I became fully invested in the story.' Annette, Jersey

'I often start books then put them down. But not this one! I honestly wanted to know what happened next. Excellent.' Pierre, Harefield

'It's a page turner indeed!' Ullrich, Stuttgart

'A brilliant read. Loved the ending.' Ken, Weymouth

'A remarkable book fully researched and highly detailed. First class. *Walking* deserves awards!' Hilary, Sussex

'Moving and poignant.' Dave, Sheffield

'Choices, consequences, and truth. When I read this I got a different view of all three.' Lucy, London

'The history and research is immaculate…. Unlike many stories I read, this one keeps seeping back into my bones. Life is short, love is fleeting, regrets should be few. I highly recommend *'Walking with a friend…'* to anyone who has ever loved and lost. Marianne, Scotland

Also reviewed on Goodreads, Waterstones & Foyles. Search:
<<Walking with a friend in the dark>>

German soldiers on the move in Jersey, Channel Islands, summer 1940

The Mortar Bunker at Corbière, Jersey, summer 2020

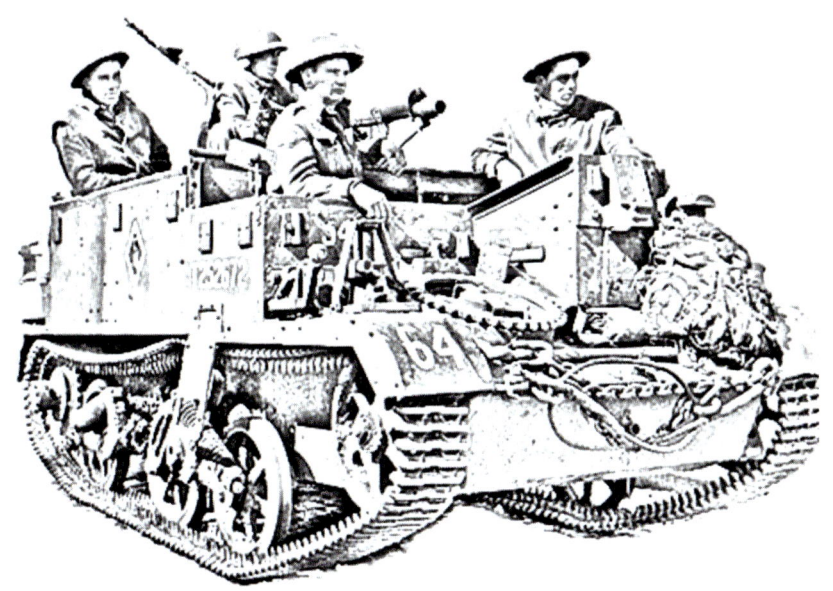

British soldiers in a 'Universal Carrier', Normandy, 1944

'The Gliders at the Pegasus Bridge', by War Artist Albert Richards, 1944

Book 1 of the von Bonn family chronicles

The von Bonn family chronicles by the same author:

Walking with a friend in the dark 2022

The craft of the father (2025)

The Wall (working title) (2026-7)

WALKING WITH A FRIEND IN THE DARK

Copyright © Martin Roberts 2022

All Rights Reserved

No part of this book may be reproduced in any form,
by photocopying or by any electronic or mechanical means,
including information storage or retrieval systems,
without permission in writing from both the copyright
owner and the publisher of this book

Although real historical figures are mentioned,
this book is a work of fiction.

First Published 2022
by
Tobydale Publishing
Email:
17eastburyroad@gmail.com

Set in Book Antiqua 10pt
v.6x

Printed by: Youloveprint, London
ISBN 978 1 0686244 0 7

Dedicated to Tabitha

A German soldier at Corbière, Jersey, summer 1943

Berlin, with the Anhalter station on the left, Easter Sunday, April 1945

Preface

We say that sometimes *fact is stranger than fiction*. In my research I have discovered inspirational true stories that are without doubt stranger more beautiful and heart-rending than any fiction.

This story begins with the German occupation of Jersey, but it is not about the history of that time in the Channel Islands. It is not a work of military fiction. Neither is it about the detail of any particular aspect of war.

Beginning on 1 September 1939, World War II was the most devastating conflict this world has ever seen, with profound and far-reaching consequences. In Europe an estimated 50,000,000 people perished. This book seeks not to glorify but instead to draw attention to the countless number of individual tragedies.

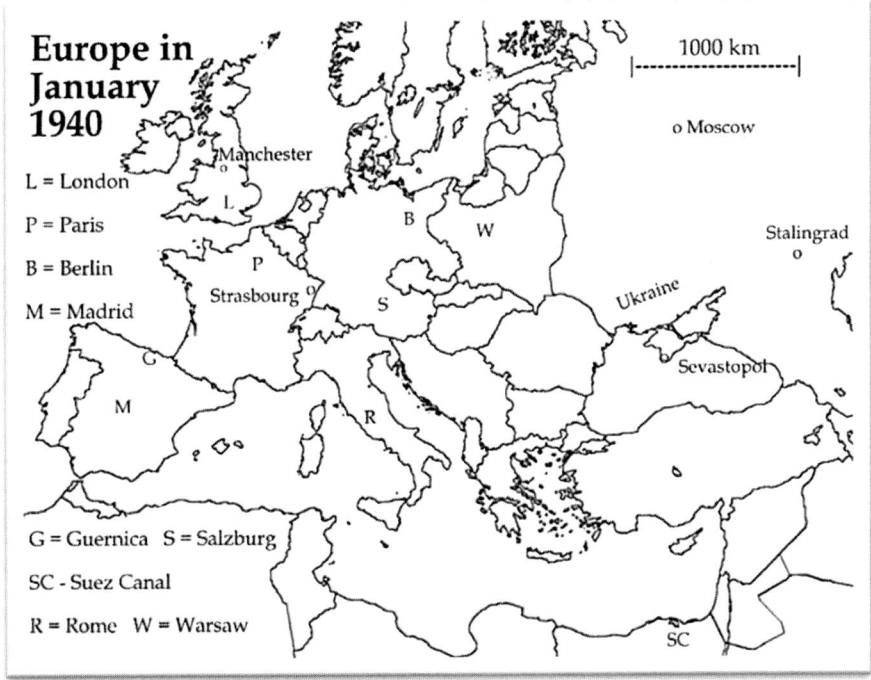

Where music is cited in the text, or a link given, it is recommended that the piece be found and played to accompany reading. The films cited are also worthwhile. YouTube hosts many of them.

MR

Inspired by true events

'Is it even always an advantage to replace an indistinct picture with a sharp one? Isn't the indistinct one often what we need?'
- Ludwig Wittgenstein

1

JERSEY

1927-1944

'True friendship can only exist between equals' – Plato

The Channel Island of
Jersey
o Mont du Vallet
Pointe
Etaquerel
Lewis Tower
St Ouen's
Pond
St Ouen's
Bay
Airport
Gorey
Mont Orgueil
Castle
Le Braye
St Brelade
St Aubin
St Helier
La Moye
Corbière
St Brelade's
Bay
Noirmont
2 km
Le Hocq

France, Germany,
Switzerland & the
Low Countries
Hamburg
Bremmen
Rotterdam
Berlin
Düsseldorf
Valognes
Amiens
Brussels
Cologne
Guernsey
Bonn
Göttingen
Leipzig
Rouen
Caen
Frankfurt
Jersey
Paris
Nuremberg
Strasbourg
Munich
Salzburg
Basel
200 Km

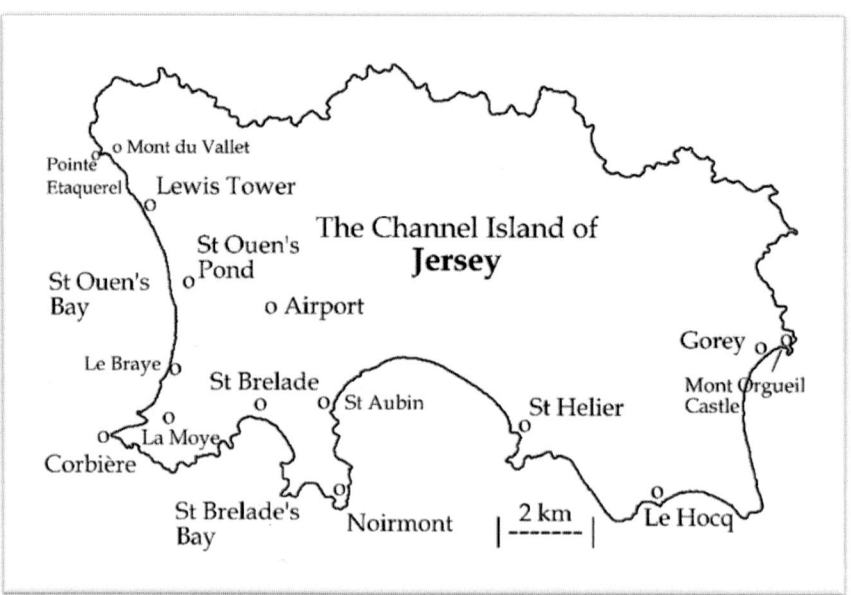

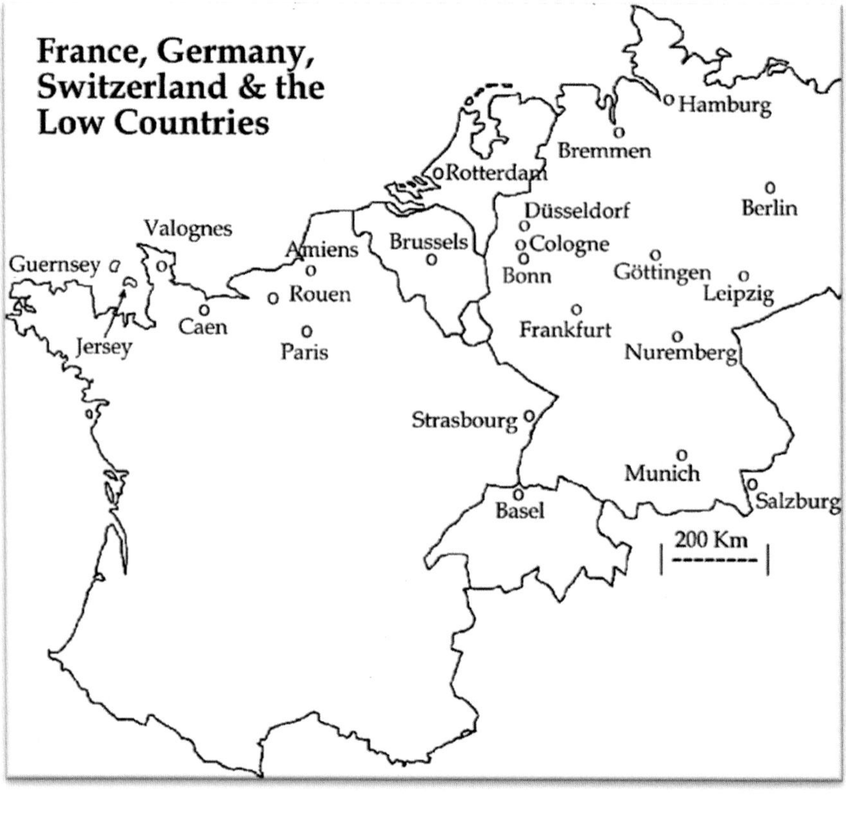

1. The Photograph, June 2018

It was my first day back at the Stanley Care Home, and I remember I'd been told to change his bedsheets.

Pulling on smelly blue rubber gloves I noticed a photograph beside his bed in an ornate pewter frame, small but big enough to be quite clear. I picked it up. A black and white of a boy holding a rifle standing next to a World War II German soldier, a sergeant perhaps? Incredibly detailed, very striking. Carefully I put it back in place next to an old photo of a nurse, and one of a smart young man in a suit and tie. There was a wooden apple too. I looked around. On the walls were many other old photos in frames.

All the guests were elsewhere, probably in the sunroom. They loved the sunroom. They sat there reading, doing jigsaws, painting, or playing bridge or chess and chattering. They loved to chatter! There was a baby grand piano in the day room, but I'd never seen anyone play it.

At that first morning briefing I'd been informed that there was a new chap called Paul Bunn that I hadn't met before and that he had no children or living relatives, but it didn't register at the time.

Mindlessly I pulled the quilt off with the top sheets, but like a clumsy fool I completely misjudged the force required, it flapped and before I knew what happened I heard the pop of the wooden apple landing on the carpet and a metallic crunch. It was the photograph, the one of the boy and soldier in the pewter frame. Oh my God! Have I broken it? I stared at it on the carpet face down. Gingerly, fearing the worst, I crouched to pick it up…

'You bloody idiot!' came a voice from behind as I pondered my clumsiness. Those were the first words he spoke to me. 'If that's broken I'll have your job.'

I had the frame in my hand and was facing away from him, my eyes tight shut. This was a truly desperate mistake. I didn't want to look to see if it was broken or turn to face its owner. I knew I'd probably be sacked no matter what I did.

I opened my eyes, turned the frame over and slowly swung around. At the same time, I glanced at the glass, which mercifully was unbroken. Then I looked up to see a proud tall old man standing in front of me.

He wasn't looking at me he was fixed on the photograph in my quivering hand. 'Give me that!' he muttered firmly. A sharp flame glinted in his eye. 'What's your name?' he asked briskly.

'I'm Katie Campbell, and I'm really sorry Mr Bunn, you are Paul Bunn, aren't you?'

I was distraught but relieved. A lucky escape - was my first reaction. The whole thing was undamaged. But now as I passed it to him, I looked again at the photo and noticed something I hadn't seen the first time: there was sea in the background.

'You don't have any idea, do you?' he said in a peeved tone. But I was captivated. What was it? Who was it? Where was it?

Jersey the Channel Islands, September 1943

The blue sky rang with the calls of Oystercatchers and Gulls. There was little wind today, but the sun was bright, and the birds wheeled and turned over the edge of the low cliff where the Germans had built a series of concrete bunkers and a huge observation tower. Their soaring flight over Corbière gave the birds the best view of the bunkers and gun emplacement, the soldiers, and of a youth on a bike freewheeling hungrily down the dusty track.

That April the boy had turned 16. He was tall, blue-eyed fair-haired and bronze skinned. Gaunt, he had the likeness of the German youths he'd seen in the posters and newsreels. Had he been better fed he could easily have passed for a young German. His looks were frequently commented upon by the soldiers at the bunkers. 'Are you sure your father is English?' they asked, and 'is your mother's name Marlene?' The boy thought all this was funny, but he wasn't quite sure why. He laughed anyway because everyone else laughed; it seemed to be some kind of soldier's in-joke.

These men were familiar. They had become the boy's friends in spite of everything. None of them could speak English or French. His way was to converse in his best Alsatian-German, which was more than good enough, as most of the men did not speak their language well. They were rough soldiers. They had typically been rough workers or labourers before the war too.

The 2nd Company Machine-gun Battalion 16 was drawn from all over Germany. They were replacements and misfits. Some had seen action in a variety of places. Many had been wounded and many were young. Some told stories of how they'd seen their comrades blown to bits, crushed by a tank, or blasted through the side of a house. They were tough men. War had made them tougher.

Today a young soldier greeted the youth as he got off his bike and leaned it against a thick concrete bunker wall. 'You're late!' he said. 'No, I'm early for tomorrow,' the boy replied with a joke that he'd heard his father use often. 'Range finding and firing practice was an hour ago,' said the soldier. 'If I had a watch, I'd know that' the boy told him tersely, reflecting on how it was that he didn't have a watch anymore. 'It doesn't matter, I know what you want,' said the soldier handing him a Mauser rifle with a telescopic sight. 'It's not loaded,' he observed. 'Danke,' added the boy, as he held up the gun and checked the chamber. 'Bitte,' said the soldier with a toothy grin.

For months now the lad had been perfecting his technique. 100, 200 and 300 metres were his preferred ranges, but he still had form at 500 and even 800 metres.

'Who am I going to beat today then?' asked the boy defiantly. Just at that very second the iron door of the bunker swung open with a squeal. Out stepped a sergeant.

****

I didn't speak to him for a week after that business. I admit it; I was scared of him and kept out of his way. However, I did go back into his room when he wasn't there to study the intricate black-and-white photograph: a clear sharp picture, taken with a high-quality instrument. A World War II German army sergeant and a young man holding a rifle standing by an odd triangular-shaped concrete wall with the sea in the background. A curious image! What is that place? Where did the old man get this? Some things were certain: this photo had been lovingly looked after and was in perfect condition. The owner clearly regarded it as very precious. There were other fine old photos in frames too. It began to occur to me that there might be more to this old man than I first imagined.

That photograph was so enigmatic that I sneaked into his room several times over the next few days when he wasn't there to study it. I looked at some of the other stuff too. His room was quite wonderful. Then he caught me looking at that photograph again…

Of the many things about the image the most striking were the details on the sergeant's uniform, buttons, even his Iron Cross medal ribbon. The detail of the belt buckle was remarkable. But the most astounding feature was undoubtedly the boy holding the rifle in his right hand standing next to the soldier and the look of simple pleasure and delight on the boy's face.

There was a glint in his eye and a self-satisfied smirk on the edge of his lips. He was holding something in his left hand; was that an apple? The soldier was smiling too.

I was so absorbed in the detail of the picture that I didn't notice him stepping up behind me…

'You again!' he said.

'Oh shit!' I said out loud with such a start that I nearly dropped it. Wincing, I turned.

'It's alright,' he said. 'I've forgiven you for the last time.'

'Aren't you going to dob me in?' I asked but I already knew the answer.

'Of course not,' he said. 'Life's too short.'

Looking back, I can certainly say that I had no idea what he meant when he said that. I also sensed this man had a story to tell. But - didn't all old people have a story to tell, the story of their lives? There were plenty of other people in the home, surely they had stories too? There was no reason to suppose that his was any more or less interesting than anyone else's. That's what I used to think - back at the beginning.

'What do you find so interesting about that photograph?' he asked.

'The details, the gun and the look on the face of that boy,' I replied.

'Oh that,' he said, and as he turned to pick up the wooden apple from the sideboard I noticed a glint in his eye and a self-satisfied smirk on the edge of his lips…

'Oh my God!' I almost shouted, *'It's you, isn't it?'*

He sat down in his armchair, apple in hand. 'You want to know who those people are, don't you?' Now he seemed far more comfortable. 'You want to know about all of it, don't you? I know you've been in here looking. I've seen you.' I had no idea he was so subtle. I thought I'd been careful, but I had definitely underestimated him.

'Yes, I'm very curious about your photograph. Where did you get it?'

'Well, as you are so persistent, I suppose I'd better tell you. Why don't you go and get us a nice pot of tea?' An unusual request, normally they ask for a cup, but he clearly had some intention as he'd asked for a pot.

Where was this going? I had no idea.

But *that* was how it started.

2. St Helier - the capital of Jersey, 28 June 1940

Films had always been an immense pleasure for Paul and his mother. The one doing the rounds at the moment was the Wizard of Oz. Everyone had seen it. The boys from church said it was 'a bit soft' but the girls he knew all called it 'magical' or 'colourful' or some such silly adjective.

It was a hot June evening and the queue for the film was short. Tickets were one shilling and nine pence for Helene and sixpence for him. They bought a quarter of boiled sweets in a white paper bag at the kiosk on the left, then went down the burgundy carpeted steps. Paul heard people chatting in the local Jersey-French language *Jèrriais,* but he couldn't follow it. They took their seats, watched the Compton piano organ rise as if by magic, tucked into the contents of the bag, and listened to the intricate music played on the instrument by a chap called Mo.

Then there was a Donald Duck cartoon that made Paul and his mum laugh.

A newsreel by Gaumont British News ran and showed British soldiers in Universal Carriers whizzing over hills. It showed the Home Guard attacking a cardboard mock-up of a German tank which even sported a painted swastika. The Nazi 'tank' was easily disabled by three flour bombs. Paul giggled at the ridiculous images. 'Those idiots wouldn't get anywhere near a real Panzer,' he told his mother. 'The Jerrys would cut them down in a second.' 'Shhhh!' whispered Helene.

Then there was a short piece about the Royal Navy laying mines in the English Channel. It said, in a cheery but pompous full English accent: '…with the fall of our allies in France, Britain must be ready for whatever the future holds.'

Not a single one of the people present in The Forum that day believed that the British Channel Islands were ready. Not in the least, and definitely not for what happened next.

As the audience sat watching the tornado in the Wizard of Oz gathering and the wind start to roar, German Heinkel III aircraft were en route from a base in northern France. Their mission: bomb St Helier.

There was a crump. The cinema shook gently. The image on the screen flickered sideways but continued. Another crump followed. Flakes of paint feathered down from the ceiling like a dusting of light snow. Then there was another crump and another.

Paul looked at his mother. The lights in the cinema came on but the film continued to roll. Paul saw that his mother was looking at him. Her face conveyed an image he hadn't seen before: *absolute shock*. 'It's bombers,' she whispered.

The tornado in The Wizard of Oz reached a crescendo. There was a loud crash and the sound of splintering glass. 'Oh Toto!' exclaimed Dorothy. Then the film came to a shuddering stop. 'Come on,' shouted Helene, 'let's get out!'

They ran up the stairs and pushed through the curtain. Paul strained his eyes in the bright June sunshine, but what struck him was the sound of aircraft engines. Not the Merlins of the British Hurricanes he had seen patrolling the skies over Jersey recently. This was a different engine sound. His mother whispered, 'The Boche are bombing us. *Incroyable!*' This shocked Paul. His mother usually moved into French for emphasis. But this wasn't emphasis, it was pure fear.

Someone in the road shouted, 'L's Allemands ont bombardé la caûchie!' (*Jèrriais: The Germans are bombing the harbour!*)

Smoke was rising from that direction. The drone of aircraft, perhaps half a dozen, haunted Paul. He would never forget that sound for the rest of his life.

Then he saw one flying in low over the harbour. It nosed down and two black bombs fell from its open bomb bay doors. 'Mother of CHRIST get in!' shouted Helene. They dived back into the cinema skidding across the tiles on their stomachs.

CRUMP, CRUMP... Blasts shattered windows above and glass rained down like hail. 'Get back inside,' someone shouted. Most already had.

The air attack continued for what seemed an eternity. Islanders were hiding in doorways - trying to see if the aircraft were coming their way. They were, but no more bombs fell. Instead, the aircraft droned in again exceptionally low. There was a pinging and rattling. It was machine-gun bullets bouncing off the sides of the granite buildings striking sparks and shattering slates. 'My God! Les Boches are strafing us. *Batards* (Bastards),' exclaimed Helene.

Paul whispered, 'Why are they doing this, what have we done to them?'

'C'est la guerre,' said Helene (It's the war). 'La guerre est arrivée à Jersey' (The war has arrived in Jersey).

This shocking injustice stayed with Paul in all the years of the German occupation. But that was only the first injustice. Many more were to follow.

On arrival the Germans billeted their soldiers in the many empty hotels houses and shops they found across the island. Farmers had not however deserted their fields and smallholdings.

Most people who wanted to leave and go to England had the chance to do so, but once the last boat had gone, Jersey knew it was on its own. After the British army and Hurricane aircraft had been withdrawn, the Channel Islands were completely undefended. Occupation was inevitable, it was just a question of when and how. Unfortunately, the demilitarisation was not communicated to the Germans who assumed, wrongly, that Churchill would as a matter of prestige not allow sovereign British territory to fall into the hands of the enemy without a fight. This assumption cost dozens of injuries and the lives of 10 innocent islanders that June day in 1940.

And so, the war came to Jersey.

Bullet marks in the walls at St Helier harbour, summer 2020

3. 'How did I get into all this?'

As I poured the tea Paul said, 'I suppose the first thing you're going to want to know is: *how did I get into all this?*'

'Get into all what? What are you talking about?' I asked.

'Get into the war and end up making friends with the Germans?'

'What!' I said with a start. He was racing away from me, racing back. He had a story to tell no doubt about that, but his first move left me absolutely stranded, I didn't know what he was talking about.

'Who is that guy in the photograph?' I asked gesturing toward it.

'That's Hans the sergeant,' he said. 'He was my friend. He ran me over on his bike in New Street in 1940.'

'Whoa! Were you Ok?'

'Let's put it this way: he was more surprised than I was,' he replied, giggling.

'New Street is in Birmingham, isn't it?' I said. 'I go through it on the train to Manchester.'

'No no! New Street in St Helier, Jersey in the Channel Islands,' he laughed. 'The Germans invaded the Channel Islands in 1940. Didn't you know that?'

I thought quietly to myself: no, I didn't. I didn't know what the Channel Islands were or where they were, I'd never heard of them. But I didn't want to show my ignorance and Paul was so engaged. I'd never seen any 91-year-old quite so animated. So, I decided to keep quiet, smile and try to make it look like I knew what he was talking about, even though I didn't. Eventually it would all make sense, wouldn't it? Anyway, the supervisors were constantly telling us to chat to the residents and befriend them, especially if they had no living relatives.

'No one really knew what to make of the Germans, I certainly didn't. I was only 13. The kids thought it was a bit of a laugh all these soldiers marching around. It didn't take long before they realised they could go up to a German, call him a bloody bastard to his face and he would just smile and say 'Wie bitte?' (Pardon?) because he didn't understand a damned word. The older people were angry and scared though. Lots of others had got away on the boats back to Weymouth before the occupation but my parents stayed because of my great-aunt and the big house,' he explained. 'I didn't insult the Germans like the lads did though. I knew better,'

He narrowed his gaze and looked away slightly, changing his inflexion, scratching his forehead. There was something about the way he said that. 'Mother had family in France: Uncle Jean in Paris and Uncle Claude who ran a hotel in Rouen. We moved to Jersey in April 1940 for my 13th birthday. We had been holidaying in Jersey for years before that.'

'You moved to Jersey from Rouen then?'

'Not really. We moved to Jersey via Paris and Rouen from Strasbourg. I was born in Strasbourg in 1927.' His *Strasbourg* came out with a distinct lilt: a slightly stressed guttural pronunciation of the 'r' and a lifted silent 'g' which was familiar, but I couldn't quite place. He noticed that *I noticed*. He studied my expression but kept silent.

Oh my God, Paul really did have a story, and it really was interesting. I thought, 'I'm talking to a war hero!' so, like a stupid fool I said, 'Are you a war hero?' He laughed so much he slopped his tea on the bed.

'Don't be daft. How can I be a war hero? I was 13 in 1940! Don't they teach you anything in school?' he exclaimed. Maybe not, I thought to

19

myself.

'How old are you?'

'21.'

'My God, are you qualified? I thought you had to be older than that to work here?'

'I'm well trained and I'm old enough.'

'Perhaps you are, perhaps you are,' he said with a lovely smile. 'Have you ever been to Jersey?'

'No, I haven't,' I said. I wasn't quite sure where Jersey was.

Oddly, as he adjusted the hearing aid in his right ear, he followed that with, 'Have you been to America?'

'Yes, I have.'

'Oh, lucky you,' he said, replacing the aid.

Then I asked, 'Haven't you been to America then?'

'Never, but I remember very clearly the first time I met an American. My father went to New York in 1936. I'd enjoy listening to your stories about America,' he told me with a thoughtful extended look.

The conversation was beginning to get interesting, but just then the supervisor Sarah came along to the open door: 'Is this where you've been?' She pulled a face which meant, *'what on earth are you doing? Back to work Katie!'* Away I trudged to the kitchen, empty teapot and cups in hand.

I must admit even after just 20 minutes I was captivated. Paul's island of Jersey had been invaded by the Germans in the war and he'd made friends with them! It was just completely startling. This old man Paul, who really was nothing to me an hour ago, who was 70 years older than me and lived in a posh care home, had me hooked. As I cycled over Kew Bridge to Brentford my mind was reeling.

I was taught history, but I didn't retain much, because none of it was real. I was just a kid. I reckoned that what happened 75 years ago was irrelevant, so I ignored it. I've always been much more interested in the future. My dad sometimes told me, 'Don't look back Katie, we're not going that way.'

In the next weeks and months, I learned that war was complicated and had profound effects. I learned from someone who was actually there; someone who was quite young at the time and really wasn't that different to me. Knowing what I know now, I feel foolish that I knew so little about the consequences of war.

4. Chess

I got to know Paul quickly in those first couple of weeks. He was different to the other characters in the home. He didn't get on that well at first and held people at arm's length. Some of the staff called him 'the mystery man.' He was new there and they didn't know how to take him. I'm not sure I did at first either, but I found myself coming back. He was a fascinating man who really stood out. Old, 91, but very fit and exceedingly mentally agile. Fiercely intelligent. Beguiling. I kept watching him, studying him. It soon became an unbreakable habit.

I love chess. So did Paul. I'd won tournaments at school, county and University level. I used to watch him play to see if I could learn from his game. He usually chose Black, played the *Sicilian Defence* and a whole sea of variations. He would torment his opponents, befuddling them; building up their hopes and letting them get ahead when actually all he was doing was laying a trap. Some of these were elementary and it was always a different trap. Sometimes he would announce, 'Mate in three,' leaving his opponent dumbfounded. After a few weeks most of them had learned not to argue although one or two insisted on trying their luck.

I noticed that he tended to be prejudiced against the readers of certain newspapers. Sometimes he deliberately played a long game with them even though he was by far the better player. He told me later that he did this so they could learn to savour their humiliation. The Times readers could give him a good game and he was always very generous towards them and their skills, *after he beat them*. Guardian readers he was gentler with. Bruce had been a salesman in his working life and was widely travelled. He and Paul got on well. Bruce was a Guardian reader. Sometimes he would go to move a piece and with a smile Paul would say, 'Are you *sure* you want to do that?'

Ha-ha! He was so funny.

His antics were quite something and in those early days I observed them carefully. He often had people in a tailspin and sometimes you really had to watch him.

In the third week I was on afternoons. At the handover meeting the morning supervisor Melissa, asked if anyone had seen Paul. Sarah, a skilled carer was the afternoon supervisor. She was a formidable character with whom you did not take liberties. None of the morning staff said anything except that he wasn't at breakfast. 'Well, where the hell is he then?' Sarah exclaimed. Ha-ha! It's making me laugh now just thinking about this. A room-by-room search began.

Looking for Paul was like looking for a lost cat, with hope, but no expectation. By 4pm it was declared that he was definitely not on the premises. They were talking about him as if he were some naughty schoolboy, but I knew from watching that he was certainly not one of those. Others in the home were, but not Paul Bunn.

At about 9pm the front door closed with its characteristic boom. It was Paul and he was carrying a large Tate Modern bag. I saw him come in and called Sarah who, unsurprisingly, came immediately carrying a characteristic scowl.

She studied him, 'Can we go to your room and talk please Paul?' Off they trooped. Oh my...!

I must admit a morbid fascination in what was going on. I considered that he was more than a match for anyone in the building, possibly all of them put together. So, trying to appear disinterested I wandered along to the closed door of his room and eavesdropped on the raised voices behind...

'You signed the documents...''I didn't sign a document that said I needed *your* permission or anyone else's...' 'It would be common courtesy to tell someone...' 'It would be common courtesy to not run this place as if it were some sort of *detention camp* for people with lots of money...' I noticed the emphasis. 'We don't run a prison camp here. People are free to come and go as they choose.' 'Ah, but they aren't, are they? They need *your* permission!' 'You've twisted my words, that's not what I said...' 'Really? That's exactly what you said. *They're you're words – not mine!'*

'I'd like you to tell me how you managed to get out...'

'I thought you said, *this is not a prison camp*? Now you're asking me how I got out. Your words not mine! If I tell you you'll block my escape route. I can't have that now, can I?'

Oh my God, he was completely running rings around her, and I found myself giggling.

'We like you Paul, but you're not making it easy for us.'

Oh shit, she shouldn't have said that!

'I'm not here to make things easy for you. I'm here to make things easy for <u>me</u>. I pay you to make things easy for me, and here *you* are making things hard! That's not how it works Sarah. Sorry! Here's how it works: I pay you, and you take care of me. The clue's in the name: Care Home.'

Oh dear. He'd wiped the floor with her.

But he wasn't finished. 'And here's another thing. Some of the people here may not have read your documents. I did. In those it <u>does</u> say that we are free to come and go as we choose. That's why I signed them. They don't mention common courtesy though. I never signed anything to say I would show common courtesy. I pay YOU to show common courtesy. Now *you* show <u>me</u> some and GET OUT!'

I quickly got away from the door and tried to make it look as if I was just passing…

Sarah came out and shut the door behind her with a thwack. Her face was white as a sheet. Off she went blazing with anger, deputised someone and then went home. For weeks after that she tried to stay as far away from Paul Bunn as she could get.

I learned something about Paul from that incident and it drew me closer: he was fearless, ruthless and independent. I envied these qualities and his directness. Others in the home would have shit themselves, literally. They would never have stood up to Sarah like that, but Paul did.

That was the first of several times that he disappeared without any warning.

The following day at about 1 o'clock he turned to me in the sunroom and asked, 'How about a game of chess then?' Alright, I said. I could hardly say no, could I?

I put Mozart's *Vesperae solennes de confessore* on the sound system and got a pot of tea. 'Good choice. Unusual,' he declared. 'Do you like classical music then?' I told him I adored it, especially Mozart. He smiled at that as he set the clock. I played Black and deployed one of the *Sicilians* (Sveshnikov) I'd watched him use to rout another guest. And he knew it.

10 moves in, I hadn't fallen for any of his irritating traps. I know he knew but he didn't say anything. I didn't say anything. I knew he was regarding me. In fact, *I was setting him a trap* all the while allowing him to move me around. I also had a solid defence and was quite secure. He knew that too; he could see it.

'You've been watching me, haven't you?' he observed dryly. I ignored that as I regard it as improper to talk in-match. I had enough about me to not look at him or indulge in whatever it was he was playing at.

By 30 moves he was up one pawn, but I had the better position because I'd sacrificed, and he didn't seem to be aware that I was closing in. Then, out of the blue he offered me a draw. What? I looked at the board. I had a good position; I almost had him. I could probably force the win in six or seven moves, but I looked at the 91-year-old and thought, 'Who am I to beat this man? He's a skilful player, he's got more to come, and I don't know exactly what he's got, so I'll take that draw.' I offered my hand.

As we shook he said, 'That's the best game I've had for as long as I can remember. Your chess is brilliant! Thank you.'

'Thank *you*,' I replied.

'You had me. Why did you take the draw?' I didn't feel like explaining.

Then he said something. 'It's because you've played schoolboys who fancied you. They were weak and eased off on you. Perhaps you've learned to be weak in return? You should've ignored that and beaten the crap out of them. Chess is only about winning. There's no other reason to play. It's in the nature of who we are. When we play a game we should only play to win. Otherwise, don't play.'

Well, I wasn't expecting that. How did he know I'd played schoolboys? How did he know they fancied me? Or was he just guessing, speculating and provoking in order to see if I would react? I did react.

'I accepted your offer of a draw out of courtesy. Why did **you** offer me a draw? Was that out of courtesy? Or was it out of weakness? I thought you said you always played to win?' I was shocked to hear myself saying such things. I never knew those sorts of things were in me.

'Well said, well said,' he replied with a marvellous grin. It was a moment. I saw him and he saw me. It was the first time.

Then to my surprise he reached by the side of his chair and pulled up the Tate Modern bag from yesterday. He fetched out a print and said, 'This is a Picasso painting called 'Chess.' I know you've been watching me play. You've been studying my game, and I feel flattered. Because you've been watching me, I want to repay the compliment, so I'd like you to have it.'

I hadn't considered anything like this before.

Then he said, 'I learned something today: you want to learn. You do, don't you?'

Now I was befuddled. I didn't know what to make of that but felt I had to say something. 'Leonardo Da Vinci was a genius engineer and artist.' I thought that was a good dodge, crude, but he'd put me on the spot. In fact, he was right, I did want to learn.

He looked at me as if summing up and continued, 'Well, he's called this

Chess. But it doesn't look much like chess, does it? It could be an image of an old woman, perhaps a stern old nun, contemplating her cocktail glass,' he grinned. 'It could be an image of someone looking at a pyramid and a perfume bottle. That could be the face of an angel. It may even be a Madonna and Child. We just don't know. But the fact of the matter is that he's called it *Chess*.'

'I'm not sure what you mean?'

'That's the whole point. It only means what we want it to mean. Picasso is saying: this is chess. From that point onwards, as soon as we know the name of the painting is Chess, we try to see chess in the image. We can't stop ourselves. If Picasso had called it *'Nun with Cocktail Glass,'* he giggled, 'we would then undoubtedly try to see the nun and her cocktail glass.' With that he could contain himself no longer and burst out laughing. He thought that was hilarious!

'So, you're saying that it's about how we see things, what we see in things? Things are not the way they seem: things are only the way we *want* them to seem.'

'Yes. Picasso has tapped into something he has realised about us: a suggestibility.'

'But he's called it *Chess*. There must be a reason why he's called it Chess.'

He gestured with his hands, 'Why does there have to be a reason? Not everything happens for a reason you know. In fact, I'd go as far as to say that in my experience a great many things happen for no reason whatsoever. In the end it's up to us. We can decide there is a reason, or we can decide that there is no reason at all. It's entirely up to us.'

'Ok, now I'm getting it. In that case I think Picasso is playing a game of chess with us.'

'Really? How interesting. What makes you say that?'

'He doesn't want us to see whatever we want to see. If Picasso was happy to let us do that then he should simply have left the painting as *Untitled*. No, Picasso wants us to see chess and he's named it Chess. After that we are in his trap.'

'How curious that you should think in terms of traps,' he observed. 'And how curious that you interpret this the way you do. Tell me, do you see chess when you look at this painting?'

'No, I don't. I see a woman's face, perhaps a mother? She is thinking about something. She looks sad.'

'Well, that's something new I must say,' and he looked at me in puzzlement then laughed that gorgeous laugh.

Afterwards the conversation drifted away from art and on to another topic which was clearly on his mind. 'How long was it before they realised I'd gone yesterday?'

'I don't know, what time did you leave?'

'I left when they were in the 6.30am handover meeting.'

'Oh my God!' I said shocked. 'That means you were gone for nine hours.'

Then to my astonishment grinning he said, *'In neun Stunden könnte ich in New York City sein und eine Bratwurst mit Senf genießen.'* (In nine hours, I could be in New York City enjoying a sausage with mustard.)

'Sie sprechen Deutsch?' (You speak German?) I muttered.

'Ja! Ich bin Elsässer,' (Yes! I am Alsatian) he replied giggling.

'Von Straßburg (from Strasbourg) ... *Elsässer..,'* I murmured, replicating his distinctive accent as an automaton. Of course he was!

With tears of laughter still pouring down his face he stopped just long enough to study my expression. In German he continued: 'The look on your face, I wish I had my camera. I don't know which is funnier, the idea of leaving here to go to New York just to get *Bratwurst mit Senf*, the thought of them not noticing until nine hours after I'd poured the mustard, or that it's taken you three weeks to discover that I am a native German speaker!' Then he broke down with laughter again. I have to admit it: he'd got me!

We were laughing so much everyone was looking and a few people came over to see if we were alright.

Eventually, after I'd got the image of sausage and mustard out of my head, I managed to stop laughing long enough to splutter something out in German, 'How did you know I spoke German?'

'Easy. I asked at the office what qualifications you have, and they told me that you studied A Level German, maths and physics. Impressive! I already knew you'd visited Manchester.'

'How did you know about Manchester?'

'Because you told me.'

'Did I?'

'Yes, when you asked me about the photograph, and I told you about Hans the sergeant,' he explained. 'I also told you that I was friends with the Germans. I thought for sure that you'd have put two-and-two together there. How could I have made friends with the Germans unless I spoke

German? It was all there. Just like with the Picasso: it's there if you want to see it. *Hiding in plain sight* is what they call that nowadays I think?' he added, giggling again.

He was right. I thought I'd been watching him, noticing him, paying attention, but I hadn't seen anything. All I'd seen was what I'd wanted to see: an interesting old man, sneaking in to look at *that photograph*, eavesdropping on his conversations, watching his excellent chess. I did all these things for me, not for him. However, he'd been paying attention to me the whole time and I hadn't noticed. There was something about him. I had a lot of care work experience, but I'd never met anyone like Paul Bunn: sharp, highly cultured and intelligent, no nonsense, multi-lingual.

Then I tried him with my GCSE French, *'Je suppose que vous parlez aussi un français parfait?'* (I suppose you also speak perfect French?)

'Bien sûr! Si vous grandissez en France, vous n'avez pas vraiment le choix!' (Of course! If you grow up in France you really don't have any choice in the matter!), he replied.

I shouldn't have been surprised, but I still was.

Our laughter continued and seemed to set everyone off. The old folks were all giggling away merrily. Someone went to put the kettle on.

He looked at me and with a lovely smile spoke again in German, 'Now that we've got that out of the way perhaps you'll stop watching me and be a friend to me instead?'

We sat in the grand bay window at the chess board, the sun shone, and we laughed together. We had our ups and downs, God knows, but that was the beginning of our friendship.

5. New Street St Helier, September 1940

In those first days that followed the chess game I was very keen to hear more stories, and Paul was happy to oblige. It was tricky trying to make it look as if I was working whilst at the same time listen and ask questions, but I created opportunities.

One of the first things I wanted to know was the business about him making friends with the Germans. I knew he spoke the language perfectly, but that didn't mean he had to take sides with them, did it? So, in a lunch break I sat and asked him what happened. He told me:

'It must have been late September 1940. I'd come out of school and cycled down New Street. I stopped and put my bike up against the kerb in front of the now empty *Louis et Cie*. Mother loved that shop and bought several hats there. The owner Monsieur Feldman always smiled and gave me bonbons from a Clarice Cliff dish. In June he'd closed up and evacuated to England. We never saw him again. He was Jewish.

I was going into newsagents looking for left over comics or anything that might keep me amused because I was getting pretty bored. Nothing was being delivered from the mainland now of course including comics. Anyway, I was minding my business crossing the road when suddenly - Thunk! A bike hit me; it sent me flying!

'VERDAMMTER IDIOT!!!' (Damned idiot!) a German soldier called out as he crashed to the ground, his rifle careering off his shoulder. He and his bike bounced across the road with a metallic clatter.

Sitting up, without any thought in German I shouted back, 'You're on the wrong side of the road, SCHEISSKOPF!' (Shit head!)

There we were rolling around in the middle of New Street causing a scene. People were staring. He got up to hit me and I got up to hit him.

'You little shit!' he shouted getting to his feet.

'*Du großer Trottel!*' I growled rolling the 'r' for maximum effect. (You great moron!)

Then he caught himself and stopped the slap he was preparing for me. 'German?' he asked apologetically.

'No, Alsatian,' I hissed, squaring up to him, fists clenched.

'You're not afraid?' he said gasping.

'Not of you, you idiot. Why would I be afraid of you? You're so stupid you can't even drive on the right side of the road.'

'My God, you're not afraid!' he repeated laughing a sort of choked laugh. If I'd hit him, it would have less effect.

Then I noticed a silver chain and crucifix around his neck that had broken loose. He tucked it back in. At that I realised my crucifix was hanging out too. I pushed it back hastily. He picked up his gun. Then to my amazement, he said, 'I'm sorry, you're right, I **was** on the wrong side of the road. Let me help you.' He was a lance corporal: *Obergefreiter - officer candidate*, with a bad scar on his left cheek.

As we dusted ourselves down and stepped onto the kerb I met him halfway, 'I wasn't looking. I should have looked, but maybe you should get a bell?' I smiled and the soldier smiled too. It broke the ice. He was in his mid-30s, quite stocky.

He clapped me on the shoulder and said, 'You're strong minded, not like these English. We came and took the Channel Islands without firing a single shot.'

I couldn't let him get away with that, so I said, 'Germany strafed and dropped bombs on completely harmless people in St Helier. I was here and I know what I saw. There were no soldiers here. There's nothing brave about bombing shooting and killing innocent people you know.'

He didn't know about the bombing and changed the subject. 'The French wouldn't have just given Alsace back to us, we had to take it. I bet they made you learn French.'

I couldn't let him get away with that either, so I said, 'Alsace is not yours, it's ours! Don't you think the people of Alsace would rather have peace than war? Don't you know that war devours what peace accomplishes?'

'Brave to use our sayings like that. You fight with words!'

'I'm braver than you and I haven't even got a gun.'

'Surely all Germans want to see Alsace come home?'

'I'm Alsatian. Alsace doesn't need to come home, it's already home. Anyway, did anyone in Alsace ask for Hitler to come? I bet they didn't. It's very rude to turn up with an army uninvited you know!' That made him laugh and we both stood there giggling.

'You've got some nerve, I'll hand you that, but keep your voice down, if anyone hears what you say it will cause trouble. What's your name lad?'

'Paul von Bonn. What's yours corporal?'

'Hans Maier. You should come and visit us at St Brelade. The lads would be extremely interested to meet you.'

'That's convenient because I live at St Brelade. I'll think about it.' That was one of father's sayings.

By this time people were walking around us on the pavement and it was time to stop making a spectacle. He said, 'We're in the hotel next to La Moye School on Route Orange. Come to the checkpoint and ask for Hans Maier. I'll see to it that they let you in. You've got some spirit, and you stand up for yourself, it's obvious you're German. Come and you'll be with comrades.'

'We'll have to see about that then, won't we?' It was another of father's stock phrases.

His front wheel was bent, and my knees and knuckles were bleeding from where I'd crashed to the granite, but even though we nearly had a punch up in the street, somehow we'd made a connection. He pushed his bike away and I pushed mine.

A few minutes later he came past me in the passenger seat of a lorry heading for St Brelade as I cycled along Victoria Avenue. He leaned out of the window and acknowledged me with a raised palm and a smile.

Perhaps I would go and visit him and his friends?'

6. 'The King of the Storks'

In the fourth week I'd just changed his sheets and sat down for a bit at his table. Paul came in with a folded copy of the Times in his hand which was open on the crosswords page. He had completed the cryptic and other things. 'Oh, I'd better go,' I said standing up. Smiling and in German he replied, 'No, I formally invite you. Please come in.'

When you looked around his room it was marvellous. There were old photos everywhere. On the bedside table in Art Nouveau pewter frames were one of a nurse and one of a smart young man in a suit and tie. There were beautiful little Art Deco porcelain figurines and plates on the flat surfaces, objects like the wooden apple, oddities of all kinds: all keepsakes. There was an old Leica camera in a battered brown leather case. His shelves held collections of English, French and German novels and poetry. There were dozens of DVD films and CDs of music in three languages. There were many books on art and architecture. There were also some old maps, mainly of northern France, but there was also a very old and battered one of Berlin.

Then I noticed a section of what looked like Russian book spines. I couldn't read them. 'Is this language Russian?' I asked.

'Yes.'

'You can read Russian?'

'Of course. How can you read Pushkin if you can't read Russian?' he said in Russian then translated.

'My God Paul, you're full of surprises,' I exclaimed. To my untrained ear he sounded Russian, a naturalised Russian speaker. Incredible.

'Everything in here is stuff I've collected along the way. Other things I left behind, but this lot here is stuff I couldn't bear to be without. I've got boxes full under my bed too.'

'Left behind? Where?'

'In Strasbourg of course.'

'You moved here from Strasbourg?'

'Yes. I have an apartment there. I needed a break. I do that sometimes.'

I shook my head in disbelief.

'My family have travel in our bones. I never like to stay in the same place too long. I get bored and then move on. Hard to get bored of Strasbourg, but just now I need a change. London will do for me at the moment. I could stay in hotels, but I like the companionship, so I'm staying here for now.'

I continued to shake my head. What on Earth was he like? 'So, where have you lived then?'

'Oh, let me see: Paris, Berlin, Vienna, St Petersburg, Rome, Prague, Bucharest,' he replied. 'I'll always end up back in Strasbourg though. You see – I'm always going away but always coming back.' He paused then with a giggle added, 'Oh, I forgot Athens, Florence, Stockholm and Copenhagen. Ooops!'

'Not America?'

'No, not America, that's a long story.' What a curious thing I thought. No wonder he wanted to know what America was like. Why had he not been there? He'd been practically everywhere else. 'I realise now that I was incredibly lucky. We could always afford to travel. My father's side was very wealthy. The von Bonns had a fantastic house built for them in Marylebone London in the Georgian time. They could afford quite fine things like motorcars and flying machines. The boys, my father Christopher and his brother George had the best education money could buy.'

'Wait a minute,' I said. 'Did you say *flying machines?*'

'Yes.'

'WOW!'

'Why the wow?'

'I love aeroplanes! I'm at Manchester studying for a master's degree in aerospace engineering.'

'Oh. You love aeroplanes too. Just like my father! He absolutely loved anything that could fly and so do I.'

This was crazy. We had more things in common.

'Ha-ha. Lovely!' he said clapping and rubbing his hands with glee. 'Well, we're going to get along like chicks in the nest!'

'Your father flew then?'

'Yes, of course. My father was *Der König der Störche*: The King of the Storks!'

'Where did he fly?'

'Hendon and Oxford University and then in the Royal Flying Corps in the Great War.'

I was astounded.

'My father was absolutely thrilled by flying and everything to do with it. Back when he was a boy there were no aeroplanes. He was amazed when Blériot flew across the channel in 1909. He asked about aeroplanes on his travels with his father but never actually saw one until 1912 when he went to the first *Aerial Derby* which started and ended at Hendon.

Three million Londoners turned out to watch the aviators fly round the city. Most people had never seen an aircraft in flight before. At Hendon Aerodrome at least 45,000 people paid for admission and my father who was 18 by then was one of them. He went again in 1913. He told me it was one of the most amazing things he'd ever experienced.'

Then the old man reached into his bedside drawer, fetched out an old grey event programme from 1913 and a photograph of an early monoplane, handed them to me and said, 'These are my father's. Be gentle with them.'

'I will,' I said as I looked at the wonderful pieces. I got a shock of pleasure from holding the programme turning its pages and looking at the ancient photo. What a thrill it must have been to see the earliest aeroplanes in flight.

Paul went on. 'My father loved every second. He had his first flight in an aeroplane that day, cost him £2. He never forgot the wind in his face and the trees and houses rushing past. He immediately enrolled at the Grahame-Wright School of flying at Hendon and the cost was £75 for *'complete tuition until the pilot's certificate is won.'* Even with inflation, the cost of learning to fly is about the same now as it was in 1913, and father soon learned. Just like the stork he was a natural, born to it. In 1914 my grandfather ordered a Sopwith Type 'SS' Biplane for him, cost £1075, but it never got delivered. The military requisitioned it because the Great War started. By then he was at Oxford of course and he joked that he probably would only have been out flying all the time anyway instead of attending to his studies.'

'I'd <u>love</u> to learn to fly. Maybe one day I will,' I said.

'An aerospace engineer has to fly, otherwise what's the point?' he quipped. I liked that.

He added, 'With all your snooping around looking at my photos I wonder if you'd noticed the one with my father in it?'

I hadn't, I'd been more interested in the photo from Jersey that I'd nearly destroyed on the first day I met him. He pointed me to a wonderful old black & white in a frame on the wall.

'My father was in the 1st 15 rugby team at the City of London School. That's him in 1912, when he was 17. I love this photo. My father is standing on the right in his suit.

I gazed at the image. Then, lifting it from his bedside table, he handed me a small portrait of Christopher in its own pewter frame that was next

to the one of the nurse. I stared at it intently, another fantastic photograph. 'You loved your father, didn't you?' I hesitated. It was perfectly obvious that he did.

'Adored him, and my mother. Adored them with every breath,' he said, almost silently.

There was a pause as I took in what this room was really full of: not memories. These things were not memories to him. These people were alive - just as alive today as they were 80, 90, and 100 years ago. *This room was full of Paul's life.* The enormity of it then struck me: I was inside his life.

He had invited me in, I couldn't refuse, could I?

7. A nurse from Strasbourg

The Stanley guests were frequently offered 'cultural outings' into central London. These could be cinema, theatre, music, opera or an exhibition, anything like that. This time it was the National Portrait Gallery for lunch upstairs and then afterwards the *BP Portrait Award Exhibition*. I had never been on one of these outings before and was looking forward to it. So was Paul. He said, 'The forecast for tomorrow is a bit showery though, bring an umbrella.' I thought we would be inside the whole time, so I didn't know what he was talking about.

Next morning Paul was waiting in the foyer looking very dapper: Trilby with a little red and white feather, suit, waistcoat and brolly. He looked fantastic. I couldn't believe my eyes. 'What are you staring at?' he exclaimed.

'Well, you scrub up nice, don't you?'

He was carrying a fabric Waitrose bag with something in it. We got into the waiting minibus. Lawrence was supervisor today. The ramp lifted up wheelchairs and people with frames like Michael. All were in good spirits as we progressed into town along the A4.

We pulled over on Charing Cross Road near a little restaurant called Gaby's with a blue sign. He turned and said, 'Gaby's is excellent, you should go.' I saw it was full. I'd never heard of it, but I didn't let on.

From there we walked and rolled a short distance down towards Trafalgar Square. The last time I was there was on a year nine school art journey in 2011.

A sudden heavy shower came over and we hastened around a slight bend and sheltered under the canopy of a theatre. He said, 'Have you ever been to the Garrick?'

'No,' I said, 'I've never been to the theatre.'

'WHAT?' he exclaimed. 'Impossible! How could you never have been to the theatre?'

'When you grow up where I did, the only theatre you know anything about is *Watermans*, but you never go,' I muttered. I had no idea why he was so indignant.

'Well, that just won't do,' he fumed. 'It won't do at all. We'll have to see about that then, won't we? I last came here in 1994 to see J.B. Priestley's *An Inspector Calls*. It was quite brilliant.'

'Lucky you,' I added taking a tone. I'd never heard of *An Inspector Calls*. Now I was getting indignant, but I tried not to let it show. He noticed and quickly changed the subject.

'Just around here is someone very special.'

'Do you mean Lord Nelson?' I asked.

'Of course not Nelson. He's irrelevant. I want to introduce you to someone far more important.'

'I thought Nelson was important?'

'Not to me Katie.'

He stood chattering deliberately to let the others get ahead of us. Lawrence glimpsed back to see if we were ok, and I raised my hand in acknowledgement. It was just us now. He said, 'My first memory of visiting her is from 1934. There were mounted Policemen, and steam was coming off the horses in the rain.'

We came around a corner and there was a tower and a statue. It was just like any statue that you would see in any other city, Manchester is full of them. The inscription read:

EDITH CAVELL. BRUSSELS. DAWN OCTOBER 12th 1915.

Then it all changed.

He walked and stood silently in front of the memorial, crossed himself and muttered a prayer.

It began to rain quite hard now, but he was oblivious, so I popped the brolly and covered us both. Then, as if in a trance, from the Waitrose bag he produced a circular garland of interwoven red poppies which was vibrant and beautiful. Humbly he stooped to place it gently on the steps at the foot of the granite statue then stepped back and bowed his head.

People passing stopped and gazed at the old man's silent ceremony, the rain noisily pelting their umbrellas. They watched him intently, some even took photos, but he just stood there staring up at the face. Tears began to roll.

After a while, his vigil ended. He turned and we made eye contact briefly again, but he said nothing. He didn't seem able or even willing to speak. I don't think he even realised I was there. I'd never seen Paul like this before.

Without saying anything he crossed the road in heavy rain, and I followed. After a moment he turned and mumbled, 'Come, let's join the others and eat.' 'Of course,' I said. I wasn't sure what had just happened.

In silence he led the way into the lift and up into the *Portrait Restaurant* of the National Portrait Gallery. We were shown to our group which was at a table by the magnificent window. I had no idea such a place existed. It was superb. We sat and Paul quietly ordered a Riesling, cakes, sandwiches and coffee.

He opened the conversation in a most unusual way, but typical of him: 'I wrote to Pius XII about Edith in 1941.'

'Who's Pius the XII?' He ignored that and looked at me. Nervously I sipped my excellent coffee.

'I got a reply too. It said, 'Whilst His Holiness recognises the brilliant dedication of the life-saving nurse Edith Cavell and the contribution of her works towards the greatness of God, nevertheless there is no proof that Edith performed any miracle.' I didn't accept that, so I wrote back. I told the Pope that when mother and I had visited her hospital in Brussels in 1938 I had seen a blue-white light in human form there. I said Edith should be canonized because she saved so many lives and that she inspired my mother to become a nurse, and in her turn, go on to save many more lives. I got another reply from the Vatican:

'His Holiness is pleased to receive the supplication but is not able to consider it any further.' It didn't seem to matter that I wrote the letters to Rome in Latin, and indeed received the replies in Latin. I think Edith Cavell is a saint and I don't care what His Holiness has to say about it.'

He continued, 'I always thought Pius turned down Edith Cavell for sainthood because she was a devout Protestant, but that wasn't it. Now I know that in 1941 if he had named a British nurse from Norfolk as a saint, it would have caused trouble for him with Mussolini and Hitler. They would have seen it as favouring their enemy. In the middle of a war His Holiness wasn't going to do that and be seen to enflame the Catholic world against Italy and Germany. I don't blame him. I wouldn't have done it either. But that doesn't mean Edith isn't a saint though.'

What he said had just sailed entirely over my head. I gathered that Pius XII was a Pope in the 1940s, but I was more interested in what Paul had said about his mother being inspired by Edith Cavell. My sister Amy is a nurse.

'The execution of Edith Cavell by the Germans at dawn on 12 October 1915, was murder and a war crime,' he said. It wasn't appropriate for me to mention that I'd never heard of her, so I kept silent. But I did have something to say and after a pause for respect I asked:

'I was very moved back there. Edith means a lot to you. If she was from Norfolk how did she inspire your mother in Strasbourg?'

'Edith was in Brussels training nurses from all over Europe when the German army rolled through in 1914. All she was doing was her job, which was keeping people alive and teaching others to keep people alive. But she put herself in grave danger by helping allied soldiers to escape. The Germans didn't like that, so they took her and shot her.' He was seething as he said that. There was total contempt in his intonation.

'There is something evil in the soul of any person that would think it right to put a nurse in front of a firing squad.' That came from the heart. I'd never heard anyone talk with such passion and conviction. There was a burning hatred in him.

'That's appalling,' I muttered. 'I'm shocked. I had no idea.'

'Somehow we must find a way to forgive, but the only way I have found over all these years is to remember that if it were not for Edith Cavell I would not be here.'

That comment shook me. There was silence as we both contemplated the words. Then he produced something else from his bag. It was the pewter framed photo of the nurse from his bedside table. He handed it to me.

'My mother was 19 and working in the family hotel in Strasbourg when the world learned of the murder of Edith Cavell. It was an international outrage. When news reached her via a smuggled French newspaper Helene

Haussmann was utterly disgusted. Don't forget that Alsace was part of Germany in those days. That did it for her. She'd had it with the Germans, and it was time to take action. She'd already seen them try to conscript her brothers. She told me, 'Edith had fallen, so I chose to go and take her place.' Mother had Christmas 1915 and New Year with her family but on 3 January 1916, she caught the train to Basel and stayed there with our long-standing family friends for a few days. Then she took the train to Paris, stayed with her pacifist brother Jean and joined the French Red Cross. She trained in a hospital there at first but by the summer she was working in a field hospital near the front line. In 1917 she moved to the Amiens sector. By 1918 Helene was a senior nurse who had seen many horrors but saved many men.'

'She's beautiful,' I said quietly. He nodded gently, smiling.

'In March, the Germans started an offensive, *Operation Michael*, towards Paris. It became a desperate defensive battle for the British forces. The Royal Flying Corps resorted to dangerous extreme low-level strafing to slow the advance.

On 26 March 1918, a British Sopwith Camel single-seater came down in a field south of Noyon. It was shot to bits. Locals dragged the pilot out of the smashed aircraft wounded and unconscious. As this was the French sector, he was taken urgently to the nearest French field hospital. He was in the back of a hay cart pulled by a black horse. Fortunately, the hospital was close by. There were many casualties there and the pilot was not considered to be in a life-threatening condition. He was placed on one side in a low-priority tent. Then he woke up wheezing and coughing blood. A nurse was passing who spotted the out-of-place pilot in British khaki-green and leather. The wheezing was coming from his chest, and no-one had noticed whilst he was unconscious and out of the way. Now he was choking to death. But the nurse knew what to do. She had seen a doctor do it but there was no time to call for a doctor: this man would die in seconds. She quickly cut open the officer's leather flying tunic, sat him up and tore back his shirt. She found a bullet hole in his chest. Bright red blood was gurgling from it as he coughed in a delirium. She threw a thick blanket over the wound back and front, grabbed a large hollow needle from a tin tray and rammed it into his chest to let the air out. The pilot screamed in pain and fell back unconscious. The nurse turned him on his side so that he could continue to breathe. And he lived. The nurse had saved his life. That man was my father, and that nurse was my mother.'

I gasped. I wasn't sure if I'd actually heard what he just said. 'Do you mean that because Edith Cavell died, you live?'

'Yes.'

A French Red Cross recruiting poster, 1916

8. Songs of storks & Strasbourg. *Always going away but always coming back*

The first thing I learned about Paul was of his deep and abiding love for his parents.

I wanted to know more, so one morning after searching for and finding Henry's lost false teeth, I sat down with him and in German asked, 'Tell me about your family and your *Heimat*.' I deliberately used Heimat as it doesn't readily translate to English.

Smiling, he spoke in his Alsatian-German: 'It would be my pleasure. I was born in Strasbourg on 28 April 1927 at the Hotel Basel 12-14 Rue De la Douane. It was the family-run hotel of my mother's parents, and we occupied the loft apartments for the first 12 years of my life.

Strasbourg is a magnificent medieval city and today it's a World Heritage Site. Quite right too. Living in the middle of it gave me many opportunities. It's a wonderful place with marvellous architecture and of course the superb Gothic *Cathédrale Notre-Dame* which is very famous. That was our local church on the Ile just behind the hotel and we attended every Sunday. You should hear the beautiful bells ringing!

We spent a lot of time away from home though: in Jersey, Paris, London, Rouen, Bonn. We also visited other German cities like Stuttgart, Frankfurt, Cologne and Leipzig, and lots of different airfields looking at aeroplanes. They even let father fly some of them. Travelling was normal for me.

We had a family saying: *'Always going away, but always coming back.'*

When you grow up in a place, that place is normal and everywhere else is measured against it. However, I was quite used to travelling, so that was normal too. I like to explore and come to know a place from the inside, from its details. Always good to go back to Strasbourg though.

I soon realised that Alsace is special: a complicated place to grow up in. I was only able to realise this later because we travelled so much and other places were just not like Alsace. It was France but we spoke French and German. Strasbourg and the region were really *very German*. It had actually been part of Germany from 1872 to 1919. Living in the hotel in the 1930s we had to be careful to identify the appropriate language. Failure to do so could cause trouble with people walking out and worse. I got a smack in the face once from a guest in the hotel who accused me of being German after he'd heard me speaking 'that cursed language' to my mother. He was a French veteran and had one leg from the first war. Mother took no pity, told him his behaviour was unacceptable, to apologise immediately, pay his bill and get out.

We spoke French outdoors mainly, it depended on who you were with. French was taught in schools. I was taught in French and partly German in a private school. When my mother grew up before the first war in the German time French was outlawed and you had to learn German in school. We all spoke the Alsatian-German dialect and French. A lot of older people lived in the country in the vineyards and mountains. Out there it was wise to open up in German as most likely they were German speakers.

My mother's family were staunch Catholics, just like my father and his family in London and Bonn. I admired my mother's parents, and they adored me, especially when I looked smart dressed in my little suit and hat on Sunday morning at Mass. In Alsace in the 30s I never saw any tension between Catholic and Lutheran we had complete mutual respect, but there was a legacy from the German time. My grandparents hated the way the region had been run by the German Kaiser and his 'Prussian fools.' They were against Germany because of the hopelessly insensitive way the Prussians tried to meddle in the Catholic affairs of Alsace. It annoyed them intensely. But the thing that really did it was when they tried to conscript Helene's brothers my Uncles Claude and Jean into the German army in the Great War. The Haussmann boys weren't having that. They both went off to Paris to avoid it. According to my mother, before the first war in the German time, Alsatian Protestants got preferential treatment over Catholics when it came to education. She hated that too. She wanted to be a doctor, but she had no chance with the system as it was. That's another reason why she went away, but she went back after the war when Alsace became French. Of course, France is a very Catholic country: was then, is now.'

Stork, stork!

Tucked away in a corner of Kew Green there is a little pond. Not many people know it's there. One afternoon I was asked to go on a 'short exercise walk' out with a group down to the pond to feed the ducks. Paul spotted me getting ready with the first aid bags and invited himself along.

The wind blew, cumulus clouds rolled across the sky and the leaves rustled. The old man was looking around enlivened and very alert to it all.

As we walked, I asked him to explain how it was that his father was English, from London, but they lived in Strasbourg. However, with Paul it was rare to get a straight answer.

Just at that moment we came to the pond, and he glanced a tall white bird over in the corner strutting around having a lovely time picking frogs. Without any warning he started singing in German:

'Storch, Storch, Langbein
Wann fliegst du ins Land hinein
Bringst dem Kind ein Brüderlein
Wenn der Roggen reifet
Wenn der Frosch pfeifet
Wenn die goldnen Ringen
In der Kiste springen
Wenn die roten Äpfel'n
In der Kiste rappeln'

Stork, Stork, Longlegs,
When will you fly into the land?
Bringing the child a little brother
When the rye ripens
When the frogs whistle
When the golden rings
Are jumping in the chest
When the red apples
Are rattling in the chest

- **Traditional German nursery rhyme**

He sang beautifully and the guests gave him a loud round of applause. Turning to me he explained, 'It's one of the songs my mother sang to me when I was young. She loved to take me out and about in the city and to the country looking at the sights sketching and painting and I loved it too.'

'That sounds perfect, but is that a stork?'

'No, it's a little egret. There are lots of them along the Thames these days, but it reminded me of my favourite bird. When I went with mother she would show me all the ducks geese and swans. We had a French song we sang about Monsieur le Canard the duck too. In the country mother showed me the delightful orchids dragonflies butterflies and birds like the crane, but of all these lovely things she would especially point out the storks flying. When I was little and I saw one, I always used to shout, 'Stork! stork!' and wave my arms around.'

'Storks?' I exclaimed.

'Yes of course. It's our bird. We get a lot of storks in Alsace. There's lots of mythology and folk stories. Even the Greek philosopher Aristotle wrote about them. He said that when an old stork has lost its feathers and can no longer fly, that its son will bring food and carry the parent on its back to safety. It's a lovely story but I never saw a stork do that. Perhaps it was one of Aristotle's flights of fancy,' he smiled.

You'd think an aerospace engineer would get a joke like that, but it sailed entirely over my head.

'Alsace has the Rhine, lots of water, plenty of tasty frogs and lots of high places to nest in. What more d'you want if you're a stork? They migrate you know. Every autumn they leave for Africa, but every spring they come back to the same place because they love it so much and are so happy there. Mother said that we were *Die Familie Storch*, (The Stork Family) and that's why we were there. Just like the storks we were always going away but always coming back, back to the place where we were happy.'

Paul might have been 91, nevertheless, he was *still* always going away but always coming back.

9. Beatrice and the Big House

How did a boy from Strasbourg happen to find himself in Jersey in the spring of 1940?

Paul explained that his true family name was *von Bonn*, which means, from Bonn. The family came to London way back in the early 1700s on the coattails of King George. He became the King of the United Kingdom even though he was German (from Hanover) and didn't speak a word of English. Back then the family were known in London simply as von Bonn. They made a fortune because they worked hard. There were no benefits in those days for anyone. If you didn't work, you died.

Many Germans lived and worked in London in the Victorian time, and they were popular because Queen Victoria had married one: her first cousin Prince Albert of Saxe-Coburg Gotha. However, the imperialist ambitions of Bismarck's newly formed Germany were colliding with British interests, especially in Africa. This caused antagonism between the countries. The Boer War (1899-1902) triggered outpourings of anti-British propaganda in German newspapers which resulted in yet more anti-German feeling in England. It was affecting business, so in 1903 Paul's Grandfather Charles von Bonn decided to change the family name simply to *Bunn* and the business to *Bunn & Co*.

All the von Bonns spoke German in the home in London and they retained strong family connections in the Bonn region of Germany. Paul's father Christopher and his brother George were born and baptised in Bonn and raised in London speaking German and English. They were French speakers too as a lot of time was spent in France on business. Between the wars when Christopher travelled widely in Germany with his family he said they were from Bonn. They spoke the language perfectly and everyone assumed they were German.

Paul never met his Uncle George. He was a Lieutenant in the British Army in the Great War but was killed at Ypres in 1917.

With his parents Christopher and Helene, Paul moved to Jersey in April 1940 when he turned 13. They travelled to take care of Great-Aunt Beatrice on his father's side, who was 80. She was a colourful character whom he adored.

He told me that according to her she had been in the West India Docks in London wandering along minding her business one day in 1880. A

Brigantine moored in flying the 'skull & crossbones' and a sea-pirate captain jumped off. He ran across the quayside, picked Beatrice up, threw her over his shoulder and carried her off on his pirate ship to his secret hideaway across the ocean on a desert island called Jersey. I can just imagine the look of wonder on young Paul's face as the ancient lady told him her story.

Whatever the truth of it was, young Beatrice von Bonn aged 20 married the Jersey captain Charles le Coyte and they acquired and renovated a house at St Brelade which is in the south-west of the island. The story went that when Paul was about three years old, he walked through the door for the first time. Instantly impressed with the lofty ceilings and space he called out, *'Wow, was für ein großes Haus!'* (Wow, what a Big House!) From that point onwards it was known simply as: *the Big House*.

He drew maps and buried his treasures, quartz crystals and seashells, in a wooden box in the sand dunes of St Ouen's. He would come back a year later with his map, find the way straight to the spot and dig it up.

Paul never met Captain Charles. He was lost at sea in 1895.

Beatrice never re-married and kept the name le Coyte. She ran the business affairs of her late husband with great skill, was highly respected and a local benefactor. If it came to her attention that someone was in any kind of strife she always stepped in, particularly financially. Paul told me it was a good thing she retained the le Coyte name. He explained that it could have caused trouble for her through the Great War if people remembered that her maiden name was von Bonn and that she was essentially German.

Paul and his parents often visited Jersey. They'd appointed a business manager for Beatrice before Paul was born. She also had a housekeeper Louise, who was a battle-axe, a housemaid Marion, who looked after her personally, who was shy and lovely, and a laundry maid Anne, who was taken on as a 15-year-old when Paul was about 10.

The Bunns assumed that Alsace would immediately see hostilities but that this war would turn out like the last one. The advancing German forces would be held back by the might of the French and British Armies. They were wrong on both counts. After war was declared in September 1939, Strasbourg was completely evacuated and became an empty city. The Haussmann and Bunn families relocated to Paris initially with 'Uncle Jean' and then took apartments. Paul lived there for six months. The shops and cafés were open, and it was as if there was no war.

It seemed like the right thing for the Bunns to move to be with Beatrice.

So, in the spring of 1940 the Bunn family had all their stuff sent to Jersey and took the train to Amiens. They cycled on to Rouen to stay with Paul's Uncle Claude in his hotel. From there they cycled-toured across Normandy and arrived at St Brelade in late April. They thought they would be safe in Jersey. They were wrong.

The Bunns could have evacuated to London, but they didn't go. Paul's father had a chronic breathing condition from when he was shot down. He needed clean air and to keep dry and warm. When he returned home in 1919 he nearly died in the Spanish Flu epidemic and then nearly died in a February 'pea soup' London smog. The family never thought it was safe for him to live in the city after that. They also thought London would be bombed, just as it had been bombed by German Zeppelin airships and aircraft in World War I. So, there were lots of reasons to be in Jersey.

On arrival Paul found school difficult. English was his third language and wasn't that good. Even though he had an English governess in Strasbourg, he described his command of the language then as 'tenuous.' He couldn't use his German for obvious reasons, but although his French was perfect his Alsace accent was quite thick. Everyone spoke English, and about half the Jersey population spoke *Jèrriais* as well. The other thing that made it difficult for him was that the churches were not well attended. The Bunns had lots of networks from church in Strasbourg. Paul found it hard to make friends in Jersey and German military control reduced freedoms still more with curfews and various bans and restrictions.

He told me, 'In 1940, lots of people left Jersey before the occupation. One of them was John Clare, the longstanding business manager of Beatrice's affairs, who was also a member of our congregation. His boys John and Charles used to come to the Big House, and we were friends. Our arrival meant that he could leave with his family and a clear conscience.'

It was no longer the free and easy idyllic holiday place of his childhood. It got more difficult. When he did go out, he found himself to be the subject of increasing interest and suspicion amongst the local boys due to his accent.

'You only learn what freedom is after you've lost it,' Paul often told me.

The Germans insisted that everyone register on brown identity cards. Christopher was born in Bonn but held a British Passport. For years he'd also held a German *Ahnenpaß*, which showed he was 'of German blood'. Mother also held a pass. Fewer questions were asked in Germany if you had one. She was German but was registered with the Jersey authorities as

French on arrival in 1940. Paul was registered on the back of his father's card as also being born in Strasbourg. These administrative details took on critical importance later.

He explained, 'Father soon established himself as a figure of respect amongst both communities, Jersey and German. The islanders were supposed to hand in their guns. However, he kept back his Webley Mk VI revolver 'just in case.' He also kept his Lee Enfield .303 and my Mauser Sportmodell smallbore for the same reason. We hid them carefully in the attic. He also gained respect for his stashed radio and willingness to share news from the mainland. Speaking perfect German was a huge advantage and he would often come to the defence of a neighbour who was having trouble with the authorities. He was utterly fearless and used to say, 'If they want to get at these innocent people, we'll have to see about that, won't we?'

Paul also gave an amusing account of how the formidable 80-year-old and his father and mother worked together to repel all borders early on:

'Great-aunt, father and mother all took a combative attitude towards the Germans. Right at the start, against father's loud protests the army tried to billet a senior sergeant from Berlin in a spare room at the Big House. He offered me chocolate, showed me his postcard collection and tried to make friends with me. 'Everyone needs to see Berlin,' he often said. I stole one of his cards! After a few days there was a massive shouting match between this Berliner and my parents ably assisted by Beatrice. They threw his suitcase out on the road, beat him up with rolling pins and saucepans and kicked him out!

Beatrice turned rolling pin in hand and told him, 'The only Germans who are going to live in this house are us!''

I soon realised that the von Bonns, or Bunns, whoever they were, had a somewhat dry sense of humour.

'An *Oberleutnant* with red epaulettes from the military police came around to investigate. He was shocked when father greeted him in flawless high German and took him into the garden amongst the flowers and roses to explain. Father confidently offered him a Wills cigarette from his silver cigarette case which he always carried, even though he never smoked. After he lit the German up with the silver lighter which he always carried, he explained that the bloody Berliner had got drunk and tried to take advantage of his wife and son and he wasn't having it. Father did so with such humble charm and respect that the officer went off apologising profusely promising that the *Hauptfeldwebel* would be disciplined internally and made to billet with the lower ranks. It was a good move as after that the Germans never again tried to foist soldiers on us.

In those early days, the Germans were taking a cautious approach in the island. They expected the United Kingdom to capitulate. They didn't want to make life difficult for themselves and didn't expect to be in Jersey very long. The initial garrison wasn't large. That changed when it became clear that British Prime Minister Winston Churchill was going to resist.

Many left, but my school survived, albeit with much smaller classes, and I began to build a small circle of friends. It wasn't easy. I was perceived as an outsider and sometimes that caused trouble. In Strasbourg I knew the inner workings and tiny details that go with growing up in a place. I didn't have any of that in Jersey. Once we got over the shock of occupation and into September and a new school year, I started to feel how little I knew about the island and its customs and ways. It wasn't as if I was free to go and find out either. There were lots of places 'you couldn't go.' Curfew was particularly hard as that autumn of 1940 came on. I didn't like being stuck indoors. Although the Big House was big, it soon began to feel not so big. There are only so many *Meccano* models a boy can build, only so many comics and annuals he can read.

It began to occur to me that making friends in Strasbourg had been easy.'

The Bunn family began to find its feet. His mother and father felt it would be politic to be seen out more and become familiar with the island. It wasn't as if there was nothing to do either. Many doctors and nurses evacuated, and this left the island short of skilled people. Helene presented herself to the General Hospital in St Helier where her outstanding nursing skills and experience were readily accepted and appreciated. 'It's all in a good cause,' as she used to say. His father approached the Bailiff's Office and offered his language skills which were also accepted. Later he taught German, which became mandatory in schools. They found ways to fit in because they had enough life experience. Paul did not, and as a result he turned to other ways by which to divert himself.

'Once we had that bust up with the Berliner and a couple of months had passed, I wondered if it might be worthwhile to cultivate the occupying forces and find out more about them. As a family we had no problem with the language or culture of Germany per se. The problem wasn't the people. The problem was the Nazi regime, the military restrictions and loss of freedoms. Everyone hated that, especially me.

In September I helped out with milking and the harvest over in one of the farms at St Peter's. This made me popular, but some of the local boys weren't so sure about my accent and they spoke about me in *Jèrriais* behind my back. I could follow only a little at first. Later I learned what the boys were really saying about me, and it wasn't flattering. For example, I distinctly recall being described as, *'Pouôrre boûse d'âne'* (a poor donkey turd). I was also told, *'Tu pensé que tu'es pus haut qu'un tchu d'un tchian'* (you think you are higher than a dog's arsehole), and sometimes simply, *'Fouaitheux!'* (Shithead!) They must have thought it was hilarious when I just smiled.

In return for helping, I was invited to spend several days making *Black Butter* with the apples. I met some nice girls: Annette and Jane who were older than me and lived in neighbouring farms. Days of peeling and peeling! We sang songs in *Jèrriais*, and I began to learn. I enjoyed that and discovering the insults. We were like the three witches in Macbeth stirring the cauldron in the smuts. Hubble-bubble! I went away with several *Bourdélot* which are apples baked with spices in pastry, delicious, and three large Kilner jars full of tasty butter. Very nice indeed.

That fun didn't last long. For some reason they closed the shops in the first two weeks of October. There wasn't anything to buy anyway. When they re-opened I did manage to find one thing I was looking for in Peter Perrio's cycle shop in New Street.

By November I was getting bored and fed up. Very few had come to visit the Big House, and I had only been to about three other houses of kids at my school or church. No-one came to stay over. Nights were long and weekends craved for. It was a sunny morning when I decided I would pay Hans and the soldiers up at La Moye a visit. At the very least I thought I could have a bit of fun and take the piss out of them. I pushed my bike up the valley, turned left, and arrived in front of the hotel.

I was confronted by two sentries with fixed bayonets and warm looking gloves. 'Halt! Sie cannot goh,' said one in hesitating English.

I smiled and began practising some of the charm I learned from father in my best German, 'Good morning! I have come to see my friend Corporal Hans Maier. Will you let me in please?'

He nearly dropped his gun in surprise.

A younger soldier laughed and said, 'We don't know you. Push off before I give you a clip around the ear!'

'Wait,' said the first one, 'he's that German boy.'

'He can't be German. The only Germans here are us.'

I corrected them truthfully, 'I am from Straßburg.'

'He's French.'

'No, you fool, listen to him. He's German.'

'I am Alsatian.'

The two sentries had a hushed discussion they thought I couldn't hear. One was sure I was faking; the other was sure I wasn't. So, I said, 'I think Hans might be a little disappointed when he finds out I was here, and you two didn't let me in. He's an officer candidate you know.'

That did the trick. 'How do you know him?' one asked.

'He ran me over with his bike in St Helier.'

'We ride on the right. You should have been looking where you were going boy.'

'I was. He was on the wrong side of the road, and he should have had a bell,' I said with a grin.

They'd heard enough and found my story and perfect German completely convincing.

The first one said, 'Alright boy, I'll go and see if he's around.'

'Thank you very much,' I said.

He disappeared off.

Five minutes passed. I chatted to the sentries. Eventually Hans came out, doing up his tunic, his breath steaming the chilly air. He said, 'Let him in lads, he's one of ours who got left behind.'

The door opened, and I stepped through. I never knew it then, but that step changed my life forever.'

51

10. The road less travelled

Paul never said or did anything wasteful of time or energy. When he asked a question of me or anyone else you could be quite sure he would listen to the answer intently. Highly observant. After a month or so he had become such a source of fascination and intrigues to me that I used to complete my shift and just hang around chattering to him. I began a diary I called 'Paul's Stories,' which is what I'm using to write from now.

With a location right next to Kew Gardens it was natural that guests were offered escorted walks almost every day with lunch or breakfast. These were popular, but I'd never been on one.

Paul's modus operandi was conversation, preferably over a plate of food with a glass of wine. In that summer of 2018, although I had learned a great deal about him, he was also genuinely interested in finding out about me.

I was pretty tired after getting off my first overnight shift, which finished around 7am. My diary says it was early August. As usual he was up and about though, in the sunroom with blankets on his legs and a copy of the Times in his hand. The air heater was blowing on him rustling the pages. He saw me coming in the reflection in the window. 'Good morning Katie,' he said, ever cheery. I was weary. 'You look tired dear,' he observed.

'Yes. Last night we had to phone the on-call doctor for Bruce. I had to sit with him.'

'I'm very sorry to hear that. I like Bruce. Is he OK?'

'Well, he's OK at the moment, but he will be assessed more fully today. Last night was busy.'

'How about we join the Kew group for breakfast then? I'll pay. The food here is typical English, i.e., crap. It's one of the things they don't tell you about in the prospectus,' he grinned. I knew that wasn't true, the food was amazing. I was hooked on his stories though, so I said, 'Yes of course.' I was knackered but wanted to go. I went home first to see my sister before she went on duty then grabbed some sleep.

At 10 I walked back to see the group crossing the road just on the Kew side of the bridge. Paul saw me approaching and waited. When I joined him, he asked, 'You live close by?'

'Yes,' I pointed, 'just over there in that tower block.' He took it in and said nothing.

We all went through the Elizabeth Gate and then directly along a path they all seemed to know well. We passed an open metal framework structure called *The Hive,* which emitted a strange humming sound, to a large ornamental lake with a statue in the middle and a stately looking building facing the Palm House. There was a lot to see, but he was watching me, 'You don't know this place, do you?' he observed.

'No. I've only ever been here twice before.'

'WHAT?' he exclaimed, 'You live less than a mile away!'

I remember I wasn't particularly impressed with that outburst, and I gave him a look which I followed up with, 'Do you think I had a choice?'

He apologised profusely. 'Mother of Christ! that came out all wrong, please accept my apology.' 'Of course,' I added. He was much more circumspect after that.

Paul had skills and knowledge that I never knew existed. But sometimes he lacked tact. He could be short-tempered and fall into passive aggression, even outright aggression, if he felt slighted. I'd seen him do it. Sometimes he blundered, like with his 'mile away' comment, into condescension. These were the times when he really infuriated me. I knew he could be charm personified, so it was all the more annoying when he came out with some patronising remark or another. He did learn though and so did I.

Walking he told me, 'My father said there were storks here before the first war. The family used to come for picnics on the District Railway. I can just remember a picnic in 1934. They had Demoiselle Cranes, and a curious Stanley Crane called 'Joey' here. It was so lovely seeing them up close.

We took seats in the sun outside *The Botanical* restaurant with its grand view of the Palm House. Geese and ducks waddled by pooping as they went. 'They're almost as bad as some of the old codgers at the home,' he said looking at the others with a cheeky grin. 'How old d'you have to be to qualify as an *old codger* then?' one asked. 'Oh, 92 at least,' he laughed. He was 91 of course.

We sat together and he had it all worked out. A bottle of Alsace Riesling was ordered while we considered breakfast. There were things on the menu I'd never heard of before and looked exotic so I chose one just to see what would turn up. Meanwhile he was pouring the wine. My co-workers looked on jealously, but I could drink because I was off duty. 'Bit early for wine, isn't it?' I observed.

He adjusted his hearing aid and glanced at his watch. '10.30. Never too early for wine. If we were back home in a café in Strasbourg we'd be onto a second bottle by now, with coffee, kugelhopf (sweet bread) and pastries,' he giggled.

Then he continued, 'So, how are you enjoying studying aerospace engineering? Sounds fantastic.' I said I loved every minute of it. But I wasn't going to let him pin me down with questions and as well as that I was beginning to learn too.

Just like in his chess, Paul had a preferred style which was to start by making it look like one thing when really he was planning something else. Not sly or cynical, just clever and sophisticated, not the kind of exchange I was used to. I never quite knew where a conversation with Paul Bunn was going to go.

I turned the tables on him. 'Where did you go to university Paul? Oxford, like your father?'

'No, not Oxford, the London School of Economics.' That was a surprise. I was sure he would have gone to Oxford. Then he turned that around and said, 'Sometimes it's not at all obvious how things will play out, is it? Did you ever think you would go to university? I must admit, when I was stuck in Jersey I never imagined I would ever see London again, let alone go to university there.'

'No,' I said. 'Nobody in my family stayed on at school. Nobody in my family even knew what university was. I'm not quite sure how I ended up at Manchester, but I have.' I studied his face.

A moment or two passed as he considered that, nodding his head; his mouth open slightly in reflection. Then he said, 'You're special. You've stepped out. You're taking the road less travelled, and I salute you!'

He raised his glass and taking a quaff recited:

'I shall be telling this with a sigh
Somewhere ages and ages hence:
Two roads diverged in a wood, and I —
I took the one less travelled by,
And that has made all the difference.'
               - **Robert Frost. From 'The Road Not Taken' 1915**

He said, 'Taking the road less travelled is a complicated business. It's profound, especially if you don't realise you've taken it. Do you know the poem?' I said I'd heard the expression *to take the road less travelled*, but never knew it was from a poem. I think my eyes must have rolled or something because he was studying me. Then I realised I was studying him: his fingers on his glass, the expression on his face. His eyes flickered, with head bowed ever so slightly.

Suddenly I realised what the poem meant. 'I see it.'

'Yes?'

'I took the one less travelled.'

'Why did you take it?'

'Because I had to.'

'Wow,' he muttered. He never used that term normally: one of mine.

'I didn't do what was expected of me. I did something else.'

I looked at him, there was a glint in his eye, a tiny nod of acknowledgement.

'The road less travelled… We are attracted to it *because* it's less travelled,' he observed.

'Yes,' I found myself saying.

He said, 'I've often wondered if I was the only one who thought this. Now I know I'm not.' That was very generous, likely to be untrue, but generous all the same.

'I was always going to leave Brentford. I don't remember thinking I'd made a choice.'

'We all make choices. They say, 'We have to live with our choices,' but actually, our lives are simply the collection of our choices, the sum totality of them. We don't live with our choices: *we are our choices.*'

I didn't really hear that bit. I was thinking about something else. 'When I look out from the balcony of the flat, I see the planes flying in and out of Heathrow.'

'I'm sure it's a magnificent view from up there.'

'On a clear day you can see St Paul's, the London Eye, Box Hill and the Crystal Palace transmitters.'

'Almost like flying?'

'Yes. Above it all: the houses and trees, and the river. I see the clouds. It's different every day. There are always aeroplanes though no matter what, coming and going.'

'I see,' he said.

Then I was startled at what came out of my mouth:

'I don't think you do *see*. I *hate* that view.'

That shook the old man so much that for once he didn't know what to say. I didn't know what to say either, so I drank my wine instead, a big mouthful.

Fortunately, breakfast was brought out right at that moment: creamy, with bread muffins and slices of ham. It looked amazing. 'Eggs Benedict, ma'am,' announced the waiter. 'Where are the eggs?' I asked. He explained, 'There is rather a lot of sauce, but the eggs are on top of the ham, ma'am.' I don't know what impressed me more, the mountain of delicious smelling thick yellow sauce, or the fact he'd referred to me twice as *ma'am*! Paul regarded me earnestly but said nothing. Probably a good thing.

I'd cut him off. That must have upset him. Then I realised I'd upset myself. I drank more wine.

He kept quiet as he ate his *Full English*. I'd found a way of silencing him without even meaning to. I had been very rude and felt sheepish. Then I stopped beating myself up and demolished the superb Eggs Benedict instead. 'This is wonderful, I've never had anything like this before,' I enthused.

'You speak so strongly. You have to know that I don't mean to upset you. Please accept my apology,' he said looking me square in the eye.

'No, I should be saying sorry to you. I'm rude. I have no manners.'

'You are who you are. Never apologise for who you are.'

'That's easy for you to say. You had advantages. I had no advantages and made no choices. I had to get away. It wasn't a choice; it was a necessity.'

'I'm sorry. I didn't ask you out to breakfast just to rub your nose in it. How can I make it up to you?'

'It's not your fault. When I said that I didn't do what was expected of me, I was kidding myself. *Nothing* was expected of me.'

'Don't say that. It can't be true.'

'It is true, but I don't think I realised until now.'

'You're studying at Manchester University on a top-level engineering course. You definitely chose that.'

'Yes, but I didn't choose to grow up on the 20th floor of a tower block where people piss in the elevator, play in crappy little parks at the bottom in grass full of dog shit, and walk along picking up needles in the alleyways on the way to the shops. I didn't choose any of that.'

I'd found myself suddenly simmering. Until that moment I never knew

I had such anger and frustration in me.

'I'm sorry,' he said in a lower tone. 'I'm learning far too slowly.'

'You haven't done anything wrong. All of this is new for me: Manchester, university education, learning. It's all wonderful. I'm learning fast. I'm lucky.'

'You took the road less travelled. I'm in awe of you Katie.'

'I took that road because I had to, but I'm not going to do what my mother did...'

There, it just came out.

The moment passed. He gave a tiny acknowledging nod but said nothing.

A little pause followed as the group finished their breakfasts. He paid then said, 'Come, let's walk.'

The rest of the morning was filled just with pleasantries. We were both reflecting on what had happened.

Paul talked about 'a step that changed his life forever,' and 'taking the road less travelled.' He had evidently done both. I had too, and he had just helped me to realise it.

He had also somehow prompted me into expressing my resentment and anger, emotions I didn't know I had, or perhaps had suppressed and forgotten.

11. The coming storm, 1938 - 1939

Whenever Paul told me any story of his or his father's flying exploits, I hung on every word. The best one was an intimate description of the day they flew a glider together from Wasserkuppe, Germany when he was 11:

'You glance down the wing and admire three buzzards circling sharing their thermal lift. They look at you, and you look at them. 'We're all birds here!' they seem to say. Instinctively you follow them. This is their element and today it's yours too. You feel the energy in the sky lifting and buffeting the heavy glider as you circle up towards the grey base of the cumulus cloud above. It's thrilling.

Behind you hear words from your father who is your instructor today, 'Keep with it! Keep turning! You have four metres per second of lift. Well done!'

The buzzards are now above you stretching their wings and showing you the way. 'Come with us. Come with us Paul Bunn!' they call.

Now you are 2100 metres above the countryside. As you approach the dark misty base of the cumulus you look to the west and see a town. 'What is that place dad?' You hear the rustle of a map. 'Fulda,' comes the reply. 'Can we go there?' 'Yes.'

You level the wings, push the stick forward and set off leaving the dancing birds to whirl between the hanging tendrils of cloud.

The fabric covering of the aircraft hums and the wooden spars creak as you cut through the bumpy air. You look down at the houses, the river, the churches, the forests and secret places. This is freedom and it's beautiful.

An hour passes as you soar over the provincial town. Then your father tells you that a storm is coming and it's time to take the glider home. There is a sadness as you realise what that means. You roll the aircraft and turn for the airfield.

Far too soon you are back at Wasserkuppe and preparing to land. You tighten your straps. Father allows you to fly the *Kranich II* down to about 200 metres altitude circling and balancing your turns. You fly well. Even though you've flown before at Dunstable he doesn't quite trust you to complete the circuit and landing. 'I have control,' he says. 'You have control,' you tell him, releasing the joystick. But he senses your disappointment and adds, 'Follow me through on the controls.'

The ground arrives and it's all over with a bump and a roll. Older

Hitlerjugend Luft (Hitler Youth Air) boys run up in their brown shirts and black shorts, your second cousin amongst them. Lifting the canopy, he congratulates you and asks where you've been. Star struck you stare at him, 'Georg, I've been in heaven!' Your answer is honest, and he looks at you with a big grin as he helps you climb out.

Your father joins you on the fragrant grass. His smile is wider than the river Rhine as he hugs you and tells you that you flew brilliantly. Mother bounces up. She is delighted too. 'I took photos!' she exclaims.'

I was thrilled to hear this story. The old man went on to explain how the rest of that day he and his father flew the *Fieseler Storch*, which was the towplane used for launching the gliders sometimes. Whilst packing the hangar at sunset, Paul proclaimed his father proudly to the gathered youths and instructors, 'This is my father: *Der König der Störche!*'

They would often visit German airfields, and his father would be invited to look around or fly the aircraft they had.

Paul and his father flying the Fieseler Storch, 1938

He showed me old photos: the Storch, members of his extended family on his father's side; the von Bonns who lived in Germany in the 1930s. He told me about them:

'I met my Great-Uncle August in Bonn a few times. He was born a year before Beatrice and was just as eccentric, with the addition that he was completely German. He thoroughly disapproved of Hitler and labelled him an uneducated liar and worse. He called the Nazis uncultured book-burning morons. August died just before the war started. His surviving children were Maximilian and Herta. Max married Maria and my second cousins Ernst and Georg were born in 1921 and 1923. We kept in touch via letters with Max and Herta as they had taken the von Bonn residence. Herta never married. I really liked her. Ernst and Georg both joined the Luftwaffe and flew as pilots. I found out after the war that both were killed in Russia.'

The Molsheim incident

At some point he told me this story:

'By spring 1939 tensions between France and Germany were running high. In my youthful exuberance and naivety, I didn't realise how strongly.

It was a lovely day just after Easter, the storks were arriving, and I wanted to see them. I cycled out of town westwards along the towpath of the Canal de la Bruche, then along the river into Molsheim. My plan was to catch the train home. It's a route we used to cycle as a family. A delightful area with vineyards, little forests and grazing. I had my paint tin and pad and sketched the storks flying and wading taking the frogs. Those birds are darlings! I painted two beautiful cranes as well. Behind were dark clouds like giant cauliflowers, and in the distance I heard thunder.

I stopped in Molsheim at a patisserie for kugelhopf. I can't resist that stuff! There were three older lads in the shop. I spoke to the storekeeper in French and didn't think anything of it. I unwrapped and started eating as soon as I walked through the door which tinged with a little bell. Then I heard the bell ting again behind me.

Next thing I knew these youths came out, pushed the bread out of my hands and trod on it. They were hurling abuse at me in German: 'Rich French boy with all your money! Don't come out here showing off.'

'You clowns don't know anything,' I told them in best Alsatian-German. Smack! I got a punch right in the eye and down I went. Then just to really piss me off they grabbed me, and stole my belt, money and watch. 'Nice watch,' one of them said, 'I'll take it.' Then they gave me and my bike a good kicking. The storekeeper came running out, but it was too late. They ran away laughing and shouting, 'Hitler is coming, and when he arrives you'd better not be here, French boy!' Bastards.

The storekeeper picked me up, dusted me off, and said he didn't know who they were. I suspected he was lying. Everyone knew everyone else in those sorts of places. He took me to a neighbour who had a telephone. The hotel was called, and father came out immediately in the car. He was absolutely furious.

****

It was market day in Strasbourg, and I'd noticed him a few weeks earlier. He was working on a wine stall with his father. He was definitely one of them: one of the *Molsheim clowns,* <u>and</u> he was wearing my watch. I reckoned he was about 14 years old to my 12, and he was going to get a surprise.

On the day I made sure I was wearing my boots. Father sometimes told me, *'Like Bomber Command: Strike Hard Strike Sure.'*

It was raining, a thunderstorm actually. I waited until his father had gone off somewhere. Then I casually walked around the side of the stall. He didn't recognise me, and it was all over in a few seconds. As I stood over him I told him, 'Nice watch, I'll take it.'

12. Not interested in being German

Paul told me that today we don't understand what the world was like back in the 1930s and '40s. He explained that the worst offenders are people aged between 70 and 85 who think they know, but they don't.

He assured me that nobody born after 1945 could possibly have any idea just how awful the 1930s and war years were for the people of Great Britain. There was poverty, virtually no benefits, and no state pension until Clement Attlee's Labour government introduced it in 1946. Lots of people died needlessly because there was no National Health Service (NHS), and people couldn't even afford to see a doctor. Labour invented the NHS in 1948 against strong Conservative opposition. When the war came it was even worse. Bombs fell, homes were destroyed, and loved ones went off to fight, often for the second time in their lives. Nobody in France or Britain could bear to think about war again because the horrific events of 1914-1918 were still a very recent memory. When hostilities opened in September 1939 it was like some great national mourning had been reawakened.

Chamberlain at Heston Airport, 30 September 1938

'People wanted to believe that the best would happen. In 1938 they were desperate to believe the Conservative Prime Minister Neville Chamberlain waving his pathetic bit of paper at Heston airport. He promised us there would be 'Peace in our time.' But he got it completely wrong. Paper is no use against people like Hitler. Less than one year after promising peace we got war. After that there were no certainties, they were gone. All you could do was rely on your friends, family and ultimately, yourself. There was a new normal. That was especially and particularly true of the occupied Channel Islands which Churchill had abandoned.'

I learned so much from Paul about growing up in the 1930s and the effects of war and occupation on the mind. What I didn't expect to learn were his motivations for doing the things he did. Some of these seemed very odd.

We went for a long walk around Kew Gardens on a beautiful early August day, Paul and quite a large group of us.

He said, 'Why did I go along to the hotel on Route Orange? Boredom, curiosity, the guns and equipment, in what the Germans thought about the war, interest in how Germans were. It's easier to beat someone when you know how they're going to play. I didn't appreciate that then, but I do now, what with everything that happened.'

'What d'you mean: *everything that happened?*' I asked.

'I couldn't have predicted what would happen after that incident in New Street with Hans. I had no way of knowing where it was going to lead.'

'Where did it lead? You told me you were Alsatian, from Strasbourg. You might have made friends with the Germans, but that didn't make you German, did it?'

'It most certainly did not. I was not interested in being German. But I was interested in what they were all about. I suppose I also craved friendship and camaraderie, there was precious little of that on offer in my circumstances. Father often told me: know your enemy and choose your battles, although I didn't always heed that advice.'

Then Paul asked, 'Do you know the German expression: 'One enemy is too many, and a hundred friends aren't enough'?' I said I'd never heard that one. 'Well, in Jersey in late 1940, I would say that I had far too many enemies and nowhere near enough friends. It wasn't possible for someone like me to continue like that for long.'

Then, as he was often wont to do, and just when it was getting interesting, he entirely turned the tables on me. He did this a lot. I was expecting him to tell me some new anecdote as we sat on a bench in the main café at the shop drinking coffee and eating cake. Instead, he asked, 'What about you? You're studying a master's degree in aerospace engineering, but why did you choose it?'

I explained that I had a long-standing interest in science and technology, that I was good at maths and physics, that I found aircraft, rockets and engines of all kinds fascinating and that I wanted to learn more. He pressed me and took a slightly different tone: 'But why did you choose that subject?'

I was puzzled. 'Haven't I told you?'

'No,' he said. 'You told me you're fascinated, ok, but what's the fascination? What is it that motivated you to invest £9000 on tuition fees, money you haven't got, on a future engineering career you can't have any certainty about, especially now that Brexit has screwed everything?'

'It's £9250 per year for four years, £37,000,' I corrected.

'Mother of Christ!' he exclaimed. I must admit, I wasn't expecting his question or any of that. He clearly wasn't interested in superficialities. He was right about Brexit too. It's ruining the British aerospace industry along with many other technical manufacturing sectors. I said I needed to think about that, but he wouldn't let me. He went on:

'That £37,000 is just the university course fees for four years. It's a staggering investment, and risky too. How do you afford to live? You've got to live for four years in term time as well. It's a huge burden for such a young person.'

'I've taken a loan.'

'How much?'

'I'd rather not say if you don't mind.'

'Ok, but now you have to work at the Stanley. It must be an awful lot of money if you are forced to take work around nosey old buggers like me. What's the interest rate?'

'Retail Price Index plus three percent. I don't know how long it will take me to pay off after I graduate, always supposing I can get a decent job.'

'RPI plus three percent interest. That's outrageous! Bank base rates are zero. Whose idea was that? Disgusting. It's a government sponsored rip-off. No wonder it'll take years. You must be pretty motivated, not just to take on a hard complex subject like engineering, but also the debt burden.' He was genuinely disturbed. He didn't know how much university education cost, or about the interest rates.

'Don't think I haven't thought about this because I have,' I said as we stood and admired the Pagoda, its dragons shining in the sun.

'What about your A Level German? Why did you do that?' I said a similar thing, that I was interested in the language and that I was good at it.

He commended me in German, 'Your German is certainly excellent. I know how you got an A star!'

Then something came out. I said, 'I thought learning German would help me in the world of engineering, perhaps even help me get a job. There are opportunities for engineers there. It's a very future facing country.'

We sat on the bench looking at the beautiful Chokushi-Mon and Japanese Landscape, I looked at him and his face fell. 'You know, Goethe wrote: 'If you're not going forwards, you're going backwards.' Well, this country is going backwards. Such a shame. You're so bright and full of life, but all the ignorant old so-and-sos who live in the past and voted Leave have screwed you forward-thinking clever young people over. You have been denied your future. Shame.'

I couldn't listen to him anymore and needed to change the subject, so I stood ready to walk back to the Stanley. Trying to be flippant and turn the conversation, with a smirk I said, 'But I'm like you: I'm not interested in being German.' He sensed my distress and took my lead.

'They're brilliant engineers though, aren't they? Got to admire them for that. I can see why you'd be interested in German aeronautical engineering; my father and I were!' We laughed, and as we walked he talked about coffee and cakes and trips to airfields in pre-war Germany with his father.

13. The shooting match

'Hans introduced me, 'Lads, this is the Alsatian boy I was telling you about. Looks as if his curiosity has got the better of him and he's finally turned up. Better late than never.' Then with a broad smile he added, 'Watch him though, this Alsatian bites!'

I was led through the building. Lots of *Heer* (army) lower ranks were wandering about. They gave me curious glances.

It was exciting. There was lots of hardware lying around and guns in racks. It was just one giant armed camp. Soldiers, including Hans, bombarded me with questions:

'You are Paul von Bonn. Alsatian?'

'Ja Hans.'

'You must be here by some sort of administrative error?'

'Nein.'

'Then why are you in Jersey?'

'Because my family moved here from Straßburg.'

'That's where you should be, in Straßburg. Not here.'

'Well, I'm here and that's all there is to it. Straßburg was evacuated and everyone had to leave, we had no choice.'

'I see. Who is your father, and where do you live?'

'My father is Christopher von Bonn, and we live on La Marquanderie, the big house on the right by the church.'

'Does your father know you're here?'

'No Corporal Hans.'

'Why have you come to see us today, Paul von Bonn?'

'Because I'm interested in the guns and weapons you have, and I'm interested in being German. You see, I was born on the wrong side of the river.' I lied.

'It seems that you were! How old are you?'

'13.'

'13 huh? Well, if you'd grown up in Germany you would already have joined the *Deutsches Jungvolk* (German Young folk) arm of the *Hitlerjugend* (Hitler Youth). It's not your fault you were born in that part of Germany where a few people speak French, it's just bad luck. Wouldn't you say so lads?' They agreed, and we all laughed together.

They had taken over the hotel. Just inside one room used to billet soldiers was a table and a large mahogany grandmother clock. I sat, and while Hans went off to get some food, studied the rather out of place timepiece ticking gently. 'The owners just left it lying around. I liked it so I took it,' said the soldat who'd nearly dropped his gun. His name was Nikolas. The windows were open, and I listened to the birds in the trees all around. They went well together and although the cuckoos had long gone, I still half expected to hear one.

'Mmm, nice clock,' I said with a smirk. 'You shouldn't have any trouble keeping it wound up, not out here.' The joke sailed entirely over the man's head, so I just giggled to myself. German you see.

Hans came back with coffee, bread, and sausage. I was hungry and tore into it. The soldiers drank the coffee, chewed the bread and smoked acrid Turkish cigarettes. The conversation continued between mouthfuls, but I was eyeing up the guns in the rack.

'Hans, can I look at your rifle?' I asked innocently.

'Yes. Here Paul, this is my Mauser,' and he passed me the weapon. 'It's unloaded,' he said as was the etiquette, but I still checked the chamber out of habit. It was the first of many occasions on which he would hand me a gun. I explored its characteristics.

'Code ce 1939 made by Sauer & Sohn for Poland. Sadly for his mother, the young man it was issued to was let down by someone and didn't go home, so I've taken it on,' Hans explained.

The wood had a good patina; overall a new and handsome piece except for almighty bullet scratches on the stock from where someone had been in a hurry to reload once.

I checked the action and removed the bolt. 'Whoa! Very smooth. How did you get the action so smooth?' But when I glanced at the soldiers they were staring at me with their mouths wide open like freshly caught mackerel on the ramp at St Brelade.

'My God boy, if you weren't in the *Deutsches Jungvolk* how d'you know weapons so well?' Hans asked.

'Guns and weapons of all kinds fascinate me. My father bought me a Mauser Sportmodell in Stuttgart for my tenth. We used to go hunting in the Vosges Mountains. Father went after the deer and wild boar with his mates. I took rabbits hares and pigeon. We Alsatians love our *Hasenpfeffer*.' (hare/rabbit stew)

'So, you can shoot then boy?'

'Better than you can drive your bicycle Hans that's for sure,' I said looking at him and pulling a face.

After a second he burst out laughing, 'You cheeky little bugger! I'll show you who can shoot!'

There followed what can only be described as the strangest shooting match I've ever been on.

Hans went off and came back with a *Feldwebel* (sergeant). He'd been briefed and didn't ask any questions except to say he wanted to be there to see a 13-year-old beat the corporal. I assured him that I would, and would he care to place a bet? The sergeant giggled and we set off through a wood.

I thought we were going out to the rifle range near Les Braye, but we veered left to a makeshift firing range in an old quarry along a soggy track through the trees and fallen leaves. As we progressed word spread and by the time we'd walked the few hundred metres to the pit we'd gathered an entourage of about 15 *Soldaten* all smoking and traipsing in the mud.

We settled down on the earthen bank as the other soldiers stood behind chattering away. Someone went down and put out two lines of five apples at 30 metres and two more lines at 60 on the ridges. Those at 60 would be hard to hit, but there was no wind today and the light was good. I fancied my chances. We shared his gun. He let me have a couple of shots just to get the trigger weight. It was a beautiful weapon, tight and slick.

By the time we'd set up the crowd had swelled, and they were teasing Hans mercilessly, 'I bet you wish you hadn't had *schnapps* (fruit brandy) for breakfast' and, 'You couldn't even hit a football, the apples are not in danger!' Hilarious, I had to laugh.

Hans was smiling throughout. It was a bit of fun to him, he couldn't lose.

He grinned, looked at me and said, 'Alright Paul, I'll go first at 30.'

He clicked the safety off and took his five shots…

The first apple exploded and the second. He missed the third apple to great applause from behind. 'Oh shit,' he cursed, smiling. He re-cocked and fired: the fourth apple exploded. He winged the last apple, and it didn't fall. 'Ooooo!' exclaimed the crowd. He scored three.

Then he passed me the weapon, safety on. I took the cold brass rounds from him and pushed them into the magazine easily, just like father's Lee Enfield. My turn, safety off.

The crowd went silent again.

I missed the first apple, corrected and destroyed the second, third and fourth apples. I drew breath again and held the strap. BOOM! The fifth apple exploded, to great applause.

Smiling, I turned to Hans. 'Four-three', I told him quietly. He liked that. 'Sehr gut!' (Very good!) he pronounced with a wide grin.

'It's not over, five more at 60,' he called, and we went again.

This was going to be much harder…

I passed him the rifle. He popped in more rounds one by one, click-click-click, and re-set the sight. As he was settling, he mumbled: 'The score is only four-three *at the moment.*' Grinning, he fired again…

The first apple exploded. Good shot! He missed, and missed, and missed. Then he destroyed the final apple with his last attempt. 'Now it's five-four,' he exclaimed with satisfied joy, slowly handing me the weapon.

'Nur *im Moment*,' (only *at the moment*) I muttered as I reloaded…

Behind I could hear matches being struck for cigarettes, pipes being lit, and the notes and coins changing hands. Acrid tobacco smoke wafted past.

I missed with my first shot, again! Then, BOOM! Reload, BOOM! I won! There was applause from behind, but I wasn't finished… Shot four, BOOM! Shot five, BOOM!

Now there was a spontaneous eruption of shouting clapping and cheering from the assembled crowd. I'd been aware throughout that Hans was watching me intently, in admiration. I felt he'd been willing me on.

Laying down the weapon I glanced at him, 'The score is eight-five, *at the moment*,' I whispered with a smirk. He had the widest smile.

Sitting up in triumph, and twisting an old German proverb, I explained to the gathered men: 'They say one should honour the old, but I say one should honour the young more!'

The soldiers laughed, cheered, and settled their bets. They looked at me in appreciation and patted me on the back saying things like, 'The *Deutsches*

Jungvolk (German Young Folk) of the Hitlerjugend has trained you well.' 'Beautiful shooting.' 'Kamerad, thank you, I won my bet,' and 'you and I will hunt in the Harz.' I liked that. They seemed ok to me, in a uniform, but just normal men. I didn't mention that I'd never been in the *Jungfolk*.

The smell of cordite lingered with the smell of sand tobacco and gun oil. It had been a hell of a shooting contest. I hadn't shot for ages and had just performed brilliantly. Hans was full of praise, 'Fantastic shooting boy!'

'Thank you,' I replied breathily. As we stood up in front of us was an officer of some kind, mid-30s. I wasn't sure what would happen next.

Looking at me quizzically he asked, 'Where did you learn to shoot boy? *Das Deutsches Jungfolk?*'

'No sir, in Alsace sir. My father taught me.'

'So, you *are* Alsatian then?' I thought he may have had a Baden accent.

'Yes sir.'

'Not French?'

'No sir, not French: Alsatian. My name is Paul von Bonn.' Hans was looking at me again grinning. I nearly burst out laughing but I thought I'd better hold it down.

'Good job. Looks like you've been entertaining the men Maier,' he said turning to the corporal.

'Yes sir,' Hans said stiffly.

'Relax Maier, we're all friends here.'

'Thank you sir.'

'Well then, the fun is over. Escort our young Alsatian sharpshooter back to the perimeter, then I want your report.'

'Yes sir,' he replied.

At this, I silently mouthed the word *Scharfschütze* (sharpshooter) at Hans and with a solemn smirk, tapped myself in the chest with an index finger.

The officer turned to me again. 'I am Leutnant Schneider and most of the time I am in command here, except when *Officer Candidate* Corporal Maier is.' He grinned at Hans who sniggered which caused us all to burst out laughing.

The Leutnant smiled, 'I knew your accent young man. You're clearly not from Bonn though.'

'No sir.'

'Maier, you're lucky he speaks such good German. If he spoke to you in his Alsatian dialect your head would explode like one of those apples.' For some reason that really amused him, and he giggled merrily.

'Leutnant Schneider, can I come to the camp again sometime?'

He said he would listen to his corporal's report and make enquiries but, 'Seeing as how wise you are and that you are obviously German,' that it should be possible.

In high spirits we walked back, full of conversation. We sat and rested on a fallen tree. From an inside pocket, Hans produced photos of his children. His daughter Ilse in a fencing outfit was holding a trophy. She looked about the same age as me. His son Otto had a model aeroplane. He was about 10. 'These are my beautiful children. Ilse is a fencing champion who will win the Olympics one day. Otto will be a brilliant pilot and fly around the world,' he told me proudly.

Then smiling he regarded me again. 'You're strong, like Ilse and Otto. You're not afraid of anything or anyone. I never met an Alsatian before. Some people back home said that your folk were weak-minded and lazy. They were dead wrong, you're just about the bravest strongest boy I ever met.'

I smiled, 'Well, I'd quite like to meet those people who said that so that I can straighten it out with them *personally*.'

'Where did you get these qualities? Who taught you?'

'My father and mother.'

We arrived back at the table and the incongruous clock. A couple of Hans' friends were sitting smoking and drinking coffee. 'We hear this boy kicked your ass Hans. Is it true?' Then they burst out laughing.

'He's better than William Tell!' Hans confessed.

This was when I chose my moment. I reached into my pocket and fetched out a fist-sized cardboard box. 'This is for you, friend,' I said offering it to Hans then symbolically placing it on the table.

'What is it?' he quizzed.

'Open it after I've gone.'

Hans and I went back to the door where my bike was under armed guard. I thanked them for that and jumped on. As I got ready, I offered my hand, we shook firmly, and I told him I'd had a great adventure. I'll always remember this; as I cycled away, he called, 'You're with friends now.'

When I got home, I wasn't sure what reception I would get.

Father was standing warming himself by the fire when I told him, and it didn't start well. Taking a tone he said, 'What d'you want to go up there for? It's not a Boy's Brigade Camp you know!'

Mother's reaction was, 'You are curious. But your father has an English expression: *curiosity killed the cat*. I don't want you getting into things you can't handle.'

Father added, 'They're not nice people, they're experienced killers. What's the fascination son?' I didn't know and didn't have any answers.

Beatrice was sat at the fireplace listening too, and she tried to help me out. She explained that if you want to catch a bird you should treat it gently. Father and I didn't know what that meant. Even mother was perplexed. Like my great-aunt that must have been quite an old one.

The conversation ranged about learning to deal with people, the dangers that *not* learning to deal with certain people might raise, but also the danger of dealing with these particular people.

Father started talking about the deserts of Sudan and Egypt, and how he'd met people who'd been through the Suez Canal to those places. He was told that someone had been stung and killed by a scorpion that was hiding in his boot when he went to put it on. The poor man died painfully in a few minutes, he never knew anything about scorpions and yet one killed him. If someone had warned him, he would still be alive. In the end father said that it was better for me to learn to deal with dangerous people because, and he used an expression he'd heard in America: *'If you can deal with them, then you can deal with anyone.'*

'As well as that son, I can tell that you are bored. None of us likes being bottled up, we're too used to our freedom. It could be good for you to get out there and learn as much as you can about these people. It's a risky investment, but it could pay off.' As it turned out, father was dead right. When it came to business he always was.

Back at the hotel Hans was opening his cardboard box. Inside he found a St Christopher bicycle bell.'

14. Death of a salesman

I came back after my two days off onto afternoons to learn that Paul's friend Bruce had passed away. He'd had a mild heart attack when I was on shift and been taken to hospital. Then there were complications. It was so sad.

Unfortunately, it had an adverse effect on Paul. At briefing I was told that in the morning he had a massive bust up with Clare who was one of my co-workers. Sarah had intervened and he'd had a go at her as well.

Lawrence was afternoon supervisor that day. He was quite young, and we got on well. He said he would keep an eye on Paul but asked for my advice which was flattering but I couldn't add anything. We went to work.

The next thing I knew I had to rush and break up a row between Paul and one of the other guests. Voices were raised and I raced to the sunroom to find Michael denouncing him as: 'A mean subversive old bastard.'

Paul retaliated brutally: 'Wow! Look at that, you've used a three-syllable word! I bet you don't know what it means though?'

'You twat!' Michael shouted, as he threw his paperback at Paul. He missed and the book skimmed fluttering across the parquet floor.

'Yah, *twat*, now that's a shorter word, more the sort you *Daily Mail* readers should be familiar with.'

I got there just in time to hear Michael shout, 'Bastard,' and Paul call back, 'Your sort have *such* a limited vocabulary.'

'STOP IT YOU TWO!' I said arriving.

Lawrence was just behind me. 'What's going on?' he called, voice raised.

As Michael was leaving the room he paused, looked at me and pointed at Paul: '*That man* is an absolute asshole.' Then off he went as fast as his 85-year-old legs and Zimmer frame could carry him.

I looked at Paul in his chair and shook my head. Glimpsing me he called, 'That's right, run away Michael, run away. No, wait, you can't!' he smirked.

Oh, that was a vicious comment!

We approached Paul who had a horrible self-satisfied look about him. As a senior was with me it was always the convention to let them lead the way. Lawrence sat next to Paul, and I stood. The room had long since emptied. A moment passed.

'Let's hear your side of it then,' he said regarding the old man earnestly.

Paul shook his head gently, narrowed his eyes slightly and stared back.

'Don't try any of your therapy strategies on me boy. They won't work.'

'I'm not proposing therapy Paul. Why? do you think I should?' That was a good answer: *combative*.

'Well said Lawrence, well said,' the old man observed dryly, smiling and gently nodding his head.

'Come on, let's have it. What happened?'

'That idiot accused me of contributing to Bruce's heart attack. I did not. I reserve the right to defend myself against falsehoods, idiots, and *Daily Mail* readers,' he grimaced.

'Ok. What did you say to him?'

'I told him he was an idiot.' He glanced at me and adjusting his whistling hearing aid added, '*Ein Trottel!*'

I looked away in irritation as he continued in his dialect: '*Der isch e Stüeck vun's Deifels Hosefüeder.*' (That one is a piece from the Devil's pants).

'Anything else?' Lawrence asked.

The old man hesitated; his face twitched. 'He took the liberty of asking me what I'd said to Bruce before he was taken ill. I told him it was none of his business.'

I watched Lawrence. He was good at this, and Paul respected him. I couldn't figure out why though. He sat there listening, biding his time.

The old man continued:

'That idiot said it had to be my fault that Bruce had a heart attack, because he was perfectly alright at dinner, and yet afterwards we watched a film together in my room and then he was taken ill. That was my fault, apparently. Now why would I upset one of my friends? Nonsense.'

'Alright. I'll have a chat with Michael about this, but I'm not taking sides because I wasn't there.'

'Well, that's lucky then because I'm not asking you to. I can fight my own battles thank you very much.'

He could be a feisty belligerent piece of work.

I really admired Lawrence for what he said next. He could have walked away but instead he was going to have the last word. 'You know Paul, you can abuse Sarah and Clare and me as much as you want. That's fine, we get paid. But please don't abuse the other guests. They pay to be here the same as you. The policy is that if anyone has a problem that can't be resolved then refer to us and we will sort it out. That's the service everyone here is paying for, and we are happy to provide it. Please don't take matters into your own hands. Let us do our jobs.'

The old man nodded awkwardly.

As we shaped to walk away Lawrence gave me a tiny glance which meant: *stay with him,* so I held back.

'How about tea?' I asked. 'Yes, tea,' Paul replied.

When I returned, he was in a quite different frame of mind, so I asked him, 'Why did you do that? You know the policy. You know we are here to sort things out.'

'I'm sick of Michael and his bullshit accusations and victimhood. As well as that, I did it to see what would happen.'

'Oh, I see. So, this is one of your little games, is it? Amusing yourself at someone else's expense? Michael is no angel, but really? Not classy. Not classy at all.'

'Alright, alright, but this place is so dull. It needs some spice.'

'Not like that. We can do better than fight over the death of a friend, surely?' That stopped him in his tracks.

He averted his gaze, lost the smirk, twitched his fingers and bowed his head. 'Yes, you're right,' he muttered quietly.

After a pause, in German he said, 'Come, do you know the card game *Böse Dame?* (German: Evil Queen) I used to play this with the soldiers in the bunkers at Corbière. It's fun.'

And with that he glossed over it. He knew what he did was wrong, but he'd done it all the same and would not climb down.

'No, show me.' So, we spent a little while playing this game I'd never heard of, conversing in German, and I sat wondering how it had all turned around so quickly.

After playing cards, I was surprised to look up and see Michael shuffling along the corridor. Lawrence was with him, and he gave me a glance. Paul stood.

Michael opened up, 'I've come to apologise. I shouldn't have said what I said about Bruce. That was quite wrong of me. I spoke out of turn. I was upset. I know you got on well with him and I know you're upset too. Will you accept my apology?'

'Of course, I accept your apology. We were both upset. We both lost a friend.'

They shook hands. It wasn't especially cordial, and I noticed that Paul didn't apologise. Lawrence noticed too and glared at him. But the matter was closed. Whatever he'd said to Michael had obviously worked.

Shortly afterwards I found Lawrence in the ready room. He observed, 'Paul has got issues. He's a sod. Did you notice how he didn't apologise?'

'Yes, I did. He's a piece of work. He respects you though. Can I ask, how did you do that? How is it that he respects you?'

'Maybe because I'm not afraid to fight him. Sometimes he goes looking for trouble. When he does, he won't stop until he finds it,' Lawrence explained with a sort of half-giggle. 'I'm dead straight with him. I just tell it how it is. I think that's what he respects. I think that's what he needs.'

'Thank you. I'll remember what you said.'

'You're welcome Katie. He really likes you; you know?'

'I think he does.'

'Keep going. He's a hard case. You must explain the secret of your success to me sometime!'

'We'll have to see about that then, won't we?' I told him.

15. Scarlet fever

Paul did not go back to the hotel again in 1940. There was severe weather and a terrific storm in the middle of November that felled hundreds of trees, one of which came down through the roof on a corner of the Big House. He and his father spent time fixing that with some local help. People were busy with the effects of the storm and coping with the increasing shortages caused by the Germans buying everything up.

Britain was getting a fearful pasting from Luftwaffe bombers, especially London, Bristol, Coventry, and Birmingham. Nowadays we call this the 'Blitz.' The Bunns heard about it on the radio. They knew what the Germans had done to Rotterdam and now that it was happening to British cities they were horrified. They worried about the von Bonns in Marylebone. Morale was low and as Christmas passed Paul didn't feel like talking to the Germans anymore. The weather was cold and snowy, and his father caught a bad chill. Overall, early 1941 was bleak. Then it got worse.

In early February word went round that a man had been shot and killed in the military zone. This incensed Paul and he decided to act. He told me what happened:

'What on earth is the point of shooting some poor bloke in the back in the middle of the night? It's not exactly as if one person is an invasion force, is it? So, I decided to go back to the hotel, find someone, and clear things up.

I arrived and the place appeared deserted. No sign of anyone although the wire was still there all out of place. I went through a side gate. Lots of trees were down but I found my way to the temporary firing range. Deserted. Just as I turned around to go back home again, I walked right into a three-man patrol, and they raised their Mausers safety off. 'Halt! What you do?' a corporal shouted.

In clear accent-free German, I called, 'Don't shoot! I have come to find Corporal Hans and Leutnant Schneider.'

'How do you know them? You must be that German boy?'

'No, I am Alsatian. Now secure your weapons, I am unarmed.' They lowered their guns and walked to examine me.

'You're lucky we didn't shoot. What the hell are you doing here boy?' snarled the corporal.

'My name is Paul, and what I'm doing here is living here. What are *you* doing here corporal? Are you a tourist?'

'You cheeky little bastard!' he said taking a tone.

I followed up: 'No, I know why you're here corporal, you're here to shoot unarmed civilians in the back in the middle of the night, aren't you?'

SMACK! I got a thump around the side of the head with the back of a fist and landed in the slush on my backside.

'You three cowards!' I shouted glaring up from the mud. 'Put those guns away, they're the only things making you brave. Put them on one side and I'll beat the shit out of all of you!'

'There's three of us, and one of you, you little twerp,' growled the corporal. 'Now get up and get out before we finish you!'

I got up and swung my fist at him connecting around the side of his head. Down he went into the sludge. Then the other two *Soldaten* went for me. I managed to connect on them a couple of times too. Bastards. The corporal got up and belted me. Down I went again.

'Yah, it'll take three of you as well you goddamned cowards.' I bellowed.

I got hauled up, handcuffed, and frogmarched off through the fallen trees with blood pouring in my eyes which made me squint. 'You bloody bastards!' I screeched.

'Shut up fool,' said one of them.

I got bundled into the back of a car and driven under armed guard to some Command Post or another. I was even madder when I got there. I was pulled out and bundled in front of someone important, but the red mist had fallen, and I was **wild**. My eyes had swelled, and I couldn't see.

'YOU MURDERING BASTARDS' I yelled at the important soldier. Whoever it was, I couldn't see, he just sat there and let me explode.

'Go on, shoot me! I dare you! That's all you lot are good for: shooting unarmed civilians in the middle of the night. There's nothing brave about that, nothing brave about *bombing Rotterdam after it had surrendered*. Nothing brave about bombing eight million innocent people in London night after night for 57 nights. Despoilers. Criminals. Nation of Goethe Bach and Beethoven despair. Bastards. VERDAMMT IHR ALLE.' (Damn you all)

A few moments passed as I heaved air into myself.

'Are you finished Paul von Bonn?' said a voice I vaguely recalled. 'You picked a fight you couldn't win. I thought you were wise. You are not. You will get yourself killed just like the man out on the Five Mile Road, and then what use will your anger be, huh?' He paused, then continued, 'First think, then act. What could you achieve by going out looking for trouble, huh?

Nothing. You could have been shot. Now Paul, stop being a damned fool. You are 13 but you will not reach 14 the way you're going. Wisdom comes with age. You must learn to control your temper, or you will not survive.'

It was Leutnant Schneider. He continued:

'You mention the genius Goethe, well here's some Goethe for **you** Paul von Bonn: *'The best government is that which teaches us to govern ourselves.'*

I said nothing and just stood there panting.

I heard Schneider tell one of his men, 'Clean him up and take him home, he lives on La Marquanderie in St Brelade in the big house on the right by the church. They speak good German. Tell his father to control his son because if he doesn't, we will.' I was plonked in a car and driven away by a first sergeant.

Father was beside himself when he saw my black eyes and blue ribs. Beatrice and mother had to physically block him from leaving the house with his revolver. They told him: 'That isn't the right way.'

Mother cried as she patched me up. 'You were hot tempered and did stupid things when you were 13 as well Christopher,' Beatrice remarked tactlessly. Mother glared at her.

It all settled quickly though as in a couple of days I was struck down with a temperature, a rash, and a white tongue. Mother said I had scarlet fever. A doctor came on a bike and confirmed it.

It was decided that I should be kept at the Big House until I recovered rather than be taken to Overdale Hospital. I was severely affected. There were no treatments in those days and mother tended to me carefully. My mental state was not good either. The boiling fever went with my boiling mind, and I lay in bed in a complete swoon.

Father reminded me of gliding, flying the Storch, the Great War, about America and about his childhood with his brother in London. I'd heard all the stories before, but it didn't matter - he told the best stories. He explained that my fight made him think of the poem *Spleen* in *Les Fleurs du Mal (The Flowers of Evil)*, like something had risen up in me and had burst out into the open:

'...And a silent horde of loathsome spiders
Comes to spin their webs in the depths of our brains,
All at once the bells leap with rage
And hurl a frightful roar at heaven...'

- **Charles Baudelaire. Les Fleurs du Mal, from:** *Spleen*

He embraced me tightly. '*Never* lose your passion; it is the right way to live. *Never* apologise for passion, never turn away from it and *always* be who you are,' he told me as tears rolled down his face. 'But don't pick fights you can't win.'

I don't remember anything about what happened after that. It was like some great St Ouen's wave had come and engulfed me and I was tumbling inside it.

The visitor

By March I was feeling better. Imagine my surprise when one windy afternoon at about 1pm there was a tap on my door and mother came in with a familiar chap following her. It was Hans. 'I've come to see how you are Paul von Bonn. Do you mind me coming?' he asked. I was thrilled.

'No Hans, come in. I haven't seen anyone for weeks. I'm glad you're here.' I meant it. I was hungry for conversation of any kind. It was special that he came to visit me.

Mother said later she wasn't sure if I wouldn't leap out of bed and belt him! I assured her that if we were going to fight, we would have done it by now. She liked that.

He came in and glancing around at my paintings of Alsace, storks, and Jersey explained, 'We heard you got caught in the restricted zone.'

'Yes Hans.'

'I don't blame you for belting that obnoxious Swabian Nazi Egeler.' He paused. 'D'you want to know something?'

'What?'

'Most of us want to belt him too.'

'He's a Nazi?'

'Of course he is, couldn't you tell?'

'My God, I didn't know. I was in too much of a rage.'

'Not all of us are like him Paul.'

'I can see that now that you are here Hans.'

'He's swine, vermin and a coward, like all those fanatics. In Poland young men died because he didn't do his duty. He's a coward, but he'll go far because he's a party man. He should be in the SS, but he can't prove his racial heritage back far enough, so he's here making our lives a misery and boring us shitless.' Pointing to his belt, he said, 'The belt-buckle may say:

'God with us' (*Gott mit uns*), but that slogan is a lie.'

Hans went on to explain the inner workings of Nazism: the cult of *Blood and Soil*. The Nazis thought the 'superior' German Aryan blood-race had emerged through ancient peasantry working on the land and was intimately connected with the soil. 'It's heathen paganism, you see it in many of the Nazi party badges and symbolism.' He told me all about the *SS* or *Schutzstaffel*. I said I didn't know much about them but through conversation with the *Hitlerjugend Luft* gliding at Wasserkuppe knew that many of them aspired to join.

He said, 'The Nazi party are evil lying bastards, corrupting the young. Only the 'racially pure' are allowed to be in the SS. Young women are encouraged to take an SS man as their partner in order to have 'pure' babies.

The party thinks the German people are special. They think everyone else is a foreigner who should be rejected and deported. They think the Jews should 'disappear.' It's shocking. Our best people have gone, fled or sent away by the regime. Even our national darling from my home city, Helene Mayer – who won a brilliant gold medal fencing for Germany in the 1928 Olympics. She won when she was only 17. Magnificent, strong, and skilful.

Helene and the truth were amongst the Nazis' first victims. They stripped away her German nationality because she is Half-Jewish, and she fled to California. But when it suited Goebbels, that cynical lying bastard invited her back to represent Germany in the 1936 Berlin Olympics. She won a silver medal and even gave the Nazi salute on the winner's podium. Newspapers were not allowed to tell the truth about her. The regime claimed credit, and then she ran back to America in fear of her life. God knows what will happen to her family still in Germany.

The Nazis and especially the *SS*, are fanatics. They will kill anyone, especially Jewish people. I saw that one night in Frankfurt. It was in November 1938. Mobs of them smashed every window of every Jewish-owned shop, then they set fire to the Höchst synagogue. They killed dozens of Jews and sent thousands away to camps. Mindless murderers.

Nazis will tell any lie as it suits them. They say it is their destiny to destroy socialism as it is a threat to the world. So, sooner or later they will attack Soviet Russia. Their devotion to the Führer is *elkerregend* (nauseating/sickening) and they are ready to do anything for him. The Nazis have given their hearts and minds to Adolf Hitler. He is their religion; they think he is some kind of Messiah. But God is *not* with them.'

'Bless you Hans, I can see that you have *not* given your heart to the Führer.'

'Only God can see the hearts of men.'

The hairs stood on the back of my neck. When Hans said that something in me stirred. It was like the click of a lock and a door opening. A light shone into a darkened room and now I could finally see him clearly.'

The old man turned to me, 'Nowadays the Nazis would be called *Right-wing racist nationalist fundamentalists.*'

I was in such a trance of listening and recalling assemblies at my Church of England secondary school that all I heard was, '*Only God can see the hearts of men.*'

Paul continued: 'I told Hans, 'It must be difficult for you, back home.'

He said, 'To view a man – Adolf Hitler – as if he were God, is blasphemy. There is no greater error, no greater sin.'

I sensed something in Hans: an agony. He was not a man of war. He could have belted me that day in St Helier, but he didn't. On the other hand, I was ready to fight a German soldier in public just to make a point. He was prepared to fight but it was against his nature.'

I had been listening intently. 'I thought you were a tough kid, someone who would take matters into his own hands.'

'No. I had been pulled out of Strasbourg, my home and a place I loved. I'd lost my freedom and was trapped in another place where I had no friends. Islanders saw me as an outsider. But then there were people like Hans and other soldiers who seemed to me to be alright. Is it any wonder that I reacted the way I did, that I went mad?'

'I can see how it happened.'

'I couldn't understand what it was that had caused German speakers to go to war again. It didn't make any sense. It wasn't rational. The German culture is in my opinion *high culture*. Some of the most brilliant people who ever lived are German speakers. As for the Nazis, they were in another dimension of evil madness. It took me many years to figure them out. I'm still not sure I have.

Hans said, 'I'm sorry Egeler and his men beat you. I won't forget that. Leutnant Schneider told me what happened. I have a long memory and so do my friends.'

'So, did he send you over here? Did Schneider send you here in order to make himself feel better?'

'No. I came because I heard you had scarlet fever, and I wanted to see if I could help.'

'Thank you Hans.'

'You have earned the respect of a great many of us just for belting Egeler. You are a young man of strong principles and people like you are exceedingly rare. When you get well come and look for me. Ask around, it's a small island.'

'Alright Hans. Thank you so much for coming today. It means a lot. I won't forget it.'

It was 4 o'clock. In three hours, I'd learned more about the Nazis than I had in the previous three years. It had been right under my nose over the river in Germany and I just hadn't seen it. I'd only seen what I'd wanted to see. I wouldn't have understood it even if I had. Only now, nursing bruised ribs black eyes and a fever did I finally realise the truth: the Nazis were godless thugs. But not all Germans were Nazis. Just because they spoke German, that didn't make them Nazis. Hans was proof.

Hans stood and placed two brown paper packages on my bedside table. 'Open those after I've gone,' he said as he turned to leave. Downstairs I heard him talk to my mother in hushed tones. It was years before I found out what was said in that conversation.

I looked at the two items and reached for a bottle shaped one first. I unwrapped it and found a spring-topped bottle of *Apfelsaft* (apple juice). The label read: *Für den Apfelmeister!* (For the apple master!) The other item was round. I unwrapped it carefully. It was a superb hand-carved wooden apple.'

16. Monster in the air, Wednesday, 8 September 1915

Paul told me another story about his father on a walk along the Thames at Strand-on-the-Green:

'My father felt his German heritage, but there was an event in London that disconnected him from it forever. This is what he recalled to me when I had scarlet fever:

'I had been over to see an old school friend. I'd flagged a Hackney Carriage on Old Street to take me back to Marylebone at about 10.30.

As we chugged along into Clerkenwell Road, I became aware of the rumbling of guns ahead of us to the right and other booming sounds.

Suddenly there was a tremendous blast and the shattering of glass away to the left down Leather Lane towards the market. My God! What was that?

The cabbie turned down the lane towards a column of smoke and dust rising in the light. It was at the corner of Portpool Lane.

We screeched to a halt, jumped out and looked up and our disbelieving eyes saw in the sky over the City an object lit by search lights. Like a giant cigar, thousands of feet above, a monster in the air: a German Zeppelin airship, and it was raining death.

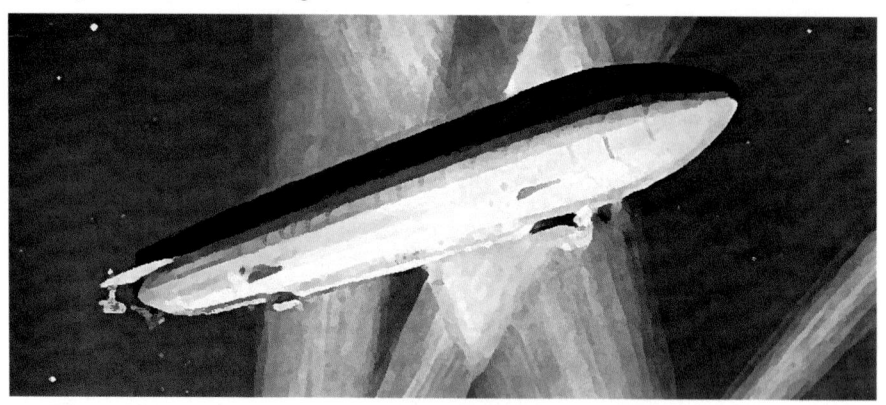

The cabbie said it was 'Laney's Buildings.'

There was screaming and people running around not knowing what to do. Then there was another much bigger blast from the direction of St Bart's Hospital that shook the ground and loosened slates which fell from nearby roofs with a sickening clatter.

Policemen came running with their lamps and we charged into the demolished building along with several locals and my driver to see if anyone was still alive. All we found were bits of tiny bodies, arms and fingers. Women in the street wailed and cursed the hateful Germans.

A catastrophe.

In the distance to the east could be heard other blasts. The cabbie and I stayed all night. We dug out survivors until our fingers bled.

The reckoning was that four children were dead. Six adults were injured and another child.

In the morning, I made my way home on foot. I passed more destruction in Holborn. A bomb had exploded in Red Lion Street and blown out the front of the Dolphin pub. They told me a man had been killed here too, Henry Coombs, and a fireman seriously injured. Queen's Square also had a huge crater in it. The bomb had narrowly missed the Hospital for Sick Children on Great Ormond Street and the Italian Hospital.

I could not let that pass. Those children and people were innocent. I walked home, washed, changed and then went to the recruiting station where I asked to join the Royal Flying Corps.'

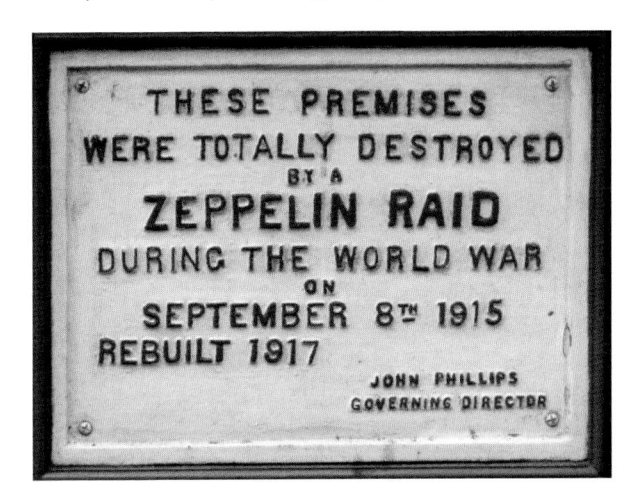

> THESE PREMISES
> WERE TOTALLY DESTROYED
> BY A
> ZEPPELIN RAID
> DURING THE WORLD WAR
> ON
> SEPTEMBER 8TH 1915
> REBUILT 1917
> JOHN PHILLIPS
> GOVERNING DIRECTOR

Author's note

Zeppelin L.13 commanded by Kapitänleutnant Heinrich Mathy bombed central London on the night of 8/9th September 1915, causing 22 deaths and 87 injured. The Dolphin pub was restored. The clock showing the time of the attack was salvaged from the ruins and can be seen today on display on a shelf to the left of the bar.

17. 'Better to bend than break'

Paul was sufficiently recovered at Easter 1941 to return to school. He had done a lot of reading and studying at home but was eager to get out again and meet those few friends he had. He told me:

'It was Sunday, and we always attended church. It was never good for my father to be out in the cold and damp. Today he wanted to get back quickly, so I let them go on ahead of me.

I was walking my bike along King Street looking in the empty shop windows, must have been early April just before Easter. My mood was foul. It was a grey day cold and windy. Very drab it all was. Everyone was miserable. Even the policeman was more miserable than usual.

I was just in front of Burton's when behind me in the road I heard the 'ting-ting' of a bicycle bell. I looked around and it was Hans. That cheered me up! I greeted him:

'I see you are finally riding on the right side of the road kamerad!'

'Yes Paul, lovely to see you too. I have even learned to ting the bell and peddle both at the same time!' he told me with a big smile.

And they say Germans don't have a sense of humour.

'Thank you so much for the juice. The wooden apple is super, I'll always treasure it.'

'I carved it for you from one of the apple trees that blew down in that massive storm in November. That tree could not bend, so it broke.'

'What did you use to carve it?'

'My bayonet of course? What else?'

'Phew!' I gasped.

'Let's go to the Soldatenheim. There's music today.'

I knew it was just around the corner at the Mayfair Hotel. We wheeled our bikes and propped them against the wall. Doing that I noticed his right hand was bandaged.

Nobody batted an eyelid as Hans took me into the wood-panelled main room. It was packed with soldiers and stank of tobacco smoke which I hated. Vanity caused me to think that someone might recognise me, but nobody did. A huge painting of Hitler hung over the fireplace which was burning logs. We stood there.

The martial music was awful, those saxophones were wasted in my opinion, but the soldiers seemed to enjoy it. I'd never been in the Mayfair before and it was quite posh, for Jersey. Hans asked if I would like some Apfelsaft. He collected the bottle of juice and some nice smelling coffee. Then we went out of the back door and sat on our own at one of the tables by the little statue there. He had something he wanted to tell me.

'How have you been Paul?' he asked.

'I'm back at school now but I'm lonely and bored.'
'I'm sorry you haven't been able to come up to see us.'
'Me too.'
'Well, what I'm about to tell you isn't good for you or me my young friend.'
'Oh?'
'My division is being withdrawn. It's already started.'
'You're leaving?'
'Yes. I'm sorry.'
'Not as sorry as I am.'
'Don't ask where I'm going. Nobody knows.'
'That'll be one less friend and I've none to start with.'
'I'm sorry. Many companies have gone already. Nikolas has gone and Schneider also - promoted to Oberleutnant.
'And the asshole who beat me up? I'm waiting for him...'
'Keep your voice down!'
'Well?'
'Egeler?' Hans leaned forward and spoke very softly, 'He had an unfortunate accident. It was just a co-incidence that I was there you have to understand.' Gesturing with a slight nod he added, 'He slipped and fell all the way.'
'Accident?'
'I told you; my friends and I have long memories.' Then I noticed he was holding his bandaged hand.
'You did that for me?'
'Not just you. After what happened in Poland that bastard had it coming.'
'Thank you for telling me this Hans.'
'You've helped me Paul, in ways you can't appreciate.'
'What do you mean?'
His eyes rolled, and he didn't answer directly. Instead, he talked about something else:
'You can speak to as many Nazi party members as you like. What they have is not real strength, not inner strength. It has been force-fed to them like when the French stuff bread down a goose. It's not real. None of what the party says is real. It's all bullshit. They say, 'God with us,' but of that there is no possibility. Not when we see their barbaric treatment of the Jews.

But Paul, you have inner strength. You have shown that young people can hang on and fight for their beliefs in spite of everything, and not weaken.'

I told him, 'You flatter me. If I don't fight for my principles, then I don't have those principles, do I? If I don't fight for my principles, then who will?'

'This is a true German value. Like the apple, it makes me think you are German at your core. We never do anything halfway, but I don't need to tell you that as you are already living proof. All children grow. So long as there are people like you there is the hope of a better future for all of us.'

'Bless you Hans. I will try not to let you down.'

'No! Don't worry about me. Worry about yourself. Your passion and hot temper have already gotten you into a lot of trouble. Schneider told me what happened. Take notice of what he said. If you're going to fight, then fight to defend yourself and only get into fights you can win.

He was telling me things about myself that I hadn't appreciated before. German values? Did I really have German values? I didn't know. There was no reason for him to lie to me.

There were other things he wasn't telling me though.

After that there wasn't that much more to say. I finished my apple juice, and we got up to leave.

In front of the Soldatenheim it seemed appropriate to say our final goodbyes. I felt bad. Just as I'd made a friend circumstance intervened to pull us apart. It didn't seem fair. We embraced, clapped each other on the back and shook hands. He said he would write, and I thanked him.

As I got on my bike and peddled away, he called out, 'I will take the St Christopher bell with me, I think I will need it. And don't forget the apple tree and our proverb Paul: Better to bend than break.'

He stayed in the gateway and held up his hand. That was it.

One or two people watched me, but I didn't give a shit about them. Once more I was in a foul mood.

Back at the Big House I greeted father warming himself at the fire and informed him that change was coming, but he already seemed to know. Rumours were ten-a-penny in Jersey throughout the occupation though. Nobody knew what was true and what was not. It was all part of the boredom. When I told him that Hans had sorted out Egeler father was pleased.'

18. The piano session

'In the weeks and months that followed there was indeed a complete change in the structure and appearance of the occupying soldiers. By the end of summer 1941 I didn't recognise any of the passing faces on bikes or in cars or trucks, and there were increasing numbers of them. I felt lonelier and more trapped than ever. My mental state fluctuated wildly. I threw myself at my studies but took most solace from music. Everyone who grew up in the 30s plays the piano you know,' he said with a smile.

'I play piano,' I told him.

'Good grief,' he exclaimed, 'we'll have to see about that then, won't we? Come, let's go to the day room.'

I took out a pile of sheet music from the stool and found Schirmer's library version of *Mozart Nineteen Sonatas*.

I lifted and propped the lid as is proper for all grand pianos. It was a baby Steinberg, an old one from about 1935 which seemed appropriate. The dust flew as I ran off a few scales and it was a bit out of tune, but I could compensate.

Guests noticed and came in. Even Mel the supervisor swung by. She said, 'I've worked here for years and never seen anyone play that. I don't think it's even in tune anymore.' She stood to watch and listen...

I sat, adjusted the stool, played a few scales, and to warm up tinkled my version of *'This Woman's Work.'* My voice is rubbish, so I didn't sing, but I know the words off by heart.

(See Author's notes at end of chapter. Dear reader – please play it.)

Paul was watching me with fascination and intent. I concluded quietly, then looked to him. Smiling and studying my face he exclaimed, 'I know that tune, it's by Kate Bush. It's beautiful. You play beautifully.'

Grinning, I told him, 'I'm just warming up.'

Flicking through the *Sonatas* before I could ask what his favourite was, he muttered simply, 'The 15th, and I will turn your pages.'

I was aware behind me that more guests were filing in to listen. When I came to the end of the first movement, I got a standing ovation. That felt good.

Bravo! Bravo! More! they called. As they did I glanced at my page turner. His eyes were closed. He shook his head ever so slightly and still with eyes closed whispered, 'That was *superb.*'

'Thank you.'

'Don't disappoint your audience. Let's finish this.'

'Yes,' I nodded turning and putting up my hands to the dozen or so guests and colleague care workers who had assembled. 'Thank you everyone. That was the first movement of Mozart's Piano Sonata Number 15. I will now play the final two movements.' My audience clapped again, and I sat and played movements two and three.

I came to the end and again the audience cheered. There must have been more than 20 by now. I hadn't played to a large audience since I was at school, and it was a lovely feeling. Blushing, I stood and bowed.

My page turner looked at me. I couldn't describe his expression; he was so happy and thrilled he looked like he was going to burst.

'Katie Campbell, YOU ARE JUST FANTASTIC! Where have you been hiding that?'

'You flatter me. My teachers at primary school noticed me in music. They got me piano lessons when I was six years old. It was subsidised by the Hounslow Music Service. I've been playing ever since.

'You play with wonderful expression.'

'I had to work at it. Dad always loves to hear me play. Mum said I reminded her of Kate Bush.' We both laughed.

He added, 'Brilliant engineer, brilliant chess player, brilliant musician, brilliant linguist, brilliant care worker, is there anything you're not good at?' I blushed again...

'Let me have a go,' he said, 'you've captured the audience for me.'

He sat, paused in a long reflective meditation, then played and sang the most beautiful song:

'She hangs her head and cries in my shirt
She must be hurt very badly
Tell me what's making you sad, Li?
Open your door, don't hide in the dark
You're lost in the dark, you can trust me
'Cause you know that's how it must be

Lisa Lisa, sad Lisa Lisa

Her eyes like windows, trickle in rain
Upon her pain getting deeper
Though my love wants to relieve her
She walks alone from wall to wall
Lost in a hall, she can't hear me
Though I know she likes to be near me

Lisa Lisa, sad Lisa Lisa

She sits in a corner by the door
There must be more I can tell her
If she really wants me to help her
I'll do what I can to show her the way
And maybe one day I will free her
Though I know no one can see her

Lisa Lisa, sad Lisa Lisa'

Sad Lisa. Words and Music by Cat Stevens
Copyright © 1970 BMG Rights Management (UK) Ltd.

He sang as if possessed by something.

When he came to the end the little audience was spellbound. His playing and singing were breathtaking, but until that morning nobody knew.

Eyes closed he stood, took a tumult of applause, then nodded his head and held himself in the moment.

All were waiting for more, but there was none. Instead, head bowed he silently took himself off through the crowd towards his room. As he passed, his glazed eyes cupped in tears, he seemed in a trance and didn't even notice me. It was as if he'd done something he hadn't meant to do, something he had no control over.

In the hush of the now quiet room, I wondered: 'Who is Lisa?'

I sensed the waiting audience, so I sat and played more Mozart and threw in a few *Bach Goldberg Variations* from the book in the stool.

It was only cycling home that I realised I'd also done something I hadn't meant to do: talk about my mother.

It didn't seem appropriate to ask about the song, and it was another year before Paul mentioned Lisa again.

Author's note

Song 1. Page 91. YouTube search: << Kate Bush This Woman's Work Vkgoeswild piano cover>> Please play – it's beautiful!

https://www.youtube.com/watch?v=gf7_nTGX8ug)

Song 2. Page 92. YouTube search: << Sad Lisa (Remastered 2020) >>
https://www.youtube.com/watch?v=bBEgvk3qB_g

Please play both.

19. Quiet years and construction 1941-1942

I had a couple of days off after the piano session. When I came back Paul was pretty quiet at first. Then, slowly but surely, he began telling me more:

'There's not much to say about life in Jersey under the occupation. It was monotonous grinding and dull.

To break it up I listened to father's jazz records. He often added to his collection on visits to London which he said had 'an excellent jazz scene.' He encouraged me to listen to the records and play. He said it showed I was growing up. I learned jazz piano with my father and by autumn 1942 we were pretty good. Mother and I often sat and played classical piano in four hands. I loved that. She would always announce it in French in the same way: *Quatre mains sont plus amusantes que deux!* (Four hands are more fun than two!) We played Schumann, Bach, Brahms, Chopin and of course Mozart. My mother was a wonderful player. She practised a lot and could play *everything*. Her playing was beautiful.

Something else I learned with father was to take and develop photographs. We brought a Leitz Focomat 2 enlarger from Paris. Father said that Jersey was so lovely that it deserved to have lovely photos taken of it. The Big House had a laundry with a sink and no window and that was perfect. We had developing cans, large bottles of chemicals for processing and plenty of film and paper. I was out taking photos all the time. Father had a Leica III camera that he'd bought in Berlin in 1934, but he'd lost it on a trip to America in 1936. In Paris he replaced it with a beautiful new IIIa. We spent hours printing. If the Germans had found out we would have been in serious trouble, but we were far too sly for them.

We all had an interest in art, especially mother. When we were in London or Paris in the 30s we always visited the galleries and bought many books and prints. The cubists and surrealists fascinated her. She said she admired Picasso, Dali and Magritte because they were able to see things other people couldn't see. I liked that. My mother taught me to draw and paint from an early age. She was an excellent teacher and very patient: she needed to be.

School was difficult. Beatrice had an extensive collection of poetry, and we brought many trunks of books with us from Strasbourg. We all had a love of German literature: Goethe, Hesse, Rilke, Schiller, Hölderlin and Heidegger. I even did battle with Nietzsche, though I deplored his aggressive atheism. You'd think this would be very odd what with the war and everything, but we didn't have a problem with German culture. My mother was born in Alsace in 1896 when it was part of Germany. My father's father was German. But that country had gone mad.

We were stunned when we heard over the radio that Germany had attacked Russia in June 1941. Luckily, we brought our set from Strasbourg and when the authorities got funny and called in the radios again later on, all we did was hand in Beatrice's, she didn't mind. Through the BBC on the radio, we were able to get some idea of what was going on in the outside world, but it wasn't good news: the Germans were winning everywhere.

I still cycled, although many of the most interesting places were now off limits. My life was in the outdoors whenever possible. I watched the birds and walked through the woods, drew, painted and took photos of the castles and towers. Jersey is a really fantastic place you know, packed with beauty and detail. Alsace also has many beautiful towers and castles.

I made myself keep a diary. I learned skills as a chef, not that there was much to cook. Mother and Marion the housekeeper taught me. In the local farms, with Jane and Annette's coaching I acquired *Jèrriais*, milked cows, made butter and cheese, helped with the threshing, made more black butter, pressed apples for cider, and even drank some of it. I learned new skills, for example, planting and picking potatoes, killing chickens ducks and rabbits, and plucking skinning and cooking them. Mother showed me how to prepare Alsatian *Hasenpfeffer*. I wasn't queasy because I was hungry, but I was still bored.

Mother was happy at the hospital and made some friends. Father made connections too and seemed to be quite popular. I was completely stuck though, trapped in a place where I once felt so happy. What I would have given to go back to Strasbourg. In my mind I longed for Alsace, watching the storks soaring and freedom.

During 1941-42 I made one or two new acquaintances: John from my congregation, who was younger than me and liked comics and annuals, and

Ted from my school who was interested in Meccano. They came around from time to time. However, it remained difficult to form any kind of friendship. Jersey was cut off and everyone was in their own private world.

The new division of German occupiers, the 319th, were of no interest to me. I missed Hans and the possibilities he offered. He didn't write. He was probably in Russia.

Now and again the anti-aircraft guns fired in the distance. We soon learned to ignore them. Planes flew over, German and British, and we learned to ignore them too.

At the end of 1941, incredibly, the Japanese attacked the American naval base on Hawaii, Pearl Harbour, and the USA declared war on Japan. For some inexplicable reason Hitler declared war on America. Father said that was the biggest mistake of them all: to declare war on a country that Germany couldn't physically attack or even credibly threaten. He flew to America in 1936 on business. He told me that America was incredible and 'Only a bloody fool would make an enemy of America.' Hitler did just that. Meanwhile, the German army was in the outskirts of Moscow. It seemed just a question of time before Stalin and the Russians capitulated.

1941 came and went. At the end of it I was so bored and inside myself that I hardly knew who I was anymore.

In 1942 it continued: boredom, hunger, rumours, anti-aircraft guns booming, boredom. I tried to break it up by cycling around with my paints, sketch pad and father's camera.

Rumours were rife. Word was that a Luftwaffe pilot stole an aircraft and flew to England in order to avoid being sent to Russia.

One thing was different in 1942. Construction workers arrived, workers from all over: France, Belgium, Holland, Spain. They set to work in a variety of places mainly around the coast. They were usually billeted in the left-over empty houses. The foreign workers were not slaves. They were paid quite well, not that there was anything for them to spend their money on. They were overseen by something called the *Organisation Todt*, or *OT* and were not treated badly. It was no problem at all to talk to them as they were French speakers in the main.

In early 1942, Russian prisoners of war started arriving too. They were used as slave workers by the OT. From the start, their conditions were dreadful, as the Germans considered them as *Unmenschlich* (subhuman). They did the nasty dangerous jobs like moving stone in the quarries and digging tunnels. The numbers of workers gradually increased. You couldn't go anywhere on the island and not encounter them. They were building bunkers all along St Ouen's Bay like at Lewis Tower and Le Braye. They put back the railway line from St Helier to Corbière which had been lifted before the war. They built other narrow-gauge railways to move the stone steel and concrete. They dug *Hohlgangsanlage* (tunnels), like in the St Lawrence valley, which they called *Ho8*. I could see all this and sometimes sneaked in to watch. In summer the island was a hive of activity, with bunker, emplacement and tunnel building going on all over.

The Russian slave labourers were being marched around. They were in a desperate state working on starvation rations. In April we even found one who had escaped, 'Yuriy', in the laundry room. Mother was appalled and said we should help him. We weren't supposed to, but we gave him some food and a bed for as long as we dared and told him to keep out of sight. After ten days mother arranged for someone else to take him. I learned some Russian as he spoke a little German. It didn't feel good to send him away but if the authorities had found out we would have been in a lot of trouble. Others came and went, and we tried to look after them, but it was a big risk.

Schooling remained difficult, but with my parents' help my studies progressed. Mother had found a book in St Helier Library: *Hugo's Russian Grammar Simplified*. She said it would be fun for the family to do something new together and break things up. Slowly, we began to learn Russian.

By harvest time I tried to work at my painting, but then I ran out of paint.

As a family we were never more together than in 1941 and '42. We joked, we read, we played music. We only had each other. I adored them all, but father was an absolute tower of strength and my best friend.

Then in September, something shocking happened.'

20. The Notice

Paul's tone began to change as he started to tell the next part of the story one colder morning in late August. We were in his room having a pot of tea. He reached into his sideboard and pulled out a wedge of newspaper cuttings. He passed one to me and explained:

'On Tuesday, 15 September 1942, Oberst (colonel) Knackfuss, who oversaw the German occupiers published a notice of deportation in the *Jersey Evening Post*. 'English born' people were to be deported with immediate effect.

Feldkommandantur 515.	Jersey, den 15. September 1942.
Bekanntmachung	**NOTICE**
Auf höhere Anordnung werden folgende britische Staatsangehörige evakuiert und nach Deutschland überführt :	By order of higher authorities the following British Subjects will be evacuated and transferred to Germany :
a) Personen, die ihren festen Wohnsitz nicht auf den Kanalinseln haben, z.B. vom Kriegsausbruch dort Ueberraschte.	a) Persons who have their permanent residence not on the Channel Islands, for instance, those who have been caught here by the outbreak of the war,
b) alle nicht auf der Insel geborenen Männer von 16 — 70 Jahren, die englischer Volkszugehörigkeit sind, mit ihren Familien.	b) all those men not born on the Channel Islands and 16 to 70 years of age who belong to the English people, together with their families.
Nähere Weisungen ergehen von der Feldkommandantur 515.	Detailed instructions will be given by the Feldkommandantur 515.
	Der Feldkommandant :
	KNACKFUSS,
	Oberst.

There followed one of the most despicable acts perpetrated by the Germans of the entire occupation.

The orders were served, we heard later that soldiers delivered notices by hand. There were many reasons why we fell within the classification for deportation, but we did not receive a notice. Father and mother made desperate enquiries and then found that we were exempted because they were working with the Germans, or in an essential service. Also, compassion was shown towards the fact that we were looking after old Beatrice.

Over the next few days there were awful scenes.

There were three sailings from Jersey in September. The third batch of 560 left Jersey on 29 September 1942, my friends John and Ted were amongst them. Altogether well over a thousand people were deported. Once again I had lost friends or had them taken. I wondered if it was something to do with me.'

He was shaking his head gently. The old man's voice was beginning to waver. He was stumbling in his speech, but he continued hesitatingly.

'After that I was in a sort of despair. Music, literature, and art could not save me. I had no-one except my parents, and I was drawn ever closer to them, my father especially. He knew what I was going through.'

His gaze wavered, and, raising a hand to his mouth, he looked away.

'I will not describe the fear panic and pandemonium caused by these summary deportations. I can't. Others can do it. I can't bear to recall it.' The old man shed gentle tears as he reached into his bookcase and fetched out a quaint looking old book: *Jersey under the Swastika*, by Philip Le Sauteur. He placed it on the table.

'Please take that book away and read it yourself. I don't want to open it. You'll soon find the entries.'

'Alright Paul,' I told him. Off I went. I also thought it best to leave him to his thoughts. I'd never seen him so upset and I was shocked. I had this impression that he was a strong old man just as he had been a strong and impetuous youth. I was wrong. With him there was always more to it, always some surprise or another, but this was an unexpected and unpleasant one. It upset me too.

I went off to the bathroom sat and turned the pages:

It was pitiful to see hundreds of people, often accompanied by young children, herding down towards the harbour, having been rooted from the homes and all that mattered most to them, now on their way to a foreign country where the general conditions were unknown to them. Many of them were not British at all, having been born of Jersey parents and brought to the Island as infants, whilst almost all of them had lived in Jersey for many years.

Exemption was given to those working for the Germans, doctors, clergy and certain essential service workers, although, in the subsequent shipments there were almost no exemptions. Certain rejections were made on medical grounds, and, in the first instance of those with more than four children. In the later batches, it almost seemed that there was a preference for deporting those with larger families.

The deportees were kept waiting about for several hours while the red tape formula was being gone through, and meanwhile the States had arranged for a picnic meal, and each person was provided with a tin each of milk, meat and beans, and a slab of chocolate, to help them while travelling to their destination. Large crowds gathered in the roads leading to, and overlooking the harbours, but, anticipating demonstrations, the numerous Germans on duty ostentatiously paraded with full kit, rifles, tommy guns and boxes of hand grenades. The singing of 'Tipperary' and other British songs by the deportees as they were leaving the pier at 9 pm was taken up by the many onlookers, whereupon the German guards quickly dispersed the crowds.

While these unfortunate people were waiting, the German officers were practising a refined form of cruelty by assuring them that they were being taken to Germany for repatriation to England (that was a lie). There were many very hurried marriages amongst those affected by the order – in some cases, girls married in order to avoid going with their British-born parents, and in others, in order that the girl might go with her man in preference to being separated.

That was ghastly. Why had they done that? Those were innocent civilians.

I went back to his room swiftly and found him standing looking out at the view across Kew Green. When he turned, I could see he was distraught, crying and shaking, breaking down sobbing uncontrollably.

'Paul. Come and sit with me here. I'm with you, I'm with you.' I helped him and he sat, and I pulled up his other chair trying to console him.

He slumped; head bowed.

'They took him,' he whispered.

'Took who? You said you weren't deported?' I held his hands.

'On Saturday, 13 February 1943.' He was sniffling, barely able to speak. 'The bastards took him.'

'Who?'

'The bastards took my father.'

Floods of tears came. He was weeping inconsolably onto my shoulder. I sat and held him. He was swimming in his thoughts, sinking, but I was there.

A colleague, Adele, was passing the open door. She came in anxiously, 'Shall I get Mel?'

'No, it's ok,' I said, 'but can you get us a jug of water and another pot of tea please Adele?' 'Sure.' Away she went.

She came back with Mel and a trolley full of tea, biscuits, cakes, and a jug of water. 'You're an angel,' I told her.

Mel took a look at Paul, then me. 'What's happened?'

I explained that Paul had been telling me about something that upset him but that I was here, and it was alright. 'Can I help at all?' she asked. I glanced at her and gestured with a little *no* shake of the head. 'Ok, you're the right person for this, so I'll leave it with you. If there is anything then call me immediately.'

'Yes Mel,' I said. Away she went.

Suddenly the room was empty again. Except that it wasn't empty. It was full of the old man's grief. The memories and mementos here - the photos of his mother in her smart nurse uniform, his father in his dapper suit and tie were all tiny now compared to the enormity of loss. I found myself sobbing too.

Minutes passed. And more minutes. Adele walked by the open door, then Mel. I gave them both nods.

I couldn't bear to see him like this. I couldn't bear that the Germans had taken his beloved father. It was too awful. Terrible questions came into my head. I chased them away, but they kept returning. Had they killed him? What happened to Helene and Beatrice? I was trying to fathom it all out, but I couldn't.

He fell asleep on my arm. That was a blessing. As I gently removed his hearing aid I saw an old scar on the top left side of his head. Hadn't noticed that before. Laying awkwardly, I could also feel a distinct lump in his left shoulder. Hadn't noticed that either. I fished out my house phone and called Mel to come and help. She came immediately, 'How is he?'

'He's asleep. Can you help me get him into bed.' Together we manoeuvred the exhausted man up and pulled a cover over him. He looked at peace and slept like a child.

'My God. What happened Katie?' she asked. We sat.

'He was telling me about a terrible experience when he was a teenager, something dreadful.'

'We had no idea. Bless you for doing this, for being there for him. He seems so strong.'

'He is strong, but something awful happened.' I couldn't tell her because I felt it was private.

'At the end of shift today I want to talk to you about grief counselling. It's about time we sent you on that course. You're such a valuable asset. Will you think about that between now and 10 o'clock?'

'Yes Mel. Thank you.'

'Stay here with him now. Be there for him when he wakes up he may be disoriented. We will swing by every 10 minutes. Call if you need me. If this goes late I'll sign for your overtime.' I had a lot of respect for her.

I went to pour the tea, but it was stone cold now of course. I sat, watched, and wondered.

He slept for hours. While he did I continued to read *Jersey under the Swastika*. It was difficult knowing that the sleeping man in front of me had been through what was written. He was distraught right now in 2018, so how bad was it in 1943? Beyond imagining.

As I looked at him and considered his loss I began to reflect. My dad always loved me, looked out for me, and did everything he could. Paul's family were very well off, but in Jersey under occupation money didn't matter. They were still hungry and hemmed in. The thing that mattered was family. In that way I reckoned Paul and I were the same.

There was something else though. In 2018 I didn't think about my own loss: the loss of my mother. I wasn't ready to think about that.

At about 3pm he stirred. He was groggy and then recognised me and where he was.

Smiling weakly and reaching out his hand, in German he said, 'Thank you Katie.'

'I'll always be here for you,' I told him.

'It's the burden. Sometimes it flattens me.' I had only the vaguest inkling what he meant. He went on, 'Thank you for walking with me.'

I called down and more tea was brought. Thank God! I needed that tea and so did Paul. The cake and biscuits got dispatched too. He didn't seem comfortable leaving the subject of Christopher's deportation like that, so he tried again. 'He told us he had our photos, then walked up onto the ship. Mother and I…' More tears came.

That was all he could do. Even after 75 years it was still too painful. It wasn't there to be explained. He settled himself:

'We got a letter from him in April that said he was in a castle in Laufen near Salzburg. It seemed to be some sort of internment camp and conditions were not severe. He said he was fine and working on machines and as a translator. He said he was ok and not to worry. That sort of work suited him as he was always tinkering about with car and aircraft engines.'

I stayed until I was quite sure he'd got back on an even keel. As for where I was, I hadn't any experience of seeing people as upset as that before, so I had no hesitation in going to Mel after the handover privately. I told her that I would definitely like to go on the grief counselling course she mentioned. She was delighted and said she would get me booked on it immediately and have overtime signed off for me too. I thanked her profusely. I told her I didn't think I'd done anything particularly special; I was simply doing my job.

She was so kind, she said, 'No, this work is hard. It looks easy but it's not. Sometimes it takes a whole lifetime for damage to show itself. As we are working at the end of life we do encounter these situations. We all need to be ready.'

'I don't think Paul is damaged. I just think he's lonely and needs a companion.'

'After today are you sure it's as simple as that? None of us saw that coming. Did you? We know Paul is an intelligent and challenging old man, but he's got things in his past that we don't know anything about. You're right about needing a companion, and it looks as if you've chosen him.'

'*I've chosen him?*' Startled I took a tone.

'Yes.'

'How is that possible Mel?'

'You're drawn to him. Can't you see it? You genuinely care about him. You've seen something in him.'

Until that moment I hadn't thought about it like that.

Mel was smiling as she said something else. 'You know, some people here think he's a manipulative old so-and-so and won't go anywhere near him. They're scared to death of him. Not you though, you've gone the other way. You like him *because* he's a so-and-so!'

My mind span. I wasn't sure if I knew what she meant. Cycling home over Kew Bridge I gave that a lot of thought.

The circle

Mel gave me the following day off, but I went in to see Paul anyway to check on him. He was slightly different, but okay, and Mel confirmed he was alright.

The next time I was in on earlies. It didn't take long before Paul came and sought me out in German, 'Come, let's play chess, we haven't played in weeks.' I had one or two tasks and said I would be ready at 11.30.

I went back to the sunroom on time and found a tuner tinkering with the Steinberg. 'They don't have a budget for that, so I'm paying for the tuning,' he told me with a wink.

It was my turn to play White and we sat with a pot of tea. His digestive biscuit dissolved with a plop into his cup as he listened to the tuner tinkling pieces from *Beatles* and *Les Misérables* melodies: *Lady Madonna, Here Comes the Sun, Who am I?* and *Bring Him Home*. She was jazzy and classy. 'Nice!' he said, and he asked the tuner to continue playing and that he would make it worth her while.

We played the game accompanied by the excellent piano, but I made a silly mistake and lost in 35 moves. Such a talented player. He gave the tuner four £50 notes, thanks, and a smile as she left.

'I see you have recovered fully then?' I enquired.

'Will you forgive me for the other day?' he asked.

'There's nothing to forgive. We don't have to talk about that, not if you don't want to.'

'Well, that's lucky then because I don't.' It was passive aggression. Typical Paul, things were never the way they seemed with him. It wasn't good enough, so I reacted:

'Please don't take that tone with me. Don't lower yourself. I thought you said we were friends?'

He gave me a look. 'Plenty of people would've told me to piss off for saying something like that and then walked out, but not you. Why? Why haven't you walked out?'

'Is that what you're trying to do? Are you testing me? Don't!'

He rocked back in his chair, spoiling for a fight. I could see it. If he wanted one of those then I was ready.

'Well?' I demanded; voice raised.

I was vaguely aware that guests were leaving the room one by one…

'Don't judge me by what you saw the other day.'

'I am not judging you! What the HELL gives you that idea? Conceit?' Now I was simmering. He was testing my patience, and he was doing it deliberately and on purpose.

Staring, he nodded his head, eyes flickering oh so slightly.

Now I was aware that the room was empty. Everyone had run for cover.

His stare continued, 'You said the right thing.'

I jumped in, 'Well, that's lucky then because it would be awful if I'd said the *wrong* thing, wouldn't it?'

'I am what you see Katie. *Please* don't judge me.'

'And I am what you see. Don't presume to judge me either.'

Then I regarded him again. '*I'll never judge you*. I will always accept you for who you are, without fail, always. Please be kind enough to do the same for me.'

He looked away. 'Things happened to me. I saw things and did things: things I can't explain, repulsive things. I don't know if I am a victim or a perpetrator.'

I told him, 'We can fight, or we can talk. I'll let you decide. If you think I'm worthy then by all means let's talk, but I don't want to fight. Be careful though, I may decide that I don't want to listen.' I got up to leave.

'Scheiße,' (Shit) he muttered.

Then I decided I wasn't going to give him the satisfaction, so I sat back down again and continued in German:

'I didn't make those things happen to you. All you are doing is making them happen again and again. For God's sake – break the circle.' Then I did get up.

He hesitated, 'No, no, please stay. You're right: *break the circle*. But don't say there was nothing to forgive because there was. I was weak.'

'Crying doesn't mean you are weak and fighting me now doesn't mean you are strong. But I think you are the strongest person I ever met.'

'And I think you're the most brilliant young person I ever met, but I am not worthy of your compassion. I'm going to ask you to accept my apology, but I wouldn't blame you if you didn't.'

'Apology accepted. Now let's stop this nonsense and move on.'

'Alright,' he said nodding.

It was enough. I knew then that there were going to be more tests and more fights. I was a timid little girl. I knew it wasn't going to be easy and that I would have to stand up to him or else lose his respect.

****

It was near the end of August. I agreed to return at Christmas and went on the grief counselling course. It helped to put some things in perspective. Paul was angry, perhaps he was grieving? Was I angry and grieving too?

Two more working weeks went by and on 14 September I finished my summer stint at the Stanley.

On my last day, a Friday, Paul came down and walked with me halfway over Kew Bridge. We stood and watched the rowers on the great river flowing beneath us.

Looking back, I think we were both in a state of mixed exhaustion and shock. He thanked me, called me an angel and said he would see me at Christmas. It was a subdued ending.

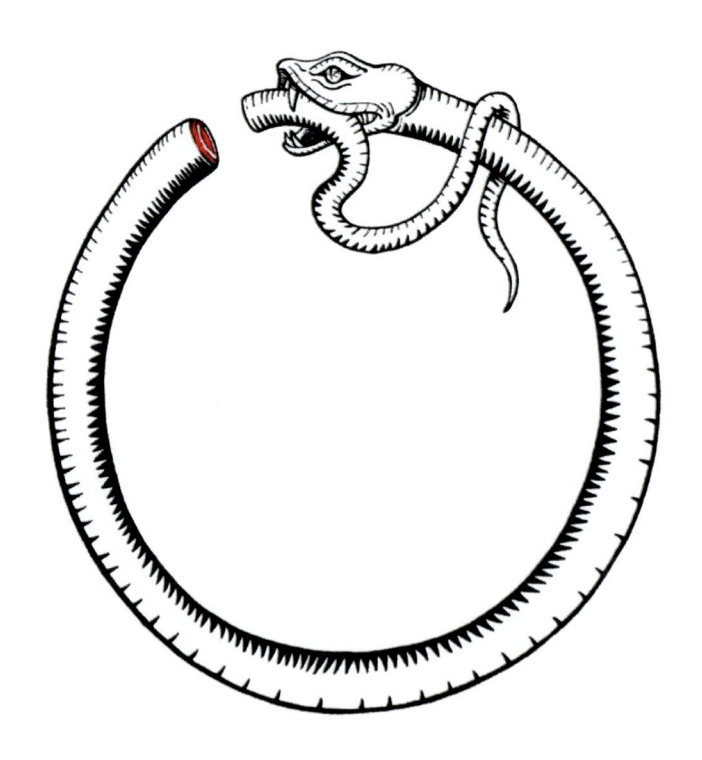

21. Slowly becoming German

In my four-week spell at the Stanley from December 2018 to January 2019 Paul mentioned his father only once. He said that in December 1942 Christopher had not been himself for weeks, and on Christmas morning he was upset because for the first time ever he and Helene had nothing for him. Paul told them he wasn't dismayed and that he felt blessed just to be their son. He told them, 'Parents are perfect presents.' Paul said his father was in floods of tears over that comment.

And then his father got taken away a few weeks later.

He said, 'I was in a sort of despair for a long time. I don't know how long, months I think. Mother was strong. She carried on as normal and was there for me, always. I'm not sure how Aunt Beatrice took it. She said, 'Your father will give them more trouble than they give him. When they piss him off he will shoot his way out and come home!' Except he didn't.

In early 1943 the Germans had taken a beating at Stalingrad and were in retreat everywhere. That gave solace. The Americans were in the war allied to the British and all the 'free peoples' who had gone to Britain to fight. The BBC radio often listed them: Polish, Norwegian, French, Belgian, Dutch, Czech, Danish, Greek. All these Europeans came to England to fight the Germans. Then there were the Indians, Canadians, Australians, New Zealanders, Rhodesians, South Africans, Kenyans and West Indians who did the same. All these so-called 'foreigners' were on our side as our Allies, it wasn't Britain on its own, far from it. Many countries battled against the Germans and Italians: the 'Enemy Axis.' The British weren't the major force. The major forces were the Russians and Americans. Even America is a foreign country you know, especially now Donald Trump is in charge. Just because Americans speak English, that doesn't make them English, does it?

The Russians were advancing westwards with armies that seemed limitless. We heard it all on the secret radio.

By spring 1943 we were in the full grip of the occupying forces, and it was turning nasty. Small offences were punished harshly. The jail was full of people who had hardly done anything. Islanders started to turn on each other. There were tales of letters being sent to the authorities: denunciations. Anyone could be an informant. Many were sent away. Jewish people were sent away. There was nothing anyone could do.

On my 16th birthday mother said she had something important to tell me. She said she knew why we hadn't been deported and needed to explain. We sat down to a gathering at the family table. We never did that, so I knew it was important. I sat with Beatrice in the bay window.

Calmly she described how when the first deportations began in September they had gone to the authorities to see if we would be deported in the future. That might have been a mistake, it was impossible to say. It came out that mother and I were not going to be deported because we were classed as *German* by virtue of our place of birth: *Straßburg Elsass*, our language and 'race.' Mother was most definitely German as she had been born in Alsace in 1896 when it was part of Germany. Father was born in Bonn to a German family and held a British Passport but was also 'of German blood', his *Ahnenpaß* said so. After France fell Hitler declared that Alsace had returned to the Greater German Reich. That meant that according to him *I was German too, just like any other boy born to a German mother and father*. She said there had been 'discussions' but father had fought against Germany and would be deported in the next wave if there was one and of course in February there was. It meant he'd known since September that he'd probably be deported. That sword of Damocles had been hanging over him. That's why he was upset at Christmas. He'd sat on that for five months and not told me.

I wasn't angry. What use would anger be? I couldn't be angry with my parents, they were protecting me, and anyway they didn't know he would be deported right up until the day it happened.

There was no question of going back to Strasbourg and no question of leaving Beatrice.

The end result was that mother and I were identified as *German* and issued with papers to prove it. We were still together and that was good. Mother said we should now obtain an *Ahnenpaß* for me. Unfortunately, there was a bad thing: next year I would turn 17. At that point, as a German, I would be conscripted into their armed services.

Beatrice made a comment, she said, 'I always knew you two were German. Now it's official.' Mother glared at her, 'We're Alsatian,' she growled. It was a very bad joke but then Beatrice was very old.

It was a serious situation. Raising her voice, something she almost never did, mother roared: 'No Haussmann has ever nor will ever take up arms for Germany. **Never!**'

My young mind looked for a solution. The only one I could think of was that mother could stay in Jersey and look after Beatrice, and I would volunteer to go to Laufen and be with father.

She said, 'They won't allow it. They told us that 'honest Germans don't get deported'. There's no chance of them letting you go.' Our little family meeting broke up with each of us going off to our own thoughts.

These were revelations, but what use were they? We were still trapped, and father was still gone. It was hopeless even thinking about it. We were in a unique position, but still totally stuck. We just had to accept it.

I was out and about as summer came on. It took my mind off things.

I came across more escaped Russian slave workers on the run in hiding and desperate for food. I took what I could to them which wasn't much, and brought some of them back to the Big House. In return they taught mother and I their language, and we learned quickly. They told us of the savagery in the east and what would happen when their 'anti-fascist' armies reached Germany: 'Everything destroy!' It was intensely worrying.

In 1943 the Allies were bombing Germany too. Just as the Germans had viciously attacked Rotterdam, London and Bristol, now the RAF and US Air Forces were destroying German cities. I couldn't calculate how dangerous being in Germany was, but I did know one thing: father was there. This bothered me a lot. Jersey was relatively safe, provided you kept out of trouble. But Germany was not safe.

I spent time watching the bunker system at Corbière being put together with massive steel rods and concrete. I wasn't supposed to be there, but I was curious. Anyway, I knew a few French and Belgians who were in a camp behind La Pulente who worked on it. I blended in well with them, my clothes were pretty tired, so I looked the part and was able to creep in. I got chatting to these workers who I recognised and walked along like everyone else. The *Organisation Todt* supervisors overseeing the constructions usually didn't check papers.

There were actually young German *Reich Labour Service (RAD)* workers in there too. I just joined in and copied what they were doing. I soon found they accepted me and chatted just as they would to any other young German working with the RAD. Anyway, according to Hitler I was German too. I did this two or three times, as not only was I bored I was also genuinely interested in what was going on with these amazing constructions. I didn't mind if I got caught. Now that I was German I thought it would be an interesting game to see what would happen if I was.

Then one day in late May I was caught. Two *OT* supervisors challenged me in poor French. I laughed and in German called them *Idioten* (idiots) as I showed them my papers and they weren't happy. 'No Labour Service papers but look, you are German! What the **hell** are you doing here?' they said. I spoke to them in my normal Alsatian brogue. 'Christ, he's Alsatian!' This was such an astounding novelty that they were flummoxed. They called over two soldiers who were shovelling cement, and just to unnerve them I struck up a conversation about German poetry. I was taking the piss out of them of course but it sailed right over their heads. None of them had heard of Goethe or Rilke, they were a young and rough lot. It was certain that they couldn't even read. Someone went off to get a senior.

Across the worksite ghostly outlines of workers could be seen coming and going through the dust. A soldier without a cap was coming our way walking awkwardly but I paid him no attention and returned to playing games with these army boys.

One looked up and said, 'Ah, here comes the sergeant. You'd better explain yourself boy.'

The group around me parted and I saw him. I couldn't believe my eyes. 'Hello Paul,' he said. It was Hans.'

22. Christmas 2018

Over Christmas I saw that Paul had recovered from his hiatus of September. There was industry in each of his days. When the weather was okay we went out to Kew Gardens with the others. When the weather was rubbish he read his favourite poetry, painted, or made a nuisance of himself at bridge or chess. He even played piano for the other guests by request once or twice a week, usually Mozart, Bach, Satie, or Chopin. *Berceuse in D-Flat, Op. 57* was a favourite, but sometimes Beatles or jazz, or show tunes from *Jesus Christ Superstar* or *Les Misérables*. He had a slight issue with his right index and little finger though.

The supervisors were impressed. Mel said I'd tamed him, but I knew I hadn't. 'Meh, he's a savage beast and only I can handle him!' I declared with a laugh. Then she said we were 'Tuning in to each other.' She came out with another gem which was that working with Paul had 'Given me an outlet.' One of her more cryptic offerings, I said surely it had to be the other way around? 'Not how it is in care work,' she told me. Perhaps she was right? The old man had transfixed me. 'He knows you are listening,' was another of her comments. She had a point there. I certainly was listening, and I wrote down all the goings on in my notebook.

Over Christmas there was building excitement as another cultural outing was approaching: a matinee of *Les Misérables* at Queen's Theatre. I got a shock when I was on duty on Christmas Day and Paul handed me an envelope at the dinner table and inside was a ticket. Smiling he told me, 'You said you'd never been to the theatre; well, you're going now!'

Les Misérables, 2.30 Saturday, 29 December 2018

We were in our seats. Paul had already overflowed in generosity towards me, but he also ensured that everyone enjoyed a glass of champagne as well. That was four bottles.

The show was absolutely magical. I can't describe it I was overwhelmed. Incredibly beautiful singing, not like anything I'd ever imagined.

Although I knew some of the tunes I didn't know the story or the relevance of the lyrics.

Of the many indelible impressions about that wonderful day perhaps the most amazing was that Paul sobbed openly pretty much from start to finish.

He'd taken a box of tissues in with him, but I had no idea why. It all started as the character *Fantine* began singing *I Dreamed a Dream*. Tears poured down his face. Most of the audience cried too and me with them. That continued through *Bring Him Home*. The old man was in floods.

The next day, Sunday, I was on duty again and he turned to me and asked, 'Is there anything you wish you'd done differently Katie?' This was a token, another one of his ploys; I'd seen this sort of thing before with him. Where was it going? It had to be connected to the show.

Innocently I said, 'Not really. I don't have any regrets. I've never had much in the way of choice.'

Paul was reflective. 'When I was in Jersey I never felt I had any choice either.' I wasn't sure he'd heard me or what he meant. Then I realised he'd mirrored my word: *choice*.

'Well, we have something in common then.'

'There are always choices,' he said. I still wasn't sure what he meant. We'd talked about choices before.

'Sounds like you made a hard choice once.'

'I've made more than one.'

'What was the difficult choice?' I said, mirroring again.

'In *Les Misérables* after meeting the Bishop, *Jean Valjean* begins to behave like a guardian angel. He comes and helps those in great need. Imagine someone you love is in great peril and that you believe you are the only person who could get them out of that situation. Imagine you have a choice. Do nothing and risk their death, or take action to save them, even though it would put you in grave danger. Can you imagine that?'

'Yes, I can.'

'Imagine you did nothing then heard that person you love had fallen. How would you feel?'

'It would be terrible. I would have to live with it for the rest of my life.' Where was this going?

He said, 'Sometimes what seems like a choice isn't a choice at all. Sometimes there is no choice.'

He left it there. Of all the many inscrutable things he'd said to me that was by far the most enigmatic.

23. Conversation at the causeway

'I was amazed to see Hans again. We embraced. 'My God Hans! What are you doing here?'

'Come, let's walk,' he said, and we went off down the causeway to the edge of the sea. 'I got in a few days ago,' he added as he moved clumsily.

I could see he was a different man to the one I'd made friends with two years ago.

We walked right down to the water. It was rough and the tide was coming in. On the left there is a tiny sandy beach, and we sat on the rocks with the sea lapping nearly to our toes. 'I never thought I'd see you again.'

'And I never thought I'd see you either. Look how tall you are! I knew it was you. When they told me an Alsatian boy was in the compound I knew it could only be Paul von Bonn.' We embraced again.

'I'm so glad you're back!'

'I'm glad to be here.'

He wasn't the same. He said, 'So many things have gone badly, but finally something has gone right, and I am here again.'

'What happened to you?' I asked. The soldier hesitated and looked away; he didn't want to respond.

'I was sent to the east, to Russia. After that I can't remember. Now they say I am not fit for combat duty.'

Horrific things had happened, so bad that for him they hadn't happened at all. He couldn't remember. He looked uncomfortable and I shouldn't have asked.

I was only thinking of myself when I said, 'I'm so pleased to see you. I have no friends.'

'How is your father, mother and great-aunt?'

There was no way he could have known.

'My father was deported in February.'

'Oh my God!' he gasped.

I know my face fell at that point and that I cried.

'Dear boy, oh my dear boy, I'm so sorry.' He knew not to ask anything more and held me tightly.

'What about Nikolas and Leutnant Schneider?'

'Dead, they're all dead, all under crosses now.'

'Christ!' I exclaimed.

'He had nothing to do with it,' he said as he reached into his tunic, fetched out and kissed his crucifix, and crossed himself. 'You once picked a fight you couldn't win, remember? Now Germany has picked a fight it can't win. We shouldn't win either. Germany has done terrible things, things for which there is no justification. We shouldn't win, and we won't.'

I wasn't sure what to say so I said nothing. We stood to walk back up the causeway.

From his tunic pocket, he produced and studied the St Christopher bicycle bell. 'I don't know anybody here, let's be friends again.'

'Yes Hans, yes of course.'

24. Death

He lay there completely silent and still. As if he were sleeping. When I looked I found myself wanting, expecting to see little movements - the tiny flickers that go with life. They didn't come.

I kept looking. There were no flickers. He was dead.

I had never seen a dead person before. Now I was sat next to one.

He had become very frail in the months I had been away. He was in bed covers pulled. His heart had simply stopped. Life had ended. His skin was pale and cool, his lips and fingernails light blue. His eyes were closed. I took his hands and placed them one over the other. There was still warmth in his body which had been alive just an hour earlier. I heard his watch ticking and took it gently from his wrist.

Infirmity, frailness, death, these things were familiar to us as workers at the home. We were young and yet we were close to the end of life. The old around us knew it. We knew it. We were trained to deal with the practicalities but sometimes not the realities.

The doctor packed her bag and began filling in forms. Name of deceased: Michael Clarke.

Later Paul quietly asked me if I was there at the end. When I told him I was he looked at me thoughtfully and said that surely I was in the company of angels.

25. Repaying evil with good

'Hans was now Feldwebel: Wachtmeister (Reconnaissance), a sergeant, in a position of authority and influence. Nobody questioned or challenged him. He had been wounded twice according to his tunic insignia. A bullet had gone through his left leg and two fingers of his left hand were missing. A doctor somewhere saw the state he was in. He'd asked to come back to Jersey and was signed into the 319th division. It was part of a recuperation process and a blessing for him and for me.

Next day he called around to the Big House. Mother and Beatrice greeted him as a long-lost friend. I'd already told them that Hans hated Hitler and the Nazis because of the dreadful things they had done, and how he expected Germany to lose the war. We went to the living room and sat.

Out of a deep tunic pocket he fetched a black box and placed it on the table.

'I'm so deeply sorry that they took your husband Frau von Bonn. It is a completely senseless action.'

Mother told him grimly, 'It wasn't of your doing Hans, we appreciate that. In Alsace we have a saying: *Der Deifel het meh ass zwölf Aposchtle.*' (The Devil has more than twelve Apostles). Hans nodded; he didn't need a translation.

'I want to help your family. I am sick of this war. Many soldiers feel as I do but nobody dares to speak up.'

She asked, 'Is it true there was a riot of soldiers at the Ritz Hotel and that the one who started it was caught, made to dig his own grave and then shot?'

'Yes. It's not wise to speak up, not wise to stick your bayonet into a portrait of *der Führer.*'

'Mother of Christ!' she exclaimed. Mother *never* swore.

'My aim is to survive this war, but I don't know how.' He turned to me, 'Your father is a good man who did nothing wrong. Now they have taken him I promise to help you and your family until your father is set free.'

'Why would you do this for us Hans?' mother asked.

His face fell again, 'I am going to repay evil with good.'

Sensing his distress, I jumped in using one of my great-aunt's sayings: 'You cannot change nature.'

Beatrice gently nodded her head in agreement adding quietly, 'Plenty of good men go to war.'

Hans looked at me then regarded the small box on the table, 'I've brought this from Frankfurt, and I want you to have it.'

I took and opened a part-used water colour paint box and glanced at him. His eyes, filling with tears, stared down. There was a story here.

Mother came, stood behind me, and placed her hands on my shoulders. 'Paul trusts you. That's good enough for me. As his mother can I ask you to do one thing Hans?'

'What is that Frau von Bonn? Tell me and I will do it.'

'Be a friend to my son.'

He turned to me, smiled, held his crucifix and replied, 'I swear by God that I will.'

Summer 1943

'Through Hans' position I quickly found myself being re-introduced to German military life and personnel and was completely accepted. It was a strange thing to find myself in amongst the very people who had sent my father away. Even stranger that I was classed as one of them. It was like a new life had started, a different life, with Hans as my trustworthy guide.

Suddenly I was no longer bored. I watched the soldiers, chatted with them and learned everything I could.

They taught me boxing and at first I got knocked down a lot because I was fairly puny, but I got stronger. Then I would get into massive shouting matches with people I didn't agree with. Hans would take me aside and tell me to calm down. It was good advice. Then I'd be boxing with a soldier I'd had a row with, and I would fight hard and get knocked down. The soldier would pick me up, help me, and say, 'Well done boy!' There was a sort of chivalry about it that made sense, but I still didn't agree with them, went back and argued and got knocked down again. I got knocked down a lot, but eventually I got good with my fists.

Sometimes Spitfires and Whirlwind aircraft attacked shipping, and the guns sprang into action. Some were shot down. I learned aircraft identification: German, American and British. The newer Allied aircraft like Thunderbolts, Mustangs and Typhoons were seen too, but you needed my father's binoculars to see the fast high-level Mosquito photo-reconnaissance aeroplanes. I heard they were causing mayhem in low-level missions on the mainland. Being made of wood, they were rarely picked up by radar, and sometimes flew ridiculously low. They were the fastest aircraft on either side and extremely hard to shoot down. The head of the Luftwaffe Hermann Göring developed a personal hatred of them. 'They are so low and accurate they could put a bomb through your front door,' one of the Luftwaffe anti-aircraft boys told me. The Germans knew they were being outgunned.

I learned about the politics of the war, the propaganda newspapers, the lies and misinformation. I knew it was lies because I would listen to the BBC on the radio. The soldiers knew it was lies too. I would chat with Hans, and he was dismissive. He didn't want to talk about the war or the Nazi regime. He hated both. A lot of the men were getting really pissed off as well. They spoke to me but didn't dare say anything openly.

There was drinking too: potato, beet or fruit vodka was a feature. As 1943 progressed, so the soldier's morale fell and fell.

I was still interested in the guns and hardware though. Once again I handled weapons like the MP40 *Maschinenpistole 40 machine gun*, Luger pistol, and handed-in revolvers and fired them in live sessions. In shooting matches with Hans, I always retained the 'apple trophy'! I was better than the best rifleman they had and took pride in showing them as often as possible. They gave me sniper training, with location, movement, camouflage, high value target identification and escape. I enjoyed that.

A couple of soldiers had good quality cameras and sometimes they took group photos or things to send home. One day after a shooting match, someone at Corbière wanted a photograph of Hans and me at what they called the 'Mortar Bunker'. Standing by the triangular wall, gun in one hand, apple trophy in the other, I turned to my friend and asked, 'Hans, what's the score, *at the moment?*' He smiled just as the shutter clicked.

I had many conversations with Germans young and old. These took place in gun pits and firing ranges, bunkers, and the backs of lorries - once even inside a captured French tank. I became a fixture, a friend to them, a confidant, a son, father confessor or younger brother, someone to tell a joke to. They told me tales of their *Heimat*: Homeland, life in their community. They told me of their families, their hills and rivers, their forests and secret places, their folktales local stories and little sayings. In return I told them about Alsace: the storks, the wonderful castles and vineyards, and hunting in the beautiful Vosges mountains with father. I learned their habits and ways and they learned mine. I learned what it meant to be German.

It was hard to listen to the stories of devastation and death. Some had lost fathers in Russia; some had lost sons in Russia. All had lost those they loved. A constant theme was death and Russia, always Russia. It was as if some great butcher's knife had been taken to Germany, its guts sliced open, and the entrails left poured across the East. Like the empty steppes their grief was limitless and surpassed even my own. Whilst many had dead fathers at least I believed mine was still alive. It was a sort of comfort.

Music was a shared passion. Neighbours joined us with their violins clarinets flutes and cellos, and we played together with mother or me accompanying on piano. My wonderful mother.

In the summer of 1943, my fully signed and stamped *Ahnenpaß* arrived. The sun shone, military bands played, and I was able to move more freely than I had for many years, but I still didn't have a father, nor any word. We had written to him in April. Then in mid-September we got a reply dated July and father was ok. It was such a relief.'

He got out a tatty old map of Jersey and told me cherished memories:

'By 1943 it was long established where islanders could and couldn't go. The north coast was out of bounds along with the headlands of St Brelade's Bay and a chunk of St Ouen's including the pond and the airport.

None of this stopped me going out and about looking around drawing and painting the birds and flowers in the lovely countryside. I enjoyed cycling the lanes especially in spring and summer. I loved the profusions of wildflowers growing from the granite walled hedgerows and the bees and butterflies. Sometimes I ran into groups of Russian forced labourers being marched somewhere and would stop and attempt conversation. Then an *Organisation Todt* guard would come back, swear and shoo me away.

I was often stopped at checkpoints. If they didn't recognise me I opened up in German, and it disarmed them immediately. I got good at doing that.'

26. The collector

'St Ouen's Bay with miles of golden sand and dunes is one of the most beautiful places in Jersey. In the south: Corbière where I was friends with Hans and the other soldiers. In the north: the wonderful windswept Mont du Vallet road, and picturesque Pointe Etaquerel that had a remarkable tower - before the Germans blew it up. This was my stamping ground. I didn't like it when they fenced it off and planted landmines in it.

Other favoured spots were the edges of the Racecourse and the golf links which didn't see a lot of putting these days due to the fact that the Germans had sunk three giant Howitzers into it. The greenkeepers were thoughtless, and the course was either completely overgrown or ruined by other constructions. They had even built a machine gun nest on the Racecourse called *Hohe*. I suppose they thought they were backing a winner there.

It was possible to get down near to the beach. Couldn't go on the beach of course because there were signs that said, 'Achtung! Minen!' sporting a jaunty skull and cross bones. These signs had to be taken seriously. Although I hadn't seen it personally, I had been told on good authority that every now and again seals would come up on the beach and be blown to smithereens. The damned fools couldn't read the signs you see. That resulted in a free meal for the seagulls which, if they weren't careful, ended in them getting blown to smithereens as well.

Early in the occupation people still liked to roam with binoculars hanging around their necks. That wasn't wise. If birdwatchers were spotted, they were quickly challenged as they were imagined to be spies. That hobby soon died out. The Germans weren't keen on sightseers and couldn't see the point of it. They had a habit of complicating things, and it was hard to answer back if you couldn't speak the language. However, there were other intrepid types who had different objectives in mind: people who were prepared to brave the rigours of occupation. I encountered one such intrepid spirit on a particularly glorious day in summer 1943.

I spotted him on the checkpoint near Le Braye, right on the edge of the barbed wire near the narrow-gauge railway line the Russians had built. He was chatting to a young sentry and had what looked like a butterfly net under his arm. This was something new; hadn't seen him before. I wandered over innocently. The soldier glanced up and in broken German English told me, 'Wo you can not goh.' I acknowledged with a nod and raised palm.

I didn't recognise the sentry or the fellow with the net and stood idly waiting for a break in the conversation. It was unusual to hear people speaking German to the soldiers. Even more of a surprise they seemed to be talking about insects! I considered the fellow's net. He had a small brass hand lens hanging around his neck too: an entomologist. I'd never met one of those. A young chap he was, maybe 21, very suntanned and fit.

As they turned to me and smiled, I enthused: *'Was für ein schöner Tag!'* ('What a beautiful day!') You should have seen the look on their faces!

Astounded, the soldier exclaimed, 'You're that Alsatian boy from Straßburg they talk about at Corbière and Ziethen. My God!' I recognised his accent from the vicinity of Stuttgart.

The chap with the net simply stared at me nonplussed.

He grinned and said to the sentry, 'Excuse me, I need to speak English to my friend.' His pronunciation wasn't great but that was good form, so I smiled and told him, 'Bravo!' The fellow gave me a sideways look...

We passed the time of day in English as the lovely sea-breeze kissed our cheeks and the shrieking gulls occasionally wheeled overhead.

Then the stranger said something I wasn't expecting. In a slightly hushed tone in *Jèrriais*, he muttered, 'Can you get us into the restricted zone to St Ouen's Pond?' We used *Jèrriais* as a secret language sometimes.

'Why would you want to go there?'

'Sorry young man. How impolite of me, I should have made introductions. My name is Wally. What's yours?'

'Paul von Bonn.'

At this the German soldier perked up and asked, 'I thought you were from Straßburg not Bonn?'

I mimicked his accent, 'Oh no, no, I come from Straßburg, and my family name is von Bonn.'

The soldier was visibly staggered and swayed back.

'Paul, your German is brilliant!' whispered Wally.

'Thank you,' I grinned.

I asked the sentry, 'Friend, will you escort us into the restricted area, to the pond? On the way you can tell us all about Stuttgart.' This was one of the tricks I'd learned, and it almost always worked.

At this, the young soldier took off his helmet revealing a shock of blonde hair. He was a particularly good specimen.

Breaking out in a huge smile he replied, 'It would be my pleasure, and why don't you tell me all about Straßburg?'

'It would be **my** pleasure, friend. Thank you for your help,' I told him.

I looked at Wally and winked and he stared back at me disbelieving.

The soldier, whose name was Leon, obligingly peeled back the rolls of barbed wire and let us through.

'You charming little bugger!' or words to that effect, Wally whispered to me in *Jèrriais*.

'I've found that Germans love a bit of flattery Wally.' He giggled at that.

Leon swung his rifle across his shoulder and bade us follow him north up the beach road. We walked alongside the railway line, past the *Steps* Bunker, past the *Bucht* anti-aircraft Box, and over the rail junctions towards St Ouen's Pond and nobody batted an eyelid. What a beautiful day!

My new acquaintance explained that he should have been at Jesus College Oxford. Hilariously, he described himself as: 'Detained unavoidably at the Führer's pleasure.' I liked that.

Every now and then he stomped off and pounced on something small in the sand and examined it with his hand lens. He seemed to be in his element.

While Wally was doing that, Leon was telling me all about Stuttgart, even though he was from Heilbronn. He'd been in a Nazi *Hitlerjugend* (Hitler Youth) torchlight parade through the streets and was of the opinion that I should be impressed, but I wasn't, not in the least. This was a common feature of all the occupying soldiers regardless of rank. They all wanted to talk about their home, their *Volk*, their *Heimat*. In their heads that's where they still were.

When we were at the pond, at a bunker system called *High Tower*, completely unexpectedly Wally announced, 'I found a rare dragonfly here two years ago: *Coenagrion scitulum*, but it doesn't seem to be here now.'

Then he said, 'Paul, have a look at these beautiful insects.' In three glass tubes were large grasshoppers which he'd collected from the dunes. He carefully took one and stretched it out to reveal superb blue-black wings.

'This is *Oedipoda coerulescens*. Isn't it lovely?' he purred. I looked and marvelled at this stranger's attention to detail.

'Do you pin them out?'

'Yes, sometimes I do,' he said, admiring his finds. 'They don't live long but look where they live. What a splendid place to live.' I wasn't totally sure. Wally was an islander. Like the storks in Alsace and the grasshoppers, in his own way he was happy to be here. On the other hand, I did not feel like I was in a splendid place. I felt like that grasshopper, trapped stretched out and examined.

'I would rather fly,' I told him idly.

'Well, that's how they got here you know: they flew. The dragonfly was a rare migrant, and this chap is a migrant as well.' I paused to look again at the silent delicate creature. 'You're a migrant too aren't you Paul? *A rare one!*' I remember I pulled a frown.

Like the grasshopper, I became silent reflecting on what he'd said. Wally was interested in rare migrants, and he'd evidently caught another one.

He wandered off back to his searching.

Meanwhile, I sat and watched the busy ants carrying off caterpillars and other booty to their anthills to be consumed.

Eventually, Leon looked at his watch, said he was due to be relieved and had to return to his post. As we walked back to Le Braye he asked the usual questions: 'Why aren't you serving your country? Why are you here?' I just looked out at the crashing waves and referred him to them saying, 'Heilbronn is a long way from the sea, isn't it?'

At the checkpoint we thanked Leon profusely adding that we hoped he wouldn't get into any trouble. Wally had left his bike at Le Braye. We reached the road and said our goodbyes. Wally gave me his address and said I should call in, but I never did.'

27. Conversations, 1943-44

'Hans explained, 'If you know about war, then you know to listen when one of your reconnaissance patrols tells you there is an ambush and a catastrophe waiting. You know when to disregard an order. My experience prevented loss of lives on many occasions. I was twice threatened with a court martial and firing squad, but I was just one man. If I'd saved two young soldiers then my life was a price worth paying. The fact that others made decisions based on stupid ideology was their problem and frequently they ended up dead because of it. Party member's blood is just as red as anyone else's, and they die in squalor in a ditch just the same.'

Paul once asked Hans how many men he had killed. 'He wouldn't answer, but he did say, 'When the enemy are in your trenches, you don't wait for them to bayonet you, you pull the trigger, you shoot them in self-defence. When threatened with death, choose to live. You **must** resist. You're dead anyway so don't go meekly, fight. Killing in self-defence is justifiable. You are no use to yourself dead.'

'Hans said that if man had no free will and no choice, then God's commandments and warnings would be in vain. It would mean that everything was predestined. It was logically impossible for there to be a God which punished man for his sins but which he nevertheless predestined him to commit. That was absurd. Instead, it was up to man to choose between good and evil. Therefore, good and evil have to go together, or else man cannot exercise a choice.' Paul said he gave that a lot of thought.

Paul told Hans that according to the folklore of Alsace, a thousand years ago there was a terrible war in that land. Seeing the murder and mayhem the hearts of the storks were filled with sorrow. They flew up to God to beg him to put an end to the war and hence their misery. However, God had no intention of interfering in man's affairs as it would have meant taking away his free will. Instead, he allowed the storks to dip their wings in black to alleviate their mourning. This is why the symbolic storks of Alsace have wings with black tips. He said his mother had explained this when he implored God to intervene against evil.

Hans was impressed with Paul's knowledge, logic and faith, after all, he was just 16 and hadn't seen that much of life. Hans asked how he could have such knowledge. 'I learn about the world from books, unlike the Nazis, who burn them,' he told him.

Hans said that in Germany children were learning only: 'Rubbish, racial theory and Nazi paganism in half-time schooling. The other half of the time they are manning searchlights or being deafened by firing anti-aircraft guns. What type of childhood is that? What type of parent or grandparent wants a half-educated child with war experience?' He despaired for children who were not getting a full education. 'It's always the children who suffer for what older people do,' he said. 'We Germans will lose our values and identity. Hermann Göring himself said, 'Whenever I hear the word 'culture,' I reach for my revolver,' and 'education is dangerous, every educated person is a future enemy.' These ghastly men have ruined our country. They lie to us, burn our books, and defile our culture. Like maggots they destroy us from the inside.'

****

'The men under Hans' command respected him and described him as considerate and devout. Meanwhile as summer turned to autumn and yet another harvest time came along he'd said very little about his home life. This marked him out, everyone spoke about their homes and lives in Germany, even the catastrophes, but not Hans.

The shooting, training and military life continued. To fit in I had to put on German pale green fatigues, but I didn't mind, I loved weapons training and shooting. I used to watch and sometimes participate in company manoeuvres, for example with the MG42 machine gun squads. By God that was a fearsome weapon.'

Then, with a typical flourish, Paul reached into a file and found a photo of Jersey soldiers setting up a MG42 machine gun. 'You can see *Obergefreiter* Emil at the back. 'MG1' is under instruction as the gun operator, that's Gustav. Karl on his left was 'MG2' - machine gun assistant. Franz is kneeling holding a spare gun barrel. He was MG3 which was the ammunition carrier. You can see the ammo box too.

The younger soldiers had been in the *Hitlerjugend* back in Germany. They said it was a sort of Boy's Brigade with guns. One told me, 'We had to spend half of our time in school and the other half doing weapons training or boxing, but I'd rather be in school. I didn't like all that fighting.'

They told me they'd heard of an SS Panzer division that was being formed exclusively of *Hitlerjugend* boys aged 17 to 19. 'Only crazy party boys from the *Napola* schools do that!' they said explaining why they hadn't.

A division was about 16-20,000 soldiers strong. It seemed incredible that such young men could serve in a fully armoured formation with tanks and heavy weapons. They had young adult officers from another SS division to lead them. I knew the SS were fanatically devoted to Hitler.

By 1943 a lot of the soldiers in Jersey were very young, older than 40, or like Hans had been wounded. One older *Obergefreiter*, Thomas, told me that the reason the SS division *Hitlerjugend* had been formed was because the war was going badly and now, 'Even our future will be sacrificed. The young always pay for the mistakes of the old.' He made me swear never to tell anyone what he'd said.

Once again I helped out on the farms and once again I found myself working with the young ladies. My *Jèrriais* was pretty decent by now. Before the other boys could begin talking about me behind my back I would greet them with, *'Bouônjour man vyi! Comme est qu'tu'es?'* (Hello old mate! How are you?) They still regarded me with suspicion. I would always be an outsider to them, and as well as that, I think they had their eyes on the girls. Not me though, I was a little young for that sort of thing.

Just before Christmas I was again relieved of my watch. I'd visited mother at the General Hospital. I walked out and straight into a group of six boys: a nasty little ambush…

'Bouônjour', (*Jèrriais; Hello*) said a youth standing in my path. Aged about 16 or 17. I didn't know him, but I'd seen him and the others around.

'Comme est qu'tu'es? (*Jèrriais; how are you?*) I replied. Then three more, all about the same age stepped forward.

One said, 'Baîse man tchu' (*Jèrriais; kiss my ass*). Another, 'Don't talk to us, Gerry lover.' Another, 'We're here to teach you a lesson.'

Two moved to block my escape. As they did another one said, 'We know you've been playing with the Germans up at Corbière.'

Scrawny underfed little runts they were. But there were too many of them. I needed to run, but I couldn't, so I tried to bluff it out:

'Tu' fouaitheux cârr'-ous!' *(Jèrriais; you shit heads clear off!)*

The tallest one regarded me and leering towards the others exclaimed, 'Oulle est sale, oulle cliut'tait ès pathais!' *(Jèrriais; it's so dirty that it would stick to a wall!)*

I told him, 'Fou pas d'ma dgeule *(Jèrriais; fuck off)*. Come on then, you little rats - I'll put you **all** in that hospital!'

He swung at me, missed, and there was an almighty punch up.

I took a some hits, but so did they. Fists and boots were flying! Blood dripped everywhere. My God, they *hated* me.

A policeman was blowing his whistle and running. The gang took off shouting: 'Un couochon d'allemands,' *(Jèrriais; a German pig)* and 'Jus'qe un couochon en manchettes verts.' *(Jèrriais; just a pig in green sleeves)*. It was true that the Germans wore green uniforms - so that was a very bad insult!

My watch was torn off in the melee. Nothing could be done so I told mother merely that I'd lost it. The watch was irreplaceable, the ripped clothes, bruises, smashed lip and black eye hard to explain.

There were no letters from father. We wrote to the camp but got nothing back. We thought the censor was cutting them out. God, I missed him.

Christmas 1943

By the time we got to Christmas I was in quite a bad state again, but I tried to keep it to myself and not bring down Beatrice and mother's morale.

Hans could see my struggles. He said things like, 'I'm sorry that you will not have your father this Christmas,' or 'I wish I could bring your father back.' These comments didn't help much, in fact they told me more about him. I felt sorry for both of us. There were lots of things he wasn't saying but I didn't have the nerve to ask.

Surprisingly, there were many soldiers at St Thomas's for Mass on Christmas Day, including Hans. On the steps afterwards he handed me a plain, brown-wrapped present and mother invited him over for Silvester (New Year's Eve).

I got the present home and unwrapped it. In a beautiful Jugendstil pewter frame was *the photograph* of him and me at Corbière after that shooting match. Incredibly generous.'

At this Paul stood and went to pick up his precious photo. He brought it back, placed it on the table, gazed at it, drew breath and then returned to his story:

'Christmas was almost a warm day. We set a place for father and opened a bottle of wine to go with the duck we were having for dinner. Since the family changed its name, the Bunns were in the hotel and restaurant trade and father was the chief wine buyer for the business in London. We always had plenty of wine in the Big House, and we kept back his favourites as a keepsake and for his return. We sat and remembered him quietly.

On Boxing Day, we had another family conference. The subject was my 17th birthday coming up in April. Mother had vowed that I would never take up arms for Germany. I told her this was ironic given that I knew how to fire dismantle clean and re-assemble practically every weapon Germany had ever produced. Beatrice said it was a waste of time teaching me how to fire guns as I had such a hot temper I didn't actually need one. It was another of her odd observations. Nevertheless, I was due for conscription and now was the time to try and work out how to avoid it. I didn't have any ideas, but I knew someone who might.

I remember on the afternoon of Silvester, 50 or 60 planes came over very high, but the guns didn't shoot for some reason. This sort of thing had been happening increasingly and it was clear to all of us that Germany was losing the war now. The BBC said so and so did some of the soldiers quite openly.

Hans arrived at 9 o'clock. He'd walked over with a torch from his billet. We greeted him warmly and put him in front of the log fire where he took off his boots. He smiled but we soon realised he was reserved. 'Thank you for inviting me Frau von Bonn, it's so kind of you.'

'Of course, Hans you are our family friend now.'

'I'm honoured, I haven't done anything to deserve this.'

'Yes you have,' I told him. 'Hans you're my one friend faithful and true. Thank you for the wonderful photo and frame.'

Mother said, 'You have done what I asked you to do for my son. Thank you from the bottom of my heart.'

Mother had cooked a *Hasenpfeffer* (rabbit stew) this time with bread, which I baked, and another bottle of father's wine. It was an absolute feast by the standards of the last three years. Then something happened.

As we were eating and before I could stop her, mother turned to Hans and asked, 'How are things back home?'

He had been enjoying everything but now his face fell.

He gently put down his cutlery, finished his mouthful and taking a napkin, dabbed his lips. He looked up. 'Frau von Bonn, I have no home. The paint box is all that's left.'

It was too late, and there, she'd said it.

I glanced at mother, who was mortified. The look she gave me said she wished she'd been told. The look I returned told her that I didn't know.

Grief stricken she slowly drew breath, then spoke softly across the table. 'Hans, I'm so deeply sorry. First your daughter taken by scarlet fever and now....' She stopped, glanced towards me but made no eye contact.

Beatrice put down her glass with a plink.

Calmly Hans spoke. 'If I had been in the shelter in Frankfurt when the bombers came, I would also be dead.'

'Oh my God...,' Beatrice muttered.

He went on, 'The world is broken. Like a smashed mirror I can never see myself in it again.'

No one knew what to say. Silence filled the room. Moments passed.

Mother hesitated, then spoke quietly: 'When those we love are taken from us, we should consider how to live; to honour them by trying to live our lives the way they would have wished.'

Hans continued, 'I feel like this also. Nothing will bring my family back. All I can do is try to live the way they would have expected of me, as a good man. But I don't know how.' His head was bowed, and tears welling.

'Bless you Hans,' Beatrice whispered, adding that we should stay quiet with our thoughts for a few moments. Then she recited a poem:

'Quiet friend who has come so far,
feel how your breathing makes more space around you.
Let this darkness be a bell tower
and you the bell. As you ring,

what batters you becomes your strength.
Move back and forth into the change.
What is it like, such intensity of pain?

If the drink is bitter, turn yourself into wine.

In this uncontainable night,
be the mystery at the crossroads of your senses,
the meaning discovered there.

And if the world has ceased to hear you,
say to the silent earth: I flow.
To the rushing waters: I am.'
- **Rainer Maria Rilke. 'Sonnets to Orpheus II', Number 29**

Tears rolled across the man's face. We joined hands around the table, his glazed eyes not seeing us.

I went and restocked the fire making it pop and hiss and then we went and sat. The soldier with us seemed now as if he were frozen. Perhaps the fire would warm him?

It was time to ask for his advice. 'Hans, they will conscript me in April, and I do not want to go and fight. Can anything be done?'

He sat motionless head down considering his response. Then he said, 'Yes,' and paused. Mother and Beatrice were listening expectantly.

After thinking very carefully he said, 'In Germany there are now millions of boys in the *Hitlerjugend (HJ)*, and they start at age 14. It used to be that boys would go from the *HJ* into the Reich Labour Service at 16 for one year before conscription at 17. The *HJ* gives 14 to 16-year-old boys part-time weapons and field training; it is a preparation for the military. The Labour Service builds installations, resupplies the Wehrmacht and is now an auxiliary military force.'

'What does that mean for my son?'

'We are not in Germany and Paul has never been in the *Hitlerjugend*. The authorities would see that he has not been prepared for conscription. He would be considered as not ready for any form of military service.' He turned, looked me in the eye and continued, 'I think you can ask to be detailed into the Reich Labour Service – RAD, and I think it would be approved.'

'I won't go to the front line then?'

'No. You would be included in work details and construction teams along with other young German workers but not at the front line. We already have these here in Jersey and you have already worked with them.'

This was a revelation. I hadn't thought to ask the young Germans in the construction teams at the bunkers or gun stands how old they were, but none of them looked over 18 so what Hans said seemed plausible.

Mother nodded and said, 'We've had some of those youngsters in the hospital when they had accidents at work, and they are all 16 or 17.'

Hans smiled. 'Yes. That's the solution. Insist that Paul go into the Labour Service, and he may even be able to stay on the island building installations here.'

Mother replied, 'The problem is that my son would be here amongst the Jersey people. He would attract attention. He would be seen as German. It could cause trouble.'

She didn't know that it already had…

'Frau von Bonn, Paul is German and so are you, but it is safer here. Jersey is safer than Germany; better for German civilians to not be in Germany.' He paused then continued, 'Anyway, I do not think the war will go on for one more year.'

He was right, being in Germany was dangerous. The war was going badly for them. Who was to say that by Christmas 1944 it wouldn't all be over?

The clock ticked past midnight. We stood and had another toast of wine, this time to 'Peace in 1944.'

Hans' words rolled around my head like marbles in an empty toffee tin: *Jersey is safer than Germany; better for German civilians to not be in Germany.* Then there was what the Russians told me the Red Army would do when it arrived there: *everything destroy.*

The BBC said the Soviets were nearly at the pre-war borders of Poland and heading west like an unstoppable red tide. Like Hans many soldiers in Jersey had seen action and were wounded on the Eastern Front. That red tide seemed like a wave of blood pouring across the continent. My father was right in its way. Germany was also getting bombed relentlessly day and night by huge American and RAF bomber fleets. Hamburg had been devastated along with many other German cities including Hans' hometown and now we knew the truth about that. Allied armies were in Italy but stuck there. In spite of lots of talk and rumours about an Allied invasion of France there seemed every chance that the Russians would engulf and annihilate Germany first. All of this scared me profoundly.

An idea entered my mind.

It was distant at first, but it came gradually into view. Hans said, *he wished he could bring my father back.* He might not be able to, but perhaps I could? I suppressed this as just another form of occupation madness.

The days of January and early February 1944 went by clear and cold, and I only saw Hans a couple of times. The bunkers were freezing, so I stayed away. But I could not keep back the idea I had. It kept re-emerging from that red ocean, those devastated cities and Hans' lost family.

I couldn't talk to mother about it. Instead, I decided to go back and see my friend to ask for his opinion and advice.

In the middle of February, I cycled up and encountered two sentries at the wire who I knew: Emil and Gustav. They told me that Hans was no longer on the island.

I was absolutely stunned.

A few days later a letter arrived from an undisclosed location in Germany.'

At this, Paul stopped, reached across and pulled out from his drawer an old and tatty envelope with a letter written in pencil. He read it to me gently translating:

My Dear Paul,   *13 Februar 1944*

I hope that you and your family will forgive me for writing like this. I am a coward and could not bear to look you in the eye and tell you I was leaving again. I have been reassigned and will probably in the next few days go east. St Christopher will be my guide.

I cherish our conversations and have learned so much from you. It is as you once said: 'One should honour the young more.' You know so much about the world and how you would like it to be. My children shall never see that world, but it is my earnest hope that you will.

One day this war will end. When it does I have faith that we will meet again and that we can live out the rest of our days together as the best of friends. Until that bright day good luck and God bless you.

Always your friend, Hans

28. The Komandant's Office

'And so, my last friend had gone. I knew that I would probably never see him again. I didn't dwell on the letter or the manner of his leaving. It was just more agony and hurt for both of us. My heart was broken.

In late February we finally got a letter from father. His address was blanked out by the censor. It didn't say much except that his breathing wasn't good. It was another jolt which kept me in a black spin, but at least he was alive.

In early March, my conscription papers arrived. My black spin got worse, and it was already bad enough.

Even though I expected them the officious looking forms still came as a shock. The day those papers arrived I called a family conference. This was important and once again we sat around the family table. It was time to do something, time to take action. I led the conversation:

'My call-up has arrived. I have an idea, and I've made a choice, a decision. You may not like or agree with it, but it's not even a choice: it's the only course of action available.'

'What is it? *what choice? what course of action?*' mother asked nervously.

'I'd like you to help me get into the Reich Labour Service and be sent to the mainland.'

'Yes, I will. I thought we had agreed on that.'

'There's more. I'm not going to fight for the Germans and I'm not going to work for them either. When I get off Jersey I'm going to Salzburg to rescue father. Then I'm going to take him to safety with our family friends in Switzerland and wait there until the end of the war.'

'My God!' she exclaimed. She was dumbfounded.

'It's not that far from Salzburg to the Swiss frontier, only 300km – about four days cycling. Someone has to get father out of danger and the only one who can do it is me.'

'*Incroyable!* But cycling from here to Salzburg is well over 1000km - a massive trip.'

'I reckon two weeks, but I'll go via Uncle Claude in Rouen, Uncle Jean in Paris and the hotel in Strasbourg. If I wait until the summer and good weather it will be easy to just stop and sleep in farms or barns en route. That's what we did when we cycled here in 1940, remember?'

'What if you get caught?'

'I have German papers. Nothing will happen.'

'I don't mean by the Germans.'

'I'm Alsatian born in Strasbourg, France. Nothing will happen. This will work. The hard bit will be joining up with him, getting him out and then cycling to safety. We'll head for our friends in Basel.'

'It's a fantastic scheme. Very daring. Very von Bonn!' added Beatrice with a proud smile.

Mother was stupefied. 'I could lose you,' she exclaimed.

'I'm already lost. They're conscripting me and I can't hide on this island and avoid it. Might as well try and turn it to our advantage. You'll lose me if I'm put in the Luftwaffe on a searchlight and strafed by a Spitfire. We could lose father if I do nothing, but I can do something. *Only I* can do this, no one else. I would never forgive myself if father died and I had done nothing.'

Mother slowly nodded her head. She knew.

'I can't stay. I will boil over. I have to do something.'

'I'll make an appointment at the Komandant's Office,' she said.

Mother came around to my way of thinking quickly. Dangerous, but I wasn't going to admit it. After nearly four years trapped in Jersey, *not* going was even more perilous: I could lose my mind. It was a wild scheme, but it had to be attempted, or I would never know, and mother knew it.

****

The appointment was on Friday, 10 March 1944, in the afternoon. We were made to wait ages.

The door opened to a smoky room. Mother spoke first extremely politely and introduced me. The Leutnant seemed impressed at once. He knew that father had been deported. My name was on the back of his record card in front of him on his desk. 'Did we feel any ill-will?' he asked.

'No,' mother replied. That was the first lie I ever heard her tell. There were plenty more to follow.

I produced my *Ahnenpaß,* and he studied it, then puffing on his cigarette asked me, 'How old are you?' 'Sixteen, sir.' He asked why we were there, and I explained that I was happy to serve Germany when I turned 17, a lie, but that I would prefer to join the Labour Service, another lie. I told him that there was no *Hitlerjugend* in Jersey for me to join and so I didn't feel prepared for military service. 'Wouldn't you rather hang around aeroplanes guard airfields and tinker about with guns and radios?' he asked. No, I said,

I wasn't interested in any of that and would prefer to work. Two whopping lies. I loved aeroplanes and had no appetite for long hard days pouring concrete like the boys over at Corbière.

It didn't take long before we had told so many lies and so convincingly that the officer was persuaded. He was positively purring when he congratulated me for: 'Feeling my German blood, wanting to do my bit and making an active choice to work hard for the Reich.' It was all utter bullshit of course. We simply told him everything he wanted to hear, and with no further questions he accepted my request.

He reached into a drawer, fished out some headed note paper and wrote a letter to the Labour Service with a handsome black bakelite Pelikan fountain pen. He put that in a tray and explained that I would be called back to have my official photo taken, a medical examination, and then, 'Probably sent to projects in northern France.' He had no idea where or when that might be, as it was out of his control. In the meanwhile, I would receive Labour Service papers and written orders detailing me to work finishing projects in Jersey in the first instance. It was the outcome I was looking for.

My 17th birthday arrived, and I was called for my photo and medical soon after. No papers came through. I wasn't going to chase them.

Eventually these arrived on 19 May along with my Labour Service badge. I was ordered to report to an unfinished 8.8cm anti-aircraft gun stand and participate in 'basic training.' After that, on Saturday 3 June I was to present myself at St Helier weighbridge for a ferry to Granville and from there to a place called Valognes near Cherbourg to join a work party. Valognes was way off my route. That didn't matter though as my plan was to steal a bike as soon as I arrived in France and head for Rouen.

I packed my rucksack and waited for the day to arrive.

Going away, 3 June, 1944

The lorry came to take me to the weighbridge. It pulled up on the gravel with a crunch and a transport corporal jumped out. I watched him through my bedroom window.

I went down and hugged Beatrice. She told me that all von Bonns were heroes, and that father and I were two more. She told me that when we got back in a few months she would lay on 'a party fit for heroes.'

Mother asked to ride with me. The corporal was alright about that, and she was allowed to put her bike in the back.

Mother looked very smart in the grubby transport. We looked at each other but hardly spoke. We had already said everything we needed to say. Tears were in her eyes.

I waved out of the lorry to Beatrice, and she waved back as we climbed up the hill and rounded the bend. It was the last time I saw her.'

This was a stunning turn of events. The old man had an endless capacity for surprise. He reached into one of his boxes and pulled out his 75-year-old Labour Service badge. It was the size of a thumbnail, red and cream with a swastika. He said, 'If you look you can see the wheat and the shovel, the blood surrounding the soil. All the usual Nazi claptrap.'

2

FRANCE

1944

'We can easily forgive a child who is afraid of the dark. The real tragedy is when men are afraid of the light' – Plato

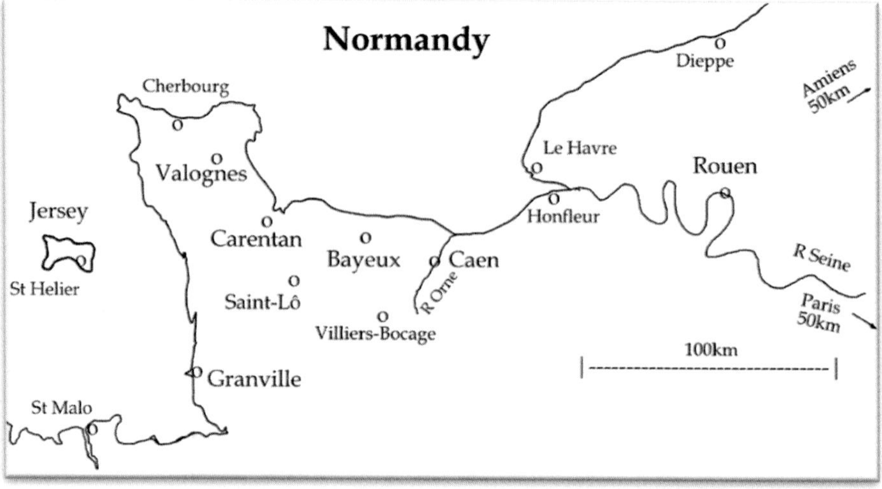
Normandy
Dieppe
Amiens 50km
Cherbourg
Le Havre
Rouen
Valognes
Jersey
Honfleur
Carentan
Bayeux
Caen
R Seine
St Helier
Saint-Lô
R Orne
Paris 50km
Villiers-Bocage
100km
Granville
St Malo

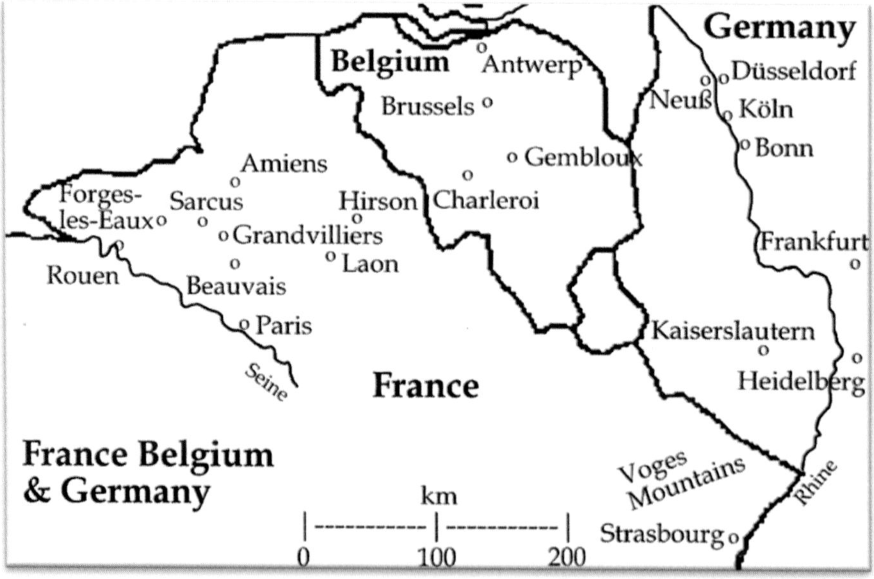
Germany
Belgium
Antwerp
Düsseldorf
Neuß
Brussels
Köln
Bonn
Amiens
Gembloux
Forges-les-Eaux
Sarcus
Hirson
Charleroi
Grandvilliers
Frankfurt
Laon
Rouen
Beauvais
Paris
Kaiserslautern
Heidelberg
Seine
France
France Belgium & Germany
Voges Mountains
Rhine
km
0
100
200
Strasbourg

1. 'What you don't know can't hurt you.' June 1944

My 2018 Christmas stint ended, and I returned to Manchester. I didn't know it then - but the journey was only just beginning, for him and for me.

As soon as I returned to the Stanley in March we went straight back to 1944. Using his old photos and a tatty yellow Michelin map of Normandy from his bookcase, Paul continued:

'I was told I was going to France to help in the construction of 'special installations.' I had no idea what these were, but it was of no relevance. At the first opportunity I was going to abscond. I had no intention whatsoever of helping the Germans or getting involved in any of their nefarious schemes. I was told that we would be travelling by road probably at night as there were frequent Allied aircraft sweeps and fighter bomber attacks on railway lines and junctions. There was sure to be a chance to break away.

Looking back now on that day when I left St Helier: Saturday, 3 June 1944, I can honestly say I was full of the power of not knowing. I had no idea what I was letting myself in for. None whatsoever.'

'What do you mean, the power of not knowing?' I asked.

'You see, I didn't know. How could I?' he said.

'Know what? What are you talking about? You constantly talk in riddles.'

'I mean, *there is a power in not knowing*. If I had known how much trouble I was going to get into, how many close scrapes, I might have made different decisions. Because I didn't know, I just went on regardless.'

'I see,' I added, but I was still confused.

'My father was in danger. I left my mother and great-aunt, then I set off and put myself in danger.' Giving a slight sigh he put down his cup with a clatter of inaccuracy. Something about what he'd said reverberated. Then I noticed he was shaking.

'What's the matter Paul?' I asked quietly.

'Bloody Nazis,' he hissed. I waited for more, but it didn't come. I made note of the expletive. Paul hardly ever swore and, unless it was in conversation with Hans, he'd *never* knowingly mentioned the Nazis.

The boat pulled away sailing on the tide around 10am on a warm morning. Grey smoke from the funnel curled across the deck flowing into the widening gap between ship and harbour. The German ensign with its blood-red Swastika fluttered on the stern. Paul's mother waved gently, her bike resting against her slim waist. In her left hand was the striking *Art Deco* turquoise handbag that Paul's father had bought for her in Paris for Christmas 1939. She loved that handbag. Paul stared and stared until he could no longer make out any detail of his mother. The vessel steered towards Granville and an unknown future.

'I kept myself to myself. I didn't feel like talking. Unfortunately, an army officer, his boards and pips showed him to be a *Hauptmann* (captain), approached me.

'Why are you not in uniform? What is your unit?'

In my straightest German I told him, 'Sir, I have no uniform, I have been sent to the *Reich Labour Service* in Valognes.'

'Were you working in Jersey?' I couldn't pick his accent. Well spoken, possibly central Germany.

'Yessir.'

I was momentarily thrown. Conversations with German military normally went along predictable lines, and this was the first one that hadn't. I wanted to be flippant and say something, but mother and I had gone to an awful lot of trouble and told an awful lot of lies for me to be here on this ship, so I reconsidered. Instead, I tried to deflect him.

'Are you going home sir?' Now it was his turn to be thrown off balance. He glanced back to Jersey, reached into his pocket, fished out his cigarette case and hastily lit up, the lighter shaking in his hand. It was the custom always to offer, but he was so flustered that he forgot.

I didn't normally have this effect on people so very politely I said, 'I'm sorry sir, I had no intention of upsetting you. My name is Paul.' I wondered what I'd said that so affected him, but after a minute or two of pulling deeply on his cigarette he calmed down a little.

'I was wounded on the Eastern Front and sent home to Nuremburg.' Ah,

Nuremburg, I knew it.

'I am very sorry to hear that captain.'

'Thank you. Then they sent me to Jersey to recover,' he said, thawing a little. He paused..., 'Now they tell me I am to report to Paris.' He paused again..., 'I will be sent east.'

'Ah, I see,' I said. It was a colloquialism that didn't fit.

'I don't think you do *see* boy.' The atmosphere chilled again. 'I *hate* it. You don't know what the war is like there. You don't know what we've done.'

'Sir, the men in Jersey told me about the war in the east - the war against the barbarous horde - against Ivan.' The captain wasn't listening, he was staring out to sea. He didn't want to talk. A few moments went by, and he was miles away. Then he turned and regarded me.

'It's as well that you don't know. You don't *want* to know either and I am not going to tell you. I will spare you that. What you don't know can't hurt you.'

'Thank you, captain.' I don't know why I thanked him; I didn't know what he was talking about. I only smiled out of politeness. He nodded and aimlessly peeled away to the stern to finish his cigarette and look back. I watched him staring as the island receded.

I took my chance to escape to the bow of the ship. I could see the French mainland very clearly now; the tiny island of Chausey and the Granville lighthouse. It was true what he said though, that *I didn't know*. I also considered the other thing he said: *what you don't know can't hurt you.*

Rounding the Pointe du Roc I observed the murderous looking guns in the concrete casemates up on the left, similar to the ones in Jersey. We approached the Avant Port virtually at full tide and were soon moored. I hadn't set foot in France in over four years, and it was a strange feeling to walk down the short plank. The circumstances had been so different when we left in 1940.

Perhaps as many as 50 soldiers disembarked and we walked up to the Zurich-Bazeilles Barracks past the Notre Dame church. The order was not jovial. I saw the *Hauptmann* and a few other ranks walking along solemnly with their kit in suitcases or rucksacks. Perhaps they all had the same orders? I glanced around. There was no chance of breaking away here, so I decided to bide my time and await a more clear-cut opportunity. I was hungry too and had an idea I would get a good meal if I stuck around.

That evening, I was fed well in the mess and despite my lack of uniform was taken just like any other German.

Incredibly, I met two Alsatian soldiers at mess. I picked them by their accents, and I was soon right back in it. My lovely Alsace! Rolf was from *Molsheim*, a town I already knew plenty about. Erich was from a tiny place called *Ittenheim*. We cycled out there a lot before the war and knew these very German places quite well. The two young soldiers were 18 and 19 respectively. They were conscripts with the '582 over on the east side of the island and of course I hadn't seen them. They greeted me like a long-lost brother, and I was overwhelmed! I'd never experienced anything like this before and loved every minute.'

Paul was a marvel. Every day it seemed, he came out with some new or astonishing thing. I reflected on my life as a 22-year-old in 2019. The world of 17-year-old Paul von Bonn in 1944 was vastly different to mine, I knew that, but perhaps some things were the same? Perhaps *not knowing* is really how all people go along? Perhaps *not knowing* is a good state to be in, useful and empowering? Inexplicably, I began thinking about my mother. Perhaps it was best to not know what happened? Perhaps I'd known once, but had chosen to forget? Is it even possible to choose to forget?

I went off to sort out Henry's false teeth. When I came back Paul was asleep wrapped in his blanket. His face was a picture of that bliss he described and for a moment I almost envied him. I woke him and helped him off to bed.

The next day after handover I found him in his usual place in the sunroom. 'Sorry I fell asleep dear.' He smiled and started again:

'You know I got mightily drunk that night in Granville with my new friends Erich and Rolf. *S'gilt!* That's Alsatian for cheers! The rest of them could drink too. They all had flasks full of the same horrible hooch: a potato vodka concoction. They claimed that one of the best things about Jersey was its potatoes. The *Unteroffiziere* had even bigger flasks. Then they started on the wine. Some of these men had been wounded and had terrible scars, some did not walk properly, but all of them talked freely under the influence of the booze. I on the other hand tried to stay tight-lipped. I was out of my depth here. I'd lived a boring life compared to these chaps, one of whom had been nearly as far as Moscow. They came from all over. Some were actually Polish-German, one was from Latvia, there was even one *Unterfeldwebel* who came from a German community in Ukraine. Compared to these guys I had no story to tell. They smiled, but all of them were drinking for a reason, and the reason was that they all knew they were going back to the Eastern Front. They didn't say it, but I knew because the Hauptmann had told me. They could be happy, for now at least. They soon wouldn't be.

It didn't take long before so much alcohol had flowed that it didn't matter what anyone said.

I sometimes got a nip of schnapps or vodka after winning a shooting contest at Corbière, but this drinking session was something else altogether. I told them about my shooting exploits, but they just laughed and told me to stop showing off. I'd never been drunk before of course.

My plan to abscond didn't get put into effect that evening as I was just too smashed and had to stagger off to bed. Then I was violently sick in the night along with Rolf. In a daze he told me, 'When we get back to Straßburg, you and I will have a few beers and some *Knack* (Alsatian smoked sausage) in one of the bars off the Place Kleber.' I told him that his plan was perfect but that he would have to pay. I staggered to a standing position and solemnly told the imaginary waiter, *'Deis Monsieur bezàhlt àlles!'* (Alsatian-German: 'this gentleman will pay for everything!') He laughed so hysterically that he fell down face first into his own vomit where he promptly slept for the rest of the night.

The next morning, I woke up to the first and arguably worst hangover I have ever experienced. I could hardly see! I got shouted at by an arsey

Luftwaffe transport corporal who stomped into the barracks amongst the beds shouting my name at maximum volume, 'Where is Paul von Bonn? Which one is he?' This was like getting bashed hard around the side of the head with the butt of a Mauser. Someone pointed him in my direction. He saw the pool of sick, pushed me out of bed, called me a useless drunken sod and a few other choice words and told me I had five minutes to get in the back of the Opel which was ready outside, or the next stop would be the military police. So much for breakfast and that good meal last night.

God, I felt bloody awful. I still remember. It was like my stomach had been pumped.

Blearily I looked at Rolf, who groaned, and told him I would see him in Straßburg at his earliest convenience. He waved his fingers numbly from his puddle.

I grabbed my stuff and heaved it out into the shocking morning light. For some unknown reason I took a photo, perhaps because I couldn't see!

There were six Luftwaffe boys loading boxes of ammunition. 'Guten Morgen Schlafmütze!' (Good morning sleepyhead!) said some sarcastic bugger. I told him to piss off. They all laughed. After lumping the boxes in, I crawled to the back and found a place to curl up. It was grey and foggy, just like my head.

Next thing I knew I was waking up in another place altogether. I heard someone say, 'Ah. The sleepyhead has woken up!' It was the same sarcastic voice I'd heard the first time, and I told him the same thing. They'd picked my accent, 'So - a bad tempered Alsatian! It should go back to sleep.' My reply was very rude.

It was lunchtime and

I was told I was in Valognes. SHIT! The transport corporal pulled up in front of the Gendarmerie where I was supposed to billet. He opened the door and went in but there was nobody there. 'Oh shit!' he muttered. He didn't seem to realise this was France and that nothing much happened on Sunday and especially nothing at all happened *au déjeuner*.

Outside again, a group of three soldiers with Mausers over their shoulders and sleeves rolled came up on bikes. One was a sergeant, older maybe late 40s, a big man - red faced with sunburn. The other two were young, maybe 18 or 19-years-old. The transport corporal flagged down the sergeant and chatted to him. The red-faced fellow looked me up and down and then waved me over.

'Let me see your Soldbuch (Paybook),' he said.

'Yes sir.' He flicked through it.

'So, RAD eh? Alright, come with me Arbeitsmann. My name is Mueller, billet with us. We'll sort you out tomorrow. Some idiot sent you here on Sunday. Nothing happens here on Sunday.'

'Yes sergeant, I can see that,' I said.

'Ah! So, you can see can you? A smart-arsed *Elsässischer*, eh?' he sneered. He'd picked my accent then deliberately mispronounced it belittling me. It was his idea of a joke. Bastard. '*Elsässischer*. A coward in the RAD because he doesn't want to fight, well there's a surprise.' He stood and poked his finger into my chest. 'Being Alsatian I don't suppose you want to work either. You *wackes* are all the same: weak-minded and bone idle.' His breath stank.

He'd called me a coward and worse: *wackes*. Calling an Alsatian *wackes* was the worst insult, and it made my blood boil. Had this been in Jersey I'd have laid into him on the spot and beaten the crap out of him, and Hans would have helped me. But I didn't want to get into a battle, not here and not with the state of my hangover. As well as that, he had a gun. So, I just said, 'Yes sergeant,' and bowed my head.

I noticed the two young *Soldaten* glimpse at each other and then look at me pityingly. One thumbed his lapel, a sign of where this sergeant would wear his Nazi party badge. I understood that and it sickened but didn't surprise me. Bloody Nazis. I didn't forget his appalling insult: *wackes*. There was no need for it. His comment about being a coward was crap as well. He was overweight and old. I was young and strong, and I reckoned he'd made a mistake.

The Luftwaffe in the back of the truck were all laughing their heads off. They were wagging their tongues and jagging their fingers into each other's chests mimicking the sergeant. The word *wackes* means: weak or wobbly. One stood up in the back of the truck and pretended to 'wobble.' Then away they chugged towards Cherbourg. Bastards.

I tromped along behind lugging my kit in a completely dejected state. The two *Soldaten* occasionally glimpsed back giving me pensive looks. We trooped along past the Hotel Beaumont which sported many officers standing around outside in the sunshine jabbering and smoking.

Further along Rue Barbey D'Aurevilly we arrived at a house more in keeping. It stank of tobacco, which I hated, but in we went. I was directed to a bedroom with three beds, one unused. The three soldiers got on their bikes and went back into town. I climbed on a bed and slept soundly.

I had no idea of the time when I woke up as I didn't have a watch. The room housed the two younger soldiers. All their kit was stowed under their beds. I pulled it out. They had army issue rucksacks and the usual assortment of kit. Nothing of any real use.

I pulled open the windows. It was a warm sultry early evening, bright with sun showing through a white sky and a light breeze from the west. My head felt better but my stomach was grumbling. I ventured downstairs.

The house was empty. In the front room were the sergeant's things and on his bed was a copy of the propaganda paper *Signal*. He had a large rucksack and various tins of something with no labels. On the dressing table I found his inevitable party badge. The mindless bastard had the round red and green *Gott Mit Uns* version.

In the back of the house there was a kitchen and large table with chairs and an open hearth. Very homely. Ravenous I pounced on the black bread on the table.

There was cheese and sausage in the cool cupboard. I couldn't believe my luck! So, with the flies buzzing around I sat and stuffed myself. Then I looked through the back door to a small cottage garden with an apple tree, onions sets, herbs, runner beans, potatoes and tomatoes all inside a flaking red brick wall. Quaint, but not as nice as the Big House. I walked out and sat under the tree, bread, sausage and sharp knife in hand. Bliss!

After all those years trapped in Jersey this was something like how I'd imagined freedom.

I looked at the white hazy sun and heard the birds calling to each other.

I felt the grass of the little garden and brushed my hand across raising its camomile fragrance. Noisy bees flew up and went on their way. It was just a gorgeous summer evening. I fell asleep under the tree...

'Where are you, you thieving little bastard?' I heard a voice shout which woke me with a start. It was Mueller and I'd eaten his food. Luckily, I didn't give a shit what anyone said, *especially and particularly* him.

My thought processes swiftly flooded with adrenaline. I wasn't going to run. Not this time.

What happened next happened very quickly.

'You greedy little Alsatian pup. You'll pay for that food!' he stormed as he burst out into the bright garden. He was on his own and had no audience to play to this time. I think he may have been drinking, but he'd gravely insulted me, and I thought: *now I'm going to show this bastard.*

I looked up and told him, 'You called me *wackes* - but it's all right, I'll give you a chance to apologise.'

'You cheeky bastard! Get up you mouthy little French parrot so I can knock you off your perch!' he blazed. 'Bloody Alsatians pretending to be with us. Come on, get up so I can beat some manners into you. You wobblies are all the same, you'll soon fall over.'

He called me *wackes*, again. That was it... *My mind raced. It said, 'Don't take that from this scum. I heard my father tell me, 'Like Bomber Command: Strike Hard, Strike Sure.'*

I did get up, *very* swiftly. In getting up with my right fist I hit him under the chin as hard as I'd ever hit anything, and it lifted him off his feet and sent him absolutely flying into the onion bed. Then, staggering over him, and gulping for breath I shouted, 'I am NOT FRENCH, NOT WACKES and NOT A COWARD. I AM ALSATIAN. Now *you* get up, so that I can knock *you* down again!'

He was a big man, and he didn't get up.

I was aware of more soldiers bursting out of the back door and into the garden. It was the two young *Soldaten*. They stood staring at the downed man. 'Shit!' one of them shouted, 'What the **hell** have you done? You're mad. You can't hit him, he's a party man. When he wakes up he'll slit your throat!'

The big sergeant was down, and he was out.

'You're lucky you got him before he got you. What's your name?'

'Paul.'

'That man *will* kill you! He shouldn't have called you that (they wouldn't even repeat the word...), but you're a bloody fool. You need to get away from here right now before he comes around.'

My fist hurt like hell. In a mist of anger, I listened to these strangers. It made sense. Now was my time to go.

'*Aus dem Staub machen,*' (make dust) said one. The other said, 'We shouldn't do this, but we know what he's like, he's a beast. He had it coming. We'll just say we don't know anything. GO NOW!'

Quickly they helped me get the sergeant's gear out and pack his big rucksack with those tins and a few other bits including the bread, sausage, his first aid kit and bivouac sheet. I ran upstairs and grabbed my stuff, my rosary and all-important papers. I made sure to take his watch and party badge, never knew when something like that might be useful.

The young soldiers giggled. One ran to the garden to look. 'He's still out for the count. My God, what did you hit him with, *Göring's Batten*? Quickly, take his bike as well you bloody lunatic.'

The sun was setting as I studied the map. I needed to head towards Carentan about 30km away southwards. I didn't dare contemplate it on the main road due to the fact I'd been told that military transports would typically travel at night. I would certainly be caught, and due to my papers, dragged back to Valognes. That had to be avoided at all costs. I needed to get out of town then stop for the night. The best plan was to track the railway line to Carentan.

In all the haste and commotion, I made sure to stop and thank these two, who apart from being young, had no reason to help me. Kurt and Horst were their names. 'You're mad,' Kurt told me, 'But we'd like to belt him too. He's a party pig,' said the other. 'The party is the reason we're here. The party will kill us all,' they said as I threw the loaded rucksack on my back and got swiftly on the bike.

As I pushed the peddles and began I heard Horst calling, 'Do something about your temper. Good luck!'

That wasn't exactly how I'd planned to get away from the Germans. I'd beaten one up, eaten his food, and stolen his gear. But the deed was done and there was no going back now.

I headed south along the road I'd been on just a few hours ago towards St Sauveur-le-Vicomte. After a short distance I turned off left into a hinterland *bocage* of hamlets and villages and crossed the railway line. I was going like lightning. Sunday evening in rural France: totally dead, nobody around. My right hand hurt like hell from where I'd belted the Nazi. I could hardly hold the handlebar due to shocking pain in the index finger.

Breezes picked up dust and hastened me along the rough roads. There was a nearly full moon, and I whizzed through a little place and then headed left again to pick up the railway line. I walked my bike along the tracks then turned off left to find somewhere to camp for the night. I came to a secluded lane and went along it but up ahead there seemed to be a lake which was odd because there were no lakes marked on my Michelin map. The tiny tree-lined track veered left away from the lake and up a slight slope. The wheat fields here were too open so I kept going until I came to an orchard on the left. This would do.

I opened the gate and pulled my bike into a corner away from prying eyes. The smell of cow shit gave me the clue it was also a pasture.

I wasn't sure where I was and wasn't going to put on my torch in order to find out. I couldn't see anything, but it seemed safe enough. After the day I'd had I thought my best plan was to find somewhere, wrap myself in the bastard Nazi's Zeltbahn bivouac sheet, camp right out of the way and just hide. I found a nice spot against a grand oak tree in the hedgerow and slept very well indeed.'

2. Monday, 5 June 1944. *The last bright day*

'I was in a corner of an orchard *avec les vaches*. I could hear them from inside my cocoon, munching and sniffing all around. Just as nosey as the ones in Jersey. There had been some rain in the night, and it was much cooler, but I was dry and warm enough in the stolen sheet. I pulled myself out and looked at my stolen watch: 5.30am. There was nobody around and it was a lovely bright day. This was rural France, there was never anyone around.

I had a pain in my right hand. My God! my index finger was swelled up at a funny angle and blue. I hadn't noticed. It didn't hurt much, but boy it looked ugly. Couldn't milk a cow with a finger like that.

'*Comment avez-vous apprécié votre camping?*' (French: how did you enjoy your camping?) came a voice from behind.

'MERDE! I muttered turning around. 'I slept very well.'

I saw her. '*What are you doing here?*' she asked.

A little older than me. She was wearing a milking smock over some overalls and wearing a white tie-over piece of fabric on her brown hair clipped by a hair band. She carried a stout stick and wore three pearly bangles on her left wrist. She was lovely.

'I'm on holiday,' I said, deliberately stupidly. Holidays were out of the question.

'You're not from around here, where are you from?'

'Strasbourg.'

'My God. You're a long way from home.'

'Yes I am. What's your name?'

'Marie, and I've come to get the cows.'

'Of course you have. My name is Paul, and I'm pleased to meet you.' *Obviously*, it was milking time.

'Should I ask what you're doing with a stolen German bike and tent?' Marie asked in a perfectly charming way.

'It might be better if you didn't ask,' I said with a grin. Then those beautiful hazel brown eyes noticed my hand.

'What happened to your hand? Let me see it.'

Marie gently took my right hand and stretched my fingers until she came to the unpleasantly blue one. She had extraordinarily strong fingers! I screeched with pain when she tried to flex it. 'I've seen this before. How did you do it?'

'It might be better if you didn't ask,' I flippantly replied.

'Tell me, stupid boy. What happened?'

'I hit a German.'

'Wow. Brave then...'

'Then I stole his bike and tent.'

'Ah! Brave **and** stupid.' It was her turn to be flippant.

'I've got his watch too.'

'Phew. A complete master criminal,' she giggled. 'You've got a dislocated finger. It goes with your *dislocated* mind. What were you thinking of belting a German?'

'He was a Nazi, and I didn't like him. He insulted me and called me a French coward. I am not a coward.'

'Bravo! You fight for the honour of France. Magnifique!' Marie said admiringly. Then slyly she added, 'Brave and stupid, but *not a coward*. Good job.' That made me laugh.

She smiled beautifully. I had never seen such a wonderful smile. God she was beautiful.

'Do you want me to fix it?'

'Can you fix it?' I asked hesitatingly.

'It has to be fixed. Papa fell off his bike when a dog ran out on the way to church once and did this. The Priest knew what to do. I watched him. I know what to do.'

The allusion to the church somehow soothed my misgivings.

'Are you a good Catholic Marie?' I asked shyly.

'Well, *I am Catholic*,' she said with a coy grin.

'I suppose you'd better fix it then,' I sighed.

'I know you are brave and stupid but because you're not a coward I'll tell you now that this is going to really hurt,' she told me quietly with a telling smile.

'I have a first aid kit,' I mumbled.

'Good, give it to me. Are you ready? Give me your hand.' She took it, felt my right index finger and gripped it, I glanced at the sky and, 'AGGGHH!'

The cows jumped and ran.

The searing pain almost made me sick, but then there was a wave of relief.

'Ok, wiggle your fingers,' she said. I held my arm out and could move that right index finger again.'

Paul looked at me across his cup of tea, wiggled his right index finger at me and smiled, 'She fixed it!'

'Marie deftly strapped up my hand using the first aid kit. 'You won't be able to cycle for a while,' she said. 'Not until it settles down. If you try you might push it out again.'

'Thank you nurse. Almost as good as my mother.'

'Your mother is a nurse?'

'Yes, she was a nurse near Amiens in the first war. She is still a nurse, a brilliant one.'

'Well then, your mother is also a true patriot. No wonder you hit that Nazi; I can only imagine what you did to him. I'm sure you belted him good and proper!'

'It was all in a good cause,' one of mother's sayings.

'Come on then, help me take the cows to milking.'

As best I could I packed my kit one handed and then we walked around and gathered up the cows. There were 10. We marched them across the small field then out onto a lane towards a farmhouse. The animals knew their way and ambled along swishing their tails. They wheeled into the large courtyard and helped themselves to the hay that was thrown all around. Chickens and cockerels wandered about. Sprawling lazily in a sunny doorway a black cat lay licking itself. We herded the cows through to the milking barn in the field behind. Très rustique.

'What is this place? Where am I?' I asked.

'You are near to the commune of Fresville, the church is over there,' she said pointing northwards. 'It's a small place. The market is in Sainte-Mère-Église over there.' She pointed south-east. 'Market day is Wednesday.'

Then I could hear aircraft engines. Lots of them. One was very high, possibly a Mosquito. Marie didn't even look up. 'We get those every day,' she said nonchalantly. 'They are Allied aircraft.'

She was right, they weren't Luftwaffe. Now that I was in Normandy the air was a lot noisier. There seemed to be the constant drone of aircraft engines near and far. 'You get used to it,' Marie said standing there with that amazing smile. Then she glanced past me back to the farmhouse. 'Look Papa! I've found a true patriot.'

Marie's father wandered across to the barn with his stick. Marie regarded him. 'Paul, this is my father Pierre.'

'How are you?' he said.

Marie jumped in: 'He's brave and stupid, but he's *not a coward.*'

'Ah, very good, we can't have any cowards around here now, can we?' His smile was almost as lovely as his daughter's.

'I'm delighted to meet you sir,' I said.

'Marie sometimes comes back with a duck or a goose that she shot, but she's never come back with a boy before. What happened? Did she shoot you?' he grinned.

'No sir. She set her cows on me, but I survived.'

'Your accent? Where are you from Paul?'

Marie interrupted again, 'He's an escaped prisoner! He killed a Nazi guard with his bare hands and took off on his bike. He did all that because the Boche insulted the honour of France. Look, he hit him so hard he even broke his fist!'

'Mmm...,' Pierre grinned glancing at my bandaged right hand. Then with a laugh he observed, 'Well, she said you were brave and stupid, now I can see why.'

'No sir, Marie is exaggerating. I'm not a prisoner and I didn't kill a guard.'

'You don't deny the other parts then?' he smirked.

'No sir,' I giggled.

'Bravo Paul!' he said. 'Where did this incident occur? and do call me Pierre.'

'In Valognes.'

'You should be safe out here. They won't come looking unless you killed him. Did you kill him?'

'I don't think so.'

'Well then, help with the milking and then you're welcome to stay with us. We don't get many visitors. Now, your accent? Where did you say you were from?'

'Strasbourg.'

'My God. That's far away!'

'Yes, but I didn't come from there. I came from Jersey.'

'Good God! How the hell did you manage that?' exclaimed the farmer.

'I will explain at dinner Pierre,' I said.

'Alright then, help Marie with the milking, then you should stay with us.'

****

The old man stood, turned, and looked at his reflection in the window glass and suddenly was full of melancholy. 'Why have you stopped? Please tell me more,' I asked.

'The army captain on the transport was right to not tell me what the Germans had done. He was right to want to protect me.' He paused.

'What do you mean?'

'That day, 5 June, the day before the invasion was *the last bright day*. It was the last day when I had a sort of innocence. But after that day I began to come face to face with all the things the captain warned me I didn't want to know. It's the same here now. To young ears it may seem as if war is some sort of romantic quest, goodies and baddies if you will. But it isn't. There is nothing romantic about innocent deaths, genocide, mayhem and suffering. Nothing romantic about doing things that cannot be undone: terrible things.'

He sighed and continued, 'Today we live in a time where millions of people want simple answers. They don't want to think or engage with complex questions. They accept simple lies and mindless slogans. The 1930s were no different. Nationalist right-wing clap trap was rampant in Europe, especially in Germany, Italy and Spain, all fascist regimes.' He was getting agitated, but he continued:

'Right now, today, idiotic nationalism is rampant in the UK, especially in England. We see it in Trump's America. It's right under our noses and it was right under our noses in the 1930s. It's there in plain sight. Mindless fact-denying populist garbage. The politics of grievance - that their problems, caused by their own laziness and stupidity are someone else's fault - immigrants, 'foreigners.' Nationalism is an easy choice for the ignorant and unthinking.'

I told him, 'Paul listen, one person can't do much…' He stopped me and spoke powerfully:

'*That's not true*. One person can save a life, and one person can take a life. Sometimes we have that choice to make.' He wavered, reflected on what he'd said, then continued:

'Mussolini in Italy was one person, so was Franco in Spain. Stalin in Russia was one person and Hitler in Germany was one person. Trump is one person. One person can poison the minds of millions. Hitler did. One person can do a lot of damage and do terrible things.'

He was right. It was obvious. He continued, 'Almost all children learn at school that words have consequences. When the Nazis used words like *Mit Uns – with us*, they really meant: *stop thinking, and you can be with us*. Their words incited millions to stop thinking.'

'You stayed at the farmhouse though?' I asked.

'Of course. Pierre said, *you must stay with us...*'

'That small phrase *with us* means a lot to you, doesn't it?'

'Yes. Marie and Pierre were compassionate and sympathetic towards me and yet I was a complete stranger to them. They didn't have to help me, but they asked me to stay with them for their own reasons. The captain also wanted to help me, and in his own way he did.'

'When the army captain told you there were things you didn't want to know he was protecting you, wasn't he?'

'Yes, and he was trying to protect himself.'

'Are you trying to protect me?'

'Yes.'

'Why?'

'Because words have consequences: choices have consequences. The power of not knowing is that it cannot frighten us. It's only afterwards when we see the consequences that we understand what we did, what that choice meant.'

'Do you wish the captain on the boat had told you?'

'No.'

'Do you wish you'd asked him?'

'No. The question wasn't there to be asked. I didn't know anything about what lay ahead. He did. Even if I had asked he would still have refused. It scared him too much and he was trying to forget, but he knew he was going back to the carnage: the life-or-death struggle.'

'Are you saying I have a choice?'

'Yes, but I'm not going to make it for you. I don't want it on my conscience. What you don't know can't hurt you, but what you do know can. If you ask me about the things that happened after that last bright day, then I will tell you as best I can. But I am asking you to think carefully of the consequences. I told you the captain was right not to tell me anything, he chose to protect me. You might want to reflect on that.'

'Shit!' I sighed.

'You have your whole life ahead of you. Do you really want the burden?

The effect it might have? Look what it's done to me.'

I didn't know what he meant when he said that.

In German he muttered, 'The wisest man knows that he knows nothing.'

'What do you mean?' I quizzed, but he was miles away in his thoughts. Then he went on:

'You don't have to get involved, not if you don't want to. But if I tell you it will be <u>our</u> story. It won't be you and me; it will be *us*.'

He was right. The old man had me thinking in a way that I'd never been required to think before.

'I will be able to accept whatever you decide Katie.'

Paul had laid it all out for me. I could just go about my business, and he would take his memories and knowledge to the grave, or we could join forces, and I would acquire his recollections. How was I supposed to decide? It was almost as if I held the power of life or death here: the power of life or death over a man's memories.

'Perhaps I should go away and think about this,' I said.

'Yes, you should take some time.'

On Box Hill

I tried not to think about any of it but found that I couldn't. *I couldn't decide to not decide*. So, I thought I'd take a long bike ride down to Box Hill at Dorking on my day off. We used to go there a lot when we were little. When I had a mother.

The forecast for Saturday morning was good. I packed some sarnies, popped on my helmet and sunglasses, and set off over Kew Bridge past the Stanley.

Cycling is good for the soul, good for meditation. It cuts through. I cycle in Manchester a lot. There are some good hills around there, it's perfect. You can empty your mind. You can ask yourself who you really are, wonder at the complexity or indeed the simplicity of it all. As an engineer I never considered myself as some deep thinker or philosopher. Maybe I was a deeper thinker than I thought I was? What is a deep thinker? How would I know if I met one? What would they know that I didn't? Did it matter?

I pushed the bike up the Zig-Zag Road it was too steep. I didn't mind getting off. It was busy at the top with lots of kids and dogs running around, like it always used to be. I sat on the grass and admired the view and beautiful trees.

I wasn't thinking about Paul, I was thinking about my mother. I could see her on a red fold out chair eating a flaky sausage roll. 'This Woman's Work' came on the radio. 'Shh, I love this,' she said turning it up and singing along.

I could see my sister Amy drinking from a pink plastic cup sitting on the woolly blue tartan picnic blanket. Dad was there in the other chair in his Brentford FC shirt, smoking a fag, reading his Daily Mirror and glancing up from time to time. 'Club's got no money and that Noades is such a piece of work,' he muttered shaking his head. He supped the coffee he'd poured from the flask. I could smell that coffee: Maxwell House. It was all a memory and as far as I was aware, nothing was missing. How would I know if there was? I recalled various images from half a lifetime ago, and the pictures were sharp. To me these things were *facts*. I could see them clearly, but they weren't real: they were memories. Are memories real: facts?

My mum Theresa left when I was nine. We never heard from her again, neither did her family in Gillingham. That's where she was from. I never liked it there. We sometimes went to see Grandma Hilda. I didn't like her either. She said unhinged things that made me feel uncomfortable. Her husband, my grandfather David, had walked out too. Seemed to run in the family. Why hadn't I seen my mother in over 10 years? Why had she made no contact?

Until that day it never crossed my mind that this might have been a *choice* she made. Why did she walk out on her own children? How could anyone do that? Was that to protect us? From what? Or was she protecting herself? What was it the old man said? 'What you don't know can't hurt you, but what you do know can.'

I never thought dad had anything to do with it. Never.

We weren't well off, but when I was 13 dad inherited a little money and he took us to Florida to the theme parks for two weeks. We had a bungalow with our own pool. Brilliant! Dad knew I wanted to go to the Kennedy Space Centre, so he took us. I have photos of me and my sister in a Space Shuttle and at the engine end of the first stage of the Apollo-Saturn V: the Moon rocket. Wonderful. That boosted my enthusiasm for science and engineering and now I was doing a degree in it.

These memories were flooding me. I felt like I was sinking in them. Perhaps that's all memory is: a river of indistinct impressions, filtered through our sense of ourselves? Perhaps that's all we are: just a collection of memories? Do we remember only what we want to remember? or, what we'd like to believe happened? Did mum really hold my hand and give me a little kiss when she left me at school every morning?

My memory of my mother stopped abruptly. I could see her face on that last day. After that she might as well have died, it was the same thing, except there was no funeral. I thought she'd come back so I didn't cry. But she didn't come back, she didn't want to be with us, with *me*. Dad said it was her choice and probably better like that. Better for me, or better for her? Dad said he didn't know. Was she displeased with me? Had I not given her the love and affection she needed, expected, felt entitled to? What about me? She wasn't there for me, to give me love. She never gave *me* the choice.

Had I been suppressing memories of mum? Because I didn't want to remember? Because I resented what she did? Or was there nothing to remember? Had I made my feelings go away, or did I simply have no feelings? I didn't know.

I sat, ate my sandwiches, and drank my cold water. Boys and girls flying kites sped by small dogs in hot pursuit.

What about Paul's memories? Wouldn't I rather have some of those? That's what this seemed like.

Paul had no family. After his death no one would know his story, not unless he shared it with me. When people die their memories disappear. How much priceless experience and knowledge is lost? If I chose to stand by, I would be colluding in the death of this man's memories. It made me uneasy to think that I could share his story but *could choose not to*.

Whatever the reasons were, I did not remember mum. She went away. I hadn't. Instead, had I spent my life trying to be the perfect daughter to an absent uncaring mother?

Listening and talking to Paul made me feel special. It's hard to explain. It made me feel good to know that he'd been through so many awful things and come out of the other side. There might be burdens - more terrible experiences, but I felt that somehow they could make me stronger. If I didn't hear Paul's story, then I would never know. I had come through difficult things too. I hadn't appreciated that until today. Would I be able to live with myself always curious, always wondering, but never knowing?

He'd offered me a choice. I knew what to do.

I dropped into the pastry outlet by Richmond station just before it closed.

I knew what he liked. Next evening when I walked out of briefing it was late, but he was still up and about. He was playing chess with Henry. As I walked in he glanced over his shoulder and winked at me. He enjoyed Henry's company and was going very easy on him.

After the game he was clearing the pieces away, and I brought a pot of tea with some cups on a tray and plonked it on the table. I followed it with the bag of pastries.

'Are we *us* now?' he asked, his face shining like the sun.

'Yes,' I said, *'I'm with us.'*

He took my wrists. *'Thank you and bless you.'*

Monday, 5 June 1944. *The Last Bright Day (continued)*

'The morning was grey with wind and low cloud and more rain was in the air. I packed my stuff in the attic.

In the traditional kitchen Marie's father sat in a large rocking chair. Another large but vacant chair stood near the fireplace. There was a bureau with a photo of a young man, envelopes and papers. The flagstone floor was laid with threadbare rugs and the air hung with the light haze of wood burning. Le petit dejeuner of bread, milk, cheese and coffee was a memorable meal, laid on just for me. Coffee only came out on special occasions, the same as in Jersey. The golden bread was warm from the kitchen oven and something like how you would imagine the clouds of heaven to taste - if they could be tasted.

Also like heaven was the smile of that golden angel Marie, who had evidently descended from one of those clouds where she had been residing. I could hardly take my eyes off her, and she knew it. I found it hard to form coherent sentences in her presence. She seemed content to sit there and let me make a fool of myself in conversation until my raggedy mind latched onto something I'd heard her father say earlier, *'…a duck or goose that she shot.'*

'Did I hear your father say that you shot ducks?'

'Yes.'

'Hardly a fair fight is it? You against a duck,' I quipped.

'Well, well, Strasbourg has finally woken up this morning! Are you challenging me to a shooting contest? You'll lose! Especially with that knackered trigger finger, stupid boy.'

How many times had she called me a stupid boy? I really didn't know.

Pierre said, 'The Germans don't like us having guns. They worry that we might shoot them. They ordered us to hand in our shotguns and rifles, but most of us didn't. We kept ours. We can't hunt with shotguns anymore. They're noisy. If any Boche heard we would be in big trouble.'

'I have a St Etienne miniature Nationale 5.5mm rim fire,' the angel beamed. 'It's a beauty. Do you want to see it?'

Pierre gave an according smile and in an aside told me, 'She's a brilliant shot, never wastes a round.'

She disappeared off and came back with an absolute little peach of a rifle: single shot bolt action, walnut stock about 110cm. I took and admired it. 'You know rifles then boy?' Pierre asked. He watched as I checked the action and removed the bolt examining the tiny pin mechanism. 'Maybe he's not so stupid,' he told Marie in another smiling aside. I looked down the rifling. Not quite two twists, right hand, six grooves. It was beautifully engineered, a masterpiece. I would *really* have liked a rifle like this.

'It's a handsome weapon and I'm very envious Marie.'

'You handle the gun like it were a new-born babe. Does your father hunt?' Pierre asked.

'I used to shoot a Mauser Deutsches Sportmodell smallbore. It's a basic weapon, not a sweetheart like this one. Father and I used to go out in the Vosges, the hunting is good there.'

'I bet you did!' he smiled.

'Are you any good though?' Marie provoked.

'Well, why don't we find out?' I smiled sensing the bandage around my almost useless right index finger.

Marie clapped with joy, 'A shooting contest. Jolly good!'

'You won't defeat her,' Pierre added in another aside, 'she'll beat the crap out of you.'

'Good, we haven't had duck for weeks,' Marie purred.

She continued, 'The Germans around here are billeted mainly in Sainte-Mère-Église which is about 4km over that way. But it's not a problem they hardly ever come over here. There aren't many and most of them are either old, slow and stupid or young, fit, and stupid. They won't come and even if they do they won't notice anyone new I'm sure of it.'

'Some of them aren't even German either,' Pierre added with a wry twist. 'They speak a gobbledegook language I never heard before, but they all have guns. They'll be out on parade, I'm sure you'll be perfectly safe.'

When Marie went upstairs her father turned to me and in a hushed tone observed, 'She really likes you, I haven't seen her this happy in years.' I just smiled.

Marie led the way back onto the lane I had come along last night with the little gun swung over her shoulder. There was a glint of water, and we turned left along a little track sloping gently down to it. 'Those are flooded fields,' she observed, 'perfect for ducks and geese, especially in winter. The Germans let the river flood so that if any paratroopers arrive they'll be drowned.'

'Why would Germans drown their own paratroopers?' I asked then realised what I'd said. Being in her company had that effect.

'Stupid boy. *Allied paratroopers* if the invasion comes here.' There, she'd called me stupid again.

'The invasion could come here?'

'*Possibly,*' she said. 'Nobody knows.'

'My God, I hadn't thought of that. Jersey is heavily defended. No one would survive invading that place.'

'Only an idiot would invade Jersey. There's nothing there but seagulls potatoes and tiny malnourished cows.'

'Hitler is defending *les îles anglo-normandes* (the Channel Islands) with one whole division. You should see the bunkers guns and minefields.'

'Only an idiot would defend all those cows potatoes and seagulls like that, but then Hitler **is** an idiot,' she giggled.

We tromped down that track in the highest of spirits full of youthful bonhomie and exuberance. On Marie's face the blossom of youth and innocence, confident and brassy, magnetic. I considered everything about her to be beautiful. She expressed freedom: freedom from any encumbrance of occupation or suppression. I felt free too - free in a way that I'd never felt before. I was finally independent and thinking completely for myself. It was all new and exhilarating.

The slope ended at the edge of an expanse of marshy waterlogged ground. Grass was growing under the water. The flooded fields were bordered to the west by the railway line I was on last night. It ran north-south. Where it was dry the ungrazed grass had grown tall in the verge.

'What is this place?' I asked as I took snapshots with the Leica.

'*Le Marais de Nouville,*' she said with a smile. 'It's our grazing land but the bastard Boche flooded it and now we can't keep so many cows. Normally it's only flooded in winter.'

I couldn't see any birds, but then she said, 'Look, there's one!'

It was a male Mallard on its own about 40 metres away. 'You pot that one and then we'll go out and get it,' she said.

'What about that water? How deep is it?'

'There's a river. You can't see it, but I know where it is, it's three metres deep. In between here and there the water is ankle deep, knee deep, sometimes more.'

She was about right with the range I reckoned, so I set the sight on the little Nationale for 40m. Now that is a bit of a shot for most shooters, but with a small calibre and iron sights in a decent wind it's a *helluvashot*. I reckoned I was good enough and as well as that I couldn't bear to have this damned girl take the piss out of me any longer. She produced a shell from a pocket, and I loaded it safety on. I found a tree on the right to brace myself against, clicked the safety off and wrapped the strap around my right arm as I'd been taught. 'Don't forget the wind,' she said.

'Shut up!' I hissed.

That poor little green and grey bird was about to have its afternoon completely ruined I thought as I drew a bead and took a breath for the shot. All I had to do was hit it. That would be enough. I didn't think about that recently dislocated trigger finger. I fired… and saw a splash over to the right. Shit! The gun was virtually silent, and the little bird sailed on oblivious.

'Well, that was rubbish!' she said chuckling.

'Shut up and give me another shell.' I muttered.

Reloading, I took aim again and made a correction on the wind and a bit more for my trashed finger. I fired. The water just in front of the bird pinged in a small plume. The duck rose up flapping its wings and ruffling its feathers. Another miss.

'You're awful,' she observed. 'Bloody useless, and you've wasted two shots. Gimme that gun, stupid boy!'

How many times had she called me stupid? I'd lost count. Handing her the rifle I realised that she was probably right.

The gun became an extension of her personality: sharp and implacable. She loaded up, pushed home the bolt, braced against the tree and blew that duck's head off in a sudden puff of green feathers. What a shot! Oh my God. What a shot! '*Incroyable!*' I screeched. '*C'est magnifique!*'

Her father was right, amazing shooting.

'Monsieur le Canard doesn't stand any chance against you, does he?'

She looked at me smiling, 'Always aim for the head.' She paused, 'and don't blame your trigger finger!'

We rolled up our trousers and took off our boots and socks. I put the camera down, and we waded in, the grass and mud oozing between our toes. She was giggling her head off! We approached the upturned duck with the water over our knees. The remnants of its feathery head were drifting across the lake blown on the wind. And then by God she started kicking water at me! 'Two can play at that game,' I called and started kicking back. Before long it was a giant splashing contest, and we were soon completely drenched. She pushed me over in the mud, I got up to push her down but then she said, 'No. Don't get mud in the gun.'

I told her, 'That's a low trick not letting me dunk you.'

'Aww poor boy!' she said. I shook my head and laughed. Now as well as being humiliated and soaked I was also caked in smelly brown gunge.

Marie took the duck and popped it under her arm like a rugby ball all the while with that giddy chuckle. Its webbed feet still seemed to me to be wiggling pathetically even though it didn't have a head. She said, 'Ducks do that sometimes,' then she laughed again. I was laughing too and shaking my head in disbelief, I had never met anyone quite like her before.

We splodged back to our boots and socks, but it was pointless putting them on. After a few minutes we set off back towards the farmhouse. With the soaking clothes it was quite chilly.

She said, 'It's fine, the oven is still going from this morning we'll soon get dried off.' As we walked she added, 'You know the boys around here have straw behind their ears *and between them.*'

'Does that mean you haven't seen any straw on me?'

'I'll keep looking,' she said. I liked that.

Back at the farmhouse she hung up the duck on a line in the kitchen. Then she put on a huge pan to boil up some water. Her father took me up to a bedroom. He said, 'This is Henri's room. In 1940 he was part of a tank squadron with de Gaulle, but a panzer shot his *Char B*, and he was captured. Now he's in a Boche prison camp. His clothes will be too big for you, but you can always roll up the sleeves and legs. Help yourself.' I was taken aback when he said that - there had been no indication.

'I'm very sorry to hear about your son.'

'It's okay, he sends us letters. One day the Allies will come, and this will all be over. We'll kick the Germans out and I'll get my son back.' He stood and went to pick up a portrait photo of Henri from the bureau. 'This is my son: a hero of France,' he solemnly announced.

I reflected on what Marie's father had said. In my case it was the other way around: it was the son getting his father back. I was glad he told me, it meant that when we came to the evening meal I could say something which showed I understood his loss. I didn't ask about Marie's mother.

A bowl full of the hot water was drawn to wash. Then I took some of Henri's clothes and dressed, rolling up sleeves and trouser legs. I took my stuff and washed it in the water. Marie happened on me doing that, 'Oh! look at this: a boy washing his own clothes, whatever next!' I hung them over the oven, took some Camembert an apple and some bread while Marie and her black cat sat and watched.

Then I slumped into the empty big chair in the kitchen. It was all very cosy and homely. Bliss.

I awoke to the gorgeous smell of roasting duck. Not only had she plucked and cleaned *Monsieur Le Canard,* now she was cooking up a storm with him. AND there was the smell of more baking bread. Could this day get any better?

By 7.30 *le diner* was ready, prepared by father and daughter. Leek & potato soup, duck with cherry sauce, bread with a poached egg, courgette and beetroot. Then cheeses. All washed down with calvados - that I hardly touched. 'That came from over the road,' said Pierre making a condemnatory observation of his neighbour's workmanship: 'It's Pays d'Auge, *apparently.*'

The conversation at table ranged widely. I listened carefully to their beautiful *Normand* French which at times sounded first like *Jèrriais,* then almost English. Meanwhile, I nibbled away at the banquet they had laid on for me savouring every crumb and trying to make it last all night, although I really wanted to wolf it down. We starved in Jersey, and I hadn't had food like this for years. Marvellous!

They understood when I told them why we went to Jersey for my great-aunt. They were interested in my father's war record and extremely impressed at how he met my mother. Pierre said, 'He gained a medal for his trouble but better than that he found love: the love of his life. He fought for France and for this I salute him! And your war nurse mother from Strasbourg is also a hero of France in the truest sense. She refused to be made into a German! Your parents are heroes of France!' I thought it prudent not to say too much, but he beat me to it. 'Alsace-Lorraine is French, always has been, always will be. *The people of Strasbourg are French.* Let me embrace you Paul, son of France!' At this he stood smiling, and I stood too. Holding up his glass he exclaimed, 'Vive la France!' Marie chirped in, 'Let me embrace you also.' It was the first time I held a girl.

When Pierre left the room for a moment I looked at Marie wondering if I'd upset him somehow. She shook her head.

'No. My father was wounded at Noyon in 1918, but he never talks about it. I think he deliberately forgot what happened. But I think perhaps that you remind him of Henri,' she explained.

The evening became more marvellous in every passing minute. Marie was quite radiant. She regarded me intently and teased me relentlessly. For example, she asked if I'd met Winston Churchill on visits to London and expressed disappointment when I told her I hadn't. She said I should have tried harder. Another one of her ruses involved our fathers. She turned to Pierre and said, 'When you fought Les Boches alongside the British in Picardy they used to talk about a *British stiff upper lip,* didn't they?'

'Oui ma chérie.'

'Papa, did you ever see a *British stiff upper lip?*'

'*Non ma chérie!*' he stated with an expressive flourish.

'Mmm...,' she paused, again deliberately, curiously. 'Well, Paul here has a British father, perhaps he'd like to show us his *stiff upper lip...* Come on Paul, we're all dying to see it!' And she pulled a face trying to make her top lip go straight, then burst out giggling. I had to laugh.

The black cat wandered over in search of duck from the table. I gave him a piece which he gobbled in two seconds flat. 'Come on my friend,' I told him, 'I'm being outnumbered two-to-one here. Help me out!' The cat looked up at me quizzically.

I glanced at Marie, and she was pulling another smirking face, 'He's on my side, always has been, always will be!'

We got to the cheese and were well filled. When her father went off again Marie looked at me and said, 'The last person to sit at the table in that chair wearing those clothes was my brother in 1940'. I gasped.

'It's good to have another man in the house,' said Pierre returning.

'Albeit a rather *thin* one,' added Marie cheekily.

'We're short-handed here, why don't you stay with us Paul?' I glanced across at the girl I'd spent a wonderful day with and my young mind span.

How could I tell them I had to leave? How could I tell beautiful Marie? I'd been thinking it through. 'I said I'd tell you how I got here. Well, it's quite easy to explain. The thing is – a lot of people in Alsace speak Alsatian-German, but that doesn't make them German, does it? because they also speak French. I was born in Strasbourg, and so was my mother. We *are* French, but we are Alsatian.'

'Oh,' gasped Marie, 'now you're going to tell us you speak German, aren't you?'

'*Ja, ich spreche elsässisch-deutsch.*'

Marie's face was a picture of astonishment.

'But you're not German! How can you be German if your mother tended wounded French soldiers, and your father got a medal fighting them?' Pierre said firmly.

'Yes sir.' Then I added, 'Just because I can speak some Russian, that doesn't make me Russian, does it?'

'My God,' gasped Marie, 'you speak Russian too?'

In Russian I said, 'I speak a little Russian. There were many Russian slaves in Jersey.' Then I translated.

The knife Marie had been holding dropped limply to the pewter plate with a clang. She looked like she was dribbling. I had finally taken the wind out of her sails.

'Paul, you are FULL of surprises!' she muttered.

'The Germans in Jersey would not conscript *les Anglais*. But they do conscript 17-year-olds from Alsace. According to Hitler I am German through my mother, place of birth and language. The Germans did conscript me, but I managed to talk my way into one of their work parties instead. That's how I got off the island and that's how I was sent to Valognes. I never planned to do any work for the Boche, I always planned to run away.'

'*Ah voila!*' exclaimed Marie's father.

There was a hole in my story, but neither of them seemed to notice they were so gripped by what I'd told them. We grabbed our calvados and took huge belts of it. Pierre re-filled the glasses. After a moment of contemplation he asked, 'What did your father have to say about that?'

Thinking about it now what I did next was quite comical. I paused, took another gulp of calvados, leaned on the great oak table and regarding father and daughter jointly explained:

'My father couldn't say anything.'

'Why not?' quizzed Marie.

'Because he's in a German detention camp.'

'My God! The Boche took your father?' muttered Pierre.

'Yes, and I'm going to get him back. He's not well. He's in danger. I have to rescue him.'

'Good God!' exclaimed Marie. She was stunned.

Pierre sat back in his chair. He drew breath and rubbed his chin. *'That's beautiful!'* were his exact words.

Marie recovered a little and was able to speak, 'Where is your father? Where have the bastard Boche taken him?'

'The last time we heard he was on the German-Austrian border near Salzburg in a place called Laufen.'

'That's so far away,' Marie gasped.

Her father drew breath and regarded me, 'You must truly love your father if you undertake a mission like this.'

'Yes, I love my father very much. When you speak of the Germans having your son, I know how you feel. So, I must regretfully decline your kind invitation. I'm going to Germany to get my father out and take him to Switzerland.'

'My God!' he exclaimed, standing again to embrace me. 'Indeed, you are courageous. Marie judged you correctly. You <u>are</u> worthy to take my son's place at our table. Bless you young man and bless your travels.' He embraced me again and I thought he would wring the life out of me! Tears were on his face. I saw tears in Marie's eyes too. I'd just found a new family and had immediately declared I was going to leave it. Marie was crestfallen. As her father held me I thought of an hour earlier and how *I'd held her.*

There was nothing more to think, nothing more to say. My mind was numb. The food was long since eaten. Just crumbs remained. We sat blankly at the table. Even the cat had gone and curled up.

Rather than have the evening completely collapse, I said, 'I want to repay my gratitude. You have been so kind to me. Can I work on the farm for a while? Nurse here can tend my wounds, I can hardly cycle anyway, and then she can teach me to shoot.' They both smiled, accepted my offer and the tension was lifted.

The weather was poor, and it was getting dark. I got all my now dry clothes and took them up to my room. Marie and her father said their goodnights. It had been a long day. Tiredness overwhelmed me but I had a full belly. Still half-clothed I climbed into bed and pulled the cover over.

Part way through I was disturbed by the droning of aircraft and booming away to the east. Somewhere was getting a pasting, but I was too tired to care.

That night I thought I heard the door creak and Marie peep around and look at me. It must have been a dream.

That was the end of the last bright day.'

The old man's eyes rolled. He was exhausted. 'Paul, that is incredible,' I said with a sigh. My mouth was dry. The old man's magnificent story had gripped me so totally, but suddenly I was aware that I hadn't moved for over an hour. It was 75 years back to that farmhouse in Normandy, but he recalled it vividly. He'd re-lived that day over and over again. Like the sharp unfaded photos he kept, nothing had been lost.

I said, 'What you've told me is *amazing. I'm humbled, I really am.'*

'No, *I'm just beginning*. This is just the beginning. I never told anyone, not even my friends. I spared them just as the German officer on the ship chose to spare me. These things have been timeless burdens.'

He'd done it again; he'd absolutely staggered me. It was one in the morning, and I thought I'd better take myself away.

Boiling point

When I saw him the next afternoon it seemed that he was still exhausted from the epic session. My mind was still reeling. He made no attempt to engage but I let it pass. It stayed like that for the next three days. Then I had two days off and changed rota coming in for the 8am from Monday. This was always more difficult as I was normally pretty tied up with general duties around the place. However, when I came across him later his mood was quite different. He wanted to say something but was holding himself back:

In the sunroom around 11, I asked him brightly: 'What d'you think Paul, pot of tea and digestives?'

He frowned a bit and said, 'Sit down dear.'

Hmm… I studied his face as we sat.

He said, 'I was relieved to talk last weekend. But since then, I have been troubled at what I told you.'

'We agreed Paul, I thought we'd agreed?' I felt my temperature rising.

'We did, but now I fear the consequences.'

'What consequences?'

'I shouldn't have told you.'

That didn't impress me one bit, and I looked him square in the eye. 'What do you mean: *shouldn't have told me?*'

'I'm sorry Katie, that came out wrong and I apologise.'

My anger increased. Changing into German, I addressed him directly: 'First, you tell your incredible story. Then you blabber on about 'fearing the consequences' and say, 'you shouldn't have told me'. You're taking the mickey. Don't talk to me about consequences Paul. Do you think I'm not strong enough? Watch me.'

The room began to empty quickly…

I felt he was playing games, and that was bad enough. But then suddenly and out of nowhere, I had thoughts of my mother and what I wanted to tell her about her *choice* to take herself away. It was an oblique connection, but it was made, and I'd boiled.

'I'm sorry, I'm sorry…' he muttered in a regretful tone, dipping his gaze.

'Don't lecture me about *shouldn't or consequences*. Never do that.'

He had tears now, but I didn't hang back. 'And don't take the mickey or play one of your games with me, I won't have it. Take your memories that are too precious to tell. Take them with you, and they will never be heard. Afterwards look around and see who cares.'

Now he was sobbing uncontrollably. I heard footsteps behind me - hastening up the hallway, but I saved the best till last:

'I thought you were brave. I am brave enough to hear your story. But <u>YOU</u> are not brave enough to tell it, Paul von Bonn!'

I'd reduced him to rubble just as Mel arrived. 'I'll take it from here Katie,' she said calmly.

He was bent forward head in hands crying with giant tears dripping on the carpet.

'No, I quit.'

'Katie, I'll talk to you in the ready room,' she said.

'I won't be there. I quit. I'm out.'

'No. NO! Make her stay Mel!' the old man pleaded. 'I've made a mistake, a terrible mistake. Make her stay.'

Then I got up and walked out.

****

I never regretted that day. Without knowing it he'd trodden on the landmine of my mother's choice to walk out. Worst of all, he'd trodden on his own choice. Why did he do that? Did he know what he was doing? I didn't think he did. For all his wisdom, all his apparent strength, he wasn't brave enough to trust his friendship with a 22-year-old student. What threat was I to him? None. He intimidated people and gave the appearance of strength, but it was all nonsense, one big game. Did I know what I was doing? I thought I did.

A week went by. I wasn't curious. He'd annoyed me too much and that was it.

I applied for a job at Waitrose in West Ealing. It was a longer cycle ride, or 65 bus then E3 and walk, but it was better paid. They called me and I went for a chat at the store. I wore my best blue suit, and it went well. The following week on the Monday morning they called me, described me as 'very personable' and offered me a position as a trainee partner to start induction on Tuesday. I accepted and didn't think anything more of Paul and the Stanley Care Home.

That afternoon the phone rang. It was Mel. 'Will you come in dear?' she asked.

'Why should I? I'm finished.'

'No, please come in Katie. If you are going to finish then at least say your goodbyes.'

I never thought of myself as an unreasonable person. However, when it came to Paul Bunn I was going to make an exception. I wasn't going to be the subject of one of his games and I wasn't going to show weakness. Going would show me as weak, and *weak I was not*. Growing up without a mother meant I wasn't weak. Getting the grades to go to a top university meant I wasn't weak. We'll see who's weak I thought as I got on my bike for the short ride over to Kew.

Mel met me at the door. 'Come in dear,' she said with a slight smile. I looked at her but said nothing.

We went to the ready room and closed the door. 'Thank you for coming in. Let me explain the situation.'

I listened and said, 'I respect you Mel, you have been really good to me, but you don't need to explain any situation. I've come out of courtesy to you and all the people here. It's been great and I have learned a lot but I'm ready to move on now.'

'Are you, Katie?'

'Yes.' I looked her in the eye. She knew I meant it. 'I've already accepted a position at Waitrose, with a pay rise.'

'Alright.' She went on, 'I don't know what was said the other day, but I have my ideas.'

'Do you Mel? I'm not going to say anything about that. If he has then that's up to him.'

I went on, 'I'm sorry I walked out, that wasn't meant to offend you, and I shouldn't have done it and left you short-handed.'

'We managed. Have you thought of how you are going to say goodbye to Paul?'

'I've already said all the things that needed saying.'

There was a knock on the door. I had an inkling I knew who it was. I looked at Mel, 'Is this a trick?' Her puzzled look said it wasn't.

'Nobody knows you're coming. I haven't told anyone.' Mel wasn't one to lie, she didn't have it in her. 'Just a minute,' she called. I had a feeling, so I went to the door. It was Henry.

'Oh, Katie. There you are. We were wondering where you were. Have you been on holiday?'

'Not exactly.'

'Come in Henry,' said Mel brightly.

'What's happened Mel? Have you sacked Katie? She doesn't look best pleased,' he observed.

'I haven't sacked Katie. Why would I? She's one of the best people we've ever had.' My ears burned. I wasn't expecting that.

'Oh, that's good. She's especially good at finding my false teeth. Always seems to know where they are.'

I laughed out loud. Well, what was I supposed to do, be the Ice Queen forever? Mel was laughing too. 'We have a very high regard for you here Katie. One person in particular holds you in the highest esteem.'

'Yes, listen to Mel,' Henry said, nodding in agreement.

'I know,' I muttered glancing away.

'Katie. Will you help me with my teeth?' Henry asked innocently.

'I'll be along in a moment,' Mel replied impatiently. Henry gave a puzzled look and went off, closing the door behind him.

Mel continued, 'I'm not going to ask you to reconsider. I'm not going to do any of that. But I will ask that you say goodbye to Paul. Don't do it for him and don't do it for me. Do it for yourself. You don't want to remember your time here for just that one day, do you?'

My mind had been made up, but by chance Mel had found a form of words: *you don't want to remember your time here for just that one day.* There might have been no words, but she chose those.

'Alright,' I said.

The phrase repeated in my head as I walked the familiar route towards his room.

He wasn't there, but the door was open. As I often did I went in and looked around. The photograph of him and Hans in the pewter frame was there in its usual place, his things were there: books, papers, shoes. I looked at his stuff. It always felt as if I would see something new. Then I began to remember what I'd said: '*Afterwards look around and see who cares…*' That was very harsh. Mean. He'd managed to bring out the worst in me.

'You came back.' It was him, in the doorway.

'Shit!' I exclaimed, just as I had that very first time.

He stood and stared. 'I don't know how to apologise for what happened.' He came in, stood by his table, then pulled out a chair. Sitting he seemed frailer now.

I joined him at the table. 'I'm sorry too, but not for what I said.'

'I know you aren't sorry. If you had treated me the way I treated you, I would have been just as unforgiving.'

'Well, we've got that straight then,' I bristled.

'Life is too short. We agreed. You were watching me and took an interest, so we started to speak.'

'You spoke, I listened, but then you… you went crazy.'

'I don't know how I could have made such a mistake, but I did. I have become weak. It's the burden, I am weakened by the burden. You are young and strong. I am a fading old man. Soon I will disappear from view. I would hate it if we parted like this. Please come back and be my friend again.'

I stared at him. 'Don't blackmail me, you're better than that. My question stands: are <u>you</u> brave enough? Because you can make the assumption that I am.'

He paused, raised a left hand, brushed his eye brow, then drew breath and glanced away. 'I don't know.'

I looked into his eyes and there was no flaw, no insincerity.

'Paul, you talked about us, *with us*. I know that I am *with us*. Are you?'

I went on. 'You said you had these memories for 75 years. If they're not coming out now, then when are they going to come out? You've had long enough to think about this. 75 years is long enough. If you aren't going to tell me that's your choice, but I want to hear your story. What's stopping you from telling it?'

I maintained a fixed gaze on him. He looked back through those blue eyes and grimaced, biting his lip.

He sighed then said, 'Now you are blackmailing me.' He paused in reflection, then continued, 'You are strong, as I was once strong. I saw it from the start.' He paused again then asked, 'Do you know the writings of Albert Camus?'

'No,' I replied quietly.

'Camus is supposed to have said: 'Don't walk behind me, I may not lead. Don't walk in front of me, I may not follow. Just walk beside me and be my friend.' A soft smile came to his lips, eyes glistening.

Reaching forward I held his wrists. Our eyes met, he gently rocked his head backwards and forwards and continued. 'Only if I join with you can the story come out, but I have become cowardly and weak. Your strength will guide me. This is something *only you* can do.' He paused, drew breath and in quiet German continued:

'You know, someone very dear once told me: 'Walking with a friend in the dark is better than walking alone in the light.'

I looked him in the eye. '**I will walk with you. Will you walk with me?**'

'I will. I swear it,' he whispered.

The sun was high and shining through the window, but in our friendship a new day had dawned.

3. A captain in the orchard

I walked with Paul down to the sunroom and after 20 minutes left him there. He smiled and waved gently and then I went off to find Mel. In the ready room I apologised and asked whether she would take me back. She said, 'You never left as far as I'm concerned.'

I was surprised by what came out next:

'He never told me what happened or what was said, so that's between you and him. But he did ask me to try to get you back. I did that because he asked me and because I work with him every day. You never saw what he was like after you went. He was devastated, dysfunctional. He stayed in his room for two days and wouldn't come out. Then he told me he wanted to pay for you personally to come back and be his one-to-one carer.'

'I will come back, but I don't want his money.'

'I know you don't.' She paused and said, 'You are a really special carer Katie. I wanted to tell you that, even if this did turn out to be your last day.'

'Thank you Mel. I won't take his money though. You'd better tell him.'

'Some of the old people here take liberties like silly children; like they want to be a child again. Not Paul. He's never once done anything like that. He is locked inside himself. Katie, you are a quite brilliant listener, and you have found a way to bring him out. Until you came we had no idea of his incredible talents: his conversation, languages or music. Such a cultured man. Bless you for that.'

'He's hard to work with. He's a fighter.'

'We've all seen it Katie. Something is there, but we don't know what it is. I don't think he knows either. You're our best carer and the best person for him. As a token of our appreciation, I've decided to offer you a rise.'

'Why would you do that? I'm unreliable and lose it with guests. I wouldn't employ me, let alone give me a pay rise.'

'Well, I'm not you, am I?' she smiled. 'You have qualities. You are loyal, compassionate and generous. Sometimes people just need a darned good shake. You have found a way to shake him. *He has shaken you* though, he must have, or you would never have walked out the way you did.'

I must admit, she was right. I hadn't thought about it like that, but she was right. How did she know?

'You don't need to offer me a pay rise.'

'That's enough! I'm authorising a rise and I'm backdating it to your first day in March. I'm also going to make sure you are paid for those days when you weren't here. Consider it an advance payment.'

'Advance payment for what?'

'For what's coming, you must know that it's all going to come out now. You've burst the dam.'

'Burst the dam?'

'Katie, you're remarkable, and you don't even know how remarkable you are,' she smiled. 'You will need to be strong. I will support you. All of us here will support you.'

'Thank you. I appreciate everything you've done for me. I will do my best.'

I cycled away and considered the events of the day, but I knew I'd done the right thing. I got home and was deeply apologetic as I phoned Waitrose to turn down their job offer.

That night I stood on the balcony looking across nighttime London and thought: Mel's right, it's all going to come in a flood now.

In sleeping, deep breath...

'Rolling over, sleep was gone, replaced by distant booming. It wasn't the wind: it was guns. Rolling over again, it didn't go away. The walls of the bedroom were brightened by flashes of light. There was a droning too, like thundering hornets with aircraft engines. In a trance I stumbled to the window. Blasts resonated every few seconds. The white glow of searchlights looking for aircraft lit the cloudy western sky. Cacophonous sounds rattled the glass. Walking to the window on the other side of the house there was a fire in the direction of Sainte-Mère-Église. There was the noise of very low aircraft moving from west to east south of the farmhouse. That sound soon moved away leaving just the blasting of the German anti-aircraft guns until, after a few minutes, that too died away.

Then the noises and lights started again, blasting, repetitive. More aircraft were coming from the west. Pierre joined me by the tall window on the landing, and we were occasionally illuminated by flashes. Then came Marie. We could easily see each other in the brightness of the lights. The deafening firing of guns was coming from all around. 'We've never had anything like this,' whispered Marie. We were standing and staring seemingly unable to move.

Approaching us from the west the sound of many aircraft got louder and lower. The German 37mm guns were monotonously pumping into the sky. 'We will be bombed!' shouted Pierre, but we were already in our rooms getting dressed hastily. 'We need to get out!' Marie called.

The deafening thunderous noise of aircraft overhead was shaking the house rattling the slates and windows. There was an explosion away to the south.

Then there was a loud smash on the roof, and I threw myself to the floor expecting death.

'GET OUT! GET OUT!' she screamed. Picking ourselves up we fell down the stairs as if pursued by devils.

Out in the farmyard, an eerie glow of light and the noise of aircraft and booming guns. Those aircraft were all around incredibly low. We stood and stared across the sky at hundreds of aircraft in the moonlight. They filled the air. Not describable. The guttural droning roar of many engines, those mad thundering hornets, was inside my skull making my teeth judder.

Senses numbed I looked around. Out of control the words, 'JESUS CHRIST,' fell from my gaping mouth.

Many aircraft now, an uncountable number. Dark like giant bats they were, all emerging from the west. Long streams of them all around. And out of them came jumpers on shadowy parachutes. *Stupefying.*

The aircraft were over our heads thundering like a perpetual storm. It was beyond the edge of anything imaginable: *beyond comprehension.*

The Germans were shooting at them furiously. They were firing everything they had, even flares. Some parachutes were on fire. I could hear the screams of men being hit as they drifted down.

The deafening unearthly drone literally drilled the sky and drummed the ground. Dumbstruck Marie and I stood and watched many parachutes go down in the area where we'd been hunting this morning: the flooded fields. Those men would likely drown.

I didn't know what to do. No thoughts or words formed in my head. I looked around. There was a large bag of some kind in the courtyard surrounded by shattered slates. It had hit the roof and come down. Nearer to us, small arms crackling and firing, light machine guns and Mausers which fizzed and popped.

Then suddenly we heard the loud crunching of branches in the orchard opposite. We ran to look with the deafening rumbling sound of the low aircraft all the while coming across our heads.

Just inside the gate a mottled green and brown parachute was caught in a shattered apple tree and a figure was underneath on the ground taking off his yellow gloves. Opening the gate, we hesitatingly approached a shadowy soldier. Marie shouted to him, 'Comment allez-vous?'

'Je suis Américain,' shouted the shadow, and turning we saw an American flag on his right shoulder.

In a strange accent the American shouted, 'Get inside, get inside! You are in danger out here.' It was hard to hear what he said as the firing and thundering of low aircraft drowned him out. I turned to Marie and said, 'He wants us to get inside.' 'You understand him?' exclaimed Marie. I nodded, 'Yes of course, he's speaking English.' 'MY GOD!' she screamed over the din.

I called to Marie's father, 'Go back, he says it's dangerous here. Go back!' Away he went.

I looked up, and amongst the booming and shooting were hundreds more parachutes, floating down through the thundering sky. They were all around raining down like giant snowflakes.

I couldn't take it in. It was not comprehendible. It was stupendous, utterly stupendous.

Awestruck, in gibbering English I attempted conversation: 'I speak English captain.' 'You speak English, that's good son, but I'm not a captain, I'm a private.' He was very busy unclipping and checking things.

'Help me pull this 'chute down son and hide it.' 'What is a 'chute?' 'Parachute.' 'Why?' 'Because I don't want the enemy to see me.' There were two opposing As in a circle in a badge on his shoulder and the word: AIRBORNE.

I tried to pull down the parachute, but it was really jammed, and I couldn't hold it with my buggered finger, I needed both hands and Marie to help me. It tore in shreds as we pulled. 'What are your names?' he asked.

'Paul, and this is Marie.'

'Thanks for helping.'

He took hold of a weapon of some sort and folded it out. 'What's that?' I asked.

'That's a gun boy.'

'I can see that captain. What sort of gun?'

'That's my M1A1 carbine and I am not a captain.'

'Sir, is this the invasion?' 'Uh-huh.' That was an expression I'd never heard before. Such a small sound but with such a large meaning. I never took it in at the time.

The droning overhead was still deafening. Further south, especially between the farmhouse and the place that was on fire, a sea of parachutes was coming down. Low like falling black clouds they were, all lit up against the searchlights and relentless anti-aircraft blasts. Small arms fire and flare after flare, everything the Germans had was aimed at the parachutists.

Now there was firing on the ground nearby. The soldier was in a real hurry. 'Tell him about the flooded fields Paul,' said Marie gripping my arm.

'Captain, the fields over that way are flooded. We saw other parachutes going down there. It's dangerous for your friends. There is a deep river and swamp, and we know where it is.' I was so overwhelmed that I wasn't sure I was even speaking the right language. My senses were addled; knocked down by the things happening around me.

'Alright son. My stick is around here, I have to find my buddies first. Then we'll come and look at your swamp.'

'It will be too late by then captain, they'll drown.'

'Well son if you want to help then you should. Go there right now. But first tell me, is there a railway line around here?' He was getting something out of one of his bags.

'Yes, it runs right through the flooded fields,' I pointed. 'Ok then go and help. If you are challenged by someone shouting 'Thunder,' you must reply 'Flash.' If you don't you'll be shot. Can you remember that?'

'Yes captain.'

We were just turning to run down to the fields where the duck hunt had occurred when the soldier stopped us and handed us a little cardboard package. 'What is it?' I asked. 'That's chocolate for you and your sister. That's for helping me.' 'Thank you captain!' I smiled in the dim light.

'You're welcome,' he said, a phrase I'd never heard before. It was the first time I met an American.

We bolted out of the open gate and headed for the flooded fields as fast as we could. We ran like the wind.

The noise of aircraft departed into the east, but there was still the incessant crackling of gunfire. In the moonlight from the slight hill, we could see the waters by the railway line broken by the splashing of paratroopers. Some were still coming down. 'Shit!' exclaimed Marie.

We ran headlong down the lane straight into two more American soldiers with their guns raised. 'Flash, FLASH!' we shouted arriving. The helmeted soldiers stopped us and stared in bewilderment lowering their weapons.

'How do you know the password?' one said in not very good French. A sergeant I thought he was. Marie gave a breakneck reply that we helped an American back up the lane and he told us to say it. The soldiers were mystified. I translated. They were stunned to hear me speak clear English. Marie explained that she knew the flooded fields were deep and dangerous and that we had come to help. Again, I translated. 'Quickly then!' called the sergeant. We ran and they trailed behind us.

We got there and straight away we saw a man struggling well to the left of where we'd shot the duck. He was thrashing and sinking, bobbing up and down. *'Allez Paul!'* Marie shouted. She charged in and I followed. We were by far the closest. There were other soldiers in the water too. Marie waved her arms and called instructions to the paratroopers where not to walk, especially the ones between us and the railway line. They didn't take any notice, so I shouted translations, and they started to move. Three soldiers without helmets were struggling with their gear. They were far away from the drowning man and hadn't seen him. The water was waist deep where we were. We just could not get there quickly enough; the mud and water were holding us back like cold treacle.

The soldier had landed right in the deep part of the river and was splashing helplessly. He was running out of life. Marie got there first. With absolutely no thought for herself she lunged for his parachute lines, but she missed! His thrashing was getting weaker, and he was being carried down by his heavy gear. Now she was tangled in his lines and fabric too. I was 15 metres behind. My blood ran cold as I couldn't see her. I waded on frozen with fear. Seconds passed like hours; the thrashing water subsided a little...

But then she bobbed back up again with lines wrapped around her arms and neck. 'PAUL!' she screamed, choked, and went down again. I leapt to grab her but there was no ground underneath me, it was the river. She came up again gulping for air but swam strongly and she had hold of the lines. I held her right arm with my usable left hand, and we swam and pulled the lines at the same time.

There was a presence behind me. Another soldier had arrived and was pulling me. He had a bright insignia bar on his shoulder. There was a blur of fabric and frantic splashing. Then we were able to stand in the waist deep water and pull the lines. We heaved the man onto his feet coughing his lungs up. He was alive.

Marie was alright. The soldier stood in a choking staggering swoon. We stopped him falling down. Two more Americans arrived, cut his lines with large daggers and supported him one on either side and we struggled back towards land through the mud. Then there was pinging in the water, bullets! Someone was shooting at us! 'Shit!' came a shout from one of the supporting soldiers. He had been shot through his left hand. I helped him support the half-drowned man and we walked them both out.

There were paratroopers all around in the fields and out in the water. An exchange of fire was occurring over to our left. The enemy had spotted us. They were taking pot shots in the broken moonlight. Some Americans were returning fire attempting to secure those still getting clear of the water. In a couple of minutes, the Germans were silenced.

We got to the dry land. Now we could talk as we took cover behind some trees. The guy with the bar gave an order to help the wounded soldier. 'I'm lieutenant in command here. Bless you both for saving one of my men,' he said in not very good French.

'You're welcome,' I said, and it caused a stir:

'You're English!' exclaimed the officer in French.

'*Non, il est français,*' Marie piped in. She was already helping the wounded man. He had been shot through the muscle between his left index finger and thumb which hung limply broken and disconnected. Marie and a soldier with a red cross on his arm sulphured and bandaged it.

We stayed close to the ground. I told the officer our names and there was a brief conversation. Marie turned to me and said, 'Thank them for coming. Thank them from the bottom of our hearts.' There were about 15 soldiers at our location on the little road. Translating I made sure they all knew what Marie had said. They appreciated it.

After about 15 minutes the marsh was clear of men and the guy who nearly drowned was on his feet and able to move. But we stayed crouched down next to the hedge. In the twilight soldiers could be seen over on the railway line heading south. The officer got out a map and turned to Marie and me and asked what the safe way would be to get to Sainte-Mère-Église avoiding the river. I translated. He turned on an impressive little right-angled torch. The soldiers were extremely well equipped. Marie told them the house on fire was in Sainte-Mère-Église.

'Ok men, follow me, let's move out,' the lieutenant called, and the group of soldiers set off heading for the fire across the boggy ground towards some houses and orchards on a slight bluff.

The men walked by, and Marie embraced each one. As she hugged the guy she pulled out of the swamp he told her, 'God bless you angel from heaven for saving my life.' I translated, and with one strong left arm he lifted her, hugged and kissed her. She was thrilled with that.

Marie called and I translated, 'Win the war for us!'

A sergeant called back, 'We will. You're with us now!'

Marie turned to me, and in delight we embraced. That soldier was right, she <u>was</u> an angel.

The aircraft had gone but there was action all around and firing including up ahead in Fresville. Carefully we retreated to the farmhouse, closed the door and bolted it. We found Pierre asleep in his rocking chair. He had started a fire, and it was blazing superbly. We were dripping wet and freezing of course.

In the kitchen nothing was said, we simply looked at each other. There was no need for words. Marie and I embraced again. It was the first time I kissed a girl. Then she went to her room, and I went to mine.'

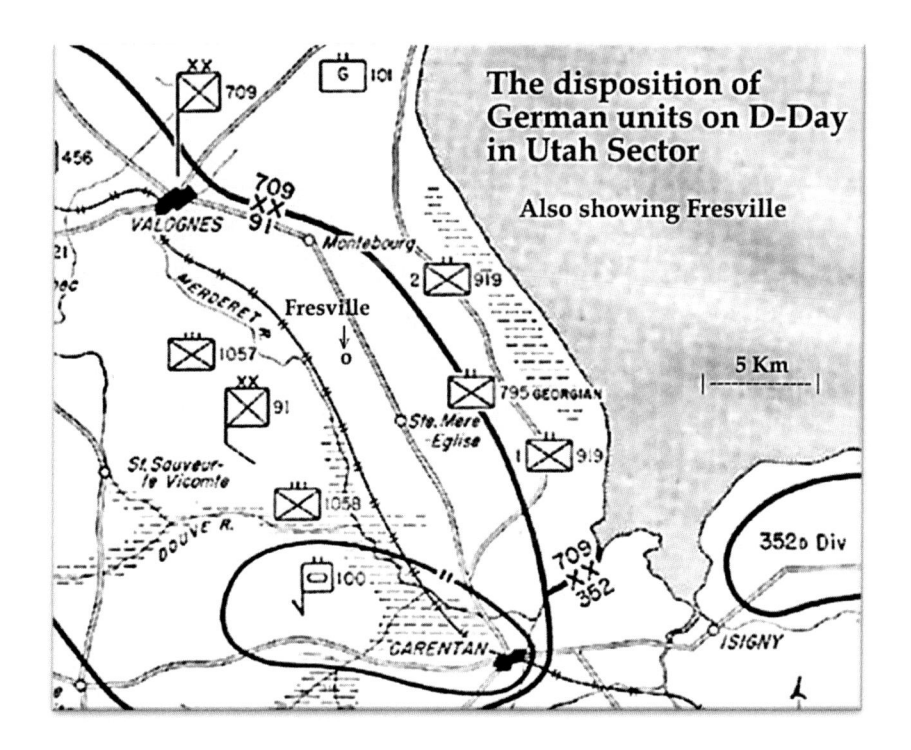

The disposition of German units on D-Day in Utah Sector

Also showing Fresville

Gliders

'I was again woken by noises, different noises. A low thud of big blasts was coming from the north in the distance: Valognes. The Allies were bombing that town. I went to look. A red haze there was, and smoke made red by many fires. I shook my head realising I could very easily have been underneath all that had I not punched the sergeant and fled. I sat on the bed and considered this in the glow of the coming morning.

Then I heard more aircraft approaching. This time the noise was coming from the opposite direction, east and further south. I went out into the courtyard and looked towards Sainte-Mère-Église. Clouds of smoke are rising from that place. The aircraft do not fly overhead as they did last night. They swerve away to the south. I see one of the giant bat-like aircraft on fire. It goes down. Surely I must be in a terrible dream.

As I rub my eyes I glimpse things flying slowly and low-down disappearing behind trees between me and the church spire. In the sky many giant bats are turning as well. I rub my eyes again as more and more of these flying things appear: bats pulling things, small and squat. Gliders.

I am incredulous again. Those must be gliders! Nothing else flies like that. Each giant bat has one glider behind it pulling it with ropes. Then I watch what happens. A glider releases and turns towards me not very high. The giant bat turns hard left to the south in a great thundering turn all the while with Germans shooting at it wrathfully. It has great American stars on its wings and body and black and white stripes. I can clearly see holes in the wings of the bat. Another glider appears and it follows the first. I pull my boots on quickly, pick up my camera and run out into the lane. Those gliders are going to fly right over the farm.

Suddenly I'm back gliding at Wasserkuppe in Germany. It's summer 1938 again, I'm 11 years old and have been working and sweating all day. Father has been flying the *Storch* towplane and I've been pushing, pulling and catapult launching single seaters with my second Cousin Georg. I'm alongside all the other young sun bronzed *Hitlerjugend Luft* devotees of this amazing thing called gliding. We spend the entire day running after gliders and pushing them back until our turn comes. I was learning to fly with my father. The excitement, enjoyment and harmony with the elements is a wonderful advocacy of youth. Suddenly I long for it, for peace, freedom, beauty. How long ago it all seems…

Now I can hear the gliders coming into land, the swish of air on the wings. Then the first one appears over the barn very low, only about 100 feet. The front is all glass. I can clearly see the two pilots, an unbelievable sight. They sail directly over my gaping mouth, then a second one over to the right. *Incroyable*. Out of that childhood instinct to chase gliders I find my feet running again to where they will arrive in a few seconds.

I glimpse up ahead. Trees thrash. The first glider has demolished a line of saplings and the ground thumps as the aircraft skids to a halt. But there is shooting. Some Germans have been waiting and they open up with a MG42 machine gun and Mausers. Hearing that, I skid to a halt in the lane about 50 yards short. The second glider goes behind the first and aims through the gap knocked down. It lands longer and to the right and I hear it crashing through a hedge. The German firing stops. Just as I decide to retreat to the farm the firing starts again. American guns return fire. There's a woof as a grenade goes off, then another. There are screams. The American firing lessens. I run trying to blot out the sounds behind me. Then I see three more gliders fly over to the landing field. I stop and try to wave them away, but they ignore me. They are flying towards death and there's nothing I can do about it. I go inside and lock the door. It takes me a minute or two to accept how close I came to running into a deadly fire fight. Blind reactive fear made me run away.

I slumped across the table staring at the dying fire, dreamed of that day in 1938 and cried my eyes out.'

The theft of the camera

'I stirred having fallen asleep at the table. Incredible as it may seem, Marie was up soon after to bring in the cows for milking. She got fresh bread from the oven with home-made butter and apple preserve for *le petit-déjeuner*. I sat and said nothing.

Outside was the sound of firing and skirmishing coming from Sainte-Mère-Église. Smoke was rising in many places. I blanked out of my mind the gliders that had landed close by. There was no sound coming from that direction.

Then we went to get the cows in. There was something reassuring about that. Except that when we got to the orchard one of the cows was lying in the corner with its stomach hanging out and ravens hopping and pecking. A stray bullet had hit it. Marie ran and shoed the birds away, but it was far too late. There were tears, although that changed when I reminded her of what happened just a few hours earlier and how so many soldiers must surely have been killed. Nothing could be done now, so we took the cows down. They moved along calmly.

In the yard I picked up the strange bag that hit the roof last night. In the house I emptied it, a trove of stuff: wool socks, a wool hat, rations, coffee, several bars of chocolate, cigarettes, and one of those clever torches. Most wonderful of all there were three rolls of 35mm black & white film which would fit my Leica camera. Brilliant! The hat was pounced on by Marie. It was her colour, and she looked good in it. Mind you, she would look good in anything.

Amazingly, the rest of that day passed without further incident. It seems incredible to me now, but we'd had enough. It was all too much. Gun fire, smoke rising, aircraft, but we kept out of the way and the doors shut. We sat, ate the chocolate and drank the strange tasting instant coffee from the American bag and stared at each other.

In the afternoon Pierre came back with another farmer and between them with axe and hacksaw they set about dismembering and breaking down the dead cow. A few more people came out and they were rewarded with great slabs of meat which they cycled home with over their shoulders. They also filled up their zinc bottles with our milk in exchange for large pots of jam and calvados. Strangely they had not much to say about what was going on. They didn't want to talk about it.

They accepted Pierre's explanation that I was a distant relative from St Lo and took me for any other French youth. I'd caught the accent, sounded *Normand* and fitted in well. The visitors were agreed on a few things; they were glad the Americans had come to kick the Germans out, they wanted it over quickly, and they didn't want to get involved.

No one seemed that concerned about all the action. Gliders had landed half a mile away and been shot up, but nobody mentioned them. I pressed two of the visitors as I wanted to find out if we were in danger at the farm. They said there had been many parachute landings and a lot of shooting. American soldiers had been seen coming through Fresville overnight and in the morning. They'd shot any Germans stupid enough to get in their way. One said he'd cycled past a farmhouse in the hamlet: 2 Route de Val, that the paratroopers had attacked because the Germans were using it as billets. There was blood there and on the road by the church. The other described watching German soldiers a few hours later scuttling along the lanes and hedgerows in pursuit. Neither wanted to acknowledge what was going on. Like me, they couldn't take it in, couldn't describe it, so instead they continued to describe the familiar. Sometimes the familiar is a comfort.

While all this was going on the booming and noise continued unabated all day. Small arms fire raged over towards Sainte-Mère-Église, there was the sound of tanks firing and howitzers. Overhead Allied aircraft circled constantly. They attacked with bombs and strafing. There were so many planes and so much anti-aircraft fire that after a few hours it just became normal somehow.

Inside, Marie and I skinned and carved up beef portions and hung them in the cool room, a messy bloody job. Those pieces of beef needed to hang for at least a week. There was some pork left and I got that out ready for dinner.

That evening Pierre and I cooked and served gammon steaks with butter and garlic, roast apples potatoes beetroot and the ubiquitous calvados and cheese. Another absolute feast. However, at table we didn't say anything about the rescue at the river and I said nothing of the gliders. It was too frightening to think about. Instead at the evening meal of 6 June 1944 we talked about normal things. Would the usual Wednesday market day in Sainte-Mère-Église take place tomorrow? We thought not. The cheeses in the cold room and the newly butchered beef would have to keep until next week. Marie said she was worried about her friends in the nearby farms, but that was soon passed over. Pierre wondered if *La Poste* would still be able to bring letters from Henri.

Marie moved on to philosophy. She asked if I'd read Baudelaire and Rousseau and was impressed to hear that I had. We sat discussing how imaginative Descartes was and how all politicians should read Rousseau's *The State of War*. All the while wildly unimaginable things were happening beyond the windows. The guns, the bombing, the blasting and the smoke were all *outside*, they were not in our world inside the farmhouse. We couldn't allow it.

Marie was widely read. Pierre sat back listening and drinking his calvados admiring her. Smiling he told me, 'Most of the kids around here can't read and do you know why? Because Marie has taken all the books from the school shelves and library and has them in her room!'

Late on yet more giant bats arrived in the south pulling more gliders, this time huge ones, unimaginably huge and long. Again, the Germans threw thunderbolts at them; again, the gliders swooped and landed near Sainte-Mère-Église. Smoke had been rising up from there all day. It was just too overwhelming. We sat at the dinner table eating cheese and discussing French literature instead of trying to consider it all.

That day, the day that came to be known as D-Day, ended almost as it had begun, with explosions and the booming of war. I pulled myself into bed completely exhausted but again with a well-filled tummy.

The next day the routine continued: milking, shooting, taking the cows back, aircraft circling and bombing, breakfast, booming howitzers, cooking bread... It was quite surreal now that I think about it. War was literally in the fields all around, but it couldn't be rendered, couldn't be broken down, couldn't be accepted. I wasn't there, wasn't part of it. If I wasn't there then I couldn't be hit by a bullet, could I? We stayed indoors and I helped Marie make the butter. Then I progressed to the bread making whilst Pierre sorted and cleaned out the pigs. Even the black cat elected to stay inside.

By the end of the second day, I'd begun to realise that I was only thinking about one thing: staying alive. Don't get injured, keep indoors, stay out of trouble. There was no thought of mother, father or my mission.

I didn't know who was going to prevail here, American or German. Nobody knew and it was better if you didn't think about it. *Not knowing* was the best way. We didn't see any soldiers down our tiny lane that day and we didn't want to. We wanted them to be somewhere else.

My new family remained wonderful to me. When Pierre and I did the evening milking on the second day he said, 'You'll be sticking around after all then Paul? Marie will be delighted.' I said I was glad to have a roof over my head and have such amazing luck to have arrived with him and his daughter. He liked that and told me I had such charm that I must have read Voltaire. I said that I had, and that I liked some of what Voltaire had to say but not all of it. Pierre suggested I talk to Marie about that as she had read a pile of books so big that he was considering building another barn to keep them in. That made me laugh. His thoughts had centred on his daughter once again, just as they had in most conversations. He was a remarkable man and a loving father.

That evening the dinner was pork with a dash of *Candide*. Marie was of the opinion that Germans, in particular Hitler, ought to be made to read it. I said he wouldn't get it as he has no sense of irony. Pierre observed dryly that Hitler couldn't read it because his Nazi brown shirts had burned every copy. With a chuckle, Marie added that this was the best of all possible worlds, so we ought to be happy with it. Meanwhile, the whizzing whirling and blasting of the war Hitler started crept ever closer.

On Thursday 8th dawn was quite chilly. Marie and I went out to bring the cows back at the usual 5.30am but this time we got a nasty shock. German soldiers were walking up the lane, eight men four on each side about 10 metres apart some with tree branches in their helmets and full camouflage. It was a reconnaissance patrol.

These usually comprised 10 or 11 soldiers. I knew there would be a MG42 machine gun pair or trio somewhere nearby. I looked but couldn't see them. Where were they? The hedgerows were in the way.

German patrols always worked in combination and tended to cover each other as well as work around their machine gun. I knew this from watching them on exercise manoeuvres in Jersey. There were likely to be other such patrols nearby all controlled from a command post in the rear. There were also likely to be mortar teams and light or heavy artillery somewhere too.

The cows were between us and the patrol causing them to stop. A young soldier with a burgundy neck scarf was at the front of the column. He rested on his Mauser and regarded us and the cows. I looked at Marie. She glanced at me as if she'd seen it all a thousand times before. At the back, a couple of soldiers lit cigarettes. The smoke of those drifted over the smell of the cows towards my nostrils.

The young lead soldier with the scarf called in poor French, 'Americaner is here?'

'No, not here,' Marie called back.

A Feldwebel came up with two others. I could hear him telling them, *'Come, we'll search the farm.'* Oh shit.

I glanced anxiously at Marie, but she was calm. Germans in combat were likely to be nervous and by their standards unpredictable. I wondered if she knew. I whispered that they were going to search the farm. She nodded her head slowly.

Completely unconcerned the cows led on through the courtyard. Two soldiers one with a machine pistol went off to search the barn, sty and outbuildings.

The soldier with the scarf and the Feldwebel remained back in the yard. 'Let us in,' he demanded. Marie opened the door.

We were met by the homely smell of baking bread. Pierre turned from his rocking chair next to the fireplace and was startled to see two soldiers in the doorway. '*Ca va,*' he said. They glared at him. 'They're searching the house,' Marie explained. 'All right,' he said.

They soon found the American bag and rations. My heart missed a beat when the Feldwebel drew a pistol and asked in a poor French accent, 'What's this?'

'We found it in the yard. That bag hit the roof,' Pierre said. The soldier seemed satisfied. He gathered up the remaining contents, coffee, rations and chocolate, and slipped them into his cylindrical ammunition canister with a clang. He took an American *Lucky Strike* cigarette, slipped it between his lips, opened the hearth door and with a taper calmly lit up. Then he offered Pierre and me the pack. We declined. So far it had gone as well as could be expected under the circumstances. Pistol cocked, the Feldwebel went upstairs followed by the soldier with the scarf. They clumped about.

I'd stashed my stuff in the attic. Then I remembered the bike! Surely the two outside would find my stolen bike? I took a deep breath and told myself that if the worst happened, I could improvise: lie, or, if necessary, run.

As they thumped back down the stairs I was horrified to see the young soldier emerge with my precious Leica camera in his hand. In poor French he said, 'This is beautiful German camera, how do you get it?' Frowning, the Feldwebel stood next to him glowering.

'That's his dead mother's camera. What d'you want with it?' said Pierre interjecting. It was the first lie he'd told.

'It's too good for you! I'll take him back where he belongs,' said the young soldier with an arrogant air.

Pierre replied, 'You'd do that wouldn't you, steal a dead mother's gift to her son? How very brave of you.'

The Feldwebel, in his poor French pronounced gruffly, 'Perhaps you prefer us to test your barn to see how gut she burns?' Pierre went silent.

Then, with a smirk aimed in my direction, the private slipped my father's camera into his tunic pocket and there was nothing I could do about it. Bastard.

The soldiers went out and closed the door with a thwack. I heard their hobnails scraping on the flagstones and their chatter as they disappeared off into the lane. I had to sit down. I was distraught. They'd taken my father, now they'd taken his camera, Leica IIIa serial 186680.

'*Bastard Boche*,' I slumped and cried. That was so clumsy. Why in hell didn't I hide that camera? Then with tears dripping on the old carpet it came to me that they hadn't noticed the stolen bike. Oh my God! If they had found that it would have been so much worse.'

A corporal in the orchard, D-Day +2

'Marie brewed coffee and handed it to me with one of her smiles. It was almost enough.

'I didn't recognise any of those soldiers, but then we don't get many soldiers down our lane,' she said as I picked over breakfast. Then we returned to the milking. We were still trying to hang on to the rhythms of normality. An hour or two went by, but I'd lost another part of my father.

As we took the cows back, I could hear pings from near the little church in Fresville itself. That was the sound of German 8cm mortars. There had to be an observer squad in the church tower directing fire at something approaching. Those things can fire about 2km but are lethally accurate at 500-1000 metres or less. There was sniping and sporadic shooting and occasionally the buzz-sound of a MG42 machine gun, but the main noise of battle was everywhere to the east. I concluded that it would be wise for us to get out of the way and stay there.

Back at the farmhouse I went upstairs and got my binoculars from the attic to see what the mortars were shooting at. I looked out to the east and saw them: American soldiers. They were walking carefully along the edges of the fields taking cover from the hedgerows trying not to be spotted by the observers in the tower. They were headed directly for our farmhouse.

Shit.

Then, to my horror, Marie called out from the upstairs window on the other side, 'The *Boche* are coming back!' I ran to look and sure enough there was a MG42 machine gun squad and about 10 other soldiers assembling in the orchard where the paratrooper had landed two days ago. They were fixing their bayonets. It looked like they were going to occupy the farmhouse and set up a strongpoint. Oh Shit.

Marie called her father to come and look. He said, 'Get your rifle and I'll get the shotgun. Let's get out of here before we get blasted.'

But I had an idea. Once the Germans took possession of the house the advancing Americans would be annihilated, and the farm would most likely be destroyed in the battle. I couldn't allow that to happen. We knew the Americans were coming, the Germans didn't. If I could delay them or put them off there was a chance the Americans would reach the house first. In the kitchen I told father and daughter my plan. I said if I didn't do something they would probably lose everything. Pierre accepted it and said he would go and try to hurry the Allied soldiers along. I told him what to say in English. Marie kissed me on the cheek with a smile and solemn 'Bon chance brave boy.' Then she went back upstairs with her gun.

I ventured out into the lane in the late morning sun with the bees and flowers and across the road to the orchard where the Germans were tooling up. Most of them were young like me.

Brazenly, I approached the squad leader who I noted from his MP40 machine pistol. 'Good morning. Thank God I found you!' The look of astonishment on his face.

'Who the hell are you, and where's your unit?' he exclaimed.

With a deliberately difficult to follow thick Alsatian accent, I waved my arm towards Sainte-Mère-Église and explained that the Americans had captured me 'over there.' I had 'tossed my dog tag and papers, stolen some clothes and escaped.' I continued:

'I've come to warn you that I just watched the Americans set up an ambush in that farm.' I pointed. 'Don't go in there, you'll be annihilated!' I rolled the 'r' of *'vernichtet'* (annihilated) for emphasis.

'Thank God you told us boy!' said the dusty soldier. 'Now, you fall in with us. What's your name?'

'Paul von Bonn sir. Yours sir?'

'I am Bauer. Very good. We have no weapon for you so join the machine gun as number three.' He ordered another soldier forward who came up and plonked the spare barrel bag and ammo tins on the ground with a clunk. Shit, I hadn't thought of that. I didn't even think my plan would work and now here I was ordered into his MG42 team.

He gave the order: *'Schützenkette, links-rechts'*, and the soldiers walked fanning out either side of the machine gun towards the hedgerow at the back of the orchard. It was a tactic I'd seen on manoeuvres in Jersey plenty of times. Now *they* were setting an ambush. The cows ran, but I hesitated. 'Von Bonn, fall in, MG3!' ordered Bauer.

A corporal with a Mauser and fixed bayonet came back. Pointing, Bauer told him to: 'sort out that Alsatian,' then walked off following his men.

The corporal moved up, 'What's wrong with you? Step lively and follow orders. Come on – let's make dust.'

I hesitated. I didn't know what to do.

He growled, 'We are in the middle of a battle, follow orders damn you!'

Over the corporal's shoulder, I watched Bauer and the machine gun team disappearing towards the hedge, but my eyes had glazed over. I wasn't going to follow them. I *couldn't* follow them. I froze.

'FOLLOW ORDERS BOY!' shouted the corporal.

He raised his bayonetted weapon, clicked off the safety, and prodded it into my chest: 'KOMM **SOFORT!**' (come immediately)

I can't explain the fear. I was sure that if I ran he would shoot me and if I stood he would bayonet me.

From away in the bushes, Bauer called out to come.

The corporal looked at me. 'Alright, stay here and die if you wish,' he sneered, and with that he flicked the safety on, lowered his weapon, picked up the ammo tins and barrel and took off towards his squad.

I tore to the house and up the stairs and there was Marie crouching with her gun braced at the window ready to shoot. Across the orchard I watched the corporal running, looking back to see if I was following.

Marie glanced at me but said nothing. I was breathless, panting. We were both shaking as I hugged her tightly. She smiled her wonderful smile, 'You are so brave,' she said quietly, tears in her eyes. But something was different.

There was a noise downstairs. It was Pierre with the Americans. I ran down and explained as best I could to another lieutenant what happened and where the Germans were setting up an ambush in the orchard. He was incredulous that I was there and speaking clear English. He ordered his men to take up positions in and around the farm behind the walls of the courtyard.

I was half an inch from being either bayonetted or shot, but I didn't dwell on it.

An uneasy *impasse* controlled the farm that day. It was a rule of war that if you opened fire you would give your position away. Accordingly, the Germans didn't attack, and the Americans didn't attack. As dusk fell nothing much changed. The battle, the sporadic shooting, mortaring, blasting, planes flying over, continued all around, but we were in another place, like in a bubble.

The front line ran along the lane just in front of the farmhouse, but there was no further action.

The Americans stayed in and around the farm. Sentries were posted and the soldiers found places to sleep including in the barn and on the sofa. Pierre made them welcome with calvados cheese ham and bread and they returned the compliment with chocolate and coffee. Smiling and wearing her American hat, Marie was holding court, chatting in the most charming and delightful way, and I translated. She wasn't quite the same towards me though.

We were together and safe, and the farm was untouched, at least for the moment. The American paratroopers declared, 'Goebbels said he wanted

Total War, now we've brought it to France for him!' My response was to talk and drink a lot of apple brandy.

One conversation was with another young paratrooper, a private, who, unlike his buddies, said he had respect for the German people. He was a New Yorker of German heritage who had seen and admired the Zeppelin airship *Hindenburg* mooring in New Jersey in 1936. It started when he asked me where I was from, and I somewhat drunkenly said Jersey. He thought I meant New Jersey, which couldn't possibly be true. Calvados can have that effect. I wanted to tell Marie and him something about the *Hindenburg*, but I fell asleep where I sat. Considering the events of that day it was a good thing there was plenty of brandy on offer. Another memorable evening.

In the night Marie came and put a woolly quilt over me.

I wasn't aware of anything else until sunrise. I woke and panicked as I realised the cows hadn't been to milking last night and this was early June. I quickly dressed and saw Marie's door was open, and her room empty. I went downstairs and she wasn't there. The soldiers were up and about assembling in the courtyard chattering and smoking.

I looked across to the orchard. There was Marie with her smile. She was in the open gateway bringing out the cows, but something was different.

The Germans had withdrawn overnight. I told them not to go near the farmhouse and they hadn't. I had bluffed them.

4. Aftermath

Paul said that until that moment he'd never told anyone about Marie or anything that happened at the farmhouse.

He was speaking from another place when he honestly asked me, 'When does youth die? When does innocence die?' I said I didn't know.

Continuing, he told me:

'When to the sessions of sweet silent thought
I summon up remembrance of things past,
I sigh the lack of many a thing I sought,
And with old woes new wail my dear time's waste:
Then can I drown an eye, unus'd to flow,
For precious friends hid in death's dateless night,
And weep afresh love's long since cancell'd woe,
And moan the expense of many a vanish'd sight:
Then can I grieve at grievances foregone,
And heavily from woe to woe tell o'er
The sad account of fore-bemoaned moan,
Which I new pay as if not paid before.
But if the while I think on thee, dear friend,
All losses are restor'd and sorrows end.'

- **William Shakespeare. Sonnet 30**

He frequently used poetry, music, metaphor or allusion to express things that he otherwise wouldn't or couldn't. This wasn't deception, it was self-protection. I didn't know how to respond to his recital which spoke of loss, pain and regret. As with many things he'd gone over the events at the farm again and again, always rehearsing but never releasing his feelings. Now it was out there, and I had been the audience. He was right, it was a burden, but he had finally started to share it.

Perhaps he loved Marie? Perhaps he never realised? Perhaps he did. Did she love him? Whatever either of them felt, he let her go. He told her he had to leave the farm. He'd lived his whole life with this knowledge.

The sonnet expressed something for him, but it offered me something too. What happened to my mother? She never told me she was leaving. Did she love me? Could she not stay? There were questions now where there had never been any before. Did my mother end up like Paul, in circularity and regret? I didn't know.

He said, 'After the incident with the corporal Marie told me she hated the Germans even more. She had her gun trained on him and could easily have pulled the trigger, but she didn't. It troubled her deeply. After a couple of days, she began using expressions like, *before you came*, and *it's so difficult now*, and *I could have killed that man*. Something was wrong. I didn't know what it was then, but I do now.

I began to wish I hadn't entered her life, that I hadn't become her friend and exposed her to that terrible choice. Then there was *my* choice. I knew that she didn't want me to leave. Perhaps I should have stayed, but I didn't, I left her.' He turned away.

This was behind his telling of the sonnet but at first I didn't see it. I thought that he finally trusted and confided in me, in the same way that he trusted Marie. I was wrong.

After a week on lates, he asked, 'How did you do it Katie?'

'Do what?'

'How did you become so brilliant when circumstances were against you?'

'Who says I've become brilliant?' It was another of his ploys. Where was this one going?

'I'm saying it.'

'I'm not brilliant *yet!*' I said in German with a smile.

'You are brilliant at doing what you do: listening.'

'It's all in a good cause,' I said with a smirk.

He lowered his voice and glanced away. 'That's one of my mother's sayings, but it won't work. You shouldn't have come back, and I shouldn't have started talking. You need to get away from me. I'm bad news. I break everything I touch.'

The moment I heard that I thought it was one of his jokes, then I immediately realised it wasn't. I had to respond:

'What are you talking about now?'

He turned and told me quietly, *'People around me end up getting destroyed.'*

I should have worked out something was coming.

'You won't destroy me.'

'I had to get away from Marie. I should've done it sooner. If you won't leave, then perhaps I should.'

That hurt, but he didn't stop.

'I upset Marie by being there. The best thing for me to do is get away from here before the same thing happens to you. I'll make the arrangements. It's time I went home.'

Bastard. I snapped. In German I told him firmly:

'You'll do no such thing Paul von Bonn. You will stay here with me. You will not walk out on us, I forbid it. You will stay here, and *you will* tell your story. You've spent far too long imagining your influence. Don't flatter yourself. You don't know what Marie was thinking, how could you? And another thing, don't flatter yourself that you will destroy me. You won't. It'll take a lot more than you to destroy me I assure you.'

That shut him up. Just to make sure, I continued in English, 'And you will not run away. You won't because you are strong. As well as that, we haven't finished, not by a long shot.' He glared at me, said nothing, stood then took himself off to bed.

I half expected him to not be there the next day, he was well capable of that. So, I took note when I came back on the evening shift and saw the light was on in his room. But he didn't come out, and he kept not coming out. That went on for four nights.

I had days off to change shift. These were difficult. Paul was on my mind constantly. When I talked to my nurse sister Amy about him, she shrugged her shoulders and said, 'He just sounds like a miserable old git. I work around people like that all day long. Surely you've got better things to do with your life than worry about him!' She was right. But now it was personal. His talk of 'destroying' me made it personal and it upset me.

I called in sick on my slated first day back on afternoons and felt bad about doing that. Before the end of the shift, I called in again and asked to speak to the supervisor. It was Lawrence.

'What's wrong Katie? You've never had a day sick?'

'It's you-know-who.'

'Thought so.'

'He's pissing me off, and I don't know what to do.'

'Thank you for telling me. You are brave for taking him on and we promised to support you. How can I help?'

'I don't know. All I know is that I'm not going to give in. I'm not going to give him the satisfaction.'

'Alright. Come in tomorrow. I'll be on duty. If he tries any of his antics I'll be with you.'

'But that's the whole thing: he won't. He'll just make an artform of avoiding me.'

'If that's his game, play it. Come in as usual, do your job, be your normal self and let him see that you won't be intimidated. I'll mind your back. He's walled up inside himself and he doesn't want to come out.'

'I think you're right; he's built a wall. I'm not scared of losing the job. I've walked out once already. I'm not scared of him either, and he knows it.'

'Ok then, I'll see you at briefing tomorrow.'

I had a strategy now, and management backing.

I slept uneasily. My mind wandered to my mother. Did she leave because she thought she would destroy something: me, my sister? Did she build a wall? To keep something out, or keep something in? I didn't know.

The next day I went in as normal. He ignored me, and the next, and the next. There was no opportunity to take the fight to him. Instead, I finished my Easter 2019 slot at the home and went back to Manchester still being blanked. Such a piece of work.

5. Carentan

I finished the second semester 2019 at Manchester concentrating on my third-year exams. I didn't send a birthday card or give Paul Bunn a second thought, I wasn't going to get distracted. Neither was I going to worry about some 92-year-old who had delusions about destroying me. Sure, something might, but not him. I restarted at the Stanley on Monday, 17 June. As far as I was concerned he could do his worst. I still needed the money for my studies, and he wasn't going to stop me.

Lawrence was on shift that first morning and I was pleased to see him. 'How's he been?' I asked.

'Normal,' he said. 'Nothing has happened. No explosions, nothing. He's been normal, coming out on trips, going around Kew, walking along the river, playing piano, and mostly thrashing people at chess.'

For a moment I thought I might be more important than that but then I realised this was the sort of hubris he indulged in, and I wasn't going to lower myself. Instead, I went back to work reflecting on Lawrence's word: *mostly*.

He ignored me on that first day, and the next. He may have thought he was needling me, but he wasn't. Two could play at that game.

On the third day I watched him play chess with Brian, a new guest. Brian beat him in 39 moves in a superb match where Paul played White. The old man was typically aggressive direct and uncompromising, but still lost.

Brian had joined soon after I left in April. He was a military man: a Falklands War veteran and had been a lieutenant in that conflict. He left the army as a major and had been working in America in engineering. He was 68 and by no means old. He had a bullet wound in his right leg and was a type 2 diabetic with a range of medical issues. He had been to Oxford University and the officer training school at Sandhurst. As soon as I clapped eyes on how he and Paul were together I sensed the 92-year-old had finally met his match. Word was that he'd beaten Paul in every game.

The old man completely ignored me, but I liked this new chap Brian who was very relaxed. He had great people skills. Nothing seemed to faze him. He was charming beyond anything reasonable. Mel said he was a gifted negotiator who could talk the hind legs off a donkey then sell them back to the donkey at a profit!

Meanwhile, I was in a different place with Paul. Once again I found myself looking from afar, watching him in Brian's company, and it was revelatory.

Brian had seen plenty of action, not just in the Falklands, but in Northern Ireland too. He wasn't giving it away though. I watched Paul ask him questions, but Brian didn't want to talk about it. Mel and Lawrence noticed as well. At a handover Lawrence told me, 'Keep watching and listening. It's going to get interesting now.' Mel added, 'Brian is a godsend, but we will need to support him. Sooner or later Paul will take a swipe at someone for Brian's benefit, just like he has for everyone else around here.' I knew she was right.

After about ten days of his blanking, I was busy on an afternoon shift. It was raining. In the sunroom Paul was once again on the receiving end from Major Brian, down two pawns playing White after 19 moves. Brian was killing him. It was bloody awesome, but the old man kept fighting and would not resign and eventually the army man had him checkmate.

Then he turned on me.

'What are you looking at? I suppose you're still learning though, aren't you Katie?' Of all the many discourteous and disrespectful things he'd said to me that was by far the worst.

'Steady on Paul, it's just a game,' Brian said looking up.

'Not to *her*. She's watching you so that she can see how to beat you. She's just biding her time,' the old man said wagging an accusing finger.

'And what's wrong with that? It's just a game. If I beat her then fine, if she beats me then fine. It's just a game.' It was a very diplomatic thing to say, but Paul wasn't having any of it.

'Not to her Brian. I'm telling you, watch her. She'll get into your head.'

I kept silent and expressionless. Brian regarded Paul casually but then stood up and in a telling way said, 'It's time for a walk. Anyone want to come?' Given that it was pouring with rain outside Paul had clearly irritated Brian intensely and he'd had enough. He pushed back his chair and off he went. Now was my chance.

'Game of chess?' I asked. He said nothing, so I said, 'I'll take that as a "yes" then,' and set up the pieces forcefully. To let him stew a bit I went off and made a pot of tea. Bringing it back and placing it firmly on the table I told him he was playing White and that I would *play to win*. He said nothing and just stared at me sullenly.

We played the game in silence, very unusual for Paul as he always talked. I won in 41 moves. It was the first time I'd managed to defeat him. He wouldn't resign though; he played the game even though it was hopeless after move 36. The tea went cold and undrunk and afterwards he got up and disappeared off to his room muttering something rude in German under his breath. What a piece of work.

I had a couple of days off, swapped shifts, then started on mornings. To my surprise he came and found me as I walked out of a briefing. 'Can we talk Katie?' he asked.

'No, I don't think so Paul. I've got things to do.'

'I need to explain, explain about us.'

'Really? I thought you'd called time on *us*. You told me you were going home, but you still seem to be here. Is that an accident?' I said hastily.

'Nicely put, well said,' he observed dryly, looking me in the eye. I returned his look.

'You know how busy mornings are. If you've got something to say then find a time that suits me rather than you.' I sighed and walked away. I thought about something he'd told me a year ago about always playing to win. Now I was playing to win. On that July morning two years ago that's where I was.

Now I blanked him. I did that successfully for four days.

It couldn't last of course. I swapped back to afternoons and one evening heard the sound of Mozart coming from the piano. That was Paul, couldn't be anyone else. In I went. He always struggled with page turning as with that gammy right index finger he usually fumbled. It was *Sonata no. 2 in F Major*, second movement, Adagio. I came in just in time to turn the page and he was able to go through it unbroken. He played beautifully. At the end, his small audience clapped. Brian was there too. Paul stood and told them, 'I couldn't have done it without Katie.' He turned to me, and that wonderful smile melted my heart.

Paul never apologised for his behaviour towards me, but then I never expected him to.

The next day I found myself sitting in conversation with him and Brian in the sunroom over a pot of tea. They definitely had a lot in common. He hadn't forgotten what Paul had said about me. I could tell Brian was puzzled by the sudden change in Paul's attitude. I noticed him. By now I was a far better watcher of people than I had been a year previously. He was right: I was still learning.

In conversation with Brian, turning to me Paul said, 'Katie here has exceptional talents. She is wonderfully gifted, works very hard and is brilliant at everything she does. She is very wise.' The old man certainly knew how to flatter me, but I knew by now that could change before the end of the sentence.

All in all, this mystified Brian, but it was the beginning of yet another one of Paul's games...

Just when I thought there wouldn't be any more surprises, I noticed a fabric Waitrose bag by Paul's chair and a large tatty brown folder on the table. Then he began talking about 1944 again. I couldn't believe my ears when, as if Brian had been present throughout the whole of the story so far, the old man began describing his departure from Marie and her father in Fresville. He started in without any introductions:

'The fighting moved away from the farm. My hand felt better, so after two days I cycled out to get information and encountered Americans marching columns of captured soldiers southwards. They weren't all German, some spoke another language: Georgian, but they spoke Russian too.'

I glanced at Brian. The look on his face was indescribable. He supped his tea and attended to the old man's account carefully.

'Cycling on the road south towards Sainte-Mère-Église I passed an American taking photos of the surrendered soldiers with a shiny little camera and a brown leather case hanging off it. I circled back to chat. He was amazed when I spoke clear English to him, but I was stunned when I noticed the camera: my camera! When I told him it was my father's he asked, 'Alright son, what's the serial number?' I was easily able to tell him Leica IIIa serial 186680, with a little Paris stamp on the bottom edge. He took the case off and sure enough there was the Paris stamp. I went on to describe the soldier who took it from me and the circumstances. 'Well, I guess it's yours and I ought to give it back,' he said handing it to me. I was overjoyed! There were tears in my eyes. I embraced the soldier and blessed him. I pushed my bike as we walked along with the prisoners, and we talked:

'Son, I'm glad you have your father's camera back. The guy I took it from won't be going home.'

'The private with a burgundy neck scarf?'

'That's the guy. He's in a ditch about two miles up that way.' He pointed up the road northwards and offered me a cigarette which I declined. He lit up, puffed the smoke, and turned his head away. There was no need to ask any more questions.'

'You're talking about Normandy 1944!' Brian gasped.

'Yes,' said the old man with a wink and a grin.

Brian glanced at me. I tried to give the appearance of someone who was surprised, but I wasn't, and he saw straight through it.

'I was thrilled with the camera. He'd only taken eight shots with it. I asked if it was possible to get to Carentan and on to Caen. He said there was a battle going on at Carentan and there was no chance of getting through. He talked about landing beaches too. I cycled up the road to see if I could find the young German and came to some tanks. When I stopped to ask what they were the Americans called them 'Shermans.' They let me climb up to have a look. That's when I noticed him in the ditch. He was still clutching his scarf. I took that scarf.'

From the brown folder Paul produced a graphic photograph of the soldier lying dead. Then he fetched out the 75-year-old burgundy scarf from the bag and placed it on the table. It was one of his classic ploys: he'd clearly staged the whole event to lead to this. Whatever game it was that he was playing, it had an impact on Brian who was visibly shaken. This was the first time I'd seen him like that. He was normally imperturbable. I noticed him, but I especially noticed Paul and the look on his face. 'I didn't take that photo,' he added. He had a mischievous self-satisfied smirk about him. I'd seen that face before.

'I cycled back to the farm and with boundless joy presented my camera. But Marie remained remote. It was hard to believe she was the same person who'd fixed my dislocated finger just a few days ago. She had lost the light in those lovely brown eyes.'

I looked at Brian. He had no idea who Marie was or of the events at the farmhouse. It still seems incredible to me that Paul just sat there and carried on his story. Who knew what his reasoning was? What was he up to with that scarf and photo? It only became clear later.

'A week or so after the incident in the orchard I prepared to leave Marie and her father and try to get to Rouen and my Uncle Claude. I helped with the milking, ate as big a breakfast as I could eat and then said my goodbyes.

Marie said she didn't want me to go but knew I had to. She asked me to write to her and I said I would. Her father embraced me tightly, thanked me generously and gave me some money.

Marie and I embraced, and we silently held our thoughts. As I cycled away in the morning sunshine I heard her call: 'Bon chance mon amour!' I glanced back and saw her lovely smile that one last time.'

He looked down, tears welling in his eyes. The memory of Marie's face was a vision he'd recalled again and again.

Nevertheless, the old man pressed on with his story:
'Sainte-Mère-Église was heavily damaged and the road to Carentan was littered with the debris of vehicles and wrecked buildings. Temporary bridges had been built to replace destroyed ones. There were little cars the Americans called 'Jeeps' whizzing around. Other soldiers were lying in the sun exhausted. There were Shermans rumbling along and big guns. Aircraft flew overhead. Everywhere local people were trying to carry on just as if nothing had happened, even though there had been an apocalypse. I cycled along and was taken simply as a passing French youth. Nobody stopped or challenged me.

There was a cloud of smoke over Carentan. The town was utterly smashed. I carried on but it was difficult to ride as there was not one undamaged building and bricks and blocks filled the road. A group of soldiers stopped me and demanded to know where I was going. I replied in French and told them I was worried about my grandmother in Bayeux and that they had to let me go to see if she was alright. It was a perfect lie, and they let me through.

I walked and lifted my bike through the charred and shattered remains. Every now and again I ventured past American soldiers sitting smoking and chatting in the morning sun. There were demolition teams clearing the unstable buildings and distraught women standing by as they watched the bodies of their loved ones being pulled from the rubble.

I got challenged twice more and both times I told the same story about my 'relative in Bayeux,' and it worked.

It was impossible to believe that just a week earlier Carentan had been some peaceful small provincial town. Now it was a heap of smouldering ruins.

The air reeked of the stench of flesh and hummed to the buzzing of flies, and I walked trying to avoid the puddles of dried blood. These sights and smells always accompanied a dead horse or other animal. None of it bothered me, it was like I was in a trance and wasn't there. I told myself I was just another local carrying on as if nothing had happened. It was good to have Carentan behind me.' With that he produced another graphic photo, this time of a smashed German tank.

Brian glanced at it. I sensed that he wasn't shocked in the way that I would once have been. He was shocked in another way. Regarding Paul he asked, 'Why have you shown me this?'

'Because you served in the Falklands, and I thought you'd understand.'

Brian got up promptly, shook his head and without saying anything walked away. There were many times when I despaired of Paul Bunn. This was just another. He was exasperating.

'Why did you do that?' I asked taking a tone.

'I don't know,' he said. Possibly a genuine answer, it was hard to tell. Whatever, it might have been a stunt to show me what he could do if he felt like it. Such a piece of work.

'Well, it might be a better idea if you started to think about it Paul, because the way you're carrying on you're going to piss people off so much that they will never talk to you again.'

'Why are you still here then?' he asked.

'Because you are,' I told him firmly.

6. West Middlesex

I left the old man to stew in his own juice, or at least that's what I thought, and went back to my duties. He went back to not talking to me again.

By early July 2019 I was on nights. I quite liked nights. I always reckoned these shifts were good for the soul, like a cycle hack around the roads between Manchester and Sheffield, you could spend time inside yourself.

Then there was a shock.

It was in the morning right at the end of my block of nights. I saw Paul come out of his room and go towards the sunroom which was his daily habit. He ignored me. Then I heard a tremendous crash of chairs and tables. I ran to find him in a heap on the floor with blood coming from a gash on his head.

He was woozy and disorientated. He stared up, and pupils dilating, told me, 'There was only one bullet left. There should have been six.' I didn't know what that meant.

On my house phone, I called Lawrence who came immediately, and he called the doctor. Helping him into a chair, Paul wanted to sleep but Lawrence wouldn't let him. The doctor came in 15 minutes.

We put him in a wheelchair and moved him to the medical room. He hated wheelchairs but didn't complain. He was nodding, his head rolling.

An ambulance came and I went with him. A paramedic put him on oxygen, but she assured me it was just a precaution.

I was beside myself. How could this happen? It took a while to get the answer.

We were taken to West Middlesex. My sister worked there and was on duty. I called her and she came over. She looked very smart in her light blue uniform, her blonde wavy hair in a tight bun under her little cap.

The old man was asleep in a bed in a cubicle. I thanked Amy for coming. It was good to see her, and I explained what happened. 'So, this is him then, your Paul?' she quizzed, 'looks fairly harmless to me.'

My big sister always had a dry sense of humour.

I went off to get coffee then we sat by his bed. Rolling over and glimpsing Amy the old man quietly muttered, *'Lisa, bist du das?'*

'What did he say sis?' Amy asked.

'I think he said: 'Lisa, is that you?'

'Who's Lisa?'

'I don't know.'

Now as he looked at Amy his eyes widened, and he told her earnestly, *'Geh nicht nach Spandau, Lisa.'*

'Don't go to Spandau Lisa,' I whispered.

'What does that mean?'

Before I could think he screamed **'Geh nicht!'** so loudly we nearly fell off our chairs. Then he passed out.

Nurses came quickly pulled the curtains and asked us what we did. 'Nothing,' we replied as they tended to him.

We waited and a doctor came. There was a flurry. Amy had to go back to work. 'Call me later sis,' she said.

The old man was ok. He'd fallen back to sleep. The doctor asked me lots of questions and pronounced that he was admitting Paul immediately with a suspected urinary tract infection and sepsis. 'He's with us now, we'll look after him and he'll be alright.'

I called the Stanley mid-morning to update them, then sat by his bed until 12pm. He slept. I dozed off too. I woke and realised I'd been on shift for 15 hours. I needed to go home. I stood and got my stuff.

Just as I turned to go I heard his familiar voice in quiet Alsatian-German. 'You're still here. It doesn't look like I'm going to be able to get rid of you.' Then we spoke in German:

'No, I'm afraid you're stuck with me Paul von Bonn,' I replied with a smile.

'Did you see Lisa? She was here a minute ago,' he hesitated. I held his hand. 'No dear.'

'Are you going to leave me too?' he whispered meekly.

'No. I told you I wouldn't leave, and I won't.' He had fallen asleep again. I was so relieved that he was alright.

A nurse asked me what he said. I replied, 'He was just saying hello.'

He was kept in, and he was in a real state. I visited as often as I could. He kept saying very odd things. Mostly he was asleep, but sometimes he woke up drowsily muttering phrases in several languages, including what I thought was Russian. Once he sat up and looking down on the floor beside his bed told me earnestly in French: *'He doesn't feel good about being in the SS now.'* Another time he growled at two imaginary Germans: *'Very good. Now you two idiots lie there and enjoy the sun quietly.'* Another time he sat up promptly from sleep, stared and in German told me solemnly: 'I finally understand who you are and why you are here.' It was incomprehensible, but I didn't ask any questions.

They kept the old man in hospital. He did have sepsis. They put him on a drip and antibiotics. He was very confused. Several times he screamed in French and German: *'The bombers are coming,'* and that we must *'get in the shelter!'* He told me he was afraid of sleeping. Amy said he had a condition called 'Delirium' that often went with those infections in old people. It caused hallucinations, mood-swings, and disassociation. I saw that. I also noticed old deep scars in his back.

At the Stanley, an urgent review of care took place surrounding Paul's condition. It wasn't anyone's fault, it was him. He'd pushed me away and I wasn't able to monitor him in my usual manner. In conversation it turned out that he'd been mean and evasive towards Sarah and Mel as well. They hadn't said anything as they thought it would make them look bad.

It was time for honesty all round. Lawrence joined me visiting on the eighth day. He came quickly to the point:

'Paul, it's time for us to re-assess where we are. It's time for some honesty and a little more co-operation from you.'

I thought the old man would explode, but he didn't. 'Yes young man. It's time.'

For a moment I wondered who it was, this was most unlike him.

'Good. We would like you to co-operate with the people here so that we can form a full picture of your care needs. Do you agree?'

'Yes Lawrence.'

That was a definite result. The question was: was this the illness talking? Would he actually do what he said, or was this merely another one of his stunts? Only time would tell. I also had to accept that I'd been mean to him, trying to pay him back for being horrible to me. That had to change.

Meanwhile, I was paid overtime to visit him every day. Paul could easily afford to go to a private hospital, but he wanted to stay at West Mid' so that my sister and I could visit. This was perfect because once again I was able to listen and give him my full attention. The three of us chatted away merrily. He was very flattering and said it was marvellous that there were two Campbells in his life now.

'Your mother must be so proud of you both,' he gestured, smiling.

I glanced at Amy. She turned, bit her lip looked at me and muttered,

'Don't say anything sis.'

****

On the last day in hospital Paul described how once he passed through Carentan he headed straight for the north coast. This was where he and his father and mother had cycled four years earlier.

He was stunned when he arrived at Vierville. 'A mighty place that was!' he said. The Americans had built a massive temporary harbour there called Mulberry. He had never seen so many ships. 'There were more ships than water, a fantastic sight. My mother would have called it *incroyable!*'

The weather was bad when he rolled down the hill into the remains of the little village. The Americans took him as a local and ignored him. He was aiming for the place where he stayed in 1940, but it wasn't there. The Germans had bulldozed it and built a concrete bunker on the site.

An apocalyptic battle had raged there too. There were hundreds of lorries and tanks and thousands of soldiers. He headed inland passing more troops and equipment and found a barn to overnight in. There were plenty of refugees and Paul looked just like any other.

The next day dawned, and the weather was appalling. A huge storm was thrashing the harbour constructions. It wasn't smart to be so near the coast, so he rode inland towards Bayeux where he encountered the British army for the first time. When he got challenged he again presented as a local youth speaking the local dialect. He carried that off quite easily, but when he mentioned he was heading for Caen he was told he had no chance as the Germans were still there.

At the end of the old man's time in hospital he had clinical assessment visits, and a psychiatric therapist came. There was a range of informal questions. This was when Paul told her of how he'd stopped for three nights in Bayeux Cathedral in June 1944. I sat and listened:

The weather was so bad and cycling so unpleasant and difficult that he decided to stay over. The town was almost undamaged, the invasion seeming to have passed it by. He made his way to the cathedral, a traditional place of safety where he knew he could rest over for a day or two until the storm blew through.

The cathedral entrance was through a small door, large enough for one person at a time to enter or leave. This door was cut from a great oak. Unlike *Notre Dame de Strasbourg*, it was very dark inside, and he only slowly got accustomed to the light. After a while he noticed a few candles glowing, spaced at regular intervals, breaking into the awful darkness. He could just make out the figures of a dozen or so servicemen standing around in this massive empty space. He said it was too dark to see the fine architecture.

Just inside the entrance was a crude block of stone. On top of that was a box of unused candles beside an open tin with a few coins inside. There were some lighted candles on this makeshift altar. Paul took and lit a candle and placed some of Pierre's money in the tin. As he looked in the dim light he saw that the place had been stripped of all furnishings. There was no high altar, no candlesticks, no pews, no pulpit, nothing. The stained-glass windows were boarded up. Everything had been removed to a safe place.

Suddenly a blinding bright light shone in the doorway and a young French boy was silhouetted there for a moment. He came inside closing the door behind him, and hesitated there at the threshold, nervous, like some wild animal about to take off. The lad was only a few feet from where Paul stood. He was aged about 10, looked unkempt and seemed as if he'd been sleeping rough.

He slowly moved towards Paul, who gave him an encouraging smile which seemed to relax him a little. Then he came and stood beside the makeshift altar, took two or three centimes from his pocket, placed them carefully in the tin and took a candle. He lit it from the flame of another, placed it in position on the altar, put his hands together, closed his eyes and prayed. Paul stood there for many minutes next to him. Then the boy made a movement, stood back, turned and smiled, walked to the door, turned once more, waved his hand as a farewell, and was gone.

In his replies to the specialist, it was clear that the young boy in the cathedral wasn't gone, not from Paul's mind. Down through the years the boy had caused the old man to ask questions without ever knowing the answers. Who was he? Had he heard his guardian angel? Had his mother sent him to pray for his brothers and sisters? Had he come to pray for his father, taken away to a camp, or something much worse? Was he an orphan without a home? What would become of him? Did this boy remind Paul of himself? So many questions and there would never be any resolution.

The specialist made lots of notes and then went away.

The day after the therapist visit Paul continued his story:

The weather on the morning of Thursday 22nd was much better, so he set off along the N-13 road towards Caen. He didn't get far. After a few kilometres at a place called Saint-Leger, he was stopped by British soldiers operating out of a little open-topped tank which he described as a 'Universal Carrier.' He again feigned being a French youth trying to 'get home to Caen,' but this time it didn't work. They told him that town was in enemy hands and shooed him away. 'It's a bloody battlefield! Anyone with any sense would have evacuated by now.' This was a problem.

He heard the noise of battle, saw aircraft circling and the smoke and dust of the front-line swirling around the fields a few miles to the south. He didn't want to run into that again. This meant he had to head north.

That area of Normandy had many memories for Paul. In spring 1940, he and his parents had caught the train from Paris to Amiens with their bikes. They wanted to show Paul the place where they had first met in 1918. They stayed a few days in an Amiens hotel and paid their respects with woven poppies at the cemeteries where some of Christopher's pilot friends were buried. Helene placed poppies at the graves of French soldiers she tended but could not save. Then they cycled on to Rouen and stayed with his Uncle Claude for two weeks. He knew he would always be welcome in Rouen.

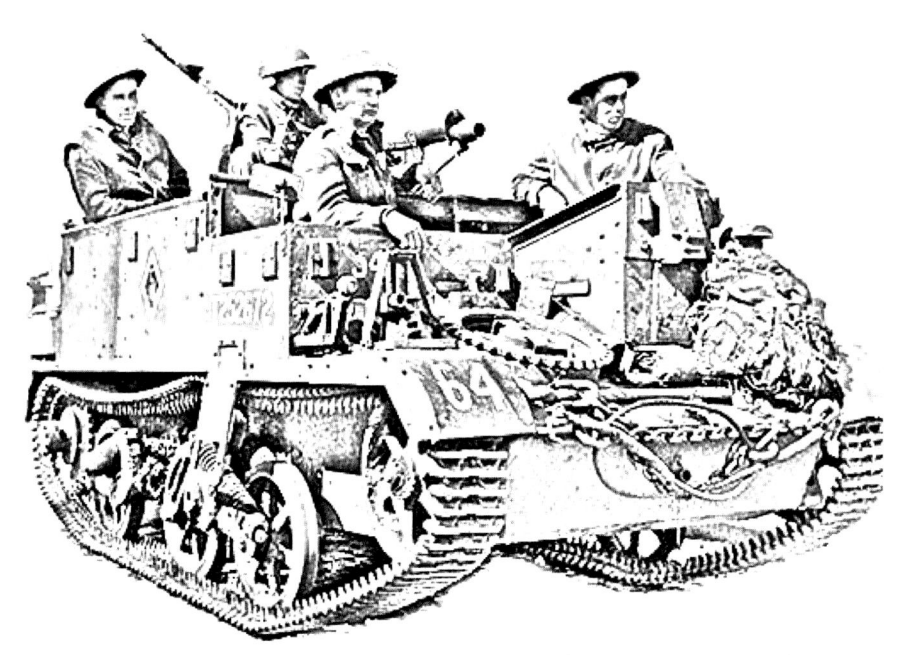

From there, the family had taken a leisurely progress towards Jersey cycling first to Honfleur. He described that little medieval town as 'gorgeous, unchanged in hundreds of years.' They continued along the coast stopping in sea-side resorts until they reached two bridges north of Caen over the River Orne and the ship canal. They crossed those then headed south-west to explore the 'wonderful medieval city and cathedral' for three days.

He knew I cycled and explained that Caen was famous for being a big venue in *Le Tour de France* cycle race and was a huge mecca for cyclists from Paris. As he was telling me this, I formed the distinct impression that he was deliberately digressing. I knew him well enough by now to understand that there was always a reason for that.

I asked what he'd meant when he talked about bullets the other day and about people in different languages. He looked at me quizzically, said he was tired and asked if we could stop. He was in hospital suffering from sepsis taking heavy antibiotics. I immediately agreed and he fell asleep in front of my eyes.

The hospital was not prepared to discharge him until they had met and briefed the care team from Stanley. On the morning, Paul was ready and dressed and a meeting held in a private anteroom.

It was agreed that Paul was physically in particularly good shape for his age due to his very fit earlier life. He had recovered well. Step-by-step, it was explained that Paul's issues were not physical, rather, they were mental and emotional. He listened impassively. They said his demonstrated behaviours were associated with 'a complex inter-related architecture of stresses, repressed memories and emotions,' and, 'Paul presents as exhibiting many of the symptoms of what today we call, Post Traumatic Stress Disorder, or PTSD.'

This seemed incredible to the assembled Stanley team. But it wasn't such a shock to me.

Mel asked how Paul could have PTSD? Surely that was impossible? No. The clinicians were agreed that the indicators were unmistakable, and that Paul should be treated according to the diagnosis. He should receive the support of a psychiatric nurse on a regular basis and those who work closely with him should receive additional training. That meant me. Details would follow. Then we went back to the Stanley in an Uber.

Paul's response was absolutely typical. The next day he went into London in a cab without telling anyone. It was left to me to 'have a word.' I didn't bother.

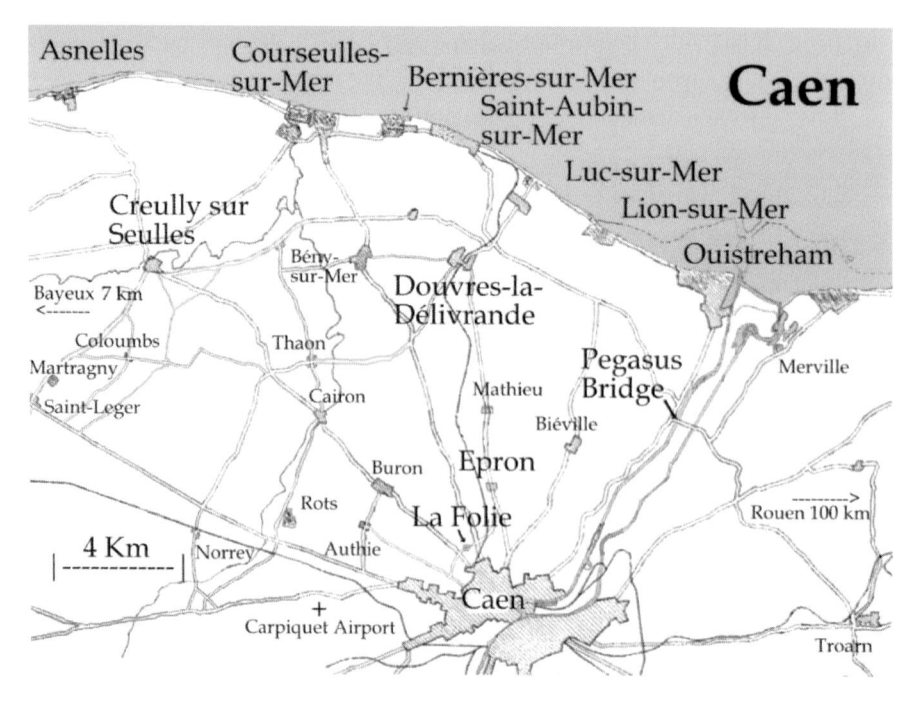

7. Café art, Thursday, 22 June 1944. D-Day+16

With Paul back at the home it was business as usual. We'd had another absolute crisis, but he went on as if nothing happened.

He was prescribed sleeping tablets but was very rude about them and anyone who suggested he take them. He was eating well and drank his favourite wines with gusto, even though he was under doctor's orders not to. He played piano and went on his usual walks. He went back to beating me at chess and just for good measure thrashed Brian a few times too.

I noticed he was writing something on the pages of a black book with his Parker pen. I had no clue what it was. The old man was once more as sharp as a razor.

If he had been testing me again, then I'd passed. I wasn't worried about mixing it with him, indeed he seemed to thrive on it. I had been testing him too, and he passed.

Meanwhile I had also passed the Batchelor of Engineering part of my degree.

One morning in mid-July Brian came and sat with me. 'He's not some kindly old man, is he?' he said. It was obvious who he was referring to. I wasn't going to agree with him even though I knew he was right. He congratulated me on my degree and asked what I was going to do with it. He said he knew that Brexit had ruined my chances of a future in engineering in the UK but that he knew people in America who were looking for top young engineers if I was interested. I expressed my appreciation but explained that I was on a four-year master course and that I would consider offers after I finished. What was really happening was that Brian was bouncing me for information about Paul. I gave him nothing. I was getting wiser.

The PTSD training helped me to help him on a daily basis. The trainer said that sufferers live in the past because they are trying to reconcile it. They seek another more desirable version of events but can never find one. They become stuck trying to 'fix' issues that cannot be resolved, and it's this conflict that causes the problems. I was told that the best way to help was simply to listen and let the sufferer find their way to the traumas. Paul said he was weak; weakened by the burden, but I didn't think he was weak at all. Strangely, I found the training was as beneficial to me personally as it was to the way I dealt with Paul. I understood myself and my issues with my mother better. I realised the questions might never get answers.

Mel's prophetic words were coming true. I couldn't put my finger on how, but they were. The training made me a better and more empathetic listener. I now heard words and phrases that kept recurring. I heard the nuances, could retain salient points, and ask meaningful questions. I became what the training called 'an active listener.' Paul sometimes said things that didn't add up: there were disassociations and confusions. Like a Picasso painting, the old man was extraordinarily complex: open to interpretation. He didn't tell the psychiatric nurse anything, he merely wound him up and told him a load of porkies which threw him off the scent. He kept Brian out of the picture too as he realised he'd annoyed him. For me though he stuck to his story. It was up to me what I saw in it.

'I cycled northwards away from the front line. Just to the west of a place called Martragny, the Allies were building a temporary airfield. Awfully close to the front line. Just a little further up the road in Martragny itself I came to a large chateau with a huge red cross pulled over the roof: a field hospital. There were lots of tents and lots of comings and goings.

I couldn't go south or through Caen, but I could go north-east. My plan was to head for the two bridges over the River Orne and the canal north-east of the city, cross and head towards Rouen that way. We had been through there in 1940. At some point I would have to enter German-held territory, I just didn't know how or where.

As I passed through a tiny place called Coulombs I saw aircraft taking off and couldn't resist going to take photos. Two British Typhoon fighter bombers roared over the hedge right in front of me with squadron markings 'EL.' Their prop wash blew me over! Through my binoculars I also saw parked up 12 twin-engined Mosquito aircraft. I'd never seen them on the ground before. Then one thundered over magnificently to land with a squeal and puff of tyre rubber. Beautiful things they were. Father would have loved them, but I grew to fear them.

It was still early in the day. I pressed on directly eastwards past hundreds, actually thousands of soldiers, artillery pieces, lorries, Jeeps, Universal Carriers and tanks some of which were flame-throwers. Some had American stars on them. To my surprise, many of the soldiers were Canadian. They had 'Canada' on their British-style uniforms and their tanks had maple leaf markings. Some even spoke French and I stopped and chatted to them. They were from Quebec.

Peculiar accents!

As I headed east I came to British Sherman tanks, soldiers, and heavy equipment. I cycled on past destroyed houses and bulldozers clearing debris away.

Eventually, I came to Benouville, crossed the disused tram lines, and arrived at the two bridges over the Orne and the Canal. British Tommies guarded them, and they were nice enough, but they were not going to let me cross under any circumstances. No amount of my pleading in French changed their minds.

Then, to my amazement just behind me at a place called Café Gondrée, I heard a woman speaking French with an Alsatian accent to a customer. I couldn't believe my ears! I wheeled my bike over towards the café and took a seat near its disused petrol pump and a Jeep parked next to it. She came and greeted me.

'Bonjour! Ça Va!' she asked. Definitely Alsatian.

'You are Alsatian?' I spoke as she passed.

'Yes young sir, from Strasbourg. You too I think?'

'Yes, from Strasbourg. I am Paul, from the Ile.'

'Incroyable!' exclaimed the hostess. About 40 I think she was. There was a baby in a crib in the open doorway of the café. Then a little one, aged about five wandered out. 'Maman!' she called, ran to her mother's hand, and hid behind her legs.

'Ah, may I introduce Arlette, ma petite chérie!' and there was her beautiful daughter in little brown boots. 'Young man you are a long way from home. My name is Thérèse, welcome!'

'I am delighted to meet you. Your little one is beautiful. Will you introduce me to your baby also?'

'Yes, of course!' I stood and walked to the crib with the shy little one holding the hand of her proud mother. She let the sleeping infant be and I looked on at the picture of contentment. 'This is Françoise. Sleeps well, even when there is shooting and big noises. I think she is used to it now. What can I get for you Paul from the Ile?'

'Anything you have, I think!'

'Well, I would love to serve you coffee and kugelhopf, but today we can only manage strange instant stuff from the British and day-old bread, that's if you don't mind.'

'Thank you Thérèse.'

It was strange to sit at a French café again. Even stranger to listen to a familiar accent, broken by occasional firing and gunshots in the distance. I wanted to ask Thérèse so many questions, but she came out with two coffees, sat, and beat me to it. 'How are you here, Paul from the Ile?'

I explained that I was a conscripted worker but managed to escape when the invasion came. It was sort of true. I told her I was going to wait until I could get safely home to Strasbourg. Then she explained, 'Well it's not as if there isn't plenty of work to do around here. There are thousands of casualties and dozens of field hospitals all along the coast. I trained as a nurse in Strasbourg and then worked in Paris. I see the wounded being brought back over that bridge every day. It's terrible.'

'An incredible co-incidence! My mother was a nurse in the first war, and she is still a nurse today.'

'Well then, why don't you go and volunteer to help as a stretcher bearer for the wounded? They will feed you and put a roof over your head. Perfect work for a fit young man like you.'

That was an excellent idea. I'd already passed a field hospital earlier.

There was nobody around. Thérèse lowered her voice and changed into Alsatian-German. 'Obviously, you speak our language. Your mother would have taught you. You know, very many wounded German soldiers are also brought over that bridge. They are in great distress and do not want to die here. Some of them are our Alsatian brothers conscripted by the Nazis. Speaking two languages you could be particularly useful, and you could wait out the war until Strasbourg is liberated. I do not think that will be long.'

She definitely had a point. I made up my mind immediately to follow that through as a temporary measure while I figured out how to cross the front line. We supped our coffee, and I chewed the day-old bread that I didn't mind. It was only then that I noticed three giant gliders in the field over on the other side of the bridge. I'd been so busy arguing with the Tommies guarding it that I hadn't noticed them.

In French I asked, 'What happened here Thérèse?'

She smiled and said, 'The Germans got a real surprise that first night. We were woken up by explosions and firing in the dark. It was about midnight. We had to hide.'

'Dear God, you and your family were in terrible danger!'

'Not for long. There was more shooting. The Germans came with a tank, but the British attacked it and stopped it. There were casualties on both sides.

Major Howard and the British had landed in those gliders. They attacked the Germans and captured the bridges. They called that *Ham* and *Jam*. They had burgundy-coloured berets and a shoulder badge of a soldier on a flying horse. That horse is called *Pegasus*. Now they have named the bridge 'Pegasus Bridge.' The British are strange!

Overnight some Commandos arrived with a crazy guy called Bill playing bagpipes. Major Howard was here and there was another battle. Lots of brave men died.'

'*Incroyable et magnifique*,' I muttered. The story of the battle at the bridge moved me deeply. It was fantastic to be able to fly such big heavy gliders and land them so close. But the most amazing thing was that the pilots did all this at night. Absolutely incredible.

'This bridge is especially important to the war effort. The British have been kind to us. They look after us like guardian angels. I think we are safe now.' A look of relief came across the mother's face. She and her family had been close to death for many hours.

There was the usual booming of guns. I looked and saw Mosquitoes carrying rockets flying incredibly low and fast. Somewhere over on the other side of the river and canal somebody was going to get a pasting.

Our conversation continued. Soldiers came by in lorries and Jeeps heading east. Occasionally heading west there were ambulances with casualties. 'Voila,' said Thérèse, 'do you see what I mean?'

I certainly did see.

Then I noticed a soldier walking back across the bridge heading towards the café. He had a cylindrical leather canister slung over his arm. Arriving,

I noticed he was a captain. He had a fabric roll of paint brushes in his pocket: an artist. Thérèse recognised and welcomed him. He threw his kit into the Jeep, sat down, and asked for coffee. Off she went. Incredibly young to be a captain I thought, he was only in his early twenties.

I leaned across and in French asked, 'Are you an artist?'

'Oui,' he said in a strange accent. I realised his French wasn't that good. Four Typhoons thundered overhead. 'Tiffies,' he muttered glancing up.

Under their din I asked with a heavily applied accent but in English: 'Can I see your paintings captain?'

He gave me a peculiar look but said nothing as he handed me the leather canister.

'I'll be careful,' I said as I opened and rolled out a watercolour with candle wax, wax crayon, and pencil.

 It was the three gliders over the bridge. Superb.'

As usual, the old man had a copy of the exact picture in his collection. He passed it to me. A fantastic image, capturing the unreal beauty of these vast engineless aircraft. 'There were other paintings, but that one was the best. I knew you would be interested in the gliders. I think you would be interested in the artist; he was an engineer like you,' he said with one of his lovely smiles.

'I was in a bit of a state when I painted that,' the captain said. He paused then in an accent I didn't recognise asked, 'You speak English?'

'Yes. My father is English, my mother is from Strasbourg. It's a long story.'

'I'm sure!' said the young soldier laughing. 'I'm Albert. And you are?'

'Paul.' He wore a burgundy *Pegasus* patch on his shoulder with 591 sewed in. 'I don't know British regiments. What is your regiment captain?'

'I was in the Royal Engineers, but I volunteered for parachute training. Then they asked me to paint the war. To help that along they made me an honorary captain. Now I get a lot of freedom to work as an artist.'

'Your painting is brilliant sir. I wish I could paint like you!'

'You paint?' he asked rolling up his work and popping it away safely into his can.

'I wouldn't call it painting sir, not compared to what you do,' I giggled. 'I haven't spent much time in England. Your accent, where are you from captain?'

'Liverpool.'

'They make Meccano there, don't they?'

'Aye lad, they do,' he answered smiling just as Thérèse came out with more coffee. Motorbikes and lorries thundered past. It was a slightly awkward situation as I didn't want to let on to her that I spoke English. I'm not sure why I was reluctant.

The artist made my mind up for me. 'Where are you going?' he asked me right out.

'I'm not going anywhere sir, I want to go home, but I can't get through the front line,' I said glancing nervously at the café hostess.

'Where is your home?' Albert asked.

'Strasbourg. It's a beautiful city, perfect for painting.' It was true. Jersey was not my real home, and I'd had an awful time there. Thérèse watched me closely. I was heading for Salzburg via Rouen and Strasbourg of course.

'Hmm, you won't be going home just yet I'm afraid,' he said with a sigh.

The three of us sat and conversed in mixed English and French and I translated as yet more planes powered overhead and the distant booming continued. I hadn't forgotten the idea of volunteering for a field hospital, so I turned to the artist and asked if it would be possible.

'Yes,' he said, 'the hospitals need as much help as they can get. There are many civilians working as porters and nurses. There are even local doctors in some of the tents.'

'Can you arrange that for me?'

'It's easy. All you have to do is flag down the next field ambulance or truck carrying casualties coming over the bridge and they'll take you to where they're going.'

I was waiting for Thérèse to blow my cover and mention my fluent German, but she said nothing. Instead, she went off to attend to her children as time was getting on.

It wasn't long before another ambulance draped with a circular red cross chugged over the bridge towards us. Thérèse came back out carrying her baby. 'Time to go,' Albert called, and he stepped into the road with his hand up. The lorry stopped and the captain explained the situation. A driver-corporal nodded his head and waved me over. I hastily grabbed my bike and wheeled it across. 'He says he's going to Number 86 General near La Délivrande. I'll pay your bill. Get in.'

He turned to pay, but Thérèse waved him away.

In the back of the ambulance were two stretchers with wounded men. There were four other soldiers sitting up with various roughly dressed wounds. There was just enough room for me. I climbed in and Albert passed up the bike. Thérèse came across to say goodbye and good luck.

'Keep up your painting Paul,' said the artist. 'I liked your description of Strasbourg. I'll visit that part of France one day.'

As the open-backed ambulance took off in a cloud of dust and fumes I waved and called back, 'It's not France, it's Alsace!'

Author's note

Albert Richards was killed by a landmine on 5 March 1945 as he was driving his Jeep. He was 25, the youngest ever Official War Artist. The work here: 'The Gliders at the Pegasus Bridge' can be seen at the Walker Art Gallery, Liverpool in Room 11 'British Art from 1880 to 1950', in a drawer. He is buried at Milsbeek War Cemetery near Nijmegen, Holland. His headstone inscription reads simply:

To the dear memory
Of Bertie our only child
"O valiant heart"

8. Casualties

The ambulance travelled west to a place called Douvres-la-Délivrande just a couple of miles from the coast. It was a large, tented camp on flat fields. On arrival Military Police emptied Paul's kit out on the ground. Of course, they found his badge and papers which showed that he was in the Reich Labour Service. They also found the Nazi Party badge. This and his German camera and binoculars caused consternation. His kit was confiscated, and he was held under armed guard. In the morning, he was put in front of a captain and asked to explain himself. He told him the truth about everything: his nurse mother, his deported father on the Austrian border, the subterfuge required to get off Jersey and the officer was impressed. 'You must love your father very much,' he observed. 'Obviously, you speak good German, and it seems you are French.'

'I'm Alsatian,' Paul told him in his customary manner.

'Alright young man, we have need of you here if you want to work.'

Paul told the captain it was in a good cause and was happy to do that.

He was given back all his kit and papers, issued with British fatigues and boots, a mug for tea, a mess tin, and a tin hat in the event of an air raid. At first they employed him digging out trenches for the ward and dormitory tents. He soon proved himself completely dependable as a factotum fetching water, moving stocks, anything.

He worked alongside the friendly nurses in their British khaki with red cross armbands. They were issued with rations of cigarettes and boiled sweets and Paul enjoyed the sweets. They lit their cigarettes from books of matches that had a white V for Victory on the cover. The food was good, served in rectangular mess tins. The weather was hot, and Paul was in a tent with itinerant local French workers who were rough, ready, and smoked so much that he had to take himself outside and sleep under the stars.

Then it started getting busy.

On Monday, 26 June, after poor weather, ambulances started arriving, and they kept arriving until Saturday, 1 July. There was a major action taking place and lots of seriously wounded soldiers were being brought in. Paul was engaged with moving them quickly out into the tents. He was sometimes asked to do double shifts or additional shifts with the Number 88 Field Hospital nearby. He worked 18-hour days and was busy to the point of exhaustion. Some were dead on arrival, some died in surgery or later. Some had arms and legs missing, some had holes in their chests. Some were patched up and sent on ships to Britain, some were sent back to their units. 'Now I understood what my mother had seen and been involved with. I admired her even more,' he explained.

Paul said that the Allies had a secret antibiotic that stopped gangrene and sepsis. It saved thousands of lives in Normandy. The Germans didn't have it. Today we know this antibiotic as *Penicillin*.

Lots of wounded German SS also came in, officers and NCOs. Because he was tri-lingual, Paul was assigned to help deal with them and translate. He was appalled to find young SS soldiers no older than he was. They were members of the 12th SS division called *Hitlerjugend*: the division he'd been told about when he was in Jersey.

He was shocked by their demeanour. 'I would have befriended them, but they were arrogant and twisted. Even though some had lost legs, feet, or arms, they were not grateful that brilliant surgeons and nurses had saved their lives. They were not like the normal 16, 17 and 18-year-olds you would meet. They were rotten. It was like they wanted to die just for the glory of it. The nurses hated them. They couldn't understand the German insults like I could.

Those boys were hard vicious bastards. They never had a proper childhood. All they'd learned was how to fight. Nothing else. They never had a choice.

No-one could feel compassion towards the SS. The boy soldiers of the *Hitlerjugend* in the hospitals were warped and ruined. I knew that older Germans could be Nazis, but I hadn't met youths who could be so fanatical. One amputee hissed that if only he had his dagger he would slit my throat, another that he would cut my balls off and feed them to me on a spoon. I sneered back that he would find that difficult with no hands. Another one shouted across a ward at me, 'Look at him. Weak-blooded Alsatian scum, a coward, and a traitor!' I would have smacked him in the face, but he'd been hit by a phosphorus grenade and didn't have a face.'

After the scramble at the end of June there was a quieter time, but there was no breakthrough at Caen. Paul still had the problem of how to get through to Rouen. He didn't arrive at a solution. It was coming up for a month since he'd left Jersey and he hadn't got far, but then he didn't expect the Allied invasion of Europe to get in the way.

The solution came accidentally and without any warning.

9. The ambush

Although he was not a soldier, Paul was willing, strong, and trustworthy. These qualities alongside his three languages meant that he was soon asked to go out to help with prisoners of war and evacuating casualties. He explained:

'On the night of 7/8 July hundreds of bombers went and smashed Caen. It seemed impossible that anything could be left alive in that fine old city. Then some sort of operation started early in the morning of the 8th, and we needed to do many return trips through the wheat fields north of the city. It was a day I've tried to forget.

We were working close to the frontline. I was in civilian clothes as my fatigues had gotten soaked with blood and buzzed with flies. I'd washed them in antiseptic soap and left them to dry. I was in the habit of carrying a kit bag with scarf, rosary, papers, binoculars and camera plus food water and a map in case I got caught out in the open. Most of us did that.

There was firing and dust in the villages to our right, with the sound of German 88mm anti-tank guns blasting away. We passed smoking Sherman tanks that had been hit by those '88s. It was getting late, and we'd already made three trips back to the hospitals with wounded from a place called Epron. These soldiers had been engaged all day edging through the fields clearing out trenches and snipers of *SS Hitlerjugend* who were fighting like wild dogs in the barns and hedgerows. We had a nearly full ambulance, but a medical orderly private and I were told to pick up one last casualty before we packed it in for the night. We headed towards a tiny place marked on the map as La Folie. Dust and smoke swirled thickly through the air. We seemed to be out on our own. Soldiers of the East Lancashire Regiment were setting up an outpost line. We had to stop near a little farm as the road was cratered and walk 200 metres with a stretcher to the casualty next to two Universal Carriers with US stars.

A staff sergeant was ready for evacuation. We put him on the stretcher. Suddenly there was a tremendous fusillade of enemy mortar fire landing all around us. A carrier was blasted into the air and landed sideways in the hedge killing the occupants. I dived for cover into a ditch pulling with me the wounded man who screeched in pain. The orderly private ran behind a farm wall with three others. There was screaming and dust and blood. Then a mortar round hit behind the wall. None of them survived. The second carrier tried to reverse hastily, with soldiers jumping into it for cover, but its track had been hit. The track unrolled and the machine fell into a mortar crater and got jammed. All the occupants promptly leapt out and ran for their lives. Another mortar round hit the first carrier and blasted it into a million fizzing red-hot fragments. Blood was spraying. A heavy piece of a carrier landed on my casualty and impaled him, and I was caught underneath his blood dripping down on me. Anyone who ran was cut down by Mausers and a MG42 from the hedgerow on the left. It all happened so quickly and there was so much dust and smoke that nobody returned fire.

Soldiers were left groaning in the dirt, their faces smashed, limbs severed. They died before my eyes as the lifeblood pumped from their shattered bodies.

Well camouflaged young Germans with SS insignia appeared out of the hedgerow. They were *Hitlerjugend*. Some soldiers had still been alive, but the youths were going around bayonetting or shooting them and then cleaning out their pockets looking for trophies, sweets, or cigarettes. Some were giggling and cursing while they did it. I thought they would bayonet me too, but they didn't see me in the ditch under the pieces of carrier and corpse of the staff sergeant. I could hear them talking about how stupid the British were coming without any tanks. Then they collected up their mortar teams and ambled after the retreating British soldiers in the gathering dusk. There were only about a dozen of them, but they had the audacity to take on two armoured carriers with just two mortars, a MG42 and rifles. All this happened in the space of about 10 minutes. It was a perfect ambush. Death could come suddenly in Normandy.

I waited until I was sure the SS had gone then climbed out of the bloody ditch. I checked my victim. In his holster was a Webley Mark IV revolver like my father's VI, except short, .38 calibre, fully loaded with six rounds. I took it and everything I could find including ammunition. Now was my chance to head south for Caen, or what was left of it.

Along the road I passed three unbroken bodies, two in German police uniform, and an SS man. They lay side by side in a little wood. Each had a single bullet wound in the back of the head, and there was a huge pool of blood.

I wandered into the ruins of the town and staggered through rubble and dust. Then I found a partially collapsed house where I hid and slept.'

He stopped, wavered, and seemed puzzled at something he'd just said.

At that point he reached down, pulled out a de-activated revolver from a box under the bed, and handed it to me. As he did he studied my face for a reaction.

Holding that cold gun in my hand suddenly made it real. He'd warned me it would be shocking.

There was something odd in what he'd said too: what were German police doing in Normandy?

Paul had this impossible habit of appearing untroubled by even the most awful recollections. With summer rain falling gently outside, he sat at the piano with his coffee and orange juice and played Eric Satie's *Gnossienne number 1*.

10. The sniper

A day or two later I joined Paul and Brian playing chess over coffee. This time the game was different. Playing White, unusually Brian went for a Queen's Gambit opening. Paul accepted the gambit and swiftly turned it into an exhibition. The army man made so many mistakes, most of them unforced, that by move 20 it was effectively all over. Brian didn't normally open that way, it was not his natural game, and the old man soon made him pay.

Paul smirked, looked at me and in German observed, 'He's an idiot today. Do you want to play Katie?' That was extraordinarily rude and provocative, but typical. 'Yes, let's play,' I said smiling for Brian's benefit and passing it off as just a normal invitation. He was up to something: all the signs were there.

He invited me to play White. Sensing an opportunity, I opened with the same Queen's Gambit and the old man accepted as before. Brian watched on feigning disinterest. I didn't make the same mistakes and dominated the centre. By move 33 he offered a draw. I declined and by move 40 I had him. 'Well played Katie, brilliant!' he said glancing at Brian who looked away, got up and went off.

He spoke in German again and regarded me across the board. 'You are no longer weak like you once were. You are strong. You have learned to be strong. You have gone against your nature, and for that I admire you even more.' It was so rude and condescending, but I let it go with a smile. I was used to it by now.

He went on, 'I've hardly ever met anyone who would fight, and I absolutely never met anyone who learned to fight as well as you do.'

'I've had a good teacher,' I replied with a grin.

'Well said Katie.'

'I'd like some of that coffee,' I asked. He nodded his head and led the way to the kitchen, empty cups in hand.

With refilled cafetière we headed to the study. We'd never been there, and he bounced along like a 10-year-old. He could be so proud, haughty, and self-satisfied, but he could also be plain and child-like, as if nothing untoward had ever happened in his life.

In the study something else new happened. He pulled out a book about Picasso and flicking through it came to what looked like a black and white picture of a painting. He showed me. 'It's a bit odd having a black and white photo of a painting, isn't it?' I observed. He looked at me as if I'd said something very silly.

'This isn't a black and white photo. This is *Guernica*,' he said softly, covering my embarrassment. 'You said you wanted to learn about art. If art does nothing else it helps us to realise the truth.'

It was another of those conversations. I reached for the cafetière and pushed down forcing the boiling water through the mesh plate. He continued, 'Look here at *Guernica*. What do you make of it?' I'd never seen or heard of it and had already made a fool of myself, so I kept my mouth shut. 'Indulge me. When you look at this, what do you see?'

'I don't know anything about this painting. I don't know where to start.'

'Start with what you see and then how you feel about it.'

'I see a shrieking woman holding a dead baby, she is looking up. I see crushed bodies, a woman with a broken leg. Another is consumed by fire. I see a severed arm holding a shattered sword. I see pandemonium and grief. I see destruction and chaos.'

'It was in the Basque country of Spain in 1937 in the Civil War. Hitler's German Nazi government was helping the fascist Franco in his bloodthirsty coup. They sent their bombers. Guernica was not a military target. Franco ordered the air attack on market day. He knew the town would be packed with innocent civilians and that the German bombers would cause maximum terror. Murdering Bastard.'

'Mother of Christ!' I gasped. Not a phrase I'd ever used, but it applied. It was revolting to think that any person could do such a thing.

'It's a massive painting, eight metres by three and a half.'

'You've seen the real painting?'

'No. I was in Caen. I don't need to see *Guernica*.'

Paul had asked me how I felt about the painting. I cared little for it. My mind was numbed. I looked at the image again searching for meaning, but there was none.

He said, 'Picasso was a genius with his words and art. There is a story that while living in Nazi-occupied Paris a German Gestapo (Secret police) officer spoke to him about a photograph of the painting. 'Did you do that?' he asked. Picasso responded, 'No, you did.' Picasso once said, 'We all know that art is not truth. Art is a lie that makes us realise truth.'

'What is the truth Paul? Who gets to determine what the truth is? You, me, Picasso, Hitler?'

'We each of us determine our own truths. But the truth shifts like the sands of the Sahara. One day it is here, the next day it is there.'

'How would I be able to distinguish the truth from a lie?'

'You can't. Truth is relative, conditional, contingent against what you choose to believe. Pontius Pilate asked Jesus Christ, 'Quid est veritas?' *What is the truth*. On hearing the answer, he declared that Jesus was not guilty of anything. Even so, by popular demand, Pilate nevertheless sent Christ to be crucified. Then he washed his hands of it. Truth had been put on trial and judged by a shouting mob who were devoted to lies and they chose the lies. Eusebius the historian tells us that later, Pilate killed himself. The truth had overwhelmed him.' At this, Paul paused and was reflective.

They read us that at school, it was from the Gospel of John. 'Are you saying that truth is just another choice, that it's up to me to decide what is true and what is not?' I asked.

'Yes. It was something Hans and I talked about a lot.'

This idea was so intuitively appealing, and yet so alien. For a second thoughts of my mother flashed into my head. What was her truth? Whatever it was, it didn't accord with mine.

This wasn't one of his set-ups. We were in a new place.

'When I was in Jersey Hans taught me so much. He had seen terrible things, but he only talked philosophically. He told me, 'It's not always easy to know what's right. The innocent feel guilty, and the guilty feel nothing. In war the truth is that you fight, or you die. When it all comes down to it, you can pretend to be someone else; someone who didn't do anything. You can say, 'I didn't kill him, the war did,' or 'the truth is, I did it in self-defence,' even if that isn't the truth. You just tell yourself. Perhaps God will forgive, but then again, perhaps he won't.'

****

'As I woke up in the ruins of Caen and glanced around it was like how I imagined hell: on fire, smoking and stinking of sulphur. Dogs screeched, yowled and ran. Mothers came out looking for sons daughters and husbands. The sky was blotted. A crackling of gunfire echoed down the streets.

Packing my stuff didn't take long. My task now was to get through the city, cross the river, and come out of the other side alive. Then I would head towards Rouen about 100km away. An easy day's bike ride, except I now had no bike, only my most prized and useful possessions. I could obtain a bike.

I picked my way in and out of smashed buildings through a lurid half-lit world of dirt and soot. Occasional shots from Mausers broke the sky.

A woman was searching in the rubble. She found me tripping over the blocks and I realised that I looked like some walking dead, caked in dried blood. She regarded me and in alarm asked, 'Have you seen a boy, about eleven years old?' She paid no attention to my shocking condition. Tears whitened her dirty face. I shook my head and pressed on. Behind me I heard inconsolable weeping.

Around a corner was a row of shattered shops.

Incredibly, there were people in the blasted remains upstairs. I could see them through the glassless windows on the first floor, and they looked back at me. A girl of about 13 ran out. 'You must be wounded?' she asked. 'No,' I replied, 'I am uninjured.' 'Come inside. My father says it's Sunday and that you must come. We have clean clothes for you.' I had done nothing to warrant such kindness, but I went in anyway and followed her up the stairs.

I entered a room unlike any I'd ever seen. Everything was broken, cups, china, glass, all in shards on the floor swept into a corner. There were buckets of water. Two small children were also there, perhaps 3 and 6-years-old, two girls. 'Come in,' said a man, the father, appearing around the corner from another room. His wife followed him. 'You are a survivor?' she asked. 'Yes,' I replied. It wasn't a lie. Incredibly, there were smiles. I still don't know how that could be, or why they helped me, but they did.

'Change your clothes. We have some spare for you. Then we will go to church,' explained the father.

I was given a small tin bath some rags and a bucket of water, and I followed through to what I thought was the back of the apartment. Except there was no back of the apartment. The block had been sheared in half.

'Don't worry, I'll build back better,' the father told me.

He passed me trousers, a shirt and a belt. I was grateful for those and washed with a small amount of their water. It felt fantastic to wear fresh clothes. 'Something happened to you,' he said as he collected my bloodied garments. I said nothing. His house was cut in half, what was there to say?

The little family carried on. They had lost everything except their lives but were still happy to share what little they had with a complete stranger. Then I heard the chattering of French voices and looked out:

A dozen soldiers, with their sergeant leading the way. Canadians they were, coming down the street. Then there was a shot. A sniper! The sergeant fell. Hastily they hauled him back around the side of a building. My blood ran cold.

It was too close to this lovely generous family. Far too close. Where was he?

Where was that sniper? First I told my family to hide, get out, do anything, because they were in great danger. Down the stairs they went, the father leading and calling to his family to go to the cellar. I never did learn their names.

I could hear the screeching of tanks not far away. Another Mauser shot rang out. I was sure it was from the attic of the adjacent building. I climbed down a pile of rubble behind the apartment and back up into the window of the first-floor next door. As silently as I could, I eased myself up the broken remnants of the stairs. This was his escape route.

After breathless moments I arrived at the attic room and there he was, stood back from the window resting against boxes looking for targets. It was another one of those *SS Hitlerjugend* and he was on a killing spree. Little bastard.

A good sniper would always be aware of his surroundings and threats to his location and *never* fire two shots from the same place. He should have a pistol handy too, so I was wary. But this guy wasn't a good sniper, he was just a boy.

I stood wondering what to do. In those moments he sighted another target and took aim for a third shot. I could feel my anger rising.

'You stupid idiot,' I hissed.

'Scheiße!' (SHIT!) the boy muttered, spinning to face me.

No pistol.

'What are you doing you bloody fool?'

'How did you find me?' He looked shocked, like I'd worked some piece of magic to be there.

'Easily, idiot. You've fired two from the same spot. You're not very good are you? Where's your pistol?'

'Lost. Stop your jabbering, come over here and be my Franz!' (Slang: observer) he demanded offering up his binoculars.

'I'll do no such thing. You've had it. They know you're here. I know you're here. You're finished. We need to get out right now, otherwise we'll be going home in boxes.'

'They don't know where I am, they haven't fired on me yet. I'm going to pot a few more.'

'IDIOT!' I growled, 'Don't you remember your training? Always only fire **one shot** from your position, if not you will be discovered. Don't make me pull my pistol on you. Come on, let's go.'

'Who are you?' the lad muttered. 'I'm not taking orders from someone who isn't even in uniform.'

He'd called my bluff. 'You will come with me now, friend. I'm telling you; their tanks are coming. Choosing to stay means choosing to die.'

'I don't mind dying. My orders are to slow them down whilst the rest of us escape the city. You should be doing the same, not trying to persuade me to leave.'

He paused, 'Who are you?'

His intense blue eyes contrasted the brown and brick orange of his camouflage smock.

'There is a young French family in the house next door. If the tanks see you and start shooting we'll die and so will they. What's the use in that?' I glared.

'What do I care about the family next door? One drop of our blood is worth an ocean of theirs.'

'What use is your blood if it's pouring through the floorboards, fool?'

I had one thing left: surprise. To my left I noticed a row of broken roof beams. Meanwhile he'd spotted another target and raising to aim muttered something unpleasant under his breath. I took a piece of beam and edged towards him. He was concentrating and it was my moment to belt him. As I moved I glanced down through the window and saw a Sherman tank on the opposite street corner. The idiot hadn't seen it.

'Don't shoot, there's a tank!' I hissed. He held fire. The Sherman was traversing its gun. If it settled on us we would die. The SS boy turned and silently watched the tank with his binoculars. I held my breath, but the turret continued rotating, searching, the sound of its engine throbbing evenly, exhaust smoke filling the street.

'We should go, right now,' I whispered, quietly and surreptitiously dropping my block of wood.

'Yes,' he replied. He turned, picked up his kit and we took off down the stairs.

I made to head left, but he held my shoulder and told me not to go that way as sappers had placed booby traps there.

I owed him for that. So, I let him lead. He had his route worked out over walls and through back yards.

We ended up in the piles of rubble behind the next block. He had a second firing location in mind.

I could have belted him with the beam, but now I was glad I hadn't. He could have shot me, but it never occurred to him. He took me as another German soldier, albeit in civilian clothes. I wanted to stop him shooting Canadians, but the only way was to kill him, and I couldn't do it.

As I followed through the ruins, he told me he was Helmut from Dusseldorf and that he was in the '25th'. From working in the hospital, I knew there were two *SS Hitlerjugend* Panzergrenadier regiments: the 25th and 26th. I said simply that I was Paul from the 26th, had 'borrowed' some clothes in order to escape from a tight spot with the Canadians and was from Straßburg. 'You were at the airfield. Pretty clever to give the Canadians the slip. They would kill you; you know.' He paused, 'Alsatian then?'

'Yes, Alsatian.'

We crouched in a broken corner surrounded by the bricks of a shattered wall.

He said, 'Come with me comrade. You're smart and keep your head. Be my spotter, we can take a few of these Canadian bastards with us and give the other lads time to clear out.' His request seemed almost reasonable...

'You're a cool customer Helmut, I'll give you that, but we need to get out of Caen, or we'll end up buried here.' It was obvious, but I explained it to him anyway.

The boy gave a dirt-caked smile and put down his gun. He was 16, and only just tall enough to qualify for the SS.

'Got any sweets?' he asked. As it happened I did, from the hospital. I reached into my bag and held out a hand offering him a choice of four. He chose a red one, unwrapped it and popped it in his mouth. 'Canadian?'

'Yes, Canadian,' I replied.

'Good work!' he giggled, commending me. I took a green sweet and smiled at the compliment. For a moment we were like children on the beach at St Brelade. All we needed was ice cream. He offered me his water flask and I drank deeply. In another reality he could have been my friend.

He said, 'A year ago I was at school. Now I'm here with you killing Canadians. What about you Paul?' It was a juddering way to open a conversation.

'I worked in a hotel. Then I volunteered.' It was a lie, but how would he know the difference?

'Volunteered, eh? Good for you! So did I.' Taking off his cap to reveal a shock of curly ginger hair, he added, 'I liked that red SS recruiting poster which said *Come to Us,* so I did.' He paused then said, 'Seen any flamethrower tanks? They're devils.'

'Yes,' I said. The Germans had them in Jersey, and I'd cycled past Allied flamethrower tanks in the Normandy Bocage.

'They have to be killed. One of those got three of my friends. You know the standing order: kill immediately, or it will send you burning to hell.'

'I know how to take out a tank. Do you take me for an idiot?' I lied, but it sounded convincing.

There was more firing, more MG42 noise. Tanks could be heard, fizzing and explosions. 'Panzerfaust!' he whispered. It was a type of anti-tank rocket launcher. We peered around a corner. There was a Canadian Sherman on the rubble. From the side, a helmeted youth appeared with a long stick. A jet of flame shot out, there was a loud blast, the left track exploded, and the machine was immobilised blocking the street. The lid of the tank was raised, and two soldiers got out. Both were shot by waiting snipers and they slid limply into the bricks. 'Mother of Christ!' I muttered. The tank lid dropped with a loud clang.

'I know those boys. Good aren't they?' Helmut beamed.

I felt sick, 'Jesus Christ...'

'HALT!' came a shout from behind. 'Hände hoch!' (Hands up!) We froze. There was a Canadian about five metres behind us...

'Use your pistol,' Helmut whispered. He'd left his rifle on the ground.

'No time to get it out. We throw bricks at him and run like hell,' I whispered back. He nodded.

'We work together, we live,' I breathed.

'Yes,' he hissed. 'Three, two, one...'

We reached for half bricks and threw. Instinctively, the Canadian put up his hands to protect himself but dropped his gun. My first brick hit him in the face. Then I was horrified to see the boy fly at the soldier. He set about him like a tiger. 'NO!' I roared. His bayonetted Enfield rifle was in the grit, and I took it and clicked the safety off.

Then there were shots which pinged off a nearby wall. We were under fire. 'Come Helmut, let's go!' I screamed pulling the kicking and gouging SS off the man. Blood was on the boy's hands. A ricochet had hit the Canadian in the back and he collapsed in a gasping heap. 'COME, FOOL!' I screeched. Helmut picked up his gun and kit and we ran like hell.

Panting we arrived in another shattered shop, a grocers. Snapping the bayonet off the Canadian's rifle I turned, pushed the boy against a wall and held the sharp dagger to his throat. 'You nearly got us killed you goddamned idiot.'

He fought me back, growling through clenched teeth, 'Why didn't you finish him you COWARD.'

'Call me a coward again and I'll slit your throat,' I hissed.

He was smiling grimly, eyes rolling.

'Alright, alright. That's our way,' he gasped breathless.

I let go of him. 'Young fool.'

He sneered and signalled to move, 'Come with me Paul. You have a rifle now, let's go hunting!'

'No. I'm not going with you, you're dangerous, clumsy and a hot head. You know the rule: NEVER let go of your sniper rifle. You did,' I blazed.

'Be my eyes then. We've got to kill them. If we don't kill them, they will kill us.'

'I'm not going with you. I'm going to find an officer and take new orders.'

It was a typical thing for a German soldier to say and Helmut accepted it without question, except he said again, 'Who are you? You're not an NCO that's for sure, but *you are one of us* I can see that.'

Those words *one of us* rang in my ears.

I picked up the Enfield, checked the magazine, which had four rounds, and turned to go. My mission was too important to piss about any longer risking death.

'You haven't got a pistol either, have you?' he laughed, 'you were trying to bluff me!'

I pulled the Mark IV from my bag and waved it at him. 'Not too bright,' I added, wincing.

'Beautiful! Give it to me, I need it. I lost mine.'

'Clumsy idiot. No, get your own. I'm leaving, I'm going to cross the river.'

The lad gave me a quizzical look then said, 'I'm coming with you. You're wise and cannot be deflected, I think you may even be my guardian angel?'

'If you're coming with me, then you'll do what I tell you. I've had enough bullshit for one day.' He nodded his head grinning in agreement.

We continued to slink southwards through the wasteland of Caen. There was less damage as we went south. Behind us was the cacophony of rifle, machine gun and tank fire. Now we were into a region where there were many more German soldiers and vehicles and a lot of activity. It was such a mess that I hardly recognised it. They were crossing the one remaining bridge over the river Orne, and sappers were preparing that with charges.

Hitlerjugend boys were putting up defences on the south side. Casually,

Helmut strolled over to one group who were building barricades and clearing cellars to make resistance nests. Then a sergeant noticed us.

'Who the hell are you and where is your uniform?'

Helmut jumped in, 'This is Paul from the 26th and he's with me. He escaped from the Canadians. He's Alsatian.'

'26th huh, Alsatian, huh? Good job, good hunters Alsatians. You his Franz then?' asked the sergeant. 'Yessir,' I replied. Another lie, but it didn't matter.

'Up that road there is a convent called Petites Soeurs des Pauvres (Little Sisters of the Poor). Go up there and dig in with this MG42 squad. Get the locals to help you, at gunpoint if necessary,' he explained.

A corporal led the way. We were a group of war hardened heavily armed little bastards. I gave Helmut the bag of sweets and walked along at the back.

Then I trailed far behind. As the squad rounded a corner I ran away from them as fast as I could.

In a doorway I emptied the Enfield rifle of bullets and threw it over a wall. I walked and then saw a local man cycling. Poor chap. I pulled my revolver on him and took his bike. Seven hours later I was in Rouen.'

I noticed that Paul was continuing to write something in a black book. He never said what.

11. Rouen

Paul had arrived in Rouen. He said his Uncle Claude and Aunt Maxine were thrilled and relieved.

They knew he was coming. Although letters from the Channel Islands were censored, Helene had written to her brother to expect: 'a package of 17-year-old Alsatian kugelhopf in early June.' The censors didn't know what to make of that, so they left it. Claude had been concerned that Paul was late. With the invasion and everything he feared the worst, so he was overcome with relief when his nephew rolled up on the stolen bike.

When they last saw him in 1940 he was turning 13 and just a child. Four years of occupation, and hardened by the Normandy battlefields, the 17-year-old looked and had the demeanour of someone quite different. He was no longer innocent and carried a loaded revolver in his bag.

He slept more or less for three days, waking only to eat and drink.

There was other particularly important news. Claude didn't say anything for a week until Paul had gotten back his sensibilities. The old man reached into his drawer, fetched out another letter and passed it to me.

'Maxine and Claude sat me down after dinner in a quiet sombre mood and handed me a letter written in French. It was in my father's handwriting. I was absolutely taken aback to see it. The envelope had a Swiss stamp and familiar looking lumpy writing. 'He sent it to our friends the Kellers in Basel, and they sent it here,' explained Claude.'

I opened it up fully and read it and the old man helped me with the translation. He knew every word by heart:

'My Dearest Maxine & Claude   *17 Mars 1944*

I hope this note does not come as too much of a surprise. I am quite well and hope you both are too.

I am writing because I fear the censor has stopped my recent letters to Jersey and I have received nothing from my family even though I know they would write. There are also other reasons why it has been difficult to keep contact. I need to explain these to you so that you can write to Helene, Paul and Beatrice in Jersey and put them in the picture. I hope that you are able to indulge my request. A letter from Rouen to Jersey stands a better chance than one from where I am now.

I have been moved to Berlin.

You will see from the address that I am no longer in any kind of camp. I have been here since August last year. It's best if I do not share details with you. Suffice to say that where I am is very much better for my health than where I was. There have been air raids, but I am close to excellent shelters.

Please do not be alarmed at what is written here. My circumstances are about as good as they could be. I have decent food and warm accommodation and am using my German language to good effect. War has forced us to make choices that we would not otherwise make.

Do write back and send me news from Jersey if you have any.
My love to you all.
Apartment 41, Arndtstraße 14, Bergmannkiez, Berlin.
Christopher

Berlin. Oh my God…
My father was in Berlin. It was shocking beyond reckoning. I thought, what now?'

12. Recalculation

'*I have been moved to Berlin*' put Paul in a spin. The effect was clear even after 75 years. He'd learned a lot in Jersey and was continuing to learn fast. He'd been in a spin before, but not like this one.

'My uncle and aunt were brilliant, but very protective. 'Stay with us until the Allies arrive,' they said. 'Your father is a brave man; he will find a way to deal with it.' There were problems with their analysis. I had been through Caen and experienced the devastation. Berlin was getting regular visits from Allied bomber fleets as well. Aside from the battle fronts Berlin was just about the most dangerous place in Europe, and my father was there. It was unbearable.

I read the letter repeatedly, lost sleep, and drank too much wine. I was going around and around. I spent a week doing that. I couldn't sit in Rouen. I couldn't go home to Strasbourg. Going back to Jersey was out of the question. In the end there was no choice: I had to go to Berlin.

When we flew, father told me, 'The best way to deal with a spin is not get into one in the first place. If you do, stop the spin with the rudder and push the stick forward.' I was in a spin. My solution was to follow father's advice, stop going around and around, and push forward again.

Claude didn't like that. He told me that many locals and workers were in *La Résistance* and to be careful. 'If the Resistance suspects you are German they will shoot you on the spot. They are everywhere, even in the construction teams.'

Paul gathered together everything he needed: maps, clothes, and rucksack. His uncle gave him his very light Duralumin *Randonneuse* bicycle. By Sunday, 23 July he was ready to go. First stop: Bonn.

13. Going away, Sunday, 23 July 1944

It was only about here, in that summer of 2019, that I began to appreciate the effect Paul's story was having on me. I was learning new things in new ways and was able to consider aspects that I hadn't before, as I hadn't known they were there. Mel the supervisor once told me that we were 'tuning in to each other.' Now I understood what she meant. He'd given me a lot to think about.

****

'As a family we were experienced cycle tourists. As soon as I was old enough, my father considered that to be eight, we got on the road. Like flying, cycling was in our blood. I didn't think that cycling from Normandy to Berlin would pose any particular difficulty. There was just a lot of it. Unlike Switzerland at least the route was mainly flat. It was pretty far, even with a stopover at Bonn. Getting away from the combat zone that I'd been in for weeks was a priority, and I just wanted a quiet unmolested journey with as few thrills as possible. Another priority was nice straight roads to my first objective: Amiens.

From Rouen I headed through Buchy towards Forges-les-Eaux. We'd been along here in 1940, and I remembered it. I didn't get very far though. I don't know why I made such slow progress. It wasn't that hilly. I left too late. I dawdled. Maybe I was daunted by what was in front of me. I don't know. In the event I only managed about 40km, and I'd wanted to cover 80-100. I also saw and heard a lot of Allied aircraft in the morning and these worried me, causing dismounts and pulls under trees or pushes into church porches. In the afternoon, the cloud came down and the air patrols stopped. The weather was closing in as the day progressed and rather than get soaked and sleep in a soggy bivouac in a hedge, I thought I'd look for something with higher comfort levels. This took longer and was more difficult than I expected. I didn't see anything of the German army though, they were still up to their necks in it back on the west side of the Seine.

As I closed in on Forges-les-Eaux I passed tempting looking barns over on the left. It was starting to rain heavily, so I headed along tiny tracks and came to a perfectly secluded rustic two-storey wooden cowshed complete with hay, *mais sans vaches*. I went up the ladder after hiding my bike, papers, and camera under some straw. I'd learned that lesson at Marie's farm.

I soon settled and wolfed down the food Aunt Maxine had prepared for me. I slept well, disturbed only by odd whooshing noises in the distance like a steam train. I slept with the revolver under my rucksack pillow.

The morning was dull. I heard planes coming over, but planes came over day and night so that was nothing new. That part of France is open with big fields a few forests and not many people. Apart from the Allied air patrols it was all very quiet, all very French.

Then I noticed a lot of bustle around a forest about 1km away to the east. I was surprised to look out of the top door with my binoculars and see a lot of Luftwaffe over there, maybe 20 or so crunching around. There was a lorry too that went along a lane and then into the forest that was heavily loaded, I could tell because it squished the mud. I didn't expect to see Luftwaffe out here in the middle of nowhere. Was there an airfield I hadn't seen? Maybe a Flak battery? With so much activity it occurred to me that something was going on. I knew the Germans wouldn't turn up at some remote forest in northern France for no reason, but this didn't look like some rear-guard action.

I took out more of the food the hotel kitchen had packed for me and settled down to consider the next part of my journey. Then I dozed back to sleep on the straw.

Suddenly there was a tremendous loud dull brrrr... like a very loud tractor but much faster and louder! Not like anything I'd ever heard before. Sort of brrrr... pulsing very quickly. Ravens squawked and flew up in all directions. I grabbed my binos and rushed to the door to see what was making the commotion. It was in the little forest! Then it seemed as if the forest had burst into a great fire, but there was no flame - just clouds, like the steam of a steam engine. The droning brrrr... continued but the forest was engulfed in a billowing white cloud. Then I heard a sort of whoosh and a tremendous blast, and a little aeroplane shot away! It wasn't like any aeroplane I'd ever seen though. Amazing! Small and grey it was, with a pipe at the back and flame coming out of it. Extremely fast! No pilot! I couldn't believe my eyes as bits fell off and the thing shot away in a northerly direction at incredible speed. How could there possibly be an airfield in that tiny forest?

'Hände hoch!' came a youthful shout from behind. 'Turn around.' I heard the sound of a MP40 being cocked. For a second I thought there was no point in turning around, I thought I was dead. In my excitement I'd gotten careless for just a moment. Now it was going to cost me.'

****

I'd cycled over Kew Bridge on a lovely early August morning. I was feeling pleased with myself. I had survived this far, and Paul hadn't managed to destroy me.

Only qualified geriatric nurses were allowed to take notes or administer medications. Only the doctor or pharmacist could make any changes to medications. This never bothered me as I knew my job was dealing with Paul, change sheets, find false teeth, make tea, and run around making myself useful. With the exception of dealing with Paul, these were all easy tasks.

Some of the guests were old and confused. Some had Alzheimer's. Some were just cussed troublemakers who were bored. Most were just pleasant old folks who read their Daily Mails and Telegraphs quietly in a corner or in their rooms. They aired their opinions to me once or twice and asked me to comment, but to be honest I didn't care for what they had to say. I just smiled sweetly. I lost count of the number of times I said, 'Yes, that's nice.' Their relatives came and went, and it was all fairly mundane.

Aside from Paul, who was the centre of my attention, I was getting bored too. I'd just got my degree and was thinking about my master's year. I was thinking about modelling, thinking about machines, and thinking about Manchester. My mind was miles away when I spotted and picked up a box of medications that had fallen under Giles' day chair, and I just put it up on the side out of the way. Giles glanced at me and smiled. He was 82 and I knew he'd been diagnosed with Alzheimer's. Since Brian left Marcus always sat next to Giles. As I walked on I remembered there was a joke in the staff room that 'Giles never smiles.' It didn't register with me that Giles had just smiled…

At the end of the afternoon handover meeting Mel asked me quietly to stay behind for a minute. Sure, I said. The door was clicked closed and Mel turned to me reached out and handed me a box of medications. It was the same box I'd picked out from under Giles' chair. With a stare she said, 'Katie, can you tell me how Marcus ended up with Giles' medication?'

Oh, Shit! Oh my God. My blood ran cold.

I wondered if I'd poisoned Marcus. I wondered what everyone else would say. Most of all I wondered at how stupid and careless I'd been. I am an engineer normally so meticulous. I felt tears welling and rolling down my cheeks. I heard someone say, 'Sit down dear.' It was Mel.

'Luckily, we always double check each other when administering meds. We spotted it was the wrong box at teatime. You made a mistake.'

I looked up, but tears were streaming, and I could hardly see.

'If you find medications hand them in to the duty supervisor immediately.'

'Yes Mel,' I heard myself say.

She paused and then said, 'But Katie, you got Giles to smile. In one day, you've managed to do something we've spent months failing to do. You did a really good thing today, well done.'

'Thank you Mel.' I felt much better.

'Off you go home and I'll see you tomorrow. From now on I want you to spend more time with Giles, I'll schedule that, okay?'

'Yes Mel. Thank you,' I gasped.

Cycling home, it seemed to me that I'd lived more in that one day than in all of the last year.

****

'I raised my arms, turned around and saw a very young soldier. I still have no idea why what came out of my mouth, came out: 'Do you fly model aeroplanes?' The binoculars were hanging around my neck in plain sight.

'What?' The young soldier in front of me was incredulous, but his machine gun was three metres away pointing at my chest. He couldn't miss. His uniform had red epaulettes with a single bird. This meant he was *ein Flieger*, a flier: the lowest rank in the Luftwaffe. Unusual for that rank to carry an MP40.

'Model aeroplanes, you fly them?'

'You're German!' he exclaimed. Saxony accent.

'Alsatian, from Straßburg,' I replied, 'and my name is Paul. Please don't point that machine pistol, you're scaring me!'

246

He lowered the gun and cautiously uncocked it. 'Yes, I flew model gliders, I started when I was 12. I am from Göttingen in *Niedersachsen* (Lower Saxony). Do you know where that is?'

'Yes, of course everyone has heard of Göttingen! There is the famous university and hospital, also the Händel music festival. I have never been there though.'

He didn't look much older than me. He asked, 'What are you doing here? It's a long way to Straßburg.'

His question put me on the spot. It seemed so unlikely that a 17-year-old boy from Straßburg would be in the roof of some barn 500km from home. Then I thought, hang on, I was sent from Jersey to Valognes to join a construction team. So, I said the only thing I could think of: 'I am a worker here, and it's a long way to Göttingen.'

'Yes – it's a long way,' he replied, his face falling. He continued, 'The special building is finished, and we are launching. Why are you here? You're German, we don't send Germans to do work like this.'

'Yes we do. The local workers can't be trusted. Half of them are with the Resistance. I was injured and had to go to the hospital. An idiot dropped a tree on me!' I lied.

'Ha-ha, very funny!' He'd finally smiled.

'I flew in a Kranich glider at Wasserkuppe in 1938.'

'Fantastic!' exclaimed the young soldier.

'What's your name?'

'Dieter,' he replied reaching into his inside pocket and fishing out a photograph of three boys with balsa wood gliders to show me. 'I used to fly model aeroplanes. That's me with my brothers in 1938. I'm the youngest, on the right.'

'Beautiful gliders Dieter! I came back, but the special building is finished, I'm with the Reich Labour Service. I've been doing my bit,' I told him. Some of it was true.

'Very good. I was in the *Hitlerjugend Luft*: *ein Flakhelfer* (a Flak helper). Now I'm here.'

I was starting to get somewhere with Dieter. I showed him my RAD badge.

For a minute I thought I was going to get away with it. Just when I was considering asking him to let me leave matters took a turn for the worse, much worse.

Downstairs the door catch clicked, and another voice shouted, 'Dieter, where are you? Are you in here?' In my mind I begged for Dieter to say nothing. I looked at him hoping against hope that he would stay silent. He didn't.

'Yes Corporal, I'm up here with a RAD worker.'

'What?' the corporal roared. He clumped up the stairs and stood. 'Who the hell are you?'

'My name is Paul von Bonn and I'm with the RAD.' The corporal was not impressed and stared at the binoculars.

'What are you doing here boy?' The *Obergefreiter* had the Flak Troop insignia. He reeked of pine resin and tobacco, but when he looked at me he smelled a rat. 'The RAD left here two weeks ago and you should've gone with them.'

'I was injured and had to go to the hospital.'

'Your accent - where are you from?'

'Straßburg,' I mumbled.

My accent was being listened to carefully by soldiers who didn't speak good German themselves. I almost laughed, but then the *Obergefreiter* said harshly: 'So, French then.' I didn't feel like laughing after that. His eyes fixed on the binoculars, 'And why d'you need those? This is a secret installation and there isn't supposed to be anyone here except us. Take him to Moser. Let him sort it out,' he ordered a stunned looking Dieter.

My heart sank. I'd almost fooled the young *Flieger*, but I hadn't fooled the *Obergefreiter*. Those binoculars made things look bad for me. Now I was for it.

As I was marched down the stairs all I could think of was something my father used to say, 'We'll have to see about that then, won't we?' It always made me smile, but today it wasn't funny. Around my neck I wore the Dienst (Service) binoculars he took from a downed German pilot in 1917.

They walked me through the mud into the muddier forest. The sun was coming out. There were small wooden huts but no airfield, not even a small one. Beyond that was a clearing in the trees with a large square concrete pad and odd-looking machinery at the base of a long structure that looked like a ski-jump ramp. I'd been skiing in Switzerland several times and seen a German film about it called *Der weiße Rausch* (The White Ecstasy) at The Forum in 1941. I saw that with mother, and it was an odd evening. A beautiful film it featured Leni Riefenstahl, a German actress who seemed to excite the full house of soldiers present. My mind was wandering. I might as well be a million miles from The Forum and Jersey. Would I ever see my mother again? Or, more likely - would I be taken as a spy and shot?

I was trudged towards what looked like a Command Post. A tough looking thing made of thick concrete just like a smaller version of a Corbière bunker. There were other small buildings scattered about. The fragrance of the pine wood was overwhelming but now I was aware of another set of scents which overpowered even that; petrol fumes and a smell like ammonia or peroxide like in the coiffurists in St Helier. These odd odours, alongside the smell of chalky mud and the immediacy of the memory of my parents were preoccupying me.

The truth was, I'd rather be anywhere than here in this forest in France.

The *Obergefreiter* roughly took the binoculars from round my neck and went into the Command Post. There were two other young sentries, and I knew if I ran I'd be shot, so I didn't run. It was then that I heard shouting and a lot of activity around the base of the ramp about 30 metres away. I was amazed to see young Luftwaffe wearing thick protective suits busily working around another of the small grey aeroplanes I'd seen from the barn. It was so small - only eight or nine metres long with silly little wings. In my head I heard mother saying, '*Incroyable!*' It was hanging from a sort of trolley. Being closer I could see that the ramp line pointed off in the direction of England. It had a pipe running through it. The aeroplane was being placed on the bottom. I could see that it was a sort of take-off ramp.

I just couldn't see how that aeroplane would fly. No propellor. It must have been a model, perhaps an experimental rocket of some sort? My father would have been very interested!

Reality returned when the door of the CP squealed open, and I was ushered inside. In front of me stood an *Oberleutnant*. He wore the yellow pilots piping on a tired-looking windbreaker jacket. He eyed me up and down. My binoculars were sitting on top of some sort of control panel. Bit odd to see a pilot amongst flak troops, perhaps he'd retained his uniform for status? There was also a photo of a Focke-Wulf 190 fighter aircraft at some dusty airfield and a pilot standing beside it wearing a parachute.

'I hear your name is Paul and that you are with the RAD from Straßburg,' said the tall officer in a thick Austrian accent. He looked rough and unshaven.

'Yessir,' I said at attention.

'Relax, you're not on duty now. I am Moser. Aren't you a little young to be so far from home on a work unit?

All I could think of was to try a tactic like the one that had worked on Dieter. 'Do you enjoy skiing sir?'

'No, I don't ski,' he replied moving forward awkwardly holding up the incriminating optics. 'What were you doing in the barn with these?'

I had my story ready.

'They are my father's sir. He gave them to me to remember him by.'
'Where is your father?'
'Russia sir.' A lie.
The Leutnant's expression changed. 'Ivan, huh?'
'Yes sir.'
He took back the binoculars and examined them carefully. 'These are Heer binoculars from 1916. Your father was in that war too?'
'Yes sir.' Not a lie. My father really *was* in the Great War.
'God. That's tough! Your father in the first war, now in Russia serving Germany again, and now his son is here in France.' Then he said, 'I know a lot of your folk were sent to fight in Russia.' By *your folk*, he meant: *Alsatians*.
'Yes sir,' I said. I'd guessed right that he'd been to Russia. Most had.

His eyes blinked when he said, 'I used to fly before they sent me there. Anyone who goes to Russia is a brave man. Your father is a brave man. Two wars. That's tough.' There was despair in the young man's voice, and a pause whilst he flew his Focke-Wulf over the Steppe... Then he came back to earth.

'Now Paul, if you are who you say you are, you will have the papers to prove it, so, papers please.'

My papers were in my rucksack in the barn, but I didn't think going to the barn was a smart idea. They would find my camera and fully loaded British revolver. That would definitely not look good for me either.

'Sir, I came from the hospital yesterday and slept in the barn. I thought my unit would be here. At the hospital, my uniform disappeared, and my papers were in the uniform.'

'Which hospital Paul?' Moser asked adding dryly, '*und Lügen haben kurze Flügel.*' (And lies have short wings)

I had no idea, so I guessed. 'Rouen, Sir.'

'Rouen has many hospitals. Which one?' he asked patiently.

'Hospital Rouen, Sir,' I said with a nice French twist then instantly realised how stupid that was. It was a total guess. I had no idea if there actually was a Hospital Rouen.

I looked at the Austrian's face and he studied mine. My tiny inclusion of a French accent had triggered some inkling of discomfort in him. But he didn't know whether there was or wasn't a Hospital Rouen. He pulled a slight grimace and nodded his head.

'Alright Paul, I'm going to find out about this hospital and contact them to see about recovering your papers. If they have your gear I'll have my corporal take you to Rouen tonight and you can return to your work party. It isn't safe for you here.'

He picked up the phone. All the while he was looking at me in a slightly quizzical way as if something didn't sit right with him. As he passed me those damned binoculars I held my breath. It was a good job they were German and not British. If they'd been British I would already be dead. He tapped the set. No answer.

He'd said it wasn't safe here. I'd heard other Germans describe places as, *'not safe.'* That had to be taken seriously. Then he said, 'The line is dead, but I'll help you get your gear back as soon as the line is restored, or I will send a runner. By the way, who is your main troop leader? I may have met him at hand-over.' He was testing me again.

I stared at him blankly. I had no idea. I knew the organisational structure of the Labour Service but nothing more. Of course I didn't know the name. The Leutnant's eyes narrowed as he stared at me. 'Well, Arbeitsmann, who is it?' I had come to the end of the line.'

****

'Three shots rang out. Along some Jersey hedgerow, half a mile away, I knew more Russian slave workers had been shot. I knew to not go and look, not for an hour or two. Bill had gone to look once and he'd been shot at by a guard, at least that's what he told us. We'd gotten used to it. We would walk along a granite bramble lane and come to large dark red patches which made the grass glisten. These patches looked like oil leaks from a truck, except they were blood. Sometimes there were bits of skull too.

I didn't associate these killings with my friends at Corbière. Hans and the men there were soldiers with a job and a sense of pride and duty. The *Organisation Todt* guards that were shooting the Russians had no humanity at all. They just pulled the trigger and walked on. I hadn't seen them do it, but I knew they had.'

For over a year now Paul had been telling me things past my reckoning, unbelievable things. Shootings, beatings, deportations, pools of dried blood: he had grown up amongst these horrors. In a way that I didn't understand, all of this was somehow normal for him.

I didn't understand fear, didn't understand hate. I had little experience of death. I took life and the expectation of long life so totally for granted that it just wasn't something I ever thought about. Paul didn't have a life like that. He'd been mortar bombed, shot at, held at gunpoint, and had seen and been close to death. He wasn't even a soldier; he was a schoolboy. How many European children had grown up in conditions like these? How many children had lost their brothers or sisters, mothers, or fathers? How many children had died? I knew it must be millions. Older Nazis had caused the war, but it was the young who suffered most. Their futures had been poisoned and taken away. They made no choices.

I was in no doubt that I had been fed a sanitised version of war from many directions: newspapers, primary school history, conservative politicians, all sorts of places. Even some of the other old people at the home had fed me 'facts' about the war. There was such a gap between their accounts and Paul's. They hadn't been there, Paul had. War was about survival. He'd used his youth and intelligence and did whatever it took to survive.

A V-1 missile being prepared for launch, near Rouen, July 1944

14. The air attack

"Who is your troop leader? Well, Arbeitsmann, who?'
I could hear the blood hissing in my ears, pulsing. My mouth was dry...
The Austrian reached out with two open palms as if pleading. 'Too many Germans have died in this war, and the last. Good Germans. Your *Haupttruppführer* might be dead anyway, killed in a fighter-bomber raid or shot by the French. How should I know? War is terrible, it brings out the worst in us. You're young and a long way from home. Your father is a long way from home. Perhaps you and I will never see home again.'

I didn't really catch what he was saying because I thought my lack of an answer was a death sentence. But I was still standing there so I began to listen. It seemed that even though he had a good reason to have me shot, he wasn't going to because I had a credible account for why I was there. He wanted to believe that I was German, and that my father was on the Eastern Front.

'Do you want to go home Paul?'

'Yes sir.'

'Well then, I will have the corporal take you back to Rouen right now and you can sort it out for yourself and return to your unit. I don't want you here.'

I was dumbfounded. All I could say was, *'Wie bitte?'* (Pardon?) I was trembling so much I nearly fell down.

The Leutnant smiled, and I smiled back. In that moment I knew his truth: all he wanted was to go home. I on the other hand, was *not* telling the truth. My father was in Berlin, not in Russia. I was heading away from Jersey and couldn't get there even if I'd wanted to.

Moser stood and walked awkwardly to the heavy door. Out of balance and holding on firmly he opened it with a graunch and we stepped outside. The sounds in the forest were sharp after the dullness of the bunker, but we could hear aircraft engines... They were getting closer fast: twin Merlin engines. I recognised that sound: *Mosquitoes*. The officer looked at me horrified. Then I was aware of a bustle further into the woods and could hear shouting again, 'Attention, Fighter Bombers. Get to your positions!'

The crew loading the aeroplane on the ramp had disappeared. Moser ran awkwardly on his artificial leg into the forest calling orders. I heard him shout, 'Run Paul, RUN!'

Two 3.7cm anti-aircraft guns were pumping rounds low into the sky in the direction the take-off ramp was pointing. I hadn't spotted those; they were in deep camouflage hidden either side of the ramp.

What happened next happened very quickly. There was a deafening explosion just outside the wood, then another. The earth shook and trembled, and soil flew high into the air. There were screams and flames. Two *Mosquitoes* flew at breath-taking speed along the ramp at about 50 feet in a shrieking thundering crescendo. My God! I panicked. I didn't know what to do. I saw the open door of the bunker. There was a choice: hide in the bunker or run. I ran.

Behind me more explosions, trees crashed to the ground, there was a metallic pinging: strafing. Men were shrieking.

I ran as if hell was opening to swallow me, the desperate mud trying to suck me back.

Then another sound, a fizzing whoosh: rockets. The Mosquitoes were firing rockets into the forest. The trees strained and broke in the tornado blast as each one crashed home. There was a tremendous crack as a missile hit and destroyed concrete: the bunker.

Only one Flak 3.7 was firing now, but there was the crackle of light arms fire: machine pistols and Mausers. There was an enormous blast, far bigger than any of the other explosions. I found myself flung face down in the mud 10 metres further on ears whistling, but I stood up and ran headlong. The aircraft soared overhead again making the air resonate with vibration that coursed through my body. I hid behind the barn and looked back. The forest was on fire now, smoke billowing. I watched the Mosquitoes turn for another attack. I couldn't hear them.

The third run poured a hail of cannon fire and rockets into the forest, at least four more hits in the centre. I lost count. The two aircraft followed this with stupendous high-speed climbing turns onto a fourth even more deadly run, with a salvo of four more missiles from the first and two from the follower. The air was filled with the smell of cordite, burning wood, mud, and concrete dust. The firing had stopped - or I couldn't hear it. The aircraft swooped around again, and I could clearly see the brown leather jacket and helmet of the pilot in the lead. His aircraft had large bullet holes in it. The second aircraft had pieces missing all over. Bits of the fin were gone, and daylight could be seen through holes in the wing and fuselage. On that last fly around, they were having a look. Then they cleared off.

I watched for a while to make sure the aircraft were gone and then stumbled back towards the installation, or what was left of it. My ears were whistling, and I was dizzy. I couldn't hear anything. I tripped, fell into the mud, and lay there.

Time passed. I don't know how long, maybe hours.

I woke up in the mangled forest then struggled through the deeply riven earth which was hot to the touch. Everything was broken, even the bunker was smashed. It had taken a direct hit.

There were soldiers, or what was left of them. They had been rendered, stripped of flesh, and looked like red jam wrapped in rags. That would have been me if I hadn't run.

There were huge smoking craters all around, charred tree stumps and shattered metal. The small aeroplane had exploded and destroyed a huge chunk of the forest.

Nothing was left alive; it was like everything had been put through a mincer. I could smell the burnt flesh in amongst the pine resin; shreds of burned meat in bits of red-soaked blue Luftwaffe uniforms. There were arms, hands, teeth, helmets with heads in. I found what I thought was Dieter. He was sitting slumped in a trench just in his shirt which was mangled in blood and wood splinters.

I walked back to the barn dizzy and shaking and pulled my bike and revolver out. I got my stuff together but fell over drunkenly. My ribs on both sides hurt. In a deaf stupor, I wandered away from the barn down the lane.

Then I thought it might be useful to have Dieter's papers, so I decided to go back and get them.

Giddy I looked around and saw more patrolling aircraft, but couldn't hear them. As I looked up I fell over again.

There wasn't anyone out here. Nobody came to see what was going on. The countryside was empty. I'd chosen my barn because it was in the middle of nowhere.

I passed three unbroken bodies, two in German police uniform, and an SS man. They lay side by side in a little wood. Each had a single bullet wound in the back of the head, and there was a huge pool of blood.

Soon I was back in the carnage of the forest.

The fires were dying down, but the craters were still smouldering. Ravens were hopping around helping themselves to the remains of the men and boys. They flew as I climbed in and out of the uprooted tree stumps.

German soldiers took great care of their papers and always carried them in their tunic inside pocket. This was the place to start looking. I searched and found the blood splattered paybook of the Austrian Leutnant, but not his body. He wouldn't be going home. Some uniforms contained pulverised flesh which poured out of sleeves and onto my boots.

Then I found Dieter's shredded body again. His legs were gone below his kneecaps. Death had come but he was serene. I sat and studied him for a long time. His face was radiant, with eyes still open, a red blush on his cheeks and not the blue tinge. As I closed his eyes for the last time I knew that angels were watching.

His tunic was missing but then I found fragments of one in a tree that had been blasted over and this turned out to be Dieter's. I reached in the pocket and picked out his blood-splattered paybook, *Hitlerjugend* (HJ) identity papers and dagger. His *Ahnenpaß* was soaked in blood. I also found some letters he'd received from home, letters from his girlfriend and his mother. He had one that he'd written complete and ready to send. Then I found a photo of his girlfriend. Finding that photo had a sudden impact.

I sat on a tree stump in the steaming remnants of the installation and studied the photo. It was signed gently in pencil, '*Your Gertrude H*' on the back. A sweet face with a winning smile, probably 18 or 19-years-old. She was wearing a casual outfit and sitting relaxing on a tree stump in a forest somewhere. It occurred to me that her Dieter had died in a forest and here I was sitting on a tree stump looking at her on her tree stump. Only an hour ago her boyfriend was alive and now I was the only person alive who knew he was dead.'

'Here, I'll show you,' he said, reaching once again into his bed side drawer.

He pulled out a wad of old brown papers and photos. He carefully chose one in particular, a letter. Then he found and passed a photo to me. I was incredulous as I turned it over and read the pencilled '*Deine Gertrude H.*'

It was the photo from that forest in 1944. Oh my God...

Then he read the letter to me in beautiful and respectful German:

'Gertrude Heckel, Mauerstraße 19, Göttingen. 6te Juli 1944

My dearest Gertie

I cannot tell you where I am in France, but I am not at the front. I have not been here long, and we are a long way from any troublemakers. I haven't shot at anyone yet and I hope I never have to, but if the time comes I will do my duty.

There are some new people in my unit who are very young. They have come from training and have not seen any action at all. I feel like a veteran! They tell me about how life is back home. A lot of us are homesick, even the Leutnant I think.

I am homesick - but more specially - I am homesick for you. I want to be with you and walk with you by the river and through the Kerstlingeröder Feld. I miss you and the good times we had.

I know that life is hard for us now, but in my dreams I know that we will be together again. I promise that I will take care of myself and come home to you.

Please give my love to my dear mother if you should see her at the Wochenmarkt.

With all my love, your Dieter XXX'

'I found myself sobbing. Dieter was a young man like me. Now his broken body was lying dead at my feet. He had a mother, a lover and although he was homesick beyond words he believed in the future. On the other hand, I was heading away from home. Where was my home anyway? Jersey? Hardly. I wasn't homesick and couldn't consider the future. My mother would be thinking about me every minute day and night, but I wasn't thinking of her. I felt cold inside. Why was I here? What was I thinking? Why was I prying into the life of this dead man? What was I doing in this forest of death? I didn't know.

I took Dieter's papers and his oval metal dog tag which indicated that he was part of *IV./Flak-Regiment 155 (W)*. He was Dieter Winkler, which means Grocer. I kept the dog tag, photo and letters. The other thing was - I didn't want Dieter to die. I had the deepest respect for him. I sensed he could help me. He lived at Mauerstraße 30 Göttingen, and I wanted him to go home to his Gertrude even though that was impossible.

Once again I thought: in another reality, he could have been my friend.

Dieter could have shot me on the spot, but he didn't. Now that I had read his letter to Gertie I knew why. He was just another kid like me. He didn't want to kill anyone. He had lived his young life, met a girl and had hopes and dreams and seemed to have a life worth living. It felt worthwhile to keep his letters and the photo of Gertie and try to find a way to return them to Mauerstraße. Even though he was dead in front of my eyes, Dieter seemed to me to be more alive than ever.

He couldn't live his life, but perhaps I could live some of it for him? Gradually I knew what to do.'

What was Paul doing? I didn't like to interrupt, but I just had to ask. So, I put down my now empty teacup and was about to speak, but then I looked again at the letter to Gertrude, and her photo. I stared at her and her pencilled signature still quite fresh and legible. Then I looked at Dieter's papers and the photograph of him. A life was there: *a life unhappened*. It seemed to me in that moment that death is just that: a life that didn't happen because death intervened. Death had intervened for Dieter Winkler, but it seemed that Paul von Bonn had other ideas for him.

There was an odd look on his face as if he were mystified by something he'd said earlier, something out of place.

After a reflective pause he said, 'My plan was always to get my father out. I had to go to Germany, and I was sure Dieter Winkler could help me in some way.'

Stunning was the word that came closest. He looked up at me and said, 'I warned you it would be hard. I told you that you might be better off not knowing.'

I found all this very difficult to cope with. I remember I welled up.

I don't know what upset me the most. Was it the thought of two dozen soldiers annihilated in the forest? Was it Paul's tale of Dieter and his girlfriend and how he sobbed on reading the letter? Or was it the thought of Paul himself nearly being blown to bits? It all hit me extremely hard. Then I looked and saw that I still had in my hand Dieter's blood-stained identity book, his letter to Gertrude and her photo and *now I sobbed* uncontrollably. The immediacy of the moment overwhelmed me just as the air attack had overwhelmed those men and taken their young lives. The old man held my wrists and passed tissues. He'd lived those moments over and over again. I looked into his eyes, and saw the mud, the tree stumps and Dieter's blood-soaked body.

After a while, I can't remember how long, he took himself off to bed. I just sat there.

It was right near the end of my shift. Lawrence was supervising. He saw I'd been crying so sent me off 15 minutes early. I got home and did not sleep. It was too awful.

The next day I went in early, hesitated but then poured the tea and took my seat.

Coming back

'The pain in my head gradually increased. I never knew ears had so much liquid in them. Pink fluid oozed out. I was dizzy, deaf and in agony. Berlin was 1000km away and it was out of the question to continue.

I kept Dieter's papers, packed my stuff and as the rain fell I began a slow cycle back to Rouen.

I had to stop several times as I was woozy. Twice I went into a hedge, once into a ditch and once into a stone wall skinning my knuckles. In the end I gave up and walked using the bike as a prop to stop myself falling over. My head was ringing, and my right side hurt like hell. It rained relentlessly, and I staggered back into Rouen looking like a drowned rat thoroughly chastened and virtually deaf.

I heaved myself around to the back entrance and into the kitchen. Maxine was shocked to see me and the state I was in: bedraggled and caked in soggy mud with blood running out of my ears and down my cheeks. Uncle Claude came and was appalled. He spoke, but I couldn't hear. He immediately called a doctor. I was in so much pain.

The doctor looked at my ears and shook her head. She said something but I had no idea. She wrote it on paper: 'What happened to you?' When I tried to speak it hurt so I simply wrote that I didn't know, which was mostly true. The doctor shook her head again. If I'd told her the truth, I don't think she would have believed that either. I had three broken ribs on the right and one on the left.

It all hurt too much. All the while Maxine was cleaning off the mud, blood and gunge with a sponge into a bowl of water on the table. The doctor produced a potion out of her big brown leather bag. I was told later that it was an opium-based concoction. I think it was laudanum. Whatever it was it laid me out good and proper. I don't know anything about what happened after that, and they kept giving it to me...

I awoke in a sort of deaf numbness. I was back in Strasbourg in the *Notre Dame* alone sitting at a pew. I could hear Mozart, coming from the walls somehow. It was *Requiem* and breathtakingly beautiful. The clarinet rose, and the strings played. Four singers appeared, opened their libretto, and sang in Latin *Recordare*. (Paul translated):

'May such great effort not be in vain
Righteous judge of vengeance,
Grant me the gift of absolution
Before the day of retribution.
Faint and weary you have sought me,
Redeemed me, suffering on the cross.'
- **Mozart. Requiem in D minor. K.626. IIId Sequentia**

This was a marvellous and miraculous swoon: a Rapture rolling across my mind like the waves on St Ouen's beach or the wind blowing in my hair on Mont du Vallet, thrilling, soaring and superb, uplifting beyond anything earthly.

Then it changed. As I looked up again the hairs on the back of my neck bristled. The singers had disappeared, and the walls of the great cathedral melted to clear glass. I heard a noise, and in the distance saw the two black & white striped Mosquito aircraft coming towards me. I was back in the forest, and it was all in slow-motion. The propellers of the aircraft rotated slowly as they levelled their wings. Suddenly it was not safe. I was out in the open again and in extreme danger. My mind said run, but my body was incapable of reaction, frozen with fear.

The Mozart morphed. The Mosquitoes unleashed their missiles and this time it was *Dies irae*:

'Day of wrath, day of anger
will dissolve the world in ashes,
as foretold by David and the Sibyl.
Great trembling there will be
when the Judge descends from heaven
to examine all things closely.'
- **Mozart. Requiem in D minor. K.626. IIIa Sequentia**

The missiles flew and *absolute terror* gripped me. Terror. Desperation. Panic. I tried to close my eyes, but they remained open. I didn't want to see how it ended. They told me later that they heard a shattering scream and ran upstairs expecting to find me dead. Instead, I was hiding under the bed screeching and wailing. I don't remember what happened after that.'

Going away again

A few days later he confessed that he was surprised at what he'd told me. This time there was no retaliation, no aggression because he'd been 'weak.' He just carried on as normal. Despite the trauma he seemed ok, lighter even.

Looking back, I'm not sure if I was surprised by this. He'd tried to not tell me, tried to push me away. He'd tried his hardest to not let the story come out. But somehow, it had. It was as if he'd finally told himself it was alright, and he'd given himself permission.

'Because I was in no state to stop them Claude and Maxine explored all my kit and this time they had questions: 'Where did you get this dagger?' 'Where did you get this Nazi party badge?' 'Who did you get this British pistol from?' The best question of all had to be: 'What the hell happened to you out there?' Good question. Even now all this time later, I still don't know.

Dieter's papers were blood-splattered but all intact. Claude had questions about those too. I told him that Dieter was about 18 and had been killed. He got upset, shed a tear, and said simply, *poor bastard*. Like his sister, my uncle was a hugely compassionate person. He could not abide death, particularly young and pointless death in a cause that was not worthy. *Bastard Nazis* was all he could hiss.

As I gradually recovered I heard reports on the radio. The Allies were hammering the Germans and getting slowly closer to Rouen. They were taking an almighty battering.'

I also felt like I'd taken a battering. When I listened to Paul it was like a sort of breathlessness took hold, the mind raced, and the blood pulsed. He had a way of describing things that no teacher of mine ever possessed nor could ever dream of. He had vividity, he had passion, and he had expression. It was the inside of his life; his inner world, and he was sharing it freely with me.

****

The Rouen bridges had been hit repeatedly by Allied air-strikes even before Paul arrived. His aunt and uncle's hotel had been popular with pilgrims to Place du Vieux Marche where the English had burned St Joan of Arc at the stake. He told me he'd always felt unnerved at the place where she died. He said the agony and fear were still there and that he could feel it.

The hotel was well away from the targeted areas. Nevertheless, air raid sirens sounded frequently, and despite his delirious state, Paul had to be escorted out to the shelter. Rouen was hit several more times. He started screaming and trembling each time the planes came over.

He tried to cycle away twice but was forced to retreat because he soon got pain breathing and couldn't keep his balance.

After about four weeks Paul had recovered much of his hearing and his broken ribs gave less discomfort. The doctor came, checked him, and admonished him for his foolish attempts to escape. He swore at her and told her he was leaving before the end of the month, no matter what.

The Germans were fleeing over the river Seine on barges and pontoons escaping eastwards.

Claude and Maxime begged him to stay. They had no children of their own and protected Paul as if he were theirs. He was adamant he was leaving, and on Saturday, 26 August 1944 he did just that. He pocketed the bottle of the opium-based pain relief 'just in case.'

He made for the same barn where he'd been five weeks earlier and slept there the night. Nothing had changed. Next day he set off eastwards again. He joked that he'd actually gotten further this time.

15. At the crossroads – Sunday, 27 August 1944

'I was cycling along the old roman road direct to Amiens through tiny unspoiled French hamlets but struggling with my breathing and balance.

You would not know there was a war going on except for the air activity all around. As I approached a tiny place, Saint-Clair, which was at a crossroads, I noticed a roadblock of farm carts and milk churns up ahead. A long way short, I stopped and checked with my binoculars. I was wise to stop. No sign of any German uniforms. This meant it had to be a Resistance roadblock. Fluent French meant I would probably be able to easily blag my way past it. However, if they searched my kit they would find two sets of German papers, a Nazi party badge, a Hitlerjugend dagger, a German camera and binoculars and a British revolver. That would not look good for me. So, I reversed back down the road until I came to an iron framed roadside crucifix at a junction. I have to confess that it hadn't registered as I went by the first time. Now I stopped and paid it my full respects, crossing myself, wrapping my rosary and kneeling.

As I was doing that I glanced right and saw two more young cyclists coming up the road from the direction of Rouen. In France it was typical to greet other cyclists with 'Bonjour,' and sometimes stop and pass the time of day. As I called my greeting they whizzed by, and one gruffly called 'Bonjour' in reply. Not French. I called to them again, 'Kameraden?'

(Comrades?) They slowed and circled around back to me.

'Sie sind Deutscher?' asked one. They *were* German...

'Alsatian, from Straßburg.'

'Very good! We are looking for the 12th SS divisional support company at Sarcus. Do you know where that is?'

'No,' I said, 'but if you go that way there is a Resistance roadblock and you'll be shot.'

'My God!' said the taller one.

'We are with the 25th Regiment. My name is Ernst, and this here is Hektor. Who are you?' the tall one went on.

'Paul von Bonn,' I replied.

'Surely you should be Paul von Straßburg?' Hektor snorted. Idiot.

They were thin, dressed in civilian clothes and had no equipment. Their bikes were rickety and old, and they looked on at mine enviously.

'We saw you crossing yourself. That superstition won't help you, you know,' Hektor added mockingly.

I wasn't going to take that from him, the SS *Hitlerjugend* or anyone else, so I said, 'That *superstition* just saved your lives. You should show some respect.' They looked at each other nonplussed, as if no-one had ever answered them back. 'Today I'm your guardian angel, you know.'

Then I added, 'If you can't respect that, then perhaps you will respect this,' and reached out my revolver.

'A British Webley pistol. Very good!' Ernst said admiringly. 'Let me see it.' As well as being someone who'd saved them from running into certain death, I was also in possession of a badge of honour. I'd earned their trust.

'Got a map?' asked Ernst. As it happened, I did, a yellow Michelin number 52 and I pulled it out. 'My God, you're full of surprises,' exclaimed Hektor. He was younger than me.

I checked the map, saw Sarcus and that we could by-pass the roadblock. I told them: 'Kommt mit mir.' *(Come with me)*

We set off rightwards at the iron crucifix and passed old farms, orchards and barns set back from the road and through fields ready for harvest. Then we turned right at the main road. We couldn't go north of course, as that was back to the roadblock. This was the Grandvilliers road.'

I had to halt the old man, something I almost never did. 'Why did you stop those soldiers? Why didn't you just let them go to their deaths?'

'I was at a crucifix. As well as that, those boys had mothers too. It was a sign,' he explained.

'We soon came to Sarcus, just a group of farms. We were stopped outside the hamlet by two camouflaged SS *Hitlerjugend* sentries with MP40 machine-pistols who emerged from a hedge. 'Kameraden! Kameraden!' Hektor called. We were told to go and report to the *Heldenklau* (slang: Hero thief) at the Command Post near the church.

In clumps of trees and hedgerows there were assorted vehicles, Kübelwagen, and motorbikes with side cars. Soldiers circulated smoking and muttering. Wounded boys sat with ravens hopping around them scavenging bread.

We found the church, then the CP. The two SS boys went in, and I followed as if I were one of them. They weren't recognised by anyone there.

An SS *Untersturmführer* (Second Leutnant) with a *Das Reich* cuff title and Iron Cross ribbon checked Ernst and Hektor's papers and found nothing untoward. I told him I was Paul von Bonn and gave him my RAD Soldbuch and the Nazi Party badge. I fished out and handed him Dieter's *Ahnenpaß* by mistake. His name was blotted by bloodstains and had no photo, so he didn't notice.

'You've seen action. RAD to Valognes. What happened after that von Bonn?'

'The invasion sir. I got separated from my unit.'

'I'm sure,' he said smiling grimly, examining the bloodied pass and nodding his head.

'I've had an awfully tough time.' My tone betrayed it all.

'I can see that von Bonn. Well, you're here with us now. How's your weapons training?'

'Good sir.'

The officer turned and muttered something to a young sergeant who went out and came back with a MG42 which was badly jammed. He placed it on a table with a brown box of spare parts and tool kit. He told me to strip and fix it. It had multiple problems, but I did it in about two minutes while the two boys from the 12th watched. Then the sergeant handed me a Mauser from a weapons rack. 'See that raven on the roof of the church? Shoot it.'

50 metres. Easier than the apple. I set the sight, braced against the door frame, pulled the trigger, and blasted the bird in a puff of black feathers. This was greeted by a 'Whoa!' from the two *Hitlerjugend*.

'Very good,' said the officer with a smile. 'We're going home to Germany. Your *Ahnenpaß* is good, you're racially pure and you're in the party. Want to come to us? (*Komm zu uns*) Want to join the SS?'

'Yessir,' I replied.

The flea

Just when I thought Paul had run out of surprises, he came out with the biggest surprise of the lot. 'You said you would never collaborate with the Nazis! I thought you hated them?'

'I did hate them. And who said I collaborated? Joining them isn't the same as collaborating with them,' he pushed me right back taking a combative tone.

'Well, if there's a difference, then it must be a pretty subtle one. How about you explain it to me?'

'I was resolved to find my father and the Germans were bound to defend their Heimatland. Now I was falling in with the 12th SS division *Hitlerjugend* who would take me there. It was expedient. All I had to do was play the game.'

'You haven't answered the question. It sounds as if you think collaborating is just a game.'

'Checkmate!' the old man exclaimed with a giggle, 'you've got me!' If you were anyone else and if this were any other place, I would have told you to piss off!'

'But that's not how we do things though, is it?' I laughed. Now we could play games with each other. We were equals. Finally, we were *us*.

He lowered his voice, 'It was a means to an end, and I **did not** collaborate. A farmer in Jersey once told me that when his dog runs to the next field, the flea hitches a ride, and the dog doesn't even know it's there. Meanwhile, the flea is getting to a place it would never get to on its own and enjoying a good feed along the way. Who's the clever one, the dog or the flea?'

'Yes, but fleas don't carry machine guns and rocket-launchers, do they?' I observed dryly.

'Ha-ha! You're on good form today Katie! The point is that in no sense is the flea collaborating with the dog. The relationship is completely one-way.'

'This just sounds like mere sophistry to me.'

'My dear Katie, there is no sophistry when your father is being held in the capital city of the enemy 1000km away. There was only one thing on my mind. Now that I was all the way out here exposed and on my own, I was prepared to do whatever it took. If that meant hitching a ride with the dogs of the 12th SS *Hitlerjugend* then so be it.' It was the pithiest comment he had ever made to me.

By now I knew Paul and understood his faith well enough to freely comment, *'Great trembling there will be when the Judge descends from heaven to examine all things closely.'*

'I am not afraid of my maker,' he said looking me in the eye. 'When the time comes with your help I will face that examination.' He continued:

'The Leutnant said I would be classed as a recruit, and that papers and an SS Soldbuch (paybook) would be organised for me once we began re-fitting. In the meanwhile, I was found an 'overall' uniform, black boots, and enough equipment. I was placed in a makeshift squad as MG2 in the first instance and given two ammunition boxes, a bag with the spare barrel and the tool kit. Werner was MG1. He had a pistol. Hektor and Ernst were also in the squad. I reported to a *Scharführer* (squad leader) called Luther with binoculars and an MP40. We were told that we were going home through hostile territory and that we needed to be ready and follow orders. Once more I became a heavily armed little bastard.

It quickly went around that I was not original 1943 *SS Hitlerjugend*. That first evening in Sarcus the dogs in my squad thought they would test me. First up was Ernst. He told me I was butcher that evening and I had to get two chickens, bring them over, kill, pluck, and clean them for him to cook. No problem. I did that in front of him with Dieter's *HJ* dagger. As a joke I stuck the two heads under the tabs on my helmet. After that my nickname was: Paul *Hahnenkopf*, 'Paul Cockerel head,' or just *Hahn*: 'Cockerel.'

Next was Hektor. He said he liked the look of my bike and would take it. I told him that if he touched it I'd kill him. I'd been looking for an excuse...

He duly picked it up. 'Very light,' he exclaimed laughing at me, 'perfect for a lightweight like you!' Before he could put it down I stood and smacked him one, flattening him. Werner and Luther had to pull me off and I hurt my right hand again, but the point was made.

Finally, *Scharführer* Luther, who was only about 20, asked me casually as we sat eating the dinner of chicken stew and bread what it was like to be '*ein elsässischer Feigling*' (an Alsatian coward). I slowly drew my HJ dagger and, staring at him, told him that if he called me a coward again I would cut his balls off, throw them in the stew and feed them to him on a spoon, always assuming of course that he had balls.

There was a moment of stunned silence.

Then everyone fell about laughing. Ha-ha! From that moment, Luther was called *Luther der Eierlose*, which means 'Luther the ball-less.' Not a very flattering name for a *Scharführer*, but he'd earned it. Luther laughed until he choked! Nobody took the piss out of me after that.

The wounded SS boys in the Normandy hospitals were loathsome. They believed they had been denied their birthright which was to die gloriously in battle. This lot were different. They saw themselves as strong because they had survived.

Overnight we moved to Beauvais in trucks, lorries, anything that had fuel. I went on the back of a bashed-up 1st SS division motorcycle with Werner and the MG42. My precious bike went on the roof of a lorry. There were a lot more soldiers in and around Beauvais.

Next day, the dogs decided to go and help themselves to whatever they could find in people's houses. It was terrible, but there was no point trying to intervene. Anyone resisting risked death. Fortunately for the inhabitants of that fine little town, we moved out that night. This time I was in the back of a 'requisitioned' truck, by that I mean stolen.

In the early hours of the morning, I awoke to find myself 150km further east at a place near the Belgian border called Hirson. Progress! That would have taken me at least two days. Getting fed and heading towards Germany, I had moved further in two days than I had in the last three months.

While we were in Hirson high ranking people came, including a General, and there was a re-organisation. I was placed with remnants of the 26th Regiment, 1st Battalion and told we would be going to Germany to be 're-fitted'. Any 'combat ready' personnel were hastily re-formed into a new command structure ready to cover the retreat.

Other rag tag bands of soldiers joined. They told us horrific stories of how the Resistance had ambushed and captured other groups, cutting off fingers and poking in eyes before finishing them off and dumping the corpses by the roadside for us to find. But the SS had done appalling things, shocking things: committed atrocities beyond imagining.

The dogs continued to help themselves to whatever they could find. Drunken nights and feasts ensued featuring brandy and pork. There was plenty of campfire singing of *Hitlerjugend* and Nazi propaganda songs too.

It was *ekelerregend* (disgusting), I hated those songs. But I mouthed the words and pretended to sing along in order to fit in. They were all too smashed to notice anyway.

Every night there was drunken boasting, and every night the boys talked of how after the 'final victory', they would settle down and get married. Their wives would enjoy the 'three Ks' of *Kinder, Küche und Kirche* (children, kitchen, and church). On one occasion Hektor, who was only about 16, stood and declared loudly: 'I'll take *der Führer's* 1000 Reichsmarks for four children!...' He paused, swayed and, aiming a comment in my direction added, '...although maybe not the church.' His voice was slurred: he was pretty gone... He brayed, 'We are SS: pure German... Any good German woman would want lots of babies from us!' Then he fell over and threw up.

On another boozy evening, I said goodbye to them as they were all classed as 'combat ready.' They joined battlegroups the next day and I never saw them again.

At first I was sure that my 'cover' would be blown, that I would say or do something stupid that would mark me out. But I *wasn't* under cover, not at all. I was taken as what I was: an Alsatian lad from the RAD. Young sure, but so was everyone else. I wasn't even the youngest. There were two wounded boys in my lorry who'd had their 16th birthdays just before D-Day. Now they were veterans. I knew Germany and its recent history and politics, and I knew the war situation and attitudes from listening to the lads back in Jersey. I even had 'letters from home' (from my father) which I got out to read occasionally, just like everyone else did, and a photo of a 'girlfriend', Gertie. It wasn't just convincing, it was normal. I cleaned my kit, took orders, and tried to get on. It wasn't difficult. I didn't talk much, as I felt that to be wise. It looked as if I was living someone else's life, but I wasn't, I was living my own.

The convoy soon entered Belgium. It was some sort of insane dream. I was with the SS: the 12th division *Hitlerjugend,* one of their own. My bike was fitted with a MG34 carrier. I even had my own Mauser and uniform.

We travelled in lorries, cars, whatever was available. It was chaotic and dangerous. Then they made me part of a 'column defence' squad travelling in a motor bike & sidecar as MG2. Around me were wounded and weakened soldiers, fleeing bands of Luftwaffe ground support units and even other RAD youngsters like me. There were air patrols of Typhoons and Mustangs which scared me shitless. All we could do was hide and hope.

The locals were hostile, and our transport barely serviceable. We went via a strange and circuitous route: Charleroi, Gembloux, and Leez. It was at Leez that I finally discovered our destination: Kaiserslautern.'

A 12th SS Hitlerjugend recruiting poster: 'Come to us'

3

GERMANY

1944-1945

'A man's duty is to find out where the truth is, or if he cannot, at least to take the best possible human doctrine and the hardest to disprove, and to ride on this like a raft over the waters of life.'
– Plato

All maps drawn by the author

1. Crossing the border. Christmas 2019

At Christmas I was able to get three days per week for four weeks at the home covering holiday slots for the full-timers. This made me popular with the staff as they were assured of time at home with their families.

I wanted to see my friend Paul, and Mel was happy for me to spend most of that first day back with him. He was in the sunroom with his favourite blanket over his legs, asleep with his mouth wide open. His cup of tea was half drunk and cold with the remains of a half decomposed digestive at the bottom: one of his trademarks. I let him sleep and went off to other duties.

About an hour later he came and found me. 'I'm delighted you're back Katie! They told me you were coming.' I was compromised with a full commode. 'Piece of work!' I groaned.

I dealt with the commode, washed, and then sprayed myself with anti-pong spray and went back to the sunroom. 'Where's the tea?' he said with that cheeky look.

It was soon like old times. Old times with Paul really were *old times*. I saw the man, his photos and heard his memories. It wasn't the 92-year-old talking though, it was the 17-year-old. Who was the real Paul? Where was the real Paul? It was impossible to say. Was it the adolescent desperate for friendship trapped for four years in occupied Jersey? Was it the young man discovering freedom in the summer of 1944 but cycling through a deadly battlefield? Or was it the feisty *SS Hitlerjugend* recruit? Perhaps it was simply this old man in a sunny room in a Kew care home in 2019? It was just like he said: he was always going away but always coming back.

I had learned about Paul, but I had learned just as much about myself: who I was and my relationship to my mother. The old man was a presence in my life while my mother was an absence. Before Paul I didn't want to be aware of that absence. Now it was fully revealed to me. In a way that I didn't understand, mum walking out meant that I had become strong. Hearing how Paul had lost his freedom and lost his father, then hearing how he coped helped me comprehend my loss.

The words of mum's song *This Woman's Work* meant something more to me now. She told me she loved the song so much that she named me after Kate Bush. But after she left I didn't want to be Kate anymore, I wanted to be called Katie. I didn't need her or the name she gave me. I needed something else.

****

It was good to be back at the Stanley, but things had changed. We were short staffed as a lot of young workers had returned to Poland, Lithuania and Spain due to Brexit. Some of the guests asked where they were and couldn't understand why they had left. Then they went back to reading their Daily Mails and Telegraphs.

Things with Paul had changed since the summer stories. I didn't notice at first we were just so pleased to see each other again.

The mind of an old person flashes on and off. Scattered thoughts congregate coalesce and flutter like moths around a streetlight. Occasionally memories break through like a jack-in-the-box bouncing on its spring. Sometimes there is intense focus with details which astound and defy reason. At other times, the image is less bright or well-focussed. Paul's mind was like this.

He'd talked about walking with a friend in the dark. As time went by and I became more attuned to his moods and manner of speech, I increasingly understood that there <u>was</u> something in the dark. When he had a bad day he left his food and told me he couldn't sleep. At these times things were bothering him. I knew because tell-tale phrases and recollections reoccurred.

****

Paul crossed the border into Germany in the first week of September 1944. He told me, 'Journeying south-east in the autumn sunshine, I recalled the ants at St Ouen's when I met Wally. How long ago was that? I really didn't know, but I remembered the sunshine and how I felt that day. The ants were carrying off anything they could find: caterpillars, other insects. All would be consumed. As I sat in the lorry being carried off, I wondered if I too would be consumed, devoured by the forces of the Third Reich?'

Our relationship crossed a border too. I was no longer in awe or frightened of him. I didn't challenge him, and he didn't challenge me. Instead, I was with him: in the lorries, on the back of the motorbike, in the conversations, and we were being carried away. I was frightened with him and for him. He was talking about the greatest trauma in human history, freely describing his part in it, and he'd never told anyone. All I could do was listen with compassion and empathy. It had always been like this between us.

The old man showed me a fabric wallet containing more photos, old money, his crucifix, and SS paybook. Astounding. There he was, on the back of the motorbike and sidecar, in his full regalia. Before I could open my mouth he said, 'I know what you're thinking, but from my point of view it doesn't require explanation.'

He was right, he knew what I was thinking, and when I considered it, I knew what he was thinking too. We had passed beyond the boundaries of questions and answers.

SS Uniform cuff title, 'Hitlerjugend'

2. Duties & training – refitting. September - November 1944

'We were at the 23e Kaserne barracks in Kaiserslautern. Here I was issued with new papers which showed my Straßburg address because I was born there. I was told that should I be killed or wounded; my mother would be informed as soon as possible. I wasn't tattooed with my blood group like the 1943 recruits. They put me into II Battalion 26th Regiment and gave me a stamped dog tag and all my kit. So now it was official: I was in the 12th SS division *Hitlerjugend*.'

****

There were many recruits with Paul at Kaiserslautern. The replacements were a peculiar mixture. About 2000 men were former Luftwaffe (Air Force) or Kriegsmarine (Navy) who had not been trained for ground combat. Some of these were in their late 40s. Others were returning wounded, or a draft of incredibly young men from the Nazi organisation for 14 to 16-year-olds: the *Hitlerjugend*, which had become mandatory during the war. They had missed a lot of schooling as most of them had been attached to anti-aircraft batteries as *Flakhelfer*. There were some groups from the same school. According to Paul, they had all been brainwashed but, he said, 'If you had grown up in Nazi Germany, you would have known no different, and you'd have been the same.' There was further indoctrination in the companies, but they hardly needed it. Paul described these youths as 'mindless.'

Nevertheless, the men and boys were taught to fight hard and kill with anything that came to hand: guns, daggers, even sharpened sticks. There were plenty of training and field exercises.

Paul was marked at first as someone who was reserved and a loner, who didn't fully fit in. In training though he was outstanding - a brilliant sharpshooter. He stood out because he spoke well, was trustworthy, honest, and compassionate, especially to the younger recruits. When the boys asked him if he'd seen any action, he looked at them, grimaced, and said simply, 'Ja.' He followed orders to the letter and spoke up for those who could not, for whatever reason. He was completely loyal to those who showed loyalty to him.

Loyalty was important in the SS *Hitlerjugend*. He had just one friend in his squad: Martin.

Also an only child, Martin was from Berlin and had been a Luftwaffe engineer. Paul said he stood out because he wasn't like the others. 'He was generous independent and intelligent.' Paul got to know him when he let slip that he'd been working on 'secret weapons' at Juvincourt airfield near Laon in France. They'd been forced to clear out when the Americans arrived, and his Luftwaffe unit had fallen back with retreating 12th SS III Battalion. When Paul casually followed that up with questions, he was astounded when Martin fetched out photos of two remarkable aircraft.

'What the HELL is that?' Paul exclaimed.

'It's a *Schwalbe* (Swallow), a Messerschmitt Me 262,' Martin explained proudly, 'a fantastic aeroplane!'

'Surely the propellors would be too small? You took them off, right?'

'It doesn't have propellors. It has a revolutionary engine called a 'Jet Turbine.' It's a type of high-pressure induction-compression engine. There has never been one before. You should see the way that thing flies!

I worked on another incredible aeroplane, the Arado 234A photo reconnaissance jet aircraft. It launched from a sort of trailer, had no undercarriage, and landed like a glider. Very high-altitude, the thing could easily fly to 11,000 metres. No Allied aircraft could get anywhere near it. They're both so fast it's terrifying. Faster and higher than a Mosquito!'

'Faster than a Mosquito?' Paul was incredulous. 'My God Martin, you're full of surprises!'

Also, like Paul, Martin was besotted with aircraft of all types, and they quickly became unshakable friends. Paul said he thought his father and I would be extremely interested in Martin's Me 262 and Arado 234.

It got out that Paul had a Webley, which he showed on a few occasions.

Asked where he'd got it, he said, 'From an English sergeant in the battle of Caen.' It wasn't a lie, and it caused awe. He wasn't supposed to have a personal pistol. After a couple of weeks, the revolver went missing. Paul told his company that if anyone had taken it, they were welcome to give it back and he wouldn't say anything. It wasn't given back, so he reported it to a senior who immediately called for a detailed search.

'The culprit was found, and a boxing match arranged.

He was ex-Kriegsmarine, bigger and older than me but woefully unfit. To loud shouts of *'Kampfhahn Kampfhahn!'* (Fighting cock!) from my squad, I beat the shit out of him in 30 seconds.

I glared at him lying on the grass they untied and took off my gloves.

They picked him up, pulled off his gloves and the Webley was ceremonially placed in his hand. He gave it back in a most pathetic way. As I took the gun I smiled and whispered that next time I would kill him, so there had better not be a next time. He whispered back that only a coward would report the matter. Calmly, I laid into him again and kicked him while he was down breaking two of his teeth and his nose. A sergeant intervened before I did him serious damage.

A watching *Untersturmführer*, Kepler, stepped into the ring and asked my name. He stood and proclaimed that these were the qualities needed in the division and the 'battles ahead.' He told the fallen man to learn his lesson about stealing and get out of his sight. Then two youths helped him stagger away.

Kepler explained to the gathered men and boys, 'When you fight, kill without pity or remorse. Know that if you don't kill them, they **will** kill you. There can be only one winner. Make sure it's you.'

The officer shook my hand and told me I'd done well, but I shrieked in pain. This time my right little finger was dislocated! I had to go to the surgeon to have it put back strapped and bandaged. To add insult to injury, I was reprimanded for having the private pistol and had a week's pay docked. However, after three days, my squad leader handed the Webley back, said he was proud of me and envious, but told me to be more careful.

The knackered finger meant I couldn't cycle away.'

There were many air attacks and Paul's regiment was moved twice during September, first to just north of the town. Then the division was ordered to move to Heilbronn, but the order was cancelled whilst his regiment was in Heidelberg. Paul explained that the Allies had launched an offensive in the north through the Netherlands and that there was talk that the division might be moved there. Such was the concern of a further Allied advance into and across northern Germany that in early October the 12th SS was ordered to move again, this time to the area southwest of Bremen.

Paul described the night train travel as, 'Chaotic but exciting. You travel across a completely black landscape on a completely darkened train. A very surreal experience. These are the times when you notice the smells: pipe tobacco, gun oil, hair cream, sausage, bad breath, even the smell of sweat in your uniform. I really enjoyed it, but the bit I enjoyed the most was that I was being taken ever closer to my father. The dog was running.'

He was now just 350km from Berlin. He joked that all he had to do was be a 'good flea' and hang on. The way things were going, the SS were going to take him all the way.

Paul was regarded as fiery, intelligent, and resourceful, easily able to solve problems and defend himself. He was identified as capable of much more than just fighting in an infantry squad. His weapons and map skills were far in advance of the standard required. In mid-October, he was moved and billeted near to the divisional headquarters in a place called Sulingen. There was a closing out ceremony, and he was given an SS dagger. Soon after that, along with a group of other 'promising' young soldiers, he was invited to volunteer to train to be a driver.

'When they asked if we had any questions, I enquired as to where the training was to take place. I was told it would be at the *Motorobergruppe Ost* (Motor group East) of the National Socialist Motor Corps in Mittweida, Saxony. This was 'due to the war situation.' I didn't know where Mittweida was, but I knew that Saxony was the region which contained Leipzig because we'd flown there before the war. It was closer to Berlin. This, and my circumstances, meant that going there and learning to drive was an absolute gift. I was the first to volunteer and congratulated for doing so. The officer told me, 'It will certainly mean promotion for you' and that, 'I had a great future ahead of me and that my country would be proud.' He had no idea. Martin saw this and stepped forward too.

My group had their orders issued, and we embarked on another series of night trains and devious routing to avoid bombed lines and bridges. On the morning of 24 October 1944, my group and I wheeled our bikes off the train in Mittweida. I was now just 165km from Berlin.'

A month in Mittweida

'The motor school was set in a sprawling country estate and the billets were good. We were regarded as important to the war effort and treated accordingly with decent food and conditions. We started on old motorbikes with relic HJ helmets, then moved on to cars and lorries.

We had smelly brown lignite coal from the local mines for the fires in our rooms, so we were able to dry out and warm up after soaking days riding motorbikes and freezing nights driving lorries with broken heaters. The vehicles were kept in old barns and coach houses and were in generally poor condition. Fixing them was part of the training and we had to get good at it as there was no recovery service. There was no time off, we were always driving or fixing. After complaints, we were told that we'd get leave before returning to the division. When Martin asked if he could go home to Berlin for a few days, the training officer told him he could, and I could go with him.

I remembered the army Berliner my family had summarily beaten up and thrown out of the Big House back in 1940. He'd tried to befriend me with his stories of 'lovely Berlin.' He even had an ancient colour postcard of the Anhalter Station which he'd been sent when he was my age. Perhaps a family heirloom. I stole that postcard, but he didn't come back to reclaim it. Father had been a few times, but my only knowledge of Berlin was his stories and of Beatrice reading me the exciting children's story *'Emil und die Detektive'* (Emil and the Detectives) by Erich Kästner and watching the delightful film in a Saturday matinee with the family in Bonn in 1937.

I requested a pass to go with Martin to Berlin starting on 22 November. We were all promoted to *SS-Oberschütze* (Private First Class), got our orders signed and the day finally arrived.

It was just us going to Berlin. With all our kit we wheeled our bikes back onto the train at Mittweida station on a frosty night. I could scarcely believe my luck.

We talked on the train all night. Martin was big-hearted and very intelligent. Not a Nazi at all, he said he'd flown *Hitlerjugend Luft* gliders before the war but failed the eye-sight test and couldn't be a pilot. He had been servicing jet engines and really didn't know how he'd gotten into all this. I had to confess that I knew what he meant. He was so generous he even gave me his map of Berlin saying he had another one at home.

We had to change trains at Leipzig. I still remember how bitterly cold that night was, but I was in good company and didn't care. In a few hours I would be reunited with my dear father.'

3. Arrival in Berlin

Berlin. Askanischer Platz mit Anhalter Bahnhof.

Paul's train moved slowly through the outskirts of Berlin in the early hours of 23 November 1944. There was a glimmer of dawn through the windows on the right side of the carriage. It was a foggy frosty morning; the haze clung to the ground. He glimpsed occasional ruined churches and streets but was surprised there wasn't more damage. The magnificent Anhalter Station was every bit as grand as in the postcard he'd stolen, but he preferred the architecture of Gare de l'Est. He told me he would much rather have been in Paris than here in Berlin, but that 'it was all in a good cause,' to use his mother's expression.

Martin and Paul exchanged addresses. Martin lived in the district of Charlottenburg near the zoo. In front of the station, they embraced then parted. Paul got on his bike and rode south to Arndtstraße in the district of Bergmannkiez. It took him 10 minutes to close the last 2.5 km of the 1200km journey. He told me:

'Cycling along Möckernstraße and over the canal, I thought I would be more excited. It was a mundane city morning and people were going to work through the mist. There were other soldiers around and I was just another. I made the left turn into Arndtstraße, passed a small park, stopped in front of the wooden double door in an arch and pulled my bike inside.

In the foyer on the right wall, I was surprised to see a beautiful original

Art Nouveau painted fresco of a tall bird: a crane. It was an unexpected delight to see that.

I'd lost myself in the occupation, lost myself in Normandy and then lost myself again here in Germany. I wasn't the same person who'd left Jersey last summer. Climbing those stairs, it felt like that painting reminded me of who I once was.

At the top I finally stood in front of door 41. The name slip said 'Jäger.' I knocked, no answer. I knocked again, no answer, I knocked again so loud that a latch clicked and the door opposite, number 42, swung open.

A young woman, perhaps 25, in a white satin night gown came out. I apologised for making a racket. She wasn't startled at my SS uniform and *Oberschütze* insignia, but I was startled at what she said:

'Ah, Alsatian eh? Far from home. Thank you for coming to Berlin to save us from the Asians!'

'Ja, Alsace is my Heimatland. Do you know the man next door Fräulein?'

'Please, my name is Greta. By what name should I address you young sir?' Very polite these Berliners.

'I am Paul, and I'm looking for the man who lives here.'

'He's away right now. He's always going away, but always coming back. That's what he told me.'

I suddenly worried, 'Perhaps he was lost in a raid?'

'No, there have been no big raids here since early October.'

Then I heard it: '…. *always going away, but always coming back.*' Yes! That was him.

After all this time, I'd learned to be careful and say as little as possible, but I wanted to be sure that the man we were talking about actually was my father. I still didn't know why or even how it was that he was here in Berlin.

I stood back giving a look of sham exasperation. Greta took note, glanced at my *Hitlerjugend* cuff title and said, 'Wait here while I get dressed.'

In a few moments she came back and beckoned me into her living room. I sat, and she took a cigarette and offered me, but I declined. Incredibly, she had coffee, which she loaded into the percolator and placed on the stove with a *woof*. I took in the well-appointed apartment and portable black gramophone player with a silver wind-up handle and a pile of what looked like jazz records on the carpeted floor. Jazz was frowned upon by the Nazis. 'You don't need to tell anyone about those, do you, SS boy?' she told me.

Ignoring that, and sipping the odd tasting coffee, I asked, 'When was the last time you saw your neighbour in 41?' I think it was crushed nuts.

'What's your business here? I thought you only existed in Newsreels! It's not every day we get SS *Hitlerjugend* in Berlin.' She seemed overly curious.

'I've just completed driver training, and I've got leave before returning to the front. I thought I'd call in.'

None of what I'd said was a lie. I was saving that for later.

'Early October. So, was he your teacher then?' That was new, I wasn't expecting that.

'Yes Greta, he taught me a lot.' That wasn't a lie either.

'Well, Richard said he was from Bonn, and that he'd spent time in Alsace hunting in the mountains.'

I observed, 'Any hunter would enjoy the Vosges mountains of Alsace.'

The man who lived at number 41 **was** my father, but he was going under the alias of Richard Jäger. It made sense, Jäger means 'Hunter' and he did love to hunt, so I continued:

'Herr Jäger is being hunted by me now, so today I am Paul Jäger!'

Greta liked that and was convinced. She stood, puffed her cigarette, walked over to a box on a shelf and fetched something out. 'These are his spare keys. As you are passing through and are one of his old students with nowhere to go, then you might as well stay here. It's empty anyway and he's a nice man I'm sure he wouldn't mind. The air raid shelter is the old round gas holder at Fichtestraße. It holds thousands and is 15 minutes fast walk to the east. If there is a raid warning just follow everyone else you'll soon find it. It's a 'mother and child' bunker but if you have a leave pass they will let you in.'

We stood and then went back to the door of number 41. She turned the key and in we went. The curtains were drawn, and it smelled a bit damp. Very sparsely furnished. I threw down my stuff on the sofa and pulled open the curtains which raised the sulphurous smell of coal soot, but bright sun shone sending rays of light through the dust.

It didn't seem possible that my father lived here. There were just a few signs: a chess board with pieces set and ready to play, and some of his favourite books by French and German authors.

I thanked my new neighbour profusely. She eyed me up. 'In these hard times we need to look after each other. There are plenty of shops in Bergmannstraße, but there isn't much in them these days. If they say they're sold out, just tell them Greta sent you, then you'll get service, I always do.' I didn't know what she meant by that. Then with big eyes and a smile she added, 'If you get cold tonight knock on my door. I'm sure we could find ways to keep warm.' Then she closed the door gently.

There was a full load of coal in the box. I felt that would keep me warmer. I'd brought rations from Mittweida. That night I got the fire blazing, ate well, and wrapped in a home-made sofa quilt felt wonderfully comfortable. I couldn't remember the last time I'd been on my own. I picked out one of father's books: *Peter Camenzind* by Hermann Hesse. His books were banned, but somehow this one had escaped the flames.

What solace, I hadn't read a book for months either.'

A menacing tourist

Paul had a seven-day pass. This meant he had to check back into his division which was assembling on the west bank of the Rhine opposite Düsseldorf at a place called Neuß by midnight on 29 November. He was never going to do that. His plan was always to find his father and run. He would work out how later. Throughout our many conversations, Paul knew the idea was totally insane and likely to fail because so many things could go wrong. Now here he was in Berlin, and Christopher wasn't there…

That first day he went to all the sights of Berlin: Unter den Linden (under the Linden trees), the Tiergarten, Friedrichstraße, the Brandenburg Gate. In typical fashion, he showed me the postcards he'd bought. In Potsdamer Platz he found the once magnificent Café Josty which featured in *'Emil und die Detektive'*, but now it was damaged and closed down.

As a soldier in uniform, he could use the trams and buses for free. He wandered around taking photos with his father's Leica camera and told me he must have looked quite the most menacing tourist in his SS overcoat!

Berlin remained a mecca for soldiers on leave. The regime did all it could to maintain an air of normality in the capital, so you could still have a good time in the bars and clubs. Paul had been saving his cash pay. He was paid two months in advance and held 150 Reichsmarks (RM). He reckoned this was more than enough, as '5RM would get you a good night out.'

There was bomb damage, bad in places, but people were going about their business pretending things were normal. They were very far from that.

There were huge concrete towers with anti-aircraft guns around the skyline. There was a massive one in the *Tiergarten* (animal garden). Colossal, it also housed a hospital and an enormous air raid shelter.

Paul was in one of the world's great cities, but he wasn't in the mood for sightseeing. The clock was ticking, his pass was running out and there was no sign of his father.

'I wasn't going back to the division: that was out of the question. Soon I would be classed as a deserter and if they found me I'd be shot. The Russians were close to Warsaw, their objective was obviously Berlin. The radio kept talking about 'heroic German soldiers' battling on the river Vistula, but two years earlier they'd been talking about battling on the Volga at Stalingrad 1,600 km to the east. After travelling over a thousand kilometres myself, I knew how far that was.

The war was lost, it was just a question of time. I didn't want to be in Berlin when the Russians arrived, I knew what they would do: 'Everything destroy.'

Berlin. Brandenburger Tor

4. Accident on Pallasstraße

'The second day, the 24th, I sat in the apartment reading and waiting for father to open the door. It didn't open. Instead, in the evening, the air raid warning sounded, and I ran down the stairs. People were in the streets heading to the east and I followed. There was the banging of anti-aircraft guns and engine noise. I immediately knew that sound as *Mosquitoes* and the fright of it caused me to run headlong pushing past everyone to the shelter which was a curious circular building just as Greta had described. As we sat in the blue-lit gloom, children screeched, and mothers chattered. After all-clear there was no damage to the area.

On the fourth day, the 26th, I decided to go over and see Martin who lived on Augsburger Straße, off Nürnberger Straße. This was near the highly stylish Kurfürstendamm with its brilliant cinemas and nightlife. We went to the zoo and watched a darling baby Hippopotamus called *Knautschke* and then we walked through the Tiergarten to the Victory Column.

Without my saying anything, Martin confided that he couldn't face going back to the division and was thinking about deserting. I told him it was a dangerous idea, but I wouldn't say anything because I was thinking about it too.

That night we went and ate *Bratwurst mit Senf* and got smashed in a bar around the corner from his parents' apartment. And I mean *smashed*. Neither of us knew what to do and we ended up hugging, crying, and falling over a lot. The bratwurst ended up on the pavement and I ended up on his very considerate older parents' sofa.

The next day, the 27th, we attempted to walk off our hangovers and set course for the zoo again. The animals looked on at us in pity. Then we progressed back to the Tiergarten. Martin knew it well as he'd grown up nearby and it was his nearest play park. We crossed bridges and arrived at a little island called Luiseninsel. He called it his secret island and had been going there all his life.

I had long since learned to trust Martin. Facing war and death, getting drunk and crying together all seemed to have a joining effect. We sat on the island and when I told him I had come from my own secret island called Jersey he was astonished. He'd never heard of it and when I told him where it was he exclaimed, 'My God, that's over a thousand kilometres away! What the hell were you doing there?' I didn't bother trying to explain.

There we were in the dull late November sunshine. We were having a lovely time nursing our heads chatting sitting on a bench next to a little wood and a statue on a secret island in the Berlin Tiergarten.

I wished I'd met Martin sooner. He was 19 and inordinately sensible. All he wanted to do was fix jet engines and stay alive. We'd already realised that we had a lot in common. He knew the war was lost and was under no illusions. The question was: how to avoid death? The Russians were coming, Allied bombers were coming, death was coming. What could we do?

Then, as if to confirm the dread, just after sunset, air raid sirens broke the evening gloom. We sprinted to the nearest shelter, which was the massive tower in the zoo garden. On the roof the guns were booming and set at a low angle. The poor animals in the zoo were screeching and wailing horribly. Now I pitied them.

As we got there, hastily showing our passes in the thronging queue of strangers, the low-level throb of *Mosquito* engines came again, and I went mad…

I screamed and ran blindly into the depths of the shelter past older working men in their overalls who were shocked to see this black dressed SS youth in such a state. Martin followed, and I sat rocking and tearing my hair. He said nothing. If he'd asked I wouldn't have been able to explain.

The all-clear eventually sounded. When we came out it was really cold. There was only one thing left to do: find another bar.

This time we headed south for Maaßenstraße which is in the district of Nollendorfkiez.

The beer was better, fresher and the effect was the same. This time though, before it got out of hand, I told Martin that perhaps we should go over to my father's place at Bergmannkiez, and he was welcome to stay. We had one more beer before we staggered off our chairs and back out into the chilly night.

I think we may have overdone it, again. It had been a day of extremes. The island conversation was as intoxicating as the booze, but the air raid was blanked away.

Martin knew the trams. On Pallasstraße, next to a colossal half-built air raid bunker, we saw an eastbound and drunkenly ran for it. He was ahead of me and jumped onto the side rail. I ran, jumped and caught the handrail but my drunken feet skidded off and crunch, down I went. My head hit the road hard and after that I didn't know much about anything.

I woke up to a shocking pain in my left shoulder and opening my eyes found I was in a hospital ward.

Martin was in a chair asleep in a stupor, and there was a terrible smell of beery vomit.

A young pretty nurse in a light blue uniform came along. Perhaps a little older than me. She cursed then went off with a bowl of sick. She came back with a tall stern-looking nun whose first words were, 'You idiot!'

'Excuse me, I'm sorry,' was all I could think to say. I couldn't move my left arm without streaks of extreme pain.

The stern nun explained briskly that I'd broken my left collar bone, but they couldn't fix it until I'd woken up. I also had a massive gash on the side of my head. She explained that it was a bad break that would be too painful to fix without general anaesthetic, but they couldn't do it as I was too drunk and had to wait until I sobered up. She added that I would just have to put up with the pain as they needed to conserve morphia for the 'more deserving cases.' Off she went in a huff.

There were some advantages though. The slim young nurse came back to check on me. She looked very smart, her blonde wavy hair in a tight bun under her little bonnet. Beautiful blue eyes. She smelled of disinfectant with a trace of beer, a unique fragrance.

I introduced myself, *'Ich bin Paul, der Idiot!'* (I'm Paul, the idiot!) and asked her name. 'Lisa,' she replied in an unknown accent.

'Thank you for looking after me Lisa. What hospital is this?'

'Saint Gertrude's. Your accent? Where are you from?' she asked thawing a bit.

'You first,' I replied giggling, but then my shoulder screamed, and I winced.

She smirked at that then told me, 'I am from Hamburg. I don't know your accent, Paul the idiot.'

'I am from Straßburg.'

'Ah. An Alsatian idiot then. Isn't Alsace part of France?' she said with a cheeky smile.

I showed faux offence. 'It's not part of France, it's part of Alsace.' By now I knew better than to try and laugh.

'No food for you until they reduce your fracture. Who is your drunken sleepyhead friend?'

'Martin.'

'He's loyal. He made sure you got here. You *SS Typen* (guys) have a strong sense of loyalty. You must be good friends.'

I'd never been called an '*SS Typ*' before and it made me feel uncomfortable. So, as she was checking my head bandage I added, 'One doesn't have to be in the SS in order to be loyal.' That made her smile.

Lisa was right about Martin though; he was my loyal friend. I'd been through so much and it had been so long since I had a friend that I could barely remember what that felt like. As I sat in a painful drunken numbness I glanced at him. Yes, he was loyal, and I thanked God that he was there to look out for me.

In the morning Martin was up and about. He'd stayed all night. Then they took me to theatre, placed a mask on my face and dripped ether.

I woke up and Martin was still there. My left arm was now supported in a sling and my head wrapped with a fresh bandage. I was given papers for my paymaster, told to present them as soon as possible and discharged from military service until 1 March. Then after a few hours observation I was sent away. I had to go back in a week.

Martin and I sat on trams, and he saw to it that I got safely back to the apartment in Bergmannkiez.

Then he went home and served out the rest of his leave. On his last day he said goodbye to his parents but didn't get on the train. He came back to my apartment. I checked to make sure Greta wasn't around before we went in, and he stayed in the spare room. Now that Martin was a deserter it was my turn to look after him.

When she returned I introduced my injury to Greta, but she was unsympathetic. 'What use are you now?' she pronounced. After that I often tapped on her door and chatted to keep her from suspecting that I was harbouring a deserter. She seemed the sort who might not be trustworthy, and it wasn't worth taking any chances.

I sorted out my pay and went on as best I could to get food, provisions and coal one-handed. Martin and I were discreet and doing ok. Still no sign of my father.

My shoulder hurt, so I used some of the laudanum I'd kept from Rouen. The following weeks and months were grim.'

'Is that the Lisa you sang about?' I enquired.

'How do you know about Lisa?' the old man replied looking mystified. I let that pass.

5. Life & death in Berlin

'After my check-up at Saint Gertrude's a few days later, I went back to the ward and found Lisa. She didn't smell so bad this time, in fact she smelled quite good, and she looked even better. 'Ah! Paul the Alsatian idiot. How are you?'

'It goes well with me and better now for seeing you Lisa.' That made her smile.

'Where is your friend?' she asked.

'He's gone back to the division.'

'Well then, he can't take me to the cinema, so that means you'll have to.'

I wasn't expecting that, but I love movies, so I wasn't going to say no.

We saw *Träumerei* (Dreaming) about the musical Schumann family in the Marmorhaus cinema in Kurfürstendamm and Lisa loved the piano playing.

A few days later I met her at the hospital. She showed me the beautiful interior chapel with its wonderful stained-glass window and superb green mosaic wall of soaring angels and sacred heart. Then we walked around the Fennsee lake which locals called 'Seepark' in those days, and the Stadtpark Schöneberg, as far as the U-Bahn station built into the bridge, and the little pond. It was lovely even at this time of the year. We were just talking and feeding the ducks. There was a milk bar, and we sat, but those blue eyes hardly smiled.

Early in December the air raid warning sounded again. The wounded could use the shelters, but I had to leave Martin. He didn't dare step out in case the neighbours saw him. It was a massive raid, not Mosquitoes this time. When I got back he was ok. He'd hidden under his bed in case the roof fell in. Mosquitoes came the next night, and again soon after, and Martin hid under the bed each time. That's just how it was. Large parts of the city were damaged, and a pall of smoke clung to it, but still people went about their business trying to persuade themselves that nothing was happening.

Then in mid-December incredibly, the radio triumphally announced a 'massive' German offensive in the west. I was aghast. Martin and I would have been in that conflagration driving lorries and motorbikes.

I saw Lisa whenever I could. We often walked in the Stadtpark. She took joy in the little sparrows that flitted down from the trees for her breadcrumbs, or moments when the sun shone in rays as a cloud passed. I knew she dealt with terrible injuries and death every day. Something had happened in her life, but I didn't ask. She didn't speak about Hamburg.

On Christmas afternoon the sun set, and I went to the nurses' home. Lisa said I could call. The lights were off because of blackout. I knocked but she wouldn't open the door. Her friend Charlotte: Lotte, came and let me in. Lisa was sat in a corner. She stood, took her coat and we walked out together into the dark. 'Tell me what's making you sad?' I asked as we walked arm-in-arm. She looked away.

On Silvester (New Year's Eve) Martin and I had our own quiet party with drink and some food. Then, and just to remind everyone, the Mosquitoes came again. The terrifying noise of those engines pursued me relentlessly as I ran headlong for the shelter. Once again I sat in the pale blue light with fists clenched shivering and shaking for what seemed an eternity.

Mothers and their children looked at me. One little girl came over and talked. Offering me her doll 'Christel,' she told me, 'She helped when my daddy didn't come back.' I glanced up but her mother looked away. She had heard every word.

Soon after Greta appeared, greeted me with the traditional 'Guten Rutsch,' which means *good slide*, and sat beside me. I pulled a grimace and didn't reply. A year ago, my mother, great-aunt, Hans and I had toasted and drank to 'Peace in 1944'. We hadn't got our wish. As the clock ticked into 1945, Greta and I took great swigs from a bottle of something quite strong.

We came out to find snow falling deeply and trudged drunkenly back to the apartment. Icicles hung from gutters and windows looking like the bars of some glass cage. She asked me to her place for schnapps. I didn't really want to go, but thought I'd better had just to keep her from suspecting anything.

She smoked and drank far too much and got rather jolly. We played her jazz records, danced for a while, and then she grabbed and kissed me. I suppose it was fortunate that I was reasonably smashed as well.

Pulling me with her, she nudged the bedroom door open, sat on her bed, and started peeling off her stockings. With those big eyes glancing up she said, 'It's very cold tonight *SS boy*, aren't you going to come over here and keep me warm?'

I only know that I woke up in my own bed on New Year's Day. I had no recollection of how I got there, and my head rang with the dull thud of yet another hangover.

During the morning there was a knock on the door. It was Greta. She gave no impression at all of what happened just a few hours earlier. She insisted that I return to her apartment and listen to Hitler's New Year message on the radio. I wasn't interested in the speech but thought I'd better go along to see if I could find out how I got back to my room.

Der Führer rattled on about 'The sacrifice of countless precious human beings' and 'the corruption of our German youth.' He had the temerity to add that, 'Aside from this, you either live in freedom or die in slavery.' All this from the person who'd ordered the sacrifice of countless precious human beings and corrupted German youth by taking them out of their schools and putting guns and rocket launchers in their hands. I'd seen their bodies strewn across Normandy. I'd seen how his lies had enslaved and destroyed. To cap it all, the heathen bastard even invoked God and thanked him, 'for the power He gave us to be stronger than misery and danger.'

Meanwhile, Greta listened attentively, and I watched her carefully. When it was all over, she turned to me and with a slight nod towards my apartment said, 'I know about your friend in there.'

My blood ran colder than the icicles hanging across the window. She'd put me in front of Hitler's message not out of politeness.

'It's alright boy, I won't tell anyone.'

I felt defeated. My knees quaked and I slumped back in her armchair. SHIT.

'The party is impatient with unconventional people. The only reason I haven't turned you in is that you're SS and so is he. You *Hitlerjugend* have sworn a blood oath to the *Führer*. You must be loyal to him until death. He expects you to do your duty.'

I muttered quietly that we had both seen too much of war and needed peace away from the frontline in order to recover our strength for the 'final battles.' It was almost true, and I sensed she wanted to believe it.

She took a cigarette, lit it, and blew out the match with a flourish.

'Last night I used your keys and helped you back into your apartment. I suspected that someone else was there and thought it might have been Herr Jäger. It wasn't though, it was your friend Martin. We spoke briefly, then he put you in bed.'

Damn. Damn. DAMN.

I sat there trying to calculate how I could have made such a mistake. Why did I get drunk with her last night? Why could I not see the danger? In any event, it was done. Now she had a hold over Martin and me.

I needed a symbol, a statement, something powerful. I stood and beckoned her to come next door to my apartment. She followed, cigarette between her red varnished fingernails.

I gestured her to sit and went to the top drawer of the cabinet. The revolver was there.

I turned with my SS dagger in hand. She looked in alarm as I pulled the blade and handed it to her saying: 'Read the inscription.'

'*Meine Ehre heißt Treue*,' (My honour is loyalty) she whispered, squinting through the reflection from the bright metal.

Looking up, she studied my face, and her expression slowly changed.

'Greta. SS <u>are</u> loyal until death. Martin saved me on the battlefield. In France I was a dead man, but he brought me out. Now I am repaying my debt. I am loyal to this man as he was loyal to me. I ask you now to respect honour. Do not interfere.'

I was shocked to hear myself say such things.

Greta drew back. She was visibly shaken and began to tremble. She caught her breath, bit her lip and eyes skyward puffed her cigarette nervously.

'Of course. I can have no idea what it's like at the front. I'm sorry I doubted you.'

After that we made small talk. Martin emerged and I explained to him how he'd 'saved me on the battlefield.' He smiled, nodded and said nothing. Greta was embarrassed. After a few minutes she said her goodbyes and left.

Martin turned to me. 'You lying bastard!' he quietly exclaimed with a smirk.

'It's all in a good cause,' I told him.'

****

Paul's descriptions of Berlin in winter 1945 were bleak:

'The walk from my apartment to the shelter was along Bergmannstraße past a big grey cemetery on the right. I often overheard people make jokes about it: 'We'll all soon be in there,' and 'at least *they* can get a good night's sleep.'

At the end of that walk was an emotionless dark shelter full of scared faces who didn't know what they would find when they came out.'

Outside snow and ice. Frozen pipes and sometimes no electricity or gas. Treacherous bone rending cold and food getting scarce. Days became battles.

His shoulder wasn't good. It was healing, but not quickly. They put it down to poor nutrition and signed him off duty for another month. Nobody was checking on any soldiers wandering around. The offensive in the west had petered out. The people's morale was doing the same.

Paul's only lightness was in seeing Lisa, but she was very troubled. He told me, 'I wanted to care for her. I could see her deep pain. Something terrible had happened.'

In early February there was another huge morning daylight air raid. Word was that Martin's parents' district had been hit. Paul and Martin rushed immediately to Charlottenburg.

They battled through obliterated streets, rubble, and slush to help the firefighters and survivors. Everything was on fire with smoke billowing through the ruins. The damage was awful. Most of the north side of Augsburger Straße wasn't there anymore. Nothing was there.

In a panic Martin ran and tore away at the remains of his shattered apartment block until his hands bled.

Nobody had seen his parents.

6. Death of a city

Martin's family was gone. He was inconsolable. Tens of thousands lost their parents, children and loved ones. It was a catastrophe, but the pointless innocent deaths went on.

Lisa and Paul sometimes stood watching the clouds of Berlin starlings flying over the ruins and rooftops. Lisa said they must be the souls of the dead finally set free.

Paul explained that going to the movies was one of Lisa's ways to escape. He remembered they saw *Opfergang* (The Sacrifice) featuring Kristina Söderbaum at Alexanderplatz. Despite the awful Nietzsche poetry at the start, he said it was one of the most beautiful films he'd ever seen, in superb Agfacolour. Set in Hamburg, it showed a world untouched by war but heavy with honour, duty, melancholy, and impending doom. Lisa hung her head on Paul's shoulder and cried on his shirt almost from start to finish, especially at the end where there is absolute heartbreak. Then she whispered that her parents were killed when Hamburg was destroyed in 1943. Her older brother had died at Stalingrad. The agony was profound. He said, 'She was lost and alone. She only had me.'

In late February there was another huge air attack. Afterwards the pall of smoke lingered over the city. The drains were blocked with rubble and rain turned the roads into lakes of stinking sulphurous black porridge. The ruined streets held the pervasive smell of soot, dust, and death.

Refugees flooded into what was left of the metropolis. This made the food shortages even worse. In March, the air attacks by Mosquitoes were nightly. Paul fled to the shelter in his SS uniform every time, and no-one challenged him, although the wardens told him to report to Alexanderplatz when he was 'fit for duty.' Martin didn't go to the shelter for fear of being reported to the authorities.

Goebbels ordered the defence of the city with bands of *Volkssturm* (People's Storm). Now not only were the young to die, but the old with them, as these elderly 'soldiers' were in no state to fight. It was madness. The war was lost. Any reserves the Wehrmacht may have had were destroyed in the December offensive in the west. Germany had nothing left.

Paul said Lisa was 'hurt very badly.' She told Paul that she liked to be near him when they walked in the park at night. They held each other often, but never kissed. He said he wanted to do more to help her, but he didn't know what.

Paul was still not fit to travel but it made no sense to stay in Berlin waiting to die. Even if he could leave, he did not want to abandon the wait for his father. There was no way of knowing where he was or even whether he was alive.

In early March defenders began putting up huge barricades at strategic places. The Russians were coming. Propaganda on the radio was putting the fear of God into Berliners. There was widespread talk of the horrors the Russians would perpetrate when they arrived in the city.

There was another enormous daytime air raid in mid-March. Paul and Martin discussed what to do and again decided to wait. Miraculously, Bergmannkiez still had only light damage, but they knew it was only a matter of time before the apartment was hit and they would be homeless like so many others.

Just a few days after the previous huge raid there was yet another shattering daytime attack. Apartments in the neighbourhood lost roofs and windows, but Paul's place was untouched.

Night after night there were Mosquito raids and night after night Paul trudged down and then back up the wooden steps to the apartment and sat shivering in candlelight. There was sporadic electricity, gas and coal. Each night was the same: a dull monotony. The city was slowly dying.

Although Paul was not yet able to attempt it, he and Martin began to prepare for their escape. The journey westwards to Bonn was about 500km. If they were unmolested they could cycle it in seven or eight days. Paul reckoned it would be better to travel as civilians and just try and keep out of trouble. The plan entailed getting hold of clothes as there were none in the apartment. This was less difficult than they imagined. Paul simply walked down to the *Karstadt* department store on Hermannplatz and bought some. It was just another bizarre example of how the city was still functioning. People were behaving and going about their business as if nothing were happening.

The evening Mosquito raids continued. They all merged into one: siren, run, sit, shiver, wait, all-clear, walk, and plod back up the echoing stairs to the apartment, sit, shiver, or doze off to sleep on the sofa under the quilt. It was all just one blur.

Paul couldn't bring himself to think about leaving. Leaving meant abandoning his father. It meant telling his friend Lisa and breaking her heart unless she came too.

On Lisa's day off, a Saturday, they walked in the Tiergarten and took photos. It was a lovely sunny day. Paul asked her to a showing that evening of the movie *Solistin Anna Alt* (Soloist: Anna Alt) which featured the brilliant pianist Anneliese Uhlig. Afterwards he would tell her about Martin and offer to take her out of Berlin. That was 24 March. They both loved the film and wonderful music:

'Lisa wore a lovely blue and white dress she'd made. Blue was her favourite colour. After the film we walked along the corridor arm-in-arm. On the stairs I told her. She seemed not to hear, stopped, then moved off slowly. I stood as the people streamed out around me. In the empty foyer, she walked from wall to wall, pacing slowly, thinking, lost in her thoughts. Then she came to me, held my hands, and spoke:

'This place is full of the dead. If we stay we'll join them. There's nothing for us here, no future.'

I said, 'You'll come with us then, with me?'

'My dear friend, you have been so kind and expect nothing in return. I want to go with you.'

As we embraced, I spoke quietly: 'I will find a way. I won't let you down. We can be together. We can be free.'

We walked hand-in-hand along Kurfürstendamm in blackout, then towards the hospital. For the first time we talked about the future. We agreed to have Easter in Berlin. If it were running, we would take the S-Bahn to Nickolassee for a walk around the banks of the Wannsee lake and then leave the city the next day.

I had to let my father go.

At the nurses' home, Lisa turned to me and explained that she was going shopping to Spandau on Wednesday to buy Easter eggs. It was so rare to see her lovely smile.

Before she went in we hugged for a long time. She stood back, held my hands and whispering told me: 'Walking with a friend in the dark is better than walking alone in the light.'

Suddenly he stopped and drew breath, eyes flickering, opening wide. 'That's enough for today,' he muttered, looking away. Then he stood and went briskly to his room.

It was most unlike him to break off like that.

7. 'Things we never knowingly talk about'

By the time we got to Christmas Day 2019 Paul had stopped talking. He left most of his dinner and didn't even have a drink with the others. Then he went off to the day room. A nod from Mel meant I had to pay him more attention. I followed and found him at the piano. He was slowly and quietly playing the little melody that I recognised as the tune about *Lisa*.

He turned to me, smiled, then reached and held my wrists in that way of his and in German said, 'Dear, go to my room and look in the bottom of the wardrobe. Bring back what you find.' I trotted off, opened the door, found a bottle of Alsatian white wine labelled *Gewurztraminer Grand Cru 1985*, and took it back. 'Put it in the ice box would you dear,' he said. He followed this with, 'Would you like to join me here in a little while?'

I had a few things that needed doing but after half an hour I was ready and got the bottle from the fridge. It looked as if Christmas night 2019 was going to be one of his special treats.

I came back and found him still at the piano playing reflectively.

I sat, but then he stopped and disappeared off to the kitchen. He came back with glasses, a cheese board, some pastries, plates, and a knife. Out of his pocket he produced a whole small, orange-wrapped cheese: *Hansi au Marc de Gewurztraminer*. Out of his other pocket he produced a corkscrew. 'Do the honours will you dear?' he said, smiling gently. We weren't supposed to drink on duty. Popping in to check on us Mel just grinned.

I put the glasses on the piano, opened and poured the golden wine and cut some cheese. The old man studied my face, smiled, then held up his glass: 'Let's toast.'

'What shall we toast?'

'Just to us dear, just to us.' Our glasses met with a clink.

I sipped the wine… Oh! That wine! That wine was like nothing I had ever tasted. Like liquid heaven. I followed it with the pungent cheese. Oh. My. That cheese! Wow!

We smiled and chatted as we drank together that wonderful wine and munched the light and delicious cheese pastries. Gorgeous! I expected conversation and more stories to follow, but they didn't.

Instead, he enquired after my family: Amy at the hospital, and my father. This was unusual. Even more unusual he said, 'Marie never spoke about her mother, and you've only mentioned yours twice. Would you like to talk about her?'

I was stunned. Then I was grateful. In all the time I knew him he only included my mother once, and that was by accident because he was seriously ill. I would have been uncomfortable talking about her.

'Can I say something Paul?'

'Say anything dear.'

'I'm so glad that we never spoke about her, but I'm happy that you've asked me now.'

'Oh?'

'If you had asked me before, I never would have told you. But you knew that, didn't you?'

He rubbed his chin and glancing down muttered, 'Well, er…'

'Thought so.'

Then he said something wonderful. 'There are things we never knowingly talk about….'

'Because we don't know them ourselves.'

'Yes,' he nodded.

We looked at each other. There was nothing more that needed saying.

Then he said, 'Our last memory of someone is like a photograph: a moment frozen in time. For us they will forever be the way they were in that moment: permanent and unchanging. For them time stands still, and they do not grow old, but we do, and we carry them with us.'

He stared at the carpet once or twice and then at around 10 with the bottle still half-full, said he wanted to turn in for the night. 'Take the wine and cheese home and enjoy it with your father and sister,' he said quietly. That wasn't right, that didn't sit well with me, he *never* left wine, but I smiled and said of course and thanked him for the lovely evening.

I reported back at handover that Paul was alright but wasn't himself. Mel said that Christmas can very often bring out the maudlin in old people, but

I knew Paul wasn't like that. He'd been through more than all of the rest of the people at the Stanley put together. As I cycled away at 11.15 I noticed the light in his room was still on.

Boxing night passed much like any other evening, except that Paul was the same. I thought there must be more I could do to help him, but I didn't know what. I asked Mel. She wasn't much help. All she said was, 'Keep an eye.'

On Silvester Paul did not stay up late.

I was only doing three-day weeks, and it wasn't long before I was due to go back to Manchester. In those days Paul was very much inside himself. I wasn't sure whether he wanted to talk or if he was holding back.

We came to the last day, a Thursday. He knew it was my last day and that we wouldn't see each other for several months, but he stayed away. The hours ticked by until just before the final handover. I decided to take the initiative, went to his room, and knocked on the door.

It was unusual for Paul to be in his room with the door closed at this time. I knocked and then knocked again. For the first time ever I called to him, 'Are you okay? Open your door.' No answer.

Concerned, I turned the handle and went in.

The curtains were open, and the lights dimmed. He was sat in the corner by the window just staring out. He didn't turn to look at me.

On his table were spread old documents, paintings, photographs, and his black writing book. Then I noticed a copy of The Times. It was open on a feature about the World Health Organisation's response to a newly identified Coronavirus: COVID-19.

Raising the light, the wind was blowing, with rain trickling down the windows. He was just sitting there staring out at the dark.

He didn't turn. Studying his face, I moved a chair to sit next to him. 'Tell me what's making you sad Paul?'

'I can't tell you,' he said hesitatingly. His look was one of perplexity and trouble.

'I'm going away.'

I didn't think he heard me, then he replied, 'I know dear.'

With a twist, I added: 'Well, we should say goodbye for now then?'

'Don't be like that,' he said quietly, shaking his head slowly.

After a long pause he continued, 'I don't think I'm ever going to see you again.' I was floored. 'I don't think I'm going to see another Christmas.'

'Don't say that!' I said slightly sharply.

'No, I think this is my last year.' He looked me straight in the eye and went on, 'There is still so much to tell you, but I don't think there's going to be time now.'

'Stop that talk!' I commanded. I couldn't believe what I was hearing. Paul was an old man who would be 93 in April. The thought whirled: *there are only so many more years when you are that age.*

'No dear. I've done my best. I've tried to tell you everything, but I haven't.'

'What are you talking about?'

'Katie, I've done things, things you can't imagine, things I can't explain.'

'What do you mean?'

'I never told you what happened in Berlin.'

'Yes you did.'

'*No, I didn't,*' he added firmly.

I was dumbfounded. 'Is it important?'

'Yes, it is important. You see, there's only me.' He hesitated as if reaching… 'Nobody knows what I did. Nobody except God… Only God can see the hearts of men.'

He began to stumble in his speech. Tears welled, but he looked at me and went on, 'I know you are an angel. I knew it from the beginning. You have been so kind. I tried, but an angel cannot be pushed away.'

'Shhh… You have helped me too.'

In German he continued, 'You have shown me the way and I am ready.'

'And you have shown me the way also.'

'But we haven't arrived yet,' he said enigmatically.

'Haven't arrived where?'

Gently nodding his head and leaning forward, in English he whispered, 'At absolution. You don't know what I've done.'

'We are together, remember? You're not walking alone. Won't you tell me?'

He bowed his head, 'I can't… I lack the strength, lack the courage.'

'You, *lack courage?* Impossible. You're the bravest man I ever met.'

'No, I'm a coward.'

'How can not telling me something mean that you're a coward?'

'No, that's not it. I've seen death knock on the door of many people.'

'Don't talk like that.'

He raised his head resolutely. 'When I was young my life was music, a book, a poem, a painting, a sandy beach, and I feared nothing. I had no doubts. But then I made choices, got involved and I learned about loss, and about death. I've seen things for a long time now, been afraid for a long time. It's not death that I am afraid of.'

Tears welled, but I held it together as best I could. 'If you are not afraid of death, then what are you afraid of?'

Seeming as if he hadn't heard he went on, 'I never wanted to learn about those things, but I did. I never wanted **you** to learn about those things, but you have. *The burden*, you have helped me with the burden. You are young and strong, I envy you. The future is yours and you have nothing to be afraid of.'

'I don't understand. What are you afraid of Paul?'

'The truth. It's been searching for me.' He wavered… 'I'm afraid because I don't know what the truth is… I don't think I've ever known.'

'The truth about what?'

He shook his head slowly. He had no answer.

I had a ticket for Manchester at 11.30am, but there was no question of leaving Paul like that. I hadn't packed, but it didn't stop us sitting and chatting all night. Like old friends we talked about anything and sat there with the rugs over our legs.

In those moments I felt like I saw the whole of his life. I had his memories, his thoughts, his reflections and feelings. I knew his moods, his strengths and weaknesses. I even had his language. We played an exceptionally long and hard-fought game of chess. It was a draw. 'Play to win Katie, always play to win,' he said as we shook hands. I smiled; I knew he was right.

As the sun rose and the low light flooded across Kew Green, I picked up my stuff to go.

In the foyer I turned, held his wrists and told him, 'Take care of yourself my friend and I will see you in April.'

'I will,' he said, adding, 'I loved our walk together. Thank you, thank you for everything.'

I ambled away in the gloom of the chill morning. Reaching Kew Bridge I looked back, and there he was framed in the light, gently waving from the open door.

8. Letters

Whitworth Park, Manchester, near the Obelisk

I returned to Manchester deeply affected by what happened over Christmas, but I couldn't do anything about it. All I could do was dive back into my studies. Then something happened.

Out of the blue on Saturday, 7 March I got a call from the Stanley. That wasn't right, I never got calls from the Stanley, so I knew something was wrong. I gulped as I heard Lawrence speak:

'He's gone Katie.'

Tears welled. 'Oh…'

'Are you there Katie?'

'Yes, yes, I'm here,' I gasped. I wasn't *here*.

'Didn't he let you know?' What did he mean by that?

'What?'

'He's gone back to Strasbourg. He wants your address so he can write you a letter.'

'Oh, oh, er…'

'He didn't tell you? Oh. I can't give him your details as that's personal information.'

'Oh, oh.'

'You ok Katie?'

'Yes, yes, thank you.'

'I don't know what to do. He wants to contact you. I can't give him your details. I shouldn't really give you his forwarding address either, but if you were here working you would have access to it. What d'you want me to do?'

I was so thrown by the whole conversation that no words came out. I choked.

'Katie, *Katie?*'

'Hello Lawrence. Yes, I'm here, just a bit shaken.'

'I can't see the difference between you being here and not being here. Also, I'm surprised he didn't give you his address. I know you two are close.'

'I don't know what to say. I'm just relieved.'

'I'm prepared to give you his address in Strasbourg. If you were here you could get that for yourself. Write to Paul and he can reply if he wants. You've done wonders with him, you two can work it out between yourselves.'

'Ok Lawrence, thank you. That sounds fair.'

'The address I have is: 6 Quai Au Sable, 67000, Strasbourg, Alsace. He left two days ago. A removal company came for his things this morning.'

'Got it. Thank you Lawrence.'

I thought something was wrong, but I was relieved. I was sure Lawrence was phoning with bad news. Paul had threatened to go back to Strasbourg before, and I knew he was strong enough to do it. Those days were gone though, and this wasn't him carrying out a threat. I knew what it was. Now I had to be strong.

On 31 January 2020, the first two cases of COVID-19 were confirmed in the United Kingdom. Nobody paid it any attention. By mid-February, the world was awash with news of the novel disease, and it was killing people. Wuhan province in China was under a strict lockdown. On 10 February, the world COVID-19 death toll surpassed that of the severe acute respiratory syndrome (SARS) outbreak from 17 years previous. I asked my friends doing Medicine and Biology what this meant, and they told me it was going to be bad, probably a global epidemic like in 1918-1919. It was ridiculous that undergraduates could see the danger, but the UK government could not. Paul had despaired at the result of the 2019 General Election.

No measures were put in place in the UK. Nothing.

Paul had been following it all in the press. It was easy to work out what he'd done.

I immediately sat and typed out a short letter to him on the computer and printed it:

Flat C, 119 Lombard Grove, Fallowfield, M14 6AN.   *7th March 2020*

Dearest Paul
I've just heard from the Stanley that you have returned to Strasbourg. I wanted to send my address so that we can correspond. I know that you do not go in for computers, emails or mobile phones. I am not one for art, but my aim now is to get practice in the art of letter writing. I will enjoy practising!
The world has entered a difficult period – which you have wisely foreseen. We need to brace ourselves for whatever lies ahead. I hope you have someone there who can keep an eye on you.
I understand why you have gone back to your beloved Strasbourg. You have described it to me many times and I wish I could be there with you enjoying coffee and kugelhopf, perhaps even with a bottle of your favourite Riesling!
Please write and keep me posted. I look forward very much to reading your descriptions of springtime in Alsace. I also hope that you can tell me more of your story.
Always your friend, Katie

I posted it directly. Half an hour earlier I'd feared the worst. Now I had just written a letter to a good friend. It bothered me to think there might not be anyone there to look after him in Strasbourg. I wanted to take care of him.

Although my worst fears for Paul were unfounded, what happened next exceeded the worst fears anyone could possibly have imagined.

As Paul had predicted, the COVID situation in the UK soon span completely out of control. On 14 March 2020, the Prime Minister said that 'herd immunity was the route through the epidemic', in other words, that everything was alright and there was no need to do anything. This was a profoundly negligent response and soon proved to be so. Nine days later on the 23rd, the same Prime Minister gave a national television address in which he instructed the British public that they must *stay at home* and 'lockdown'. By refusing to accept reality and moving too slowly he'd made the most serious mistake since Chamberlain in 1938, but he never admitted it.

I realised that I would be stuck in Manchester without money, as I could not work at the home at Easter. I couldn't apply for any of the government schemes either. All I could do was write a letter to my bank. Fortunately, I was able to reach an understanding with them.

On 27 March, a letter arrived with a French stamp and my address written in black fountain pen. It was Paul:

6 Quai Au Sable, Strasbourg, Alsace.   24th March 2020

Dearest Katie

Thank you so much for your letter. I worried that my leaving Kew in haste would upset you. I meant to let you know, but it didn't turn out like that I'm afraid. Please accept my apologies.

You're right: I had to leave. I'm so glad I did. I got back just before lockdown. You will have seen that Italy is very severely affected. France moved quickly to a complete lockdown, but I was able to attend to my affairs before it all closed up.

The rules allow me to employ a maid, Anna. She speaks many languages, gets my shopping and bread, cooks and runs around after me. She also turns the pages when I play piano. Don't worry, nobody could do that better than you!

Everything is closed, so there is no chance of coffee and kugelhopf I'm afraid. However, I was able to secure a supply of Riesling, though how long it will last is another matter...

My apartment overlooks L'Ill which has trees along it, and Pont Sainte Madeleine. We are not quite in spring just yet, but when it arrives it will be quite lovely here, it always is.

I have been reading, writing, painting, and playing Mozart Bach and Chopin on the piano, although not as well as you I fear. It could take a while to play a game of chess by letter, but we could try!

Hopefully, this lockdown will be relaxed soon, and I will be able to get out to watch the storks once again. They're always going away but always coming back you know.

I don't have your phone number and wouldn't impose in any event. I thought I would write more, but now it's come to it I find that I've been stuck indoors most of the time and don't have that much to say.

What I do want to say though, is that I miss your company very much.

In friendship always, Paul

9. The empty space, April 2020

It was lovely to receive Paul's letter. I could hear his voice so clearly. I was relieved that someone was helping him. I could hear his piano playing too, even the occasional hicks with his right index and little fingers.

This was the first national lockdown, and there was little to do except study and reflect. A very strange time when almost nothing moved. In Manchester, Oxford Road through the university area normally swarms with students like a Jersey anthill. Now it was a barren empty space, with virtually no life.

I soon realised that I didn't have much to say either, just like Paul. I decided that a computer printout letter was too impersonal, so I invested in a swish blue Parker fountain pen, nice paper, and a bottle of black ink. Thus equipped a hand-written letter ensued which seemed much more appropriate. I posted it on 31 March. I wrote that I was getting bored and that my studies were suffering because I needed the interaction in the Engineering Department. I told him I was starting to formulate my master's thesis and beginning to consider what I would do after I completed my degree. Then I realised he might find that all a bit dull.

There was a government directive to empty hospitals into care homes. This proved to be a deadly miscalculation.

I got calls from Mel and Lawrence at the Stanley to tell me Giles, Marcus and then Henry had all died of COVID, and that several others were seriously ill. That was terrible to hear. It was desperate that their families could not be there for them.

Easter came and went. The country was at a complete standstill, a very reflective time. I thought a lot about what Paul had told me. I thought about my mother too.

Then on Saturday, 18 April, a crisp white envelope arrived from France. This one had my address in different handwriting. Odd. I opened and unfolded the single page. In English it read:

Avocat Eckhart, Rue des Hannetons, Strasbourg, 67000, France.   14th April 2020

Dear Ms Campbell

We are the appointed executors for Monsieur Paul Bunn of 6 Quai Au Sable, Strasbourg.

It is with the deepest regret that we write to inform you that Paul Bunn passed away in his home on Easter Sunday.

It was his express wish in the circumstances of his death, as his closest friend, you be advised immediately.

We appreciate that it is exceedingly difficult to receive such sad news in this manner. Please accept our most sincere condolences.

We are sorry to state that the regulations in force at this time mean that it will not be possible for mourners to attend his funeral. The arrangements for this have been made by us. A simple ceremony of burial will be held at Cimetière municipal Saint-Urbain at the family grave conducted according to his faith and wishes. This will be held at 11am on Monday, 20 April.

All the affairs of Monsieur Bunn have been placed in the hands of Avocat Eckhart. Following legal process, we will write to you again at the proper time to advise you of the next steps.

Again, our deepest condolences.

Eckhart, Avocat

10. Mam Tor

He was gone.
I should have been prepared but I wasn't.
I cried. I cried for quite a while. A long time...

I got on the bike and cycled my favourite route through the Peak District: New Mills and Chapel-en-le-Frith to Mam Tor. It was a nice April day, cool and bright, so I just went.

Cycling cleanses and purges. That's why I enjoy it. Then I walked up Mam Tor and took a selfie. I cycled on to my favourite café: the Penny Pot at Edale station. Closed, empty and far away, it was how I felt that day.

Manchester via the A57, a long downhill, was exhilarating as always, and I arrived at the empty house after dark.

Monday 20th was a lovely day. I wondered if there would be music in Strasbourg at his funeral and concluded there wouldn't be. He would have wanted music. So, at 11am French time I sat out in the back yard, lit a candle, and put on *Fauré's Requiem: VII. In Paradisum*. Sublime music. My vigil felt right.

I sat, listened, and wondered about a great many things.

Paul also deserved a wake. I may have been on my own, in an empty house, but he was going to have that wake. I donned a mask, went to Fallowfield Sainsbury's, and bought the nicest bottle of Riesling and the best coffee and cheese pastries I could find. I also found some lovely fresh red roses in the Shell garage.

I had no keepsake or photo, but in my room I placed the roses in a small vase on my electric piano behind the burning candle. I spent the rest of the day playing music and thinking about him and our many weeks and months of conversation.

What would life be like without Paul and his stories?

11. Dappled light, May - July 2020

In early May, another crisp white envelope arrived. The letter invited me and my legal representatives to come to Strasbourg for the reading of Paul's Will. I was startled.

The letter clearly stated that 'individual attention' would be extended and that hotel suites would be provided for 'my party.' I had no idea what that meant. It went on to state that if I did not have legal representation, 'A range of reputable firms are known to us that we could recommend in London,' and that, 'The Bunn (formerly von Bonn) family have used Taylor's of Bishopsgate for over 200 years. You may wish to consider them.' Finally, the letter said that: 'All costs would be found from the estate as a courtesy to you.'

What did this mean? I didn't know. I asked my father and sister. They had no clue, except dad said, 'Perhaps the old man left you something?'

I can't remember the exact order of things and may have forgotten parts, but I did phone up Taylor's. Despite the difficulties imposed by home working, I was called back within the hour by the senior partner, Mr Ralph Taylor. He explained that he was aware of me and of Paul's passing and offered his deepest condolences. He said he would be happy to represent me, but that it would be better if a meeting could be arranged and that he would clear his diary at my request. I said I didn't know what was happening. He was incredibly charming and polite and suggested a meeting in Manchester 'At my convenience.' Here he would try to explain what he could and the service he could offer. When I asked how much his time would cost, he said simply, 'Not a penny.' I put down the phone and my hand was shaking. Later I called on his personal number to say that social distancing restrictions meant that I could only meet him in an open space and suggested Whitworth Park in Manchester, in the centre circle on a bench next to the obelisk. The time set was 11am, 1 June.

He was by far the smartest man in the park. Charm personified, after introductions Ralph explained that he knew Paul had lived in Kew in a care home recently. I said that's where I came to know him. He also said that he knew Paul had gone back to Strasbourg. 'Typical,' he said with a tut and a smile, adding, 'always going away, but always coming back, typical Bunn behaviour!' In his 70s, I asked Ralph how he knew Paul. With a tear in his eye, he said simply, 'Always. I've always known Paul Bunn.' That was enough. I offered him my condolences, and asked him to represent me, even though I had no idea what that meant. He was visibly shaken. 'It would be an honour to continue to serve the family. Thank you. I would shake your hand, but I'm not allowed!' He said he would have papers drawn up and sent for me to sign. He told me he was aware of Avocat Eckhart, and that he would make all the arrangements and oversee them personally.

We walked, socially distanced, back to his car: a black Range Rover waiting on Oxford Road, with masked up driver. 'I'd offer you a lift, but that's probably not allowed,' he said with a grin. Just before he opened the door he said, almost as an aside, 'Paul was a wealthy man, did you know?' I said I didn't but knew he was extremely generous. Ralph paused for a moment, looked at me, but said nothing. Then he got in the car, lowered the window, unhitched his mask and with a smile said, 'I'll see you in Strasbourg.' I was none the wiser for that meeting, I still had no idea.

Papers arrived and were duly signed and returned.

Eurostar and TGV was arranged via the grand Paris Gare de l'Est to Strasbourg for 12 July.

The train pulled in and the timing was good. I wheeled my suitcase to the Régent Petite France which is over a narrow bridge in a beautiful location on an island in the river Ill. After checking into my room, I asked at the desk where I could buy three red roses. There was a duty to perform.

I went out and headed for the *Cimetière municipal Saint-Urbain*. In the office in the passageway arch they gave me directions to the family grave. Wandering to the quiet corner, suddenly there in gold were the names of Helene, Christopher and Paul.

I'd brought the candle from Fallowfield and now it found its final home. I lit it and placed the three roses on the grave in front of their names. Sobbing a little I had private words for my friend in German. Then I put *Gabriel Fauré's Requiem* quietly on the speaker once more. He would have liked that.

Walking back, I explored Strasbourg that Paul loved so much. What a marvellous city. He was right - a wonderful place to grow up in. So many alleys, nooks, and crannies. Endlessly interesting and intricate medieval architecture, and the absolutely brilliant cathedral which was his local church. I made sure to visit the nearby Hotel Basel, and the venue for tomorrow's 11am meeting: *6 Quai Au Sable*, Paul's apartment by the river.

The morning was sunny and bright, and I'd slept well. The marvellous cathedral bells were ringing as I took the leisurely walk along the water's edge back to the apartment. I knocked and a smart maid dressed in black opened the door with a prompt curtsy and '*Mademoiselle.*' She introduced herself in French as Anna and I thanked her for her service to Paul.

There was a fine marble staircase, but a lift brought us up to a quite magnificent drawing room filled with the scent of fresh coffee and beautiful yellow roses. Chairs and a table were arranged and there were papers. I recognised Ralph and he introduced me to Fernand Eckhart, Senior Partner.

The room was bathed in perfect light reflected from the water outside. Passing clouds gave shade then bright sun. We took the wonderful coffee and pastries and exchanged pleasantries about my journey from London. I'm not sure now what impression I gave with my starry eyes and posh Waitrose interview look. Noticing this, the two lawyers drew back and let me walk slowly around the room and step out onto a balcony taking in the superb view across the river.

Surely this was some other world, a dream of some sort? Little bronze statues, porcelain figurines, prints, paintings, photos, all were adorned in this room lit with the mirrored glow from the water. My eye was caught by a distinctive sketch next to the window: two interlocked faces of a young woman in white and blue. A Picasso. Signed original. Superb.

Fernand approached, 'Yes, it's a Picasso. From 1954. This isn't my favourite though; I prefer the one upstairs.'

I was feeling dizzy. Now would be a good time to sit down I thought.

It was only after I sat that I caught sight of it on the marble mantlepiece: *the photograph*, the one of Paul and Hans in Jersey. And there was the photo of his dear mother in her nurse uniform and the one of his father from 1912.

There was his Leica camera and wooden apple. It was overwhelming, too much for me.

I sat and sobbed for quite a while. Anna came with tissues. The gentlemen saw me distressed and didn't take their seats. Instead, they disappeared off somewhere. They only came back when I was quite settled, and Anna gave a signal. I liked her already.

Fernand took his seat, and Ralph sat next to me. From somewhere two note-takers materialised. They were introduced and took their seats with a smile, one notary for each lawyer. Then Fernand spoke:

'Welcome to Strasbourg and welcome to the apartment of Paul Bunn. We are here today to mark the passing of our dear friend and to read his Will in the presence of witnesses.' He paused, then addressed me directly:

'Katie today is a day which will change your life forever. As you enriched Paul's life, so it was his dying wish that he enrich yours.'

I was distracted, looking at the dappled light reflected from the rippling water outside, the shadow patterns on the wall and how they tumbled and danced across the photograph on the mantelpiece. Delightful.

'With minor variations, Paul has named you as the sole beneficiary of his entire estate. His business interests, properties, this apartment, and everything in it are yours.'

At that moment the shadow on the photograph moved from Paul's face, the light fell on him, and I could see that self-satisfied smirk once more.

'I only want the photograph,' was apparently what I said, but I don't remember. There was a long pause and after that I stood, went to collect it from the mantelpiece and placed it on the table in front of me.

'I think you would like a moment?' said the lawyer. He stood and Ralph and the others followed him, and the room emptied. I took the photograph and held it to my heart. Then I cried again.

I don't remember much about the days that followed it was all a haze which passed me by.

I stayed in Strasbourg, I was planning to anyway and remained in the Régent. I didn't have the nerve to stay at the apartment amongst all of Paul's things. Ralph had to go back to London, but I asked that his notary Toby stay over. A skilled linguist, he became my legal counsellor. I had tickets to go home but realised there was no need, and anyway Strasbourg was such a beautiful city, why leave it?

More things were explained: the properties all across Europe, the companies, the investments, the five aircraft in a private hangar including a *Fieseler Storch*. To this day it remains overwhelming to me.

After a week I called Amy and dad and instructed them to come to Strasbourg. Both refused saying how could they just drop work? This meant I had to go home.

Travelling across France I wondered how to tell my sister and father. By the time I got to St Pancras I'd figured it out. I got back to Brentford and went up in the lift. It was an anti-climax. Amy was out on night shift, and dad was in the pub. I remembered why I didn't like that place.

Eventually I managed to synchronise them. As we got in the black cab I said we were going for a nice meal in the West End as I had important news. Amy teased saying she was looking forward to meeting him. I just giggled. Dad looked quite good although he couldn't understand why I wouldn't let him wear his Brentford FC football shirt.

How do you tell someone that you've just inherited a fortune? Not the sort of thing that happens every day. The setting was right though: the *Portrait Restaurant* of the National Portrait Gallery. 'What's this all about Katie?' dad asked as we sat admiring the superb view.

I produced two bottles of Paul's *Riesling* from my cold bag which seemed most appropriate. Amy piped up and said she'd never heard of it and would have settled for Prosecco, then added, 'How can you afford *this place*?' I just smirked.

Just at that moment the young waiter arrived and somewhat indiscreetly told me there would be corkage for the wine and ice bucket. Giving him a look, I told him plainly that if he charged me corkage there would be no tip and that I and my friends on Facebook would never set foot in the place again. Amy stared at me with her mouth open. Even dad seemed startled. The waiter looked at me totally nonplussed. To help him along, I changed to a quieter tone and suggested that it would be in his interests not to charge corkage. He nodded his head, walked off and came back with two ice buckets and a corkscrew. Later he received a *very* generous tip.

Suitably cooled, I poured the wine, broke my news, and proposed a toast to 'My dear friend Paul Bunn.'

'What? That old man?' exclaimed my sister.

'Yes, him!' I grinned.

Dad stroked his chin. 'So, he did leave you something.'

12. Learning to fly

A lot of things happened in summer 2020. There were some imperatives though:

First, leave Brentford. Second, learn to fly.

Paul said that an aerospace engineer has to fly, otherwise what's the point? I always liked that.

I moved out to a hotel near Fairoaks, cycled to the airport and flew every day. *'Complete tuition until the pilot's certificate is won.'*

I studied hard, saw my shadow cross the clouds and by the end of two weeks I had my Private Pilot's Licence.

I called Anna, who speaks many languages, including Russian, a little English, and French and German with a strong Alsatian dialect, and asked her to arrange one of the rooms for me. A month after the Will reading I moved, and Strasbourg is now my home.

There are eight bedrooms to choose from. Mine is the light and airy one with a balcony overlooking the river next to the piano room which contains the most magnificent *Grotrian-Steinweg* grand. It's in tune too, and I am able to practice daily. The other Picasso is here: a highly stylised sketch of a keyboard and player in greys, reds and black. I prefer the one downstairs.

On the day I moved in, Anna noticed me in the drawing room studying the painting of the young woman in white and blue. She came over and explained, 'Paul said he bought it years ago because it reminded him of someone called Lisa.'

The envelope

Then Anna described how Paul had left 'something for me'. She went away and came back carrying a large thick grey fabric envelope.

'What is it Anna?'

'I don't know, but he said it was particularly important that I see it safely into your hands.' She passed it to me.

Inside were two leather-bound ledger style writing books, one with a green cover, the other black, and many old photos, papers and sketches. Curious, I flicked the black one open and immediately recognised Paul's fountain pen script. Then I realised I was holding the black book he'd been writing at the Stanley. Just a casual glance told me he'd written about 1944-5. It was his story, the one we hadn't managed to finish, *but he had*.

The enormity of it gripped me, and I began to shake. I had to sit down.

He had finished the story.

I stared at Anna. 'What is it?' she asked.

'Something special...' I whispered, as tears welled once more.

'Paul said it was special too. He was writing even on the day he passed. He said you would know what it was.'

He'd done it again: sprung an incredible surprise on me. On top of all the most amazing things, now this.

In a daze, I loaded up a flask of Anna's lovely coffee, got my sunhat and glasses, packed the black book in my backpack and set off. On the way to *Cimetière municipal Saint-Urbain* I bought *kugelhopf* and three red roses.

At the grave I sat on the bench and poured the coffee. Sipping it, I told him, 'Piece of work!'

I got the book out. He'd picked up the story in various places, but the real detail started when he was recovering in Rouen. His written description of his mental and physical state was much worse than what he'd told me. They'd sedated him with opium (laudanum) on many occasions, twice to stop him leaving. When he finally did get away, he'd sneaked out of the hotel in a delirious state at five in the morning without telling anyone. That was quite a different version of events. Elsewhere there were minor variations in his written account, but essentially it was the same.

Paul had deliberately not told me. He couldn't tell me. He'd written it all down and, at the very end, had told himself instead.

13. Bittersweet, 25 - 26 March 1945

I smiled as I sat reading the old man's handwriting. Turning the pages of the black book, I came to the place where he'd left off before Christmas. Paul wrote (verbatim):
'Just before dawn on Palm Sunday, a key stuttered in the lock, and the door pushed open. I looked up from under the quilt on the sofa and there in the dim light stood my father.'

His father had returned! It was wonderful to read. I glanced up to look at the family grave again with their names in gold lettering. They were reunited.

I didn't want the story to end. Then I realised it didn't have to. Their story was mine now, it didn't have to end. I think it was about here that I decided I would write it all down, the whole story from the beginning.

I ate the kugelhopf, sipped the coffee, and read what Paul had to say.

As the words came off the page it was easily possible to imagine that moment in the Berlin apartment. In the black book he wrote (verbatim):
"My God! Paul, it's you, it's you!'

In the tight embrace neither of us knew what to say. Neither of us wanted to let go. There were tears.

Father was thin, gaunt even, tired and drawn. He picked up his suitcase and gently shut the door, as if he didn't want anyone to know he was there. 'Shh... speak quietly in French, the walls have ears,' he whispered.

We sat and stared at each other. He said he'd forgotten what anyone else looked like, except Helene and me. He pulled out the photos of us he carried. He said he needed to stare just to check that it really was me. We stood and embraced again.

He'd brought food and coffee. Proper coffee. Still staring, we talked and talked whilst waiting for the gas to come back on, and then we ate and drank together for the first time in two years. Thick black bread and *Kirschmarmelade* (Cherry jam) from a tin and real bitter coffee. That jam was oh so sweet!

Martin appeared and was introduced. With his father and mother in a mass grave this moment was hard for him, and he wept openly. 'My parents at least have each other's company,' was all he could say over my shoulder as I held him. Then he went away, dressed in his civilian clothes and set off into the cold late March morning saying he was going to see what he could find. I knew he couldn't cope with it, but he was taking a chance going out.

In the sunlight in the window, we stood.

Father asked: 'Why are you here?'

'I've come to rescue you. I've come to take you home.' Tears welled again and we embraced.

'Why? You haven't told me why.' It was a typical challenge; he hadn't forgotten how. 'Why did you risk your life coming here?' There was frustration in his tone.

For me it was not a matter of thought or reflection. It was simply something I had done.

I stared at him, 'I had to do it.' It was the perfect answer because it was true. 'Why haven't you escaped?'

'What makes you think I haven't escaped?' he said with a self-satisfied grin. There was his old air of casual confidence again. Two years away and nothing had changed. Such an amazing man.

'What?' I exclaimed.

'Did you really think they could hold *me*? Do you imagine that I haven't *chosen* to be here?'

'You've chosen to be here?' I was incredulous.

He looked at me. 'Yes.'

'Why? Why are you here risking everything? For what?'

'I'm doing something only I can do.'

'What could that be? What can *only you* do?'

He hesitated. 'If I tell you it will put you in danger.'

'DANGER... Don't talk to me about danger. I've come halfway across Europe through a bloody battlefield and been bombed, blown up and shot at. I've lived a lie for four months in this God forsaken city. Don't talk to me about danger.'

'What makes you think I haven't done *exactly the same*? We are not so different.'

'What? What could you possibly be talking about?'

'Yes, I suppose you're entitled to an explanation,' father garbled, lowering his head.

'Oh. You *suppose* do you? Don't be an arse. Stop this crap and come with me right now,' I fumed. I'd never sworn at him before, but he'd earned it.

'My work here is too important.'

'What work? What work is so important that you will not come home with me?'

'Paul, I'm working for British military intelligence. I have been since 1934. You just haven't seen it.'

CHRIST!

I was speechless, shaking.

'Son, what did you think we were doing all those years when we were touring Germany? Remember when you were growing up, going to those airfields, looking at and flying all those aeroplanes? Visiting all those places with the Leica camera, taking all those photos? Why d'you think I went on the *Hindenburg* to New York?'

I was staggered. Dumbstruck.

I'd spent my whole life seeing him as my father. I wanted him to be my father. But I'd only seen what I'd wanted to see, what I expected to see. Things were not what they seemed.'

I stood up with the book in my hand and walked around repeating, 'OH MY GOD!' Anyone passing would have thought I was insane. Years ago, Paul told me that things are only the way we *want* them to seem. Now I saw the understatement.

I paced about the family grave staring at their names.

In the black book, Paul wrote of how his father saw deportation from Jersey as an opportunity. After arriving at Laufen detention camp in early April 1943, Christopher asked to speak to the authorities. He knew he wouldn't survive a winter there. He had to do something. It was expedient. He proved he was 'of German blood' when they checked his *Ahnenpaß* and extended family in Bonn. Then he charmed them. They asked if he would teach German, and he agreed knowing this would bring him into better circumstances.

Christopher explained to Paul how there were tens of thousands of British prisoners of war in various camps around the Reich. Some of these agreed to join a small band of British SS volunteers called *das Britische Freikorps* (The British Free Corps). In late August 1943, he was assigned to them in a camp in a southern suburb of Berlin and began teaching German. Paul wrote that his father was also 'keeping an eye.' There was another intelligence officer hidden in that grouping who was not named. He also heard mention of an Englishman 'working with the Germans', who had been in prison in Jersey when the Germans arrived in 1940, also unnamed.

During the winter, *das Freikorps* moved to a northern suburb, then in February 1944 they moved to Hanover. Christopher made sure he stayed in Berlin working as a translator.

He was increasingly regarded as valuable to the German war effort and became completely trusted. As an asset he was paid and looked after, and in November 1943 given the apartment of 'a person who had been denounced to the Gestapo and deported.' He was given an alias by the authorities: Richard Jäger, 'for his safety and protection,' though from what was unclear.

Then he was detailed to teach German to French SS recruits. These were collaborators who had cleared out of France as the Allies pushed east during 1944. Many of them became the *Waffen-Grenadier-Brigade der SS 'Charlemagne.'*

In fact, Christopher was a subversive operative, using his languages, charm and inter-personal skills to subtly give the enemy conflicting advice and undermine his confidence. He was also a surveillance officer, collecting information and reporting it back by invisible ink and coded letters to British intelligence via Switzerland, Portugal and Sweden.

Christopher told Paul that the *SS Britische Freikorps* was a 'bloody shambles' and that his work was done. He had managed something similar in the French SS '*Charlemagne*' Brigade. They had been upgraded to division status, sent to fight the Russians in East Pomerania and annihilated.

Berlin was in such a state of melt-down by late March 1945 that Christopher, or Richard, whoever he was, could effectively disappear and nobody would notice. That's how he'd returned to his apartment, and that was when he found his son waiting for him. Paul wrote (verbatim):

'Father stood there and explained everything, and it made sense. All except for one especially important detail. When I looked him square in the eye and asked about the circumstances of his deportation from Jersey, he went deadly silent. I could feel my anger rising... In the long silence I realised an awful truth:

'You allowed yourself to be taken, didn't you?'

'Yes.'

I snapped, hit him in the mouth with a right fist, and down he went.

'You bastard!' I told him as he lay on that carpet.

'I'm not going to say I'm sorry if that's what you want. I had to go. I had to get back into the game. I was no use to anyone wasting my time in Jersey,' he growled sitting up staring back and feeling his broken lip.

'Get up so I can knock you down again! What about **me**? What about mother? *Wasting your time* were you? Bastard! You weren't wasting your time – you were being my father, at least that's what I thought. But you chose to leave us and come to this hell hole, to play a game!'

'Slaying these monsters is above everything. If we lose, we lose EVERYTHING, can't you see that?'

'I lost YOU. Then I went mad. I changed into THIS because YOU went away. Can't **you** see that?'

'It was necessary. If I shorten the war by one minute, or save the life of one innocent child, it would be worth it.'

'What about us? What about *your* child? What about your wife? What about our lives? Are the lives of others worth more?'

'Well said son, well said. But it was necessary. War forces us to make sacrifices and accept larger truths.'

'Don't pose as someone dealing in truths when you could not tell **me** the truth.'

He blinked his eyes and nodded his head in a form of acceptance.

Standing over him, nursing my right hand, I thought and then dared to ask the worst question:

'Mother knew. She knew you let yourself be taken, didn't she?'

'No. She knew nothing.'

I slumped into the sofa holding my head in my hands. I was crushed. He'd lied to mother as well.

Father stood, straightened himself up, wiped the blood from his lip, then sat next to me on that dingy maroon sofa and tried to explain:

'Would it have made any difference, had you known? If I had told you, would you have tried to stop me, and would you have succeeded? You already know the answer.'

'Why didn't you tell me? Why didn't you tell mother? Why did you hide the truth from us?'

'The truth is dangerous. You and your mother didn't need to know the truth. There was nothing you could have done with it. You were on an island and making friends with the enemy. You were growing up. If you had let anything slip we would all have been shot. Don't you see that? I couldn't tell you.'

'JESUS CHRIST!' I muttered through clenched teeth. 'You took that decision all on your own then? You presumed to choose for us, without telling us? And send us through hell. **How could you?**'

'I had to fight, and if necessary, kill. These Nazis are sent from a hell much worse than the one you Beatrice and your mother were in. The battle wasn't in Jersey, the battle was elsewhere. You understand this, you always have. Even if you had known why I left, would it have stopped *you* leaving?'

He paused then quietly added: 'I'm sorry I left you.'

Of course he was going to leave Jersey. He had to go, and so did I. It was unavoidable.

He continued. 'You, your mother and I, we are all very much alike. The proof is right here in this room. You are strong and I am so proud of you.'

We stood and embraced again, and I told him I loved him very much. More tears came. He was right, I did understand.

He returned to the window and warmed himself in the morning sun. Then he turned back to me and said, 'Son, give me a few days to tidy things up. Then let's go home.'

14. Bad Friday

Paul had written so vividly that it could all have happened yesterday. My appearance at the Stanley had triggered the intense memories which had brought us to here. I didn't cause the events of 1939 to 1945, but I did cause him to remember them. Were these memories like the treasured shells he used to bury in a box in the sand dunes of St Ouen's? Or were they tormenting devils that should have remained locked away?

It made me think about mum. She chose to leave. I never understood why. Paul's father had left and when the truth came out it hurt. My mother knew the truth. Perhaps that truth would hurt me too? Perhaps it was better that I didn't know? Paul was who he was *because* his father went away. Now I understood that I am who I am *because* my mother went away. The old man knew this. He'd known all along.

Paul told his father about his journey to Berlin and showed him the Webley revolver. He told him about Martin and his nurse friend Lisa and his plan to leave Berlin with them directly after Easter.

Christopher warned Paul to be careful of Greta. He was sure she was the one who'd denounced the previous occupant of number 41. Paul said he'd described himself to her as *Richard's* former student, told him that Martin was a deserter, and that Greta knew because of his indiscretion on New Year's Eve. Christopher said that the SS uniforms counted for a lot, as did Paul's 'honour' warning; it was a perfect response. But that currency wouldn't last for ever. 'She hasn't done anything, but that doesn't mean she won't. These Berliners show deference but wear your uniform and carry the Webley at all times,' Paul's father advised.

Meanwhile, Greta returned to her apartment the next morning, which was Monday, 26 March. Christopher tapped on her door to say hello again after being away. He wanted to gauge her mood.

She was edgy, hungover, bleary-eyed and sat smoking non-stop. She was scared to death at the thought of the Russians arriving. She complained that she didn't like Easter because there would be no dancing, so she had to make up for it elsewhere. Then she complained that it was 'too solemn' anyway and that this year 'they ought to make it a celebration.' In Paul's book he comments that you would be hard pressed to find a single street in Berlin where anyone would have anything to celebrate. Then Greta talked about Good Friday and told Christopher that she couldn't see anything good about it.

On Wednesday there was a massive daytime air raid to the west of the city in Spandau.

On Thursday Martin went out in his uniform and overcoat but didn't come back to the apartment. This had never happened before. He wasn't the sort to just take himself off and not return. Bad weather meant there was no Mosquito raid, so he wasn't in a shelter. They went out to look for him. No sign of Martin.

On Good Friday morning he still hadn't returned. Paul was anxious to get out of Berlin, and he wanted Martin to come. He thought he knew where to find him. He was able to ride now, took his revolver 'just in case' and set off, leaving his father sitting by the fire warming himself.

He made good time despite the debris in the roads.

Pulling onto Tiergartenstraße he cycled until he arrived at the Großer Weg entrance to the Tiergarten which led directly to Luiseninsel, Martin's secret island. Paul wrote (Verbatim):

'There were two police and an SS *Charlemagne* Unterscharführer. I noticed his dagger. They stopped me and asked for my papers. The SS examined those and in a French accent said, 'Paul, huh. Signed off injured. But active service for you tomorrow boy.'

'Yessir.'

'There will be plenty of work for us when the reds arrive. Where will you report?'

'Alexanderplatz sir.'

'Very good. You have received the right orders, even though they are not written here. Why have you no written orders from your paymaster?'

He had gouge marks by both his eyes, with fresh blood seeping.

'My division is not here. The paymaster told me to report to Alexanderplatz sir.'

He looked at my cuff title and said something like, 'Why are you here if your division isn't? An SS deserter is the worst kind of coward.' He paused, considered me, but seemed satisfied.

'Yessir.'

Then they walked off along Tiergartenstraße.

I went and found Martin on his island. He was dead hanging from a tree with a chalk sign around his neck which said:

ICH WAR ZU FEIGE
MEIN VATERLAND
ZU VERTEIDIGEN

I WAS TOO COWARDLY
TO DEFEND MY
FATHERLAND

He was still warm.

15. In the garden

I looked up and saw the two police and SS man moving away. Below me, black boots were pacing fast. The distance between those boots and the three men was closing rapidly. In a pocket a right hand was holding a cold fully loaded revolver. The first one was going to be the Unterscharführer...

They heard my hobnails, stopped, turned, and saw me.

Someone said, 'Stay out of it.'

Another voice said, 'Yes Peter?' It was the French SS. Somehow I'd arrived right next to him. The two police were gazing at me in perplexity. I looked at them.

One said, '*Hitlerjugend,* like you. Do you know him?'

'My name is not Peter, and yes – I do know him.'

I heard: 'String him up like the other one...'

I growled, '*You murdering bastards,*' and something in French at the SS.

There was the flash of a dagger, a struggle, a blur, noises.

I walked away from three unbroken bodies, two in police uniform, and an SS man. They lay side by side in a little wood. Each had a single bullet wound in the back of the head, and there was a huge pool of blood.

Then, somehow, I was back on Martin's island washing blood from my hands in the water and cutting him down.

I looked at his face, bit my fingers and wept as I closed his eyes for the last time.

Then I set off to St Gertrude's. I had to go and find Lisa.

She wasn't there. Nobody knew where she was.

Her friend Lotte saw me, put back my dislocated right index finger and gently strapped it.

She said nothing, but then very quietly and slowly explained that on Wednesday Lisa had gone to the weekly market at Spandau town hall to look for Easter eggs and a gift for her boyfriend. 'That must be you,' she said. Her face fell. 'There was a raid on Spandau on Wednesday. I'm so sorry.'

We cried as she cleaned and stitched up knife wounds in my back that I didn't even realise I had.

I have no memory of anything after that or of how I got back to the apartment.

Father was waiting. 'What happened?'

'They found Martin and executed him.'

He saw my black eyes and bloodied face and clothes and got out a first aid kit.

After he checked my stitches we sat in front of the fire. He held my wrists and explained, 'There was nothing you could have done.'

'Yes there was,' I whispered.

Then I told him I went after the lynching party but didn't know what happened. He said:

'Whoever fights monsters should see to it that in the process he does not become a monster. If you gaze long enough into an abyss, the abyss will gaze back into you.'
- **Friedrich Nietzsche. 'Beyond Good & Evil'**

'Did you kill them?' he asked quietly.

Silently I got out the revolver and examined it. I noticed that three bullets were spent.

He looked at me, studied my eyes, but said nothing.

Then I told him that my friend Lisa was dead, lost in an air raid.

I was numb. Beyond weeping.

For a long time, I stared into the flames of the fire blaming myself for Martin and Lisa's deaths.

In another reality I could have loved Lisa. But I couldn't save her.

Then we heard the lock catch of our neighbour's door click. It was Greta. My mind went red.

Next thing I remember, and before either father or I knew what was happening, I was standing up revolver in-hand heading next door. Father blocked my route.

'Stop. This isn't the right way.'

'She denounced Martin, now she must pay,' I told him.

'NO! You don't know that. Even if you confront her she will only deny it. What use will that be? Killing in self-defence is one thing, but murder makes us as bad as them.'

'I lost my friend, and someone has to pay,' I growled.

'Not like this. We're all paying now. If you kill in cold blood it will always be your truth. Don't go that way.'

I looked at him. 'Is Nietzsche right then - that there is no God? Or is he so bored in heaven that he enjoys watching us die like worms suffering and crying? It doesn't look like he's interested in truth. Who wants a God like that? What use is a God like that?'

'Son, you and I have stared war and death in the face: we have stared into the abyss. No surprise that we don't like what we see. Don't make it worse. Don't make it worse for yourself.'

I didn't go next door. Instead, I slumped down and stared at the gun in my hand wondering what the truth might be.

The plan

That evening beside the fire we sat and talked about escape. Father had lived for years in wartime Germany and thrived. He always had a plan.

He was a brilliant pilot with a lot of experience, and knowledge of practically all German aircraft. He'd flown most of the non-fighter single-engine types. When I mentioned to him about getting a bike and cycling out, he said, 'We'll never get out like that. They'll have roadblocks everywhere and we won't have the papers. We'll be shot.'

'What do you suggest then? Walking, driving, train?'

'None of those. We will leave on Easter Day. Everywhere will be quiet. Tempelhof Airport will be quiet. I've had that place under surveillance, and I know what they're up to in there. I've talked to plenty of pilots, and I've walked in and out lots of times. I know my way around.'

'You're surely not suggesting that we fly out?'

'That's exactly what I'm suggesting. I'm so sorry that your friends Martin and Lisa won't be coming with us.'

'Mother of Christ! You're serious!'

'They have three *Fieseler Storch* in there at the moment. We'll just borrow one.' He looked at me, smiled and at the same time opened his suitcase, and there was a Luftwaffe Colonel's uniform and Luger pistol folded inside. My amazing father.

'What if they start shooting?' I asked.

'We shoot back.''

16. Flight of the Storch

At the Stanley, Paul told me many examples of people stealing aeroplanes and flying out. In May 1941, even Hitler's Deputy Rudolph Hess stole one. He took a Messerschmitt Bf 110 twin and flew to Scotland to try to persuade Churchill to join Germany before the attack on communist Russia. He gloried in the fact that he'd gone to see and touch the bits of it in the Imperial War Museum in London. Plenty fled to England in stolen aircraft: Poles, Czechs, Belgians, French - anyone with access who knew how to fly the types. He said he thought Germans had flown off Jersey in stolen aircraft, certainly there was plenty of talk, but he wasn't sure if anyone had actually done it. German pilots had even broken out of British prisoner of war camps, stolen RAF aircraft and tried to fly home. A German stole a Messerschmitt Me 262 jet aircraft and escaped to neutral Switzerland in 1945. Stealing aeroplanes was commonplace.

I remembered that Christopher had flown the Storch as a glider towplane on many occasions in Germany before the war. Preparing and flying one would pose no difficulty. I also knew that Paul had a Storch in his private collection hangar at *Aéroport de Strasbourg*. I thought he had it because he liked the name: Stork. But that wasn't it at all, there was another reason. In his black book this is what Paul had to say:

'It was Easter Sunday, and we got dressed to the embers of the dying fire. Father looked pretty slick in his uniform. 'I see you have been promoted, Herr Oberst!' I teased. He just smiled and told me: 'We'll have to see about that then, won't we?' I always liked it when he said that.

As we walked in the dawn light I asked him how the hell he'd managed to acquire a Colonel's uniform? Quietly he told me that the chap who owned it wouldn't be needing it anymore. He added that his boots fit so he took those too.

333

We arrived just at sun rise in a cold clear morning. Father was right: nothing was moving. He explained that Tempelhof was not a military airfield. By now the priority was to have all the armed forces deployed out on the Eastern Front defending Berlin against the Russians, so there were few guards. They had foreign workers there building and repairing aircraft, but they were all inside and unsecured. They weren't going to stop us. The Storch were reconnaissance aircraft, easy to fly with a very short take-off run. All we had to do was gain access and find the one with the most fuel in it. We walked around the concrete perimeter wall until we came to a suitable spot across some railway lines and scrambled in through a bomb hole.

The place was vast and empty, but father knew where to find the few serviceable machines and we set off at pace.

The three aircraft were under the concrete and steel canopy on the leftmost side of the main terminus building to the left of the foreign worker huts. There was a pile of broken and cannibalised aircraft and the tail of a Stuka dive bomber sticking out of a hangar.

One Storch was unserviceable and had its wings folded back. He'd already briefed me to look at the under-wing fuel gauges which hang down for ease of reference. The one he found had ¾ full tanks and a good battery charge state. He quickly beckoned me over to help prepare it, and I threw my rifle and kit in below the rear mounted MG34 machine gun. Under the instrument panel he found a checklist. I pulled off the rudder and elevator clamps, checked free movement on the control surfaces and removed the wheel chocks. He checked the oil and got underneath to drip the tanks to make sure there was no water, then he checked the wing main pins for security. In the door I found a metal pocket with useful maps. He checked magnetos off and fuel on, then turned the propeller three times. It was all fairly breathless work. He took an iron bar and hammer and smashed the fuel pump of the unserviceable Storch. Then we pushed our aircraft out.

Unfortunately, we had attracted some attention, and two young grey uniformed boys walked towards us from the direction of the main hall.

The question was whether to get in and go and risk getting shot at or try another strategy. I knew what father would do. 'Get in,' he said.

He walked off to greet the young soldiers while I peered anxiously out of the back seat trying not to look concerned. The soldiers stood to attention, saluted the senior officer and they chatted. Father got out his silver cigarette case and offered them both. Then he lit them up with his silver lighter in his familiar and casual way.

The conversation felt like it went on for hours, but it probably didn't. I was shitting myself. Then, to my horror, they all three began walking back to the aeroplane. I held my breath and got the revolver in-hand.

Giving me a nod, father got in and did up his straps.

One young man with a Mauser over his shoulder stood at the open door. He spoke: 'We hope you get well soon; appendicitis is a dangerous thing. Your father will look after you.' Even more amazing: he had a Colmar accent. He was Alsatian!

I groaned, closed my eyes, threw my head back and said nothing. Meanwhile, father primed the engine with the yellow lever. He tried to start it, but it wouldn't start!

Cool as you like, father unstrapped, got out, gathered up the crank handle and showed the Alsatian how to crank the engine at the port on the other side from the door. Then he got in and tried again. The youth cranked like hell, spinning the propeller and chugga-chugga-chugg-brrr... The engine fired up in a cloud of grey smoke which left the soldiers coughing and spluttering. Father taxied out a little as the two looked on.

There were a few pensive moments as the engine temperature rose, then father took the brake off, and we taxied out. The wind was light and variable and all we had to do was negotiate a few bomb holes in the concrete. He set the flaps with the chain mechanism, gunned the engine and in 15 seconds we were away.

I've never been so relieved in all my life.

Over the headphones I heard my brilliant father *Der König der Störche* say, 'They won't shoot at us now, they won't fire on their own aircraft.'

We turned left and flew over Berlin gaining height all the while. I looked out and took a photo of the Anhalter station. (page 6)

To the east, in the distance, was the haze of the battle raging at the River Oder. We picked up the River Spree and flew keeping it on our right. Below us: Berlin, magnificent, but choked in smoke and destruction. There was the Brandenburger Tor and the Tiergarten.

Then I saw Martin's island and turned my head away.

Climbing, we flew a compass heading of 250 degrees. Father pointed out the heavily damaged Charlottenburg Palace on the right and the Olympic Stadium. Climbing further he pointed out Spandau with its distinctive fortress island.

The buildings were smashed with smoke still rising. My dear Lisa was under that rubble.

We flew over the Wannsee lake. Lisa and I would never walk together beside it.

I never told anyone about Lisa, and no one knows her story or even that she ever lived. But in my mind she is free, and I am walking with her: walking with a friend in the dark.

Father was exhausted. On the intercom passing Potsdam he told me he couldn't concentrate - couldn't keep his mind on the flying, so he asked if I would take over. This Storch was a training aircraft which had been adapted to dual controls and instruments. I gave him the food and flew the aircraft. He ate then dozed off to sleep. Now I was flying him to safety.

Aristotle was right.

The Storch was easy to fly. Calculations showed that at the 130km per hour cruise speed it would take two hours to reach our destination: Göttingen.'

17. Göttingen

'I picked up the River Elbe and flew past Magdeburg on our right. It had been destroyed.

In those days, the airfield for Göttingen was about 2km out of town to the north-west. Today it's a giant trading estate, there's even a place to play crazy golf. In April 1945, the thought of landing there filled me with dread.

As we came in over the old city we noticed that the marshalling yards had been bombed. Some of the river bridges were down, but I spotted a crossing into the centre. First though we had to land and not be shot.

There wasn't much going on; the airfield appeared to be abandoned. It had five big hangars on the north side. We taxied up over the grass in front of the leftmost, rolled the doors open, pulled the Storch inside and left it there. It was almost out of fuel anyway. I loved that aeroplane.

It was only as we were leaving that a Leutnant, and two young soldiers came and challenged us.

As before I had my hand on the revolver, but father was as cool as ever. After salutes cigarettes and pleasantries, he explained, 'I've come with my son from Berlin, and he has appendicitis. The hospitals there are full and anyway are staffed by those damned French surgeon-butchers.

The hospital here is the best in Germany, and it still has trustworthy Germans in it. So Leutnant, if you don't mind, we'll be leaving now.' They were apologetic that they had no car or fuel to spare to drive us. Away we walked, appropriately slowly.

Father had several reasons to be in Göttingen, but I had only one.

Bells rang as we wandered into town on that bright Easter Sunday morning. Sullen people regarded our uniforms and then went about their business. There were no other soldiers around, but it didn't seem to puzzle them at all to see a smart middle ranking Luftwaffe officer and a young *SS Oberschütze* with a rucksack wandering their streets asking for directions. They were past caring.

Eventually we approached a place I'd only seen in my imagination: Mauerstraße 30. Just a plain wooden door in an average cobbled street in a small German city.

We were 30 metres away when the door opened, and two women emerged: a young lady and an older woman. Without saying anything, father and I followed them right and then left into St Michael's church. We sat at the back as the Easter service was conducted. At the end, the congregation filed out, the two women with them. They eyed father up as they walked past. They were not happy to see us in our uniforms and neither was anyone else in church that day. I knew the young woman was Gertie. She had cut her hair short, but I recognised her from the photo.

After a respectful time, we walked once more back to Mauerstraße 30. I knocked on the door. It opened, and the younger woman stood there. She spoke gruffly: 'You. I saw you at church. What do you want?'

338

I opened up, 'Miss, please, I am sorry to trouble you. I have come to see Frau Winkler. Is she in?'

Behind her down a corridor, the older woman appeared. 'What do they want?' she called.

'Frau Winkler, is it you? My name is Paul von Bonn, and this is my father Oberst von Bonn. Can we come in please?'

'What's your business here?' Gertie said, blocking the doorway.

'Bitte, Fräulein, I am here with something important for you and Frau Winkler, *something from Dieter.*'

'Oh. Oh... In that case, come in,' she said with a look of startlement.

We were silently ushered through past a front room to a simple homely kitchen of flagstones and oak sideboards and invited to sit at the table where candles had burned away. Dieter's mother spoke:

'Forgive me young sir, I would have thought that your father from the Luftwaffe would speak?'

'No Frau Winkler, I have nothing to say,' father said quite solemnly, taking off his cap and bowing his head. Without speaking, I reached into my bag, fetched out everything of Dieter's and placed it all on the table: his dog tag, letters and papers. Finally, I produced the photo and his last unsent letter which I handed to Gertie. At the sight of these, the two women wept openly and grasped each other's hands which they held tightly. Gertie stood and comforted the bereft mother that last letter clutched in her right hand.

Father and I went off to the front room where we took seats. Here we saw family photos: mother, father and three boys. There was a copy of the one of Dieter and his brothers with their gliders.

A length of time passed. Then the two women came and sat with us in the front room. Frau Winkler spoke:

'Thank you for coming. We were informed in September that Dieter was missing and had received no word. He always wrote and was a faithful son. We hoped he had been captured but heard nothing more and now we know the truth. His father and two brothers are also gone, in Russia.' She held her hand across her mouth, as if she felt guilty in saying it and wanted to stop the words coming out.

It was too terrible. I reached and held her wrists. 'I am so deeply sorry that your husband and your sons are victims of war. My sincerest condolences,' I whispered.

'My deepest condolences Frau Winkler,' father added, almost silently, bowing his head.

Slowly, a form of normality took over. We were treated as family even though we were the long-awaited envoys of death. Coffee was produced, bread and cherry jam. We ate and talked and were entirely accepted.

Dieter's mother did not ask me how he died.

After an hour, she said, 'I should like to repay you for your kind mission, which you were not bound to undertake. I invite you to stay with us for as long as you wish. Will you stay with us?'

With us was a phrase I hadn't heard in a long time. I glanced at father. His slight nod made it clear that he agreed with me. 'Yes Frau Winkler, if it is no trouble to you then we will gladly accept your offer,' he said. There seemed no reason for her to make that invitation.

She continued, 'Please call me Katharina. The war is over. There is no sense any longer in being inhospitable and this is Easter Day after all. I would like you to stay with us.' It was agreed.

Handing Dieter's identity papers back she refused them and quietly told me, 'I want to remember him as my little boy, not as this man of war.'

Father suggested it would be better if I dressed as a civilian. It was a difficult moment when Katharina told me to help myself to Dieter's jacket and clothes.

Later we went out and joined the low-key Easter procession from the church through the fine old town. We walked slowly behind the banner and past the statue of *Das Gänseliesel* (Little Lisa with the Geese) around the streets. In the afternoon we took food parcels to the elderly and war-wounded. Unfortunately, there was a consequence to this.

It was lovely to stay in the Winkler house in those days and Katherina was a very gracious host. The same could not be said of the city which was of sour temperament. I took Göttingen as if it were Berlin: a place where you could disappear, anonymous and impersonal. Father did disappear. He said he had business at the university. He never said what. However, I didn't disappear and my presence on the streets was a mistake.

The Winklers had a vegetable stall at the market in front of *Das Gänseliesel* which was on Tuesday, Thursday and Saturday. I helped out on the stall and kept busy moving bags of produce. Katharina was glad of my company. Gertie was there too. Her family stall sold millinery, cotton, wool, scrap dresses and fabrics, anything to do with sewing and knitting.

There was a lot of talk of when the Americans would arrive. Nobody knew what they thought about that, but they all agreed that it had to be any day. They knew the military defenders had gone. I got so engrossed chatting to Gertie and her friends that it didn't register that I was a young man in a town where there were no young men. On the streets were mostly children, women, and the elderly. One or two of them looked at me but said nothing.

On a sunny Thursday, we'd been at the market for a couple of hours when two smart looking fellows with hats came to the stall. They weren't your run-of-the-mill customers. Older men they were, in their 40s. They were interested in me in particular, but they started with the stall holder:

'Good day Frau. Papers please,' said one with a brown suit and hat, turning his lapel to show his party badge.

'Not until I see yours. Nobody has ever asked for my papers before. Who are you, strangers? and what's your business here?' Katharina was in no mood for his crap.

The other one, in a black leather trench coat, studied me. 'What about you boy? Shouldn't you be at the front? Let's see your papers.'

'How dare you!' accused Katharina. 'Why aren't YOU at the front? If you are so interested in the front, why don't you take yourself there right now and leave us in peace.'

'Don't take that tone with us Frau. Papers please,' the one with the brown hat persisted.

'No!'

The market had gone quiet and with shocked faces people regarded the awful stand-off.

'Come with us then, both of you,' they demanded waving orange Gestapo identity cards.

Quietly I told them, 'You two idiots are making a mistake. Leave my mother and I'll go with you to sort this out.' They looked at me quizzically.

Katharina had described them as strangers. They didn't know the town. This meant I could lead them past St Johannis church to an arch through a row of houses I'd noticed on the procession.

We got into the seclusion of the arch, and I rounded on them: 'It would be a pity if your sort survived this war.'

'What did you say boy?' brown hat exclaimed nonplussed.

At that I handed them Dieter's papers. It bought me five seconds to reach in his jacket pocket, get the revolver in-hand and summarise my options.

The one in black studied the papers and looked me up and down. 'These papers are no good, *Dieter*. You're a deserter, aren't you?'

'How about you two idiots walk away, huh? The war is over. Frau Winkler has lost a son in France and two sons and a husband in Russia, and all for nothing. Don't come here looking for trouble. Walk away.'

My revolver was pointed at the stomach of the one with the brown hat and the other would have no time to react.

'TRAITOR!' the other one exclaimed. 'We've been hanging cowards like you!' he guffawed.

I cut him off. 'NO, YOU are the cowards. Where have YOU served? France? Russia? No, you have served in the only place that would have you: the sewers. What have YOU lost? A son? A daughter? A wife? NO, YOU are the traitors. YOU have killed good Germans. YOU have killed Germany.'

Brown hat growled, 'Keep your pious speeches boy. You will come with us. We're going to make an example of you. Don't make me draw my pistol in the street.'

I snarled: '**No**. *You will come with me, and I will make an example of you*. I have *my pistol* trained on you right now.'

They glanced at my right hand in-pocket. It betrayed their doubt.

'You are bluffing. You have no pistol!' brown hat scoffed.

'Deserters are cowards, and you're a coward,' said the other.

'Call me a coward again, and I **will** shoot you.'

There was a moment. I was ready…

Blood hissed in my ears, my eyes alert to any movement.

I drew the Webley slowly, all the while aiming right at brown hat's stomach. 'I'll take your pistols now then gentlemen, as you are too cowardly to use them. Take them out slowly one at a time, put them on the ground, walk away and we will all survive this war.'

I picked up their Lugers, put them in my pockets and told them, 'You have chosen wisely. Now come and I will show you the way. Walk in front of me. Don't make a fuss or it will be the end for you.'

Dutifully, they walked ahead as I guided them back towards the airfield, then northwards on a track by the side of the river. Then we crossed to the west side on a bridge. I walked them for over an hour. They were unfit and sweated profusely. Occasionally they looked back, yelled a few names at me and said they'd cut my head off. I called them idiots and after a while they wearied and gave up their jabbering. As we walked I told them they'd better not come back to town because if they did I'd be waiting. I marched them westwards across fields and along lanes. They appeared exhausted.

Suddenly, in the middle of nowhere, I saw their sweaty faces again, and there was a struggle…

Afterwards the grass glistened red, and they were laying down, side by side, silent and still. I told them to enjoy the sun quietly.

Walking back along the river, I stopped to wash my hands. When I looked up I saw Lisa on the other side. I was so sure it was her that I began to run and look for a place to cross. I got there and realised it was a young silver birch tree, the river reflecting its shimmering blue-white light. I sat and stared at that tree for a long time.

Back at Mauerstraße I found father who embraced me tightly. Katharina had told him about the bust-up at the market and they were desperate to see me. I started to tell him, but I wasn't sure what had happened.

He said, 'Well, thank God you're safe, but you look like you've been in another fight?' I regarded him in puzzlement. Blood was oozing from my throat and fingers. My back was soggy with blood from ripped stitches, my nose was bleeding, and my right little finger was dislocated again. I put it back myself this time.

Father continued, 'We're not safe here, we must go to another house.'

He could be a master of understatement.

Because of the incident at the market, father was invited to go through Herr Winkler's wardrobe. He had died at Sevastopol in April 1944.

Katharina suggested we go to the Heckel house and stay there until the Americans came. Frau Heckel kindly agreed, and that's what we did.

Gertie's brother and father were away at war.

While we were there, Gertie gave me back Dieter's letter. She pressed it into my hand with her photo and told me it would be better if she forgot him. She said she'd lost hope long ago.

We didn't have to wait long for the Americans. On Saturday, 8 April 1945, the citizens of Göttingen were told to hang white sheets of surrender from their windows. We also had to hand over any weapons. I didn't.

When I looked at the revolver there was only one bullet left.

The next day, in the afternoon, American Jeeps and lorries rolled into the market square. I went out to watch, and Gertie stood with me.'

18. A new life, April 2021

I descended to 5000 feet as I passed Metz with 70 nautical miles to go and let down again to 4000 feet at 25. It's always lovely to see the Vosges mountains from the air.

Strasbourg tower was co-operative, and I was Number 1. The circuit for runway 23 brings you in over Molsheim. Today I could see it very clearly in bright sunshine. On the powered glide I remembered Paul's *Molsheim Clowns* and decided to pay the town a visit.

The King Air twin turboprop is easy to fly, with power to spare, and I taxied to the apron smoothly and promptly. I parked up then wheeled my bike off the aircraft and through customs. Despite Brexit it did not invite any comment from the officers as they recognised me. Then I cycled into town.

Anna greeted me with coffee, fresh kugelhopf and her customary smile. We chatted in German and caught up. She commended me for 'attacking the language.' I had to laugh. I asked if she might like a trip to London for her English, and delighted me when in good English she replied, 'We'll have to see about that then, won't we?'

After lunch, in the piano room I played from Paul's well-thumbed copy of Chopin's *Berceuse in D-Flat, Op. 57*. Then I returned to the drawing room with its Picasso and perfect light and sat writing whilst listening to James Heather's beautiful piano piece, *Immortal Beloved*.

I always follow a custom. On every arrival I go to the family grave with three red roses which I place beneath the headstone, one for each: Helene, Christopher, and my Paul. I always sit on the nearby bench studying the scene and Strasbourg skyline. He had chosen of course to be with his beloved parents, and they had chosen to be here. The Bunns were always going away but always coming back. Now it was my turn.

Sometimes I brought coffee in a flask, kugelhopf and pastries, sometimes I brought wine. Today it was Anna's coffee. I took the thermos, poured, then drank and followed it with a slice of kugelhopf. Paul would have enjoyed that and sitting there telling me another story. My eyes always fill at this point.

Next day, with a view to catching the train home just as Paul had in 1939, I cycled out of town westwards along the towpath of the Canal de la Bruche. I was delighted to stop and watch lots of storks in the nearby fields and flying overhead. Next, along the river into Molsheim in pleasant spring sunshine. A charming and very Alsatian place. I wondered where the bakery might have been where Paul got bashed and robbed in 1939. He got drunk with a lad from Molsheim in summer 1944.

In the Town Hall square, I sat at the Café Patrick Eck, a boulangerie patisserie. Was it here in 1939? It looked as if it could have been. Eck is an old Alsatian-German name.

A young waitress came out and addressed me in English, which was a bit disappointing, although I did look a lot like an Australian backpacker. In Alsatian-German I ordered their best Gewürztraminer, coffee and pastries. It would be rude not to. Looking shocked, in Alsatian dialect the young lady swiftly corrected her error: 'Oh, excuse me, you are Alsatian!' She came back quickly and served the wine with a smile which I returned with a nod and self-satisfied smirk. I asked if she was a student at Straßburg? Not yet she said, but she was saving up to study music: piano and violin.

I couldn't possibly drink the whole bottle so I invited her to join me, but she said her 'Urgroßopa Rolf' (great grandpa Rolf) would not approve. I asked for the cork and popped the bottle in my rucksack. In so many ways I am still a student.

I tipped her 100 Euros. She ran after me to tell me there was a mistake. No mistake, I replied. Later, under the saucer, she would find the card from my Foundation.

345

19. The green island, 29 August 1945

The RAF *Avro Anson* flew in through showers across the green island of Jersey. It turned right over the headland and lighthouse at Corbière, flew across St Ouen's Bay and settled on the powered glide from the west to the airfield. On board were a mixture of other aviators and returning islanders.

Coming in over the sand dunes and hedgerows, the undercarriage was lowered, and flaps set. A gentle landing and short taxi to the apron followed. The passengers walked to the terminal building followed by the two pilots. There were no formalities.

Two civilians, a father and son, were offered a lift from an RAF sergeant, but they declined. They explained that they wanted to breathe the moist air of the Channel Islands again as they had been away for too long and would enjoy the walk. The sergeant nodded his head.

The son carried a camera and packed rucksack and the father a smallish suitcase. They headed right and ambled south along the Quennevais Road.

As they walked, the father was intrigued to hear his son's stories of this place. It rained but they never noticed.

They crossed a bridge and railway line and came to Red Houses. Walking over, they began the descent of La Marquanderie as the rainwater gushed down the road. Then the cloud passed, and the sun shone brightly.

A big house on the right by the church came into view with blue sea behind. They stopped for a moment, looked at each other, smiled, hugged, then continued.

They crunched across the gravel of the drive and knocked on the door. It opened, and there was a cry of delight.

ENDE

The Big House at St Brelade, Jersey, summer 2020

Dear reader, music should have the last word. So, to finish, please listen to *'On the Nature of Daylight'*. YouTube Search: <<Max Richter - On the Nature of Daylight (Arrival) // Piano Cover>> by Caliko
https://www.youtube.com/watch?v=ZfXe2VOG244

Katie Campbell

About the author

Martin is a retired primary school headmaster and school inspector. He has a lifelong interest in the history of World War II which began with listening to the stories of his mother, father and grandparents. In 1969, aged 10, he discovered the abandoned German defences of Jersey on a family holiday. He has visited the Normandy battlefields many times. Martin is also a keen aviator and accomplished glider pilot.

He lives in Ealing, London with his partner Sharon. Their son Toby is at Manchester University studying linguistics.

Martin's mother's maiden name: Audrey Mary Bunn.

Helen Keller 1880-1968

Deaf and blind from an early age, the title: 'Walking with a friend in the dark (is better than walking alone in the light)' is one of Helen's many profound and remarkable quotations:

'Life is a succession of lessons which must be lived to be understood.'
'Life is either a great adventure, or it is nothing.'

Acknowledgements

My thanks and appreciation to all who have helped me on the journey. Particular thanks to my long-suffering partner Sharon for her patience and listening skills and my son Toby who is the same age as the protagonists. To Ken Boult who came with me to the Normandy battlefields and museums, for his constructive criticisms and technical knowledge. To my inspirational colleague and historian Paul Musetti. To my long-standing school friends Charles Williams, John Paul who provided sounding boards for ideas, and Dave Walter for his proof reading. To my neighbour Nicholas Chennells for his positivity. To Dr Ulrich Willenburg of Stuttgart for tidying up my sloppy German. To Jersey War Tunnels (Ho8), and Jersey Museum which assisted primary research. To the Channel Islands Occupation Society (CIOS) who literally opened doors for me. My personal thanks to Damien Horn who runs and owns the Channel Islands Military Museum at Lewis Tower, Jersey. His outstanding collection of materials and stories (and patience with me) was an inspiration. My thanks to Annette Campbell (née Kemp) of St Ouen's Jersey, for her help after an incredible piece of serendipity at the Albert Hall. Finally, though not least, to Helen Evans, who gave me belief. To all of you – thank you.   **MR January 2022**

Music lyrics not in the public domain. On page 92:
Sad Lisa
Words and Music by Cat Stevens
Copyright © 1970 BMG Rights Management (UK) Ltd.
Copyright Renewed
All Rights Administered by BMG Rights Management (US) LLC
All Rights Reserved Used by Permission
Reprinted by Permission of Hal Leonard Europe Ltd.

For two years attempts were made to contact the publishers of 'Jersey under the Swastika' (page 99-100). No replies were received.

Further sources of information, photo & drawing credits
All images are from the author's private collection or sourced from archives in the public domain and are from the period. Below is a list of some of the best sources of information. The author is not a re-enactor.
https://www.bundesarchiv.de The Federal Archive of Germany
https://www.iwm.org.uk/collections/photographs The Imperial War Museum (IWM)
https://www.archives.gov/ US Government National Archives (NARA)
https://www.bac-lac.gc.ca/eng/discover/military-heritage/second-world-war/Pages/introduction.aspx The Library and Archives of Canada
https://www.theislandwiki.org/index.php/Jerripedia My thanks to Mike Bisson for his assistance and advice.
<<Gliders at Pegasus Bridge by Albert Richards>> reproduced on page 221. Copyright has expired.

A Call to Action!

If you enjoyed *Walking*, then please review on the appropriate platform: Goodreads, Waterstones, Foyles or Amazon/Kindle, with FIVE STARS! Find me on Facebook & eBay. There is an occasional blog on Goodreads.

Promotional videos can be found on YOUTUBE by searching:
Martin Roberts 1944   See them and send the links to your friends!

The second book is currently being researched & written. If you would like to receive free chapters, then email Martin on: 17eastburyroad@gmail.com We meet Katie Campbell in her new life, and we meet Christopher Bunn in the period 1933 – 1952. The German airships: *LZ-129 Hindenburg & LZ-130 Graf Zeppelin II* are featured. We also find out more about Katie's mother…
Working title: << **The Craft of the Father** >>

Rear cover: Fieseler Storch type B-0. D-IKVN. Serial number 625. Believed to be a demonstration model owned by the Fieseler company, 1938

Front cover: 'Memorial to the fallen' Wilgartswiesen church, Rhineland-Palatinate, Germany. Sculptor Richard Lenhard, 1938

Printed in a UK CarbonNeutral® factory using FSC certificated paper, within a ISO14001 Environment Management System where no dry waste goes to landfill.

Mauerstraße 30. Göttingen, April 1945

Das Gänseliesel (Little Lisa with the Geese). Göttingen, summer 2020

The Victory Column, Tiergarten, Berlin, 24 March 1945

Das Gänseliesel, Göttingen, 1952

Paul's apartment: Arndtstraße 14, Bergmannkiez, Berlin, summer 2020